D0482484

DISCARDED FROM
GARFIELD COUNTY PUBLIC
LIBRARY SYSTEM

DISCARDED FROM
GARFIELD COUNTY LIBRARIES
Garfield County Libraries
New Castle Branch Library
402 West Main Street
New Castle, CO 81647
(970) 984-2346 • Fax (970) 984-2081
www.GCPLD.org

Passenger

nger

ALEXANDRA BRACKEN

HYPERION
Los Angeles   New York

For Mom—

In all of history, there has never been anyone with a heart as beautiful and strong as yours.

Copyright © 2016 by Alexandra Bracken

All rights reserved. Published by Hyperion, an imprint of Disney Book Group. No part of this book may be reproduced or transmitted in any form or by any means, electronic or mechanical, including photocopying, recording, or by any information storage and retrieval system, without written permission from the publisher. For information address Hyperion, 125 West End Avenue, New York, New York 10023.

First Edition, January 2016
10 9 8 7 6 5 4 3 2 1
FAC-02003-15288
Printed in the United States of America

Library of Congress Cataloging-in-Publication Control Number: 2015031657
ISBN 978-1-4847-1577-2

Reinforced binding
Visit www.hyperionteens.com

SUSTAINABLE FORESTRY INITIATIVE   Certified Sourcing
www.sfiprogram.org
SFI-00993

THIS LABEL APPLIES TO TEXT STOCK

It matters not how strait the gate,
How charged with punishments the scroll.
I am the master of my fate:
I am the captain of my soul.

WILLIAM ERNEST HENLEY

BHUTAN
1910

PROLOGUE

As they ascended, retreating farther from the winding trails that marked the way to nearby villages, the world opened to him in its purest form: silent, ancient, mysterious.

Deadly.

Nicholas had spent the better part of his life on the sea, or close enough to catch its perfume of fish and brine when there was a good wind. Even now, as they approached the monastery, waiting for it to appear through the heavy cover of mist and clouds, he found himself turning back, futilely searching beyond the towering peaks of the Himalayas for the hazy line where the sky met the curve of rippling water—something familiar to anchor himself to, before his courage disappeared along with his confidence.

The trail, a winding series of stairs and dirt, had stretched at first through the pine trees dripping with moss, and now hugged the sheer, vertical cliffs into which the Taktsang Palphug Monastery had somehow, impossibly, been built. Lines of bright prayer flags fluttered overhead in the trees, and the sight eased some of the tightness in his chest; it reminded him instantly of the first time Captain Hall had brought him to New York Harbor and the new frigates had been festooned with flags of every make and pattern.

He shifted again, a small, careful movement that would ease the sting of the rucksack's straps digging into his shoulders, without sending himself plunging over the open side of the trail.

You've climbed the rigging any number of times, and you're frightened of heights now?

Rigging. His hands itched to touch it, to feel the spray of the sea kicked up by wind and his ship charging through the water. Nicholas tried to set his shoulders back, toss sand over the burn of resentment in the pit of his stomach before it could catch fire. He should have been back by now—he should have been with Hall, with Chase, rolling over the crest of each passing wave. Not here in a foreign century—the nineteen hundreds, for goodness' sake—with an incompetent sop who required Nicholas to help button his new coat, lace his boots, knot his scarf, and position his ridiculous floppy hat, despite having two hands of his own and, to all appearances, a brain in his skull.

The leather sack slung around his neck slapped heavily against his side as Nicholas continued his climb toward where Julian stood, one leg braced against a nearby stone—his usual pose when he thought ladies were around to admire him. But now Nicholas couldn't begin to fathom whom he was attempting to impress—the few birds they'd heard on their walk through the damp forest? Had he always been this way—dramatic, vain, with a complete lack of consideration—and Nicholas so blinded by the wonder of finding a so-called brother, a new life with possibilities of comfort and wealth and adventure, that he'd willingly ignored it?

"Now, chap, come here and take a look—this is the Tiger's Nest, you know. Damn this infernal mist—"

Nicholas did, in fact, know. He made a point to read as much as he could about whatever location the old man sent them to, so as to figure out the best ways to keep the ever-reckless, ever-stubborn Julian alive. Nicholas was constantly working from a deficit of knowledge, of training. When he'd realized the family would never truly provide a real education for his traveling, he'd begun to wonder if it was intentional, a way to keep him in his lowly place. The thought had enraged him enough to cause him to spend most of his meager funds on history books.

"Bhutan's Buddhism guru Padmasambhava—according to legend, of course—flew here on the back of a tigress," Julian continued with a grin that had gotten them out of any number of scrapes and trouble—the smile that had once softened Nicholas's heart and temper, always teasing out forgiveness. "We should pop into one of their meditation caves on the way back. Maybe you can have yourself a little think. Have a look at that view, and tell me you won't miss traveling. How, in the whole of your small life, would you ever have come here otherwise? Put that foolish notion away, will you?"

Rather than throw a punch at his smug face, or send the metal tip of the pickax strapped to his back on a similar path, Nicholas shifted the rucksack again and tried not to focus on the fact that he was, yet again, being crushed under the weight of Julian and his belongings.

"It looks as though there's a storm coming in," Nicholas said, proud of how steady his voice sounded, despite the rattle and hiss of the resentment he felt building again inside of him. "We should make this climb tomorrow."

Julian flicked a bug from the shoulder of his pristine coat. "No. I had to leave that bearcat back in the speakeasy in Manhattan, and I want to get back for a quick tumble before returning to the old man." Julian sighed. "With empty hands, yet again. Sending us out into the middle of nowhere for something that probably doesn't even *exist* at this point. Classic."

Nicholas watched as his half brother twirled his walking stick around, and began to wonder what the monks would make of them: the preening, ruddy-haired prince in new mountaineering gear, poking around their sacred spaces looking for lost treasure, and the dark-skinned young man, clearly the servant, trailing behind him like a trapped shadow.

This isn't how it was supposed to be.

Why had he left? Why had he signed the contract—why had he *ever* trusted this family?

This isn't who I'm supposed to be.

"Buck up, old man," Julian said, with a faint punch to Nicholas's shoulder. "Don't tell me you're still sore about the contract."

Nicholas glared at Julian's back as he turned away. He didn't wish to speak of it, didn't wish to think of it either—the way Julian had shrugged and merely said, *I guess you should have read the terms a bit more closely before you signed it.* He'd escaped enslavement by this family once, yet, in the end, he had only sold himself back into servitude. But the old man had talked of impossible things—of magic, of voyages, of money beyond his wildest dreams. Five years of excitement had hardly seemed like a sacrifice at the time.

The moment he had realized he would only ever be a valet to a half brother who would never, ever, not in a thousand years, acknowledge him publicly as such, Nicholas had merely swallowed the bile rising in his throat and finished retying Julian's cravat the way he preferred it to be styled. Since then, he'd never felt so aware of time. Each passing second chipped away at his resolve, and he was afraid to find out what disastrous fury might spill out of him when his defenses were whittled away.

"We should turn back and make camp," Nicholas said finally, avoiding Julian's assessing gaze. "Start again tomorrow."

Julian scoffed. "Afraid of a little rain, are you? Don't be such a pill, Nick. The climb's a snap."

It wasn't the climb itself he was worried about. Already, the air felt thin in his lungs; his headache, he realized, had less to do with Julian's incessant prattling and more to do with how perilously close they were now to the heavens. His knees felt as though they'd turned to sand; his hands were drained of any sensation at all.

I could leave him here. Run.

Where could he go that they couldn't find him? Not back to Hall; not back to his own natural time. Not even to find his mother.

Nicholas glanced at the spread of steel-gray clouds rolling through the mountain range, sliced neatly by the Himalayas' long, jagged necks. On a ship, he would use the ocean and the vessel itself to gauge the intensity of an approaching storm, and form a plan to see it through safely. Now he had neither; there was only the faint prickle at the back of his neck to warn him as distant thunder cracked and echoed through the empty mountains.

"The old man had better be right this time," Julian said, starting up the trail again. From where Nicholas stood, it looked like an endless ribbon of steps that had been draped over the rough, rocky face of the cliff, rising and falling with the natural shape of the landscape. "I'm tired of this game of his—the blasted thing is lost. Even *he* doesn't win sometimes."

He always wins, Nicholas thought, fingers curling into fists at his side. *I am never going to be free of any of them.*

"All right, come on then, Nick. We've a journey to make," Julian called back. "And I'm hungry enough to eat a horse."

The first fat splatter of rain caught him across the face, sliding down his cheek to drip off his chin. It was a strange, trembling sort of moment. Nicholas felt caught in that instant, glancing around for some form of temporary shelter, which he knew Julian would demand, rather than risk getting his boots wet. Aside from the *choten*—the low white buildings that sheltered the elaborate, brightly colored prayer wheels—there were a few small covered ledges where mourners had placed conical reliquaries of ashes.

"There!" Julian let out a sharp, joyful cry, pumping a fist into the air. The mist shrouding the monastery had settled, as if the rain had dragged it down. It sat like the foggy surface of a lake, disguising the thousands of feet between the ledge and the sheer, rocky drop below. "Where's the camera? Break it out, will you? No one around to see it anyway—"

The thunder that exploded overhead ricocheted like cannon fire through the mountains. Nicholas's whole body tensed, cringing away from the deafening roar. No sooner had it faded than the heavens opened up and rain poured down from the clouds, momentarily blinding him with its strength. Nicholas let out a startled gasp as the pounding intensified into a solid sheet of water, a surge he'd only ever witnessed once at sea when his ship had drifted toward the edge of a hurricane. Rivers of rain were washing down from the ledges above, pouring around him, nearly carrying his feet out from under him.

Julian—

Nicholas spun back toward the edge of the trail just as Julian turned to shout something to him, and watched Julian's left foot disappear as the muddy ledge crumbled beneath it.

As he dove, throwing himself across the distance, a single thought slammed through Nicholas's mind: *Not like this.*

"Nick! *Nick!*" Julian had managed to grab on to the fractured remains of the ledge, his hand already sliding out of his sopping wet glove as his full weight dangled over a vast spread of air, stone, mist, and trees. Nicholas crawled the last few feet between them on his stomach and was reaching, reaching, and the contents of the rucksack were rattling, digging into his back—

Julian's face was bone-white with fear, his mouth moving, begging, *Help me, help me—*

Why should I?

This family—they'd taken everything from him—they'd taken his true family, his freedom, his worth—

A cold, bitter satisfaction filled him to the core at the thought of finally taking something back.

Because he's your brother.

Nicholas shook his head, feeling the force of the rain start to carry him toward the ledge. "Reach up—swing your arm up—Julian!"

A look of determination crossed Julian's mud-smeared face as he thrust his free arm up, trying to catch Nicholas's grasping hand. Julian sacrificed his grip on the ledge to swing himself up; Nicholas lunged forward and caught his fingers—

The weight he'd been holding disappeared as Julian's hand

slipped out of the glove, and his dark shape slipped silently down through the feather-soft mist, parting just enough for Nicholas to see, at the bottom of the ravine, a burst of light as Julian's body broke apart into glittering dust.

There was a boom and rattle from miles away, and he knew the passage they'd come through had just collapsed. Blood roared in Nicholas's ears, chased by his own soundless scream; he did not need to look, to search through the haze and rain, to know that time itself had stolen Julian's broken body, and dissolved it into nothing but memory.

NEW YORK CITY
Present Day

ONE

THE AMAZING THING WAS, EACH TIME SHE LOOKED AT them, Etta still saw something new—something she hadn't noticed before.

The paintings had been hanging in their living room for years, in the exact same spot behind the couch, lined up like a movie reel of the greatest hits of her mom's life. Now and then, Etta felt something clench deep in her stomach when she looked at them; not quite envy, not quite longing, but some shallow cousin of both. She'd done her own traveling with Alice, had hit the international violin competition circuit, but she'd seen nothing like the subjects of these paintings. Nothing like this one, of a mountain with its spiraling, shining path up through the trees, toward the clouds, to its hidden peak.

It was only now, leaning over the back of the couch, that Etta noticed Rose had painted two figures working their way up the trail, half-hidden by the lines of bright flags streaming overhead.

Her eyes skimmed over the other paintings beneath it. The view from the first studio Rose had lived in, off Sixty-Sixth Street and Third Avenue. Then, the next painting: the steps of the British Museum, spotted with tourists and pigeons, where she'd done portraits on the spot after moving back to London. (Etta always loved this one, because her mom had painted the moment that Alice had first seen her, and was walking over to scold Rose for skipping school.) The dark, lush jungle reaching out to caress the damp stone of the Terrace of the Elephants at Angkor Thom—Rose had scraped together enough money by the time she was eighteen to fly to Cambodia and sweet-talk her way into working on an archeological dig site, despite her complete and total lack of qualifications. Next was the Luxembourg Garden in full summer bloom, when she'd finally studied at the Sorbonne. And below that, perched on the back of the couch and leaning against the wall to the left, was a new painting: a desert at sunset, cast in blazing rose gold, dotted with crumbling ruins.

It was the story of her mom's life. The only pieces of it Rose had been willing to share. Etta wondered what the story was with the new one—it had been years since Rose had had the time to paint for herself, and even longer since she'd used the paintings as prompts for bedtime stories to get a younger Etta to fall asleep. She could barely remember what her mom had been like then, before the endless traveling to lecture on the latest restoration techniques, before her countless projects in the conservation department of the Met, cleaning and repairing works by the old masters.

The keys jangled in the door, and Etta jumped off the couch, straightening the cushions.

Rose shook out her umbrella in the hall one last time before coming inside. Despite the early autumn downpour, she looked almost pristine—wavy blond hair, twisted into a knot; heels damp but not ruined; trench coat buttoned up all the way to her throat. Etta self-consciously reached up to smooth back her own hair, wishing she'd already changed into her dress for the performance instead of staying in her rainbow-colored pajamas. She used to love the fact that she and her mom looked so much alike—that they were a matching set—because not having to see her father looking back at her from a mirror made it easier to accept life without him. But now, Etta knew the similarities only ran skin-deep.

"How was your day?" Etta asked as her mom flicked her gaze down at her pajamas, then up again with a cocked eyebrow.

"Shouldn't you already be dressed?" Rose answered instead, her English accent crisp with the kind of disapproval that made all of Etta's insides give an involuntary cringe. "Alice will be here any moment."

While Rose hung up her coat in their small apartment's even smaller coat closet, Etta dashed into her room, nearly slipping on the sheet music spread over her rug and almost tumbling headlong into the old wardrobe that served as her closet. She'd picked out the ruby-red cocktail dress weeks ago for this event, but Etta wavered now, wondering if her mom would think it was too informal, or somehow too cutesy with the ribbons that tied at each shoulder. This was a private fund-raising event for the Metropolitan Museum of Art, and Etta didn't want her mom's bosses to think she was anything less than a true professional.

Etta wanted to see her mom smile again when she played.

She put the red dress away, pulled out a more serious, subdued black dress instead, and sat down at her desk to start her makeup. After a few minutes, her mom knocked on the door.

"Would you like some help with your hair?" Rose asked, watching her in the mirror that hung on the wall.

Etta was perfectly capable of taming her hair, but nodded and handed her the bundle of bobby pins and her old brush. She sat up straight as Rose began to work the tangles out of her hair, smoothing it back over the crown of her head.

"I haven't done this since you were a little girl," Rose said quietly, gathering the waves of pale blond hair in her hand. Etta let her eyes drift shut, remembering what it felt like to be that small, to sit in her mom's lap after bath time and have her hair combed out while listening to stories of her mom's travels before Etta was born.

Now she didn't know how to reply without sending Rose back into her usual tight, cool silence. Instead she asked, "Are you going to hang up the new painting you finished? It's really beautiful."

Rose gave one of her rare, soft smiles. "Thanks, darling. I want to replace the painting of the Luxembourg Garden with this one—don't let me forget to pick up the hardware for it this weekend."

"Why?" Etta asked. "I love that one."

"The play of colors will work better," Rose explained as she plucked one of the bobby pins off the desk and pinned Etta's hair back into a twist. "The flow of darkness to light will be more obvious. You won't forget, will you?"

"I won't," Etta promised and then, trying her luck, asked, "What is it of?"

"A desert in Syria . . . I haven't been for years and years, but I had a dream about it a few weeks ago, and I haven't been able to get it out of my head." Rose smoothed the last few stray strands of hair back and spritzed hair spray over them. "It did remind me, though—I have something I've been meaning to give you for ages." She reached into the pocket of her old, worn cardigan, then opened Etta's hand and placed two delicate gold earrings in her palm.

Two brilliant pearls rolled together softly, knocking against small, heart-shaped gold leaves. What Etta sincerely hoped were dark blue beads, not actual sapphires, were attached to the small hoops like charms. The gold curved up, etched in meticulous detail to look like tiny vines. Etta could tell by the quality of the metalwork—slightly rough—and the way the designs matched imperfectly, that these had been painstakingly handcrafted many years ago. Maybe hundreds of years ago.

"I thought they'd go beautifully with your dress for the debut," Rose explained, leaning against the desk as Etta studied them, trying to decide if she was more stunned by how beautiful they were, or that her mom, for the first time, seemed to genuinely care about the event beyond how it would fit into her work schedule.

Her debut as a concert soloist was still a little over a month away, but Etta and her violin instructor, Alice, had started hunting for fabric and lace together in the Garment District a few days after she found out that she'd be performing Mendelssohn's Violin Concerto at Avery Fisher Hall with the New York Philharmonic. After drawing out her own sketches and ideas, Etta had worked with a local seamstress to design her own dress. Gold lace, woven into the most gorgeous array of leaves and flowers, covered her shoulders and artfully climbed down the deep blue chiffon bodice. It was the perfect dress for the perfect debut of "Classical Music's Best-Kept Secret."

Etta was so tired of that stupid label, the one that had chased her around for months after the *Times* article was published about her win at the International Tchaikovsky Competition in Moscow. It just reinforced the one thing she didn't have.

Her debut as a soloist with an orchestra had been coming for at least three years now, but Alice had been staunchly opposed to making commitments on her behalf. As a young girl with crippling stage fright, one who'd had to fight with every ounce of nerve she possessed to overcome it at her early competitions, she'd been grateful. But then Etta had grown out of her stage fright and suddenly was fifteen, and sixteen, and now close to eighteen, and she'd begun to see kids she had squarely beaten making their debuts at home and abroad, passing her in the same race she'd led for years. She began to obsess over the fact that her idols had debuted years before her: Midori at age eleven, Hilary Hahn at twelve, Anne-Sophie Mutter at thirteen, Joshua Bell at fourteen.

Alice had dubbed tonight's performance at the Met her "soft launch," to test her nerves, but it felt more like a speed bump on the way to a much larger mountain, one she wanted to spend her whole life climbing.

Her mom never tried to convince her not to play, to focus on other studies, and she was supportive in her usual reserved way. It should have been enough for her, but Etta always found herself working hard for Rose's praise, to catch her attention. She struggled to gain it, and had frustrated herself time and time again with the chase.

She's never going to care, no matter how much you kill yourself to be the best. Are you even playing for yourself anymore, or just in the hope that one day she'll decide to listen? Pierce, her best-friend-turned-boyfriend, had shouted the words at her when she'd finally broken things off with him in order to have more time to practice. But they'd risen up again and again as a hissing, nasty doubt in the six months since then, until Etta began to wonder, too.

Etta studied the earrings again. Wasn't this proof her mother cared? That she *did* support Etta's dream?

"Can I wear them tonight, too?" Etta asked.

"Of course," Rose said, "they're yours now. You can wear them whenever you like."

"Who'd you steal these from?" Etta joked as she fastened them. She couldn't think of a time in her mom's forty-four years when she could have afforded something like this. Had she inherited them? Were they a gift?

Her mom stiffened, her shoulders curling in like the edges of the old scroll she displayed on her desk. Etta waited for a laugh that never came—a dry look that acknowledged her stupid attempt at humor. The silence between them stretched past the point of painful.

"Mom . . ." Etta said, feeling the stupidest urge to cry, like she'd ruined whatever moment they'd been having. "It was a joke."

"I know." Her mother lifted her chin. "It's a bit of a sore spot—it's been years since I had to live the way I did, but the looks I used to get from others . . . I want you to know, I have *never* stolen anything in my life. No matter how bad things got, or how much I wanted something. Someone tried to pull a fast one on me once, and I've never forgotten what that felt like. I almost lost something of your great-granddad's."

There was a hum of anger behind the words, and Etta was surprised that her first instinct wasn't to back off. Her mother so rarely spoke about her family—less than she spoke about Etta's father, which was next to never—that Etta found herself reaching for the loose thread and hoping that something else would unravel.

"Was it your foster father?" Etta asked. "The one who tried to steal from you?"

Her mother gave a humorless little smile. "Good guess."

Both parents gone in one terrible Christmas car accident. Her guardian, her grandfather, gone after little more than a year. And the family that had fostered her . . . the father had never laid a finger on her, but from the few stories Etta had heard about him, his control over Rose's life had been so rigid, so absolute, it was a choice between staying and suffocating, or the risk of running away on her own.

"What was it?" Etta asked, knowing she was pressing her luck. "The thing he tried to steal?"

"Oh, some old family heirloom. The truth is, I only kept it for one reason: I knew I could sell it and buy my ticket out of London, away from the foster family. I knew your great-granddad had bequeathed it to me so I could make a choice about my future. I've never regretted selling that old thing, because it brought me here. I want you to remember that—it's our choices that matter in the end. Not wishes, not words, not promises."

Etta turned her head back and forth, studying the earrings in the mirror.

"I bought these from a vendor at an old market—a *souk*—in Damascus when I was about your age. Her name was Samarah, and she convinced me to buy them when I told her it was my last trip, and I was finally going back to school. For the longest time, I saw them as the end of my journey, but now I think they were always meant to represent the beginning of yours." Rose

20

leaned down and kissed her cheek. "You're going to be wonderful tonight. I'm so proud of you."

Etta felt the sting of tears immediately, and wondered if it was possible to ever really capture a moment. Every bitter feeling of disappointment was washed out of her as happiness came rushing through her veins.

There was a knock at the door before Alice used her keys and announced her arrival with a cheerful "Hullo!"

"Now, get going," Rose said, brushing a piece of lint off Etta's shoulder. "I need a few minutes to change, but I'll meet you over there."

Etta stood, her throat still tight. She would have hugged her mom if Rose hadn't stepped away and folded her hands behind her back. "I'll see you there?"

"I'll be right behind you, I promise."

A ROLL OF FIRE BREATHED THROUGH THE NOTES, RATTLING THE breath in Etta's chest, and sank down through her skin to shimmer in the marrow of her bones as she and Alice slipped inside the still-empty auditorium.

She could admit it; this violinist . . . Etta looked down at the program she had picked up. Evan Parker. Right. She'd heard him play at a few competitions. She could admit that he *was* decent enough. Maybe even a little good.

But, Etta thought, satisfaction slinking through her, *not as good as me.*

And not nearly good enough to do Bach's Chaconne from Partita no. 2 in D Minor justice.

The lights dimmed and swept across the stage in bursts of shifting color as the technicians in the booth made last-minute

PASSENGER

adjustments to match the mood of the piece; Evan stood in the middle of it, dark hair gleaming, and went at the Chaconne like he was trying to set his violin on fire, completely oblivious to everything and everyone else. Etta knew that feeling. She might have doubted many things in her life, but Etta had never once doubted her talent, her love for the violin.

They had no choice which piece of music the museum's board of directors had assigned each of them for that night's fund-raising performance, but some small, sour part of her still stewed in envy that he'd been picked. The Chaconne was considered by most, including herself, to be one of the most difficult violin pieces to master—a single progression repeated in dozens of dizzying, complex variations. It was emotionally powerful, and structurally near perfect. At least, it was when played by her. It *should* have been played by her.

Her piece, the Largo from Sonata no. 3, was the last of the violin set. The piece was sweetly stirring, meditative in pace. Not Bach's most complex or demanding, or even the brightest in its colors, but, as Alice said time and time again, there was no cheating when it came to Bach. Every piece demanded the full force of the player's technical skill and focus. She would play it flawlessly, and then the whole of her attention would be on the debut.

Not on her mom.

Not on the fact that she now had no one to text or call after the event to give an update to.

Not on the fact that one night could determine her whole future.

"You would have done a bang-up job of the Chaconne," Alice said as they made their way to the side of the stage, heading to the green room, "but tonight, the Largo is yours. Remember, this isn't a competition."

Alice had this magical look about her, like she would be at home in front of a hearth, wrapped in a large quilt, telling nursery rhymes to sweet-faced forest critters. Hair that, according to pictures, had once been flaming red and reached halfway down her back was now bobbed, as white as milk. Turning ninety-three hadn't dulled any of her warmth or wit. But even though her mind was as sharp as ever, and her sense of humor twice as wicked, Etta was careful to help her up the stairs, equally careful not to hold her thin arm too tightly as one of the event coordinators led them to the green room.

"But also remember," Alice whispered, grinning broadly, "that you are *my* student, and you are therefore the best here by default. If you feel inclined to prove that, who am I to stop you?"

Etta couldn't help herself; she laughed and wrapped her arms around her instructor's shoulders, and was grateful to have the hug returned tenfold. When she was younger, and just starting out on the competition circuit, she couldn't go onstage until she'd had three hugs from Alice, and a kiss on the head for luck. It made her feel safe, like a warm blanket tucked around her shoulders, and she could disappear inside the feeling if she needed to.

I have Alice.

If she had no one else, she had Alice, who believed in Etta even when she was playing at her worst. Of the two Brits in her life, she was grateful that at least this one seemed to care and love unconditionally.

Alice pulled back, touching Etta's cheek. "Everything all right, love? You're not having second thoughts, are you?"

"No!" God, she couldn't give Alice *any* excuse to cancel the debut. "Just the usual nerves."

Alice's gaze narrowed to something over her shoulder; Etta started to turn, to look and see what it was, only to have her instructor touch one of her earrings, her brow wrinkling in thought. "Did your mum give these to you?"

Etta nodded. "Yeah. Do you like them?"

"They're . . ." Alice seemed to search for the word, dropping her hand. "Beautiful. But not half as beautiful as you, duck."

Etta rolled her eyes, but laughed.

"I need to . . . I think I ought to make a call," Alice said slowly. "Will you be all right to start warming up by yourself?"

"Of course," Etta said, startled. "Is everything okay?"

Alice waved her hand. "It will be. If I'm not back in a few minutes, make sure they let you have your turn onstage—you'll need the most time, since you couldn't make the dress rehearsal. And the Strad—which one are they giving you again?"

"The Antonius," Etta said gleefully. It was one of several Strads in the Metropolitan Museum of Art's collection, and the very first one she'd been allowed to play.

"Ah, the golden child. It'll take a bit of work to get him to behave himself," Alice told her. "I don't care what your mother says about preserving them for the future. Holding incredible instruments hostage in glass cases. You know that—"

"—the longer you silence a violin, the harder it is for it to find its true voice again," Etta finished, having heard the argument a hundred times before.

A Strad—a Stradivarius—one of the stringed instruments crafted by the Stradivari family of northern Italy in the late seventeenth, early eighteenth centuries. The instruments were legendary for the power and beauty of the sound they produced. Their owners didn't describe them as mere instruments, but like humans—temperamental friends with moods that could never be fully conquered, no matter how skilled the player.

No matter how lovely her own violin was—a Vuillaume copy of the "Messiah" Stradivarius she had inherited from Alice—it was still just that: a copy. Every time she thought of touching the real thing, it felt like sparks were about to shoot out of her fingertips.

"Back in a bit, duck," Alice said, reaching up to give her an affectionate tap under the chin. Etta waited until she was safely down the stairs before turning back to squint her way through the darkness.

"There you are!"

Etta turned to see Gail, the concert organizer, hustling and wriggling over the stage as best she could in her long, tight, black dress. "The others are backstage in the green room. Need anything? We're running through warm-ups one by one in order, but I'll introduce you to everyone." She looked around, a flash of disappointment crossing her face. "Is your instructor with you? Rats, I was hoping to meet her!"

Alice and her late husband, Oskar, had both been world-renowned violinists, and had retired to New York City when Oskar became sick. He had died only a year after Etta started taking lessons from Alice, but at five, she'd been old enough to form a true impression of his warmth and humor. While Alice hadn't played professionally in years, and hadn't had the heart to try after Oskar passed, she was still worshipped in certain circles for a breathtaking debut performance she'd given at the Vatican.

"She'll be back," Etta promised as they made their way to the green room. "Will you introduce me to everyone? I'm sorry I couldn't make the dress rehearsal."

"Evan couldn't make it, either. You'll be fine—we'll get you situated."

The green room's door was open, and a current of voices, pitched with excitement, rolled out to meet her. The other violinists studied her with blatant curiosity as she walked in.

They're wondering why you're here. She squashed the voice down and sized them up in return as Gail went around the room and rattled their names off. Etta recognized two of the three men present—they were older, near retirement age. Evan, of course, was still onstage. The organizers had balanced out their number with three women: an older woman, herself, and another girl who looked to be about Etta's age. Gail introduced her only as "Sophia," as if no last name were necessary.

The girl had tied her dark, nearly black hair back from her face and pinned it up into an old-fashioned twist. She wore a plain white shirt tucked into a long, dark skirt that fell to her ankles, but the outfit wasn't half as severe as the expression on her round face when she caught Etta studying her, trying to place whether they'd crossed paths at a competition.

"Mr. Frankwright, you're up," Gail called as Evan made his way in and introduced himself. One of the old men stood, was handed a gorgeous Strad, and followed.

No one seemed in the mood to talk, which was fine by Etta. She put on her headphones and listened to the Largo all the way through once, eyes shut, concentrating on each note until her small purse accidentally slipped off her lap and the lip gloss, powder, mirror, and cash she'd shoved into it went scattering across the tile. Evan and the other man helped her scoop it all back up with faint laughter.

"Sorry, sorry," she muttered. It wasn't until she began to replace everything that she realized there was a small, cream-colored envelope tucked inside.

It can't be, she thought. There was no way . . . her mother hadn't done this for her in *years.* Her heart gave a joyful little bump against her ribs, flooding with the old, familiar starlight as she tore the envelope open and shook its contents out. There were two sheets of paper—one was a rambling letter that, to the casual eye, was filled with chatter about the weather, the museum, the apartment. But there was a second, smaller piece of paper included, this one with the shape of a heart cut out from its center. When laid over the first, the message changed; the heart gathered the rambling, nonsensical words into a simple phrase: *I love you and I am so proud of who you are and what you'll do.*

She used to leave Etta notes like this every time she had to travel for work, when Etta had gone to stay with Alice—little reminders of love, tucked inside her overnight bag or in her violin case. But the longer she looked at it, Etta began to feel herself drift away from that initial burst of happiness. Her mom wasn't exactly a sentimental person when it came down to it; she wasn't sure what to make of this, especially on top of the earrings. Trying to thaw their relationship after freezing it over in the first place?

Etta checked her phone. A half hour until the concert.

No texts. No missed calls.

No surprise there.

But also . . . still no Alice.

She stood up, setting her purse down on the chair and slipping out of the room to check on her. Her instructor had seemed almost confused earlier, or at least startled. It was entirely possible someone had trapped her in conversation, or she was having a hard time getting ahold of whoever she was trying to call, but Etta couldn't turn off the panic valve, the prickle of something like dread walking down the back of her neck.

The auditorium was empty, save for the ushers being briefed on the evening by an event coordinator. Etta hustled up the aisle as fast as she could in her heels, catching the last few notes from the violinist onstage. She'd be up soon.

But Alice wasn't out in the hall, cell phone pressed to her ear. Neither, for that matter, was her mom. They weren't loitering in the museum's entrance, the Great Hall, either—and when she checked the steps, all she found were pigeons, puddles, and tourists. Which left one possibility.

Etta turned back toward the steps up to the European paintings collection and slammed into someone, nearly sending them both tumbling to the ground.

"Ah—I'm sorry!" Etta gasped as he steadied her.

"What's the rush? Are you—" The man stared down at her through silver-rimmed glasses, lips parted in surprise. He was older, edging into middle age, or already there judging by the streaks of gray in his otherwise jet-black hair. Etta took one look at him and knew she'd nearly mowed down one of the Met's donors. Everything about him was well-groomed; his tuxedo was immaculate, a dark red rose tucked into the lapel.

"I wasn't looking where I was going," she said. "I'm sorry, I'm so sorry—"

He only stared at her.

"Anyway," she rambled, backing up to continue her search, "I hope you're okay, I'm so sorry again. . . ."

"Wait!" he called after her. "What's your name?"

Etta jogged up the steps, her heels clacking loudly against the marble. She made her way through the exhibits, waving at the security guards and curators, to the elevator that would take her to the conservation wing. Her mom might have needed to stop by her office, or maybe she had taken Alice up for privacy.

The wing was all but abandoned, save for a security guard, George, who nodded in recognition as she passed by and continued down the hall.

"Your mom's in her office," George told her. "Came up a few minutes ago with a lady blazing at her heels."

"Thanks," Etta said quickly, ducking around him.

"Don't you have that concert tonight?" he called. "Good luck!"

Concert, practice, warm-up—

"—haven't listened to me in *years!*"

She almost didn't recognize Alice's voice in its anger; it was so rare for the woman to raise it. It was muffled by the closed door, but still powerful enough to rage down the hall and reach her ears.

"You don't get to make this call, Alice," her mom continued, sounding far calmer. Etta's knees felt like water as she stood outside the office door, pressing her ear against it. "I'm her mother, and contrary to your opinion, I do know what's best for my child. It's her time—you know this. You can't just pluck her off this path, not without consequences!"

"Damn the consequences! And damn you too, for thinking

of them and not of her. She's not ready for this. She doesn't have the right training, and there's no guarantee it'll go the right way for her!"

Not ready for this. Alice's words ripped through her mind. Not ready for what? The debut?

"I love you to death, you know this," Rose continued. "You've done more for the two of us than I could ever express or thank you for, but stop fighting me. You don't understand, and you clearly don't know Etta if you're underestimating her. She can handle it."

Between the hummingbird pulse of her heart and the numb shock spreading through her veins, Etta had to replay the words again and again before she could understand that her mom was actually fighting for her—that it was Alice who was trying to hold her back.

She's going to cancel the debut.

"And you clearly don't love her the way I do, if you're so ready and willing to throw her to the wolves!"

Alice is going to cancel the debut.

The one she'd given up real school for.

The one she'd given up Pierce for.

The one she'd practiced six hours every day for.

Etta threw the office door open, startling Rose and Alice enough to interrupt the furious staring contest they'd been having across her mother's desk.

"Etta—" her mom began, standing quickly. "Shouldn't you be downstairs?"

"I don't know," Etta said, her voice thin with anger as she stared at Alice. "Should I be downstairs, or should I just go home? Is *this* too much for me to handle, too?"

Her stomach churned as Alice raised a hand toward her, trying to beckon her into the office, into the soothing trap of her arms. Like Etta was a child all over again, and needed to calm down.

There was something sharp, assessing, in Alice's eyes that instantly brought about a tremor of panic in her. She knew that look. Etta knew exactly what she was thinking.

"I think, duck, we *should* go home." She turned and met Rose's even gaze. "We can finish our discussion there together."

Etta felt her heart give a kick, then another, until she felt her pulse rioting in her ears, and the temperature of her blood start to rise.

"I've given up everything for this . . . *everything*. And you want me to just walk away? You want me to cancel, to delay *again*?" she demanded, trying to keep the pain lancing through her from twisting the words into a whisper. "You don't think I'm good enough, do you?"

"No, duck, no—"

"Don't call me that!" Etta said, backing out of the office. "Do you realize I don't even have a *friend* left? You told me I needed to focus if I wanted my debut. I gave it all up! I don't have anything else!"

Concern broke through even her mother's anger as she shared a glance with Alice. "Darling, that's not true—"

Alice reached for her again, but Etta wasn't having any of it—she didn't even want to *look* at her, let alone be reasoned with.

"Etta—*Henrietta*," Alice tried, but Etta was past the point of listening, of caring what either of them had to say.

"I'm playing," she told her instructor, "tonight, and at the debut. I don't care what you think, or if you believe in me—I believe in myself, and there is literally *nothing* in this world that can keep me from playing."

Alice called after her, but Etta turned on her heel and stormed back down the hall, keeping her head up and her shoulders back. Later, she could think of all the ways she might have hurt the woman who had practically raised her, but right now all Etta wanted was to feel the stage lights warm her skin. Free the fire fluttering inside her rib cage. Work her muscles, the bow, the violin, until she played herself to ash and embers and left the rest of the world behind to smolder.

THERE WAS ALWAYS A MOMENT, JUST BEFORE SHE PUT HER BOW to the strings, when everything seemed to crystallize. She used to live for it, that second where her focus clicked into place, and the world and everyone in it fell away. The weight of the violin cradled against her shoulder. The warmth of the lights running along the lip of the stage, blinding her to everyone beyond it.

This was not one of those moments.

A flustered, panicked Gail had met her in the hall, and dragged her backstage as guests began to file into the auditorium.

"I thought you said I'd have time to rehearse!" Etta whispered, nearly stumbling as they took the stairs.

"Yes, *twenty minutes ago*," Gail said through gritted teeth. "Are you all right to just go out there? You can warm up in the green room."

Panic curled low in her belly at the thought, but Etta nodded. She was going to be a professional. She needed to be able to take any hiccup or change in plans in stride. What did it matter that she'd never played on this stage? She'd played the Largo hundreds of times. She didn't need Alice standing by, waiting to give her feedback. She would give Alice proof that she could handle this. "That's fine."

Michelle, the curator in charge of the Antonius, met them in the green room. Etta actually caught herself holding her breath as the Antonius was lifted out of its case and placed gently into her hands. With the care she'd use to handle a newborn chick, Etta curled her fingers around its long, graceful neck and gladly accepted its weight and responsibility.

Ignoring the eyes of Sophia, the dark-haired girl watching her from the corner, Etta set the bow to the violin's strings, crossing them. The sound that jumped out was as warm and golden as the tone of the instrument's wood. Etta let out a faint laugh, her anxiety buried under the fizz of excitement. Her violin was a beauty, but this was an absolute prince. She felt like she was about to melt at the quality of each note she coaxed out of it.

She's not ready for this. She doesn't have the right training, and there's no guarantee it'll go the right way for her. . . .

Etta closed her eyes, setting her jaw against the burn of tears rising in her throat, behind her lashes. What right had Etta had to yell at Alice like that? How could she think *her* opinion was somehow more accurate than Alice's, when the woman was lauded the whole world over, when she'd trained dozens of professional violinists?

A small, perfect storm of guilt and anger and frustration was building in the pit of her stomach, turning her inside out.

What had Pierce told her? *You'll always choose playing over everything else. Even me. Even yourself.*

Etta couldn't even argue with him—she had made the choice to break up with him. She loved him in a way that still made her heart clench a little, from memory alone. She missed the light-headed giddiness of sneaking out at night to see him, how reckless and amazing she'd felt when she let herself relax all of her rules.

But a year after they'd gone from friends to something more, she'd placed second in a competition that she—and everyone else—had expected her to win. And suddenly, going to movies, concerts, hanging out at his house, waiting for him outside of his school, began to feel like lost hours. She began tracking them, wondering if Alice would let her debut with an orchestra sooner if she dedicated those precious minutes to practice. She pulled herself deeper into music, away from Pierce.

As she had done with everything but the violin, she'd shrugged him off, and expected that they could go back to the way they'd been for years—friends, and Alice's students. The only way to get through the breakup was to *focus*, to not think about the fact that no one called or texted her, that she'd chased away her only friend.

Just a few weeks later, she'd run into Pierce in Central Park, kissing a girl from his school. Etta had spun on her heel to walk, and then run back up the path she'd just taken, cut so neatly in half by the sight that she kept looking down, as if expecting to see her guts spilling out of her skin. But instead of letting herself cry, Etta had gone home and practiced for six straight hours.

Now not even Alice believed in her.

She should have asked Gail for a minute, a second, to get her head and heart straightened out. Instead, when the woman appeared, chattering into her headset, Etta found herself following her, walking out into the flood of soft blue light on the stage. The applause rolled over her in a dull wave.

Don't drop it, don't drop it, don't drop it. . . .

Etta found her mark and took a moment just to study the violin, turning it over in her hands, fingers lightly skimming its curves. She wanted to still everything that was hurtling through her as she stood under the stage lights; to freeze the fizz of disbelief and excitement, remember the weight and shape of it in her hands.

The Grace Rainey Rogers Auditorium in the Metropolitan Museum of Art wasn't the grandest venue Etta had ever performed in. It wasn't even in the top ten. But it was manageable, and more importantly, hers to command for a few minutes. Seven hundred faces, all masked by shadows and the glare of the lights high overhead as they shifted into a final, rippling blue that reminded her of the ocean, with wind moving over the surface.

You have this.

The applause petered out. Someone coughed. A text alert chimed. Instead of sinking into that calm, the deep concentration, Etta felt herself hovering on the surface of it.

Just play.

She dove into the Largo, pausing only for a steadying breath. Seven hundred audience members stared back at her. Two bars, three bars . . .

It crept up on her slowly, bleeding through her awareness like light warming a screen. Her concentration held out, but only for another few seconds; the sound that began as a murmur, a growl of static underscoring the music, suddenly exploded into shrieking feedback. Screams.

Etta stumbled through the next few notes, eyes frantically searching the technician's booth for a sign about whether she should stop or keep going. The audience was still, gazing up at her, almost like they couldn't hear it—

It wasn't a sound a human could produce; not one anyone could get without ravaging an instrument.

Do I stop? Do I start over?

She crossed strings and flubbed the next three notes, and her anxiety spiked. Why wasn't anyone doing anything about that sound—about the screaming feedback? It crashed through her eardrums, flooding her concentration. Her whole body seemed to spasm with it, the nausea making sweat bead on her upper lip. It felt like . . . like someone was driving a knife into the back of her skull.

The air vibrated around her.

Stop, she thought, desperate, *make it stop—*

I'm messing up—

Alice was right—

Etta didn't realize she'd stopped playing altogether until Gail appeared, white-faced and wide-eyed at the edge of the stage. Pressing her face into her hand, Etta tried to catch a breath, fighting through the sensation that her lungs were being crushed. She couldn't look at the audience. She couldn't look for Alice or her mother, surely watching this play out in horror.

A nauseating wave of humiliation washed over her chest, up her neck, up her face, and for the first time in Etta's nearly fifteen years of playing, she turned and ran off the stage. Chased by the sound that had driven her off in the first place.

"What's the matter?" Gail asked. "Etta? Are you okay?"

"Feedback," she mumbled, almost unable to hear herself. "Feedback—"

Michelle, the curator, deftly plucked the Antonius out of her hands before she could drop it.

"There's no feedback," Gail said. "Let me get you a glass of water—we'll find a place for you to sit—"

That's not right. Etta swung her gaze around, searching the faces of the other violinists. They would have heard it—

Only, they clearly hadn't. The sound of the feedback and her own drumming heart filled the violinists' silence as they stared back with blank faces.

I'm not crazy, I'm not crazy—

Etta took a step back, feeling trapped between their pity and the wall of sound that was slamming into her back in waves. Panic made the bile rise in her throat, burning.

"Go!" Gail said frantically to one of the older men. "Get out there!"

"I've got her."

The dark-haired girl, Sophia, stepped out of the green room, reaching out to take Etta's arm. She hadn't realized how unsteady she was until the arm Gail had thrown around her lifted, and she was forced to lean on a stranger a whole head shorter than her.

"I'm . . . I'm fine. . . ." Etta muttered, swaying.

"No, you're not," Sophia said. "I hear it, too. Come on!"

The easiest explanation was that she'd snapped, that the stress had gotten to her, but . . . someone else had heard it, too. It was as alive and real for her as it was for Etta, and it flooded reassurance through her system to know she hadn't lost it, that she hadn't just crashed and burned because her stage fright and anxiety from childhood were colliding with the way Alice had doubted her.

Etta thought, just for a moment, she might cry in relief. The sound moved like burning knives beneath her skin as Sophia expertly wove them through the dark backstage area and out a side entrance that dumped them directly into the dark, silent museum, just at the entrance of the Egyptian wing.

Wait, Etta wanted to say, but her mouth couldn't seem to catch up to her mind. *Where are we going?*

"It's coming from over here," Sophia said, tugging her forward.

Etta took a step toward the Egyptian wing, and the sound grew more intense, the oscillations quicker, like she was working a radio dial and tuning until she found a signal. Another step, and the pitch rose again into a frenzy.

Like it was excited she was paying attention.

Like it wants me to find it.

"What is that?" she asked, hearing her own voice shake. "Why can't anyone else hear it?"

"Well, we're going to find out—Etta, right? Let's go!"

In the dark, the Met wore a different, shifting skin. Without the usual crush of visitors clogging the hallways, every small sound was amplified. Harsh breathing. Slapping shoes. Cold air slipping around her legs and ankles.

Where? she thought. *Where are you?*

What are you?

They moved beneath the watchful gaze of pharaohs. In the daytime, during the museum's regular hours, these rooms radiated golden light, like sun-warmed stone. But even the creamy walls and limestone gateways were shadowed now, their grooves deeper. The painted faces of sarcophagi and gods with the heads of beasts seemed sharper, sneering, as the girls followed the winding path through the exhibits.

The Temple of Dendur stood alone in front of her, bleached

by spotlights. There was a massive wall of windows, and beyond that, darkness. *Not here.*

Sophia dragged her past the pools of still waters near the temple, and they ran past statues of ancient kings, past the gateway and temple structure, through to the small gift shop that connected this section of the museum to the American wing. There were no docents, no guards, no security gates; there was nothing and no one to stop them.

Nothing and no one to help her.

Go find Mom and Alice, she thought. *Go home.*

But she couldn't—she had to know. She needed—she needed—

The blood drained from her head, until she felt as dizzy and light as the specks of dust floating through the air around her. It was like passing into a dream; the halls were blurring at the edges as she walked, devouring the gilded mirrors, the rich wooden chests and chairs. Shadows played with the doorways, inviting her in, turning her toward one of the emergency stairwells. The sound became a pounding, a drum, a call louder and louder and louder until Etta thought her skull would split from the pressure—

A deafening shot ripped through even the feedback, startling Sophia to a skidding stop. Etta's whole body jerked with the suddenness of it. Awareness snapped against her nerves; the stench of something burning, something almost chemical.

She saw the blood first as it snaked across the tile to her toes.

Then the milk-white head of hair.

The thing was a crumpled body.

Etta screamed, screamed, screamed, and was drowned out by

the pulsing feedback. She pushed past a startled Sophia to get to the body on the cold tile, heaving, a sob caught in her throat, and dropped down to her knees beside Alice.

Breathing, alive, breathing—

Alice's pale eyes flickered over at her, unfocused. ". . . Duck?"

Blood sputtered from her chest, fanned out against Etta's hands as she pressed them against the wound. Her mind began to shut down in its panic.

What happened? What happened?

"You're all right," Etta told Alice, "you're—"

"Shot?" Sophia said, leaning over Etta's shoulder. There was a tremor of something in her voice—fear? "But who—?"

A shout carried to them from the other end of the hall. Three men in tuxedos, one of them the man in glasses she'd bumped into in the Great Hall, followed by a security guard, seemed to come toward them in slow motion. The emergency light beside them caught a pair of glasses and made them glow.

"Call 911!" Etta yelled. "Somebody help, please!"

There was a slight pressure on her hand. Etta looked down as Alice's eyes slid shut. ". . . the old . . . familiar places . . . *run*. . . ."

Her next breath came raggedly, and the next one never came at all.

The scream that tore out of Etta's throat was soundless. Arms locked around her waist, dragging her up from the ground. She struggled, thrashing against the grip.

CPR—Alice needed help—Alice was—

"We have to go!" Sophia shouted into her ear.

What the hell is going on?

The door to the stairwell directly behind them scraped open.

Loose hair floated around Etta's face, clinging to the sweat on her cheeks and neck.

The stairwell was so brightly lit compared to the rest of the building that Etta had to hold up her hands to shield her eyes.

The humming . . . it was as if the empty air on the edge of the landing, just above the stairs, was moving, vibrating in time with the sound. It shimmered the way heat did when it rose from sidewalks on an unbearably hot day. The walls leaned in toward her shoulders.

"Sorry about this."

She was shoved forward, and the world shattered. A blackness ringed the edges of her vision, clenched her spine, dragged her, tossed her into the air with crushing pressure. Etta lost her senses, her logic, her thoughts of *Stop, help, Mom*—she lost everything.

She disappeared.

ETTA DIDN'T SURFACE BACK INTO REALITY SO MUCH AS SLAM INTO IT.

Hours, days—she wasn't sure—a small forever later, her eyes flashed open. There was pressure on her chest, making it difficult to draw a breath. When she tried to sit up, to open the path to her lungs, her joints cracked. Her arms and legs cramped as she tried to stretch out, to feel in the darkness—they struck something hard and rough.

Wood, she thought, recognizing the smell that filled her nose. *Fish.*

She coughed and forced her eyes open. A small room unfolded around her. The wood floor dipped violently to the right, as if someone had upended one side of it.

As the bright sparks cleared out of her vision, and her eyes adjusted to the dark, Etta dragged her legs in and her chest up, so she could sit up in—what was this? A large cradle, a bunk bed built into the floor and bolted to the wall.

The museum . . . what was going on?

There had been some kind of . . . some kind of an explosion. . . .

Where were the cold tile floors of the stairwell? Where were the fire alarms? Her heart was in her throat, fluttering like a desperate animal. Her muscles felt like they'd been carved out of wood. She reached up, trying to scrub the burning sensation from her eyes, erase the black spots still floating there.

Alice. Where was Alice? She had to get to Alice—

The fuzz of static in her ears burst like the first clap of rain from a thundercloud. Suddenly, Etta was drenched in sound. Creaking, groans, slamming footsteps, pops of explosions in the air. Screams—

"—forward—!"

"Behind me—!"

"—the helm—!"

The words took shape, strung together like dissonant chords, smashing cymbals. The room was clogged with silvery smoke.

This wasn't the stairwell; this wasn't any office in the Met. The walls were nothing more than panels of dark unfinished wood. When she turned, she could just make out the shape of a chair and a figure cowering in it, arms clasped over her head.

"Hello?" she scratched out, surging forward on unsteady feet. She was caught again by shock, the feel of rough fabric against her arms and legs. For the first time since she'd come to, her adrenaline slowed to a complete stop.

She wasn't wearing her black dress.

This was . . . it was floor-length, some kind of pale shade Etta couldn't make out. She ran her fingers over the bodice, tracing the embroidery in disbelief. The dress had her upper arms and chest in a chokehold, making it difficult to move.

"Oh!"

A girl's voice. The figure in the chair moved, rising to her feet. A trembling memory flickered through Etta's mind. *The girl.* The girl from the concert. Etta charged forward, knocking her aside to get to the crack of light she could see just beyond her—a door.

She pushed me in the stairwell, she shoved me forward—once she had the first glimmer of memory in place, the rest fell into line behind it.

"No—no—we must stay down here!" the girl cried. "Please, listen to me—"

Etta's fingers ran along the wall until they found a latch, and she burst out of the cramped, dark room. A thick cloud of smoke rose up to meet her, and light flooded her eyes, bleaching the world a painful white. Etta felt hands at her back again, which made her fight harder to move forward, to feel her way through the smoke until her foot caught something and she went tumbling down.

Don't think, just go! Etta reared up, then stopped. Her wide, white skirts were spread out over a man, flat on his back.

"I'm sorry, I—" she choked out, crawling over to make sure he was all right. "You—"

His pale blue eyes stared up at the ceiling, shock and anguish twisting his features into a stiff mask. A trail of gleaming buttons on his absurdly old-fashioned coat had been torn open and the shirt beneath was splattered with—with—

Oh my God.

"Sir?" Etta's voice cracked on the word. He wasn't moving. He wasn't blinking. She looked down, mind blank as it took in the dark liquid coating her skin, her chest, her stomach, the dress.

Blood. Her snowy white skirt was drenched with thick, crimson blood. She was crawling through that man's blood. *I'm crawling through his blood.*

What is this?

Etta was up and on her feet before her mind registered moving, and headed toward the source of the light from above. The smoke reached out to smother her, locking tight around her neck. Glass lanterns crashed around her, exploding like pale fireworks. She kept going toward the light until her knees struck something—stairs. Etta grabbed her skirt, hauled the thick layers of it up around her waist, and started to pull herself up, not caring that she was crying, just looking for fresh air and a path out of this nightmare.

Instead, she climbed into the mouth of another one.

THE ATLANTIC
1776

TWO

HELL AND DAMNATION—NOT THE BLOODY BELL, TOO!
Nicholas swung around, slamming his fist into the next face that tried to block his path. The thing was in pieces—hot, smoldering fragments scattered around the deck. And, unfortunately, *in* various parts of the bodies that had fallen when the grenade struck.

It had been impossible, in the thick of things, to form a true assessment of how badly the *Challenger's* gunners had savaged their prize. Now that he was past the initial wave of violence that followed the boarding, Nicholas had had the chance to conduct a quick survey for himself on the state of the *Challenger,* and now, this captured ship. He tallied up each defect in the ship's outward perfection. All three masts were standing—holding for now, if only just, despite the thrashing they'd taken; the mizzenmast, toward the rear of ship, seemed to be shivering and swaying like a drunkard with each faint breeze. The sails had been torn and punched through, but his prize crew could make quick enough work of replacing them. Once, of course, this ship's crew surrendered.

47

Nicholas moved with the ship, catching the next spray of salt water full across the face. Most importantly, he noted that the ship wasn't taking on water insofar as he could tell. The gunners hadn't struck her below the waterline—which meant they had managed to disable the ship without wrecking her.

Nicholas refused to give in to the flighty, half-drunk feeling that victory was within arms' reach. Before the day was out, he'd start sailing his first ship back to port as prize master.

He would finally be able to cut himself loose from his past.

Still—the damn idiots should have struck their colors first thing. Would have saved every party involved from a bloodstained affair, not to mention an ungodly headache for the carpenters. How unfortunate that sailing was one of the few occupations where a man could be praised for failing, so long as he did it bravely.

This ship—*my ship*, he thought stubbornly, because it would be, once the ship's officers admitted to themselves the inevitable fact of their defeat—was a lovely piece of work, all damage from the *Challenger* and boarding party aside. A three-masted vessel, the foremast square-rigged, the mainmast carrying a large fore-and-aft mainsail, with a square main-topsail and topgallant sail above it. The moment they'd spotted the sails in the distance and her British colors, the *Challenger* had fallen on it like a shark. A fast, sleek schooner streaking after its fat prey. With speed on their side, it had hardly mattered that they were outgunned sixteen to twelve. The merchant vessel was a plum prize for the crew of the *Challenger* after weeks of fruitless hunting around the waters of the West Indies, but it was also the target he had been hired to track, and capture.

He was loath to admit the real reason they had stalked the

waters, searching for it. Ironwood wanted the two women, the passengers, who sailed upon it.

The sudden shift of air at his back, the splatter of hot, salty sweat against his skin—Nicholas dove hard to the right, slamming his shoulder into the wood as a tomahawk sliced down behind his head.

The cannon smoke had choked the air from the moment the ships had exchanged broadsides, and the dismal breeze of the day refused to carry it off and clear the field. It was all fruitless fighting now; the result was obviously in his boarding party's favor. Nicholas tried to find purchase against the ever-growing tide of bodies and blood staining the deck.

The sailor with the tomahawk stalked forward through the chaos of clanging steel and the earsplitting explosions of flintlock pistols firing.

The wood under him bounced as Afton, one of the *Challenger's* mates, fell inches from Nicholas, his chest shredded by balls of lead, his face a death mask of outraged disbelief.

Anger roared through Nicholas, heating him at his core as he felt for a weapon. His own flintlock had been fired, and there'd be no reloading it in time. Throwing it would only stun the man, and would be a waste of a damn good pistol at that. Nicholas plucked a knife from a tangle of rigging someone had cut away. A deer-horn handle, ornately carved. His outlook on the situation brightened considerably.

The short, stout sailor with the tomahawk charged toward him screaming, eyes glassy, face gleaming with sweat and soot. Nicholas knew that look, when the burn of bloodlust had set in and you gave yourself over to the pounding rhythm of a good, hard fight.

His right shoulder burned as he lifted his unloaded pistol from his side, pretending to take aim. The gray light caught the muzzle, making it glow in his hands. The seaman drew up short so quickly that his feet nearly slid out from under him. He was close enough for Nicholas to smell him—the acrid sweat, the gunpowder—to see his nostrils flare with surprise. The sailor's grip on the tomahawk eased, just for a moment, and Nicholas threw the knife. He imagined he could hear the *thwack* as it pierced the sailor's meaty neck, and felt some grim satisfaction that he'd hit his mark.

The fight was finally slowing as more of the men realized the fact of their defeat. Bodies began to ache, and powder cartridges emptied; where there had been shouts, there was now a growing silence. The knife was lodged in the side of the sailor's neck—he must have turned just before it struck. He'd given himself a bad death, drawing the whole business out as he drowned in his own blood. Nicholas leaned over him, instinctively bracing his weight against the swelling sea.

"Sent . . . down . . . to . . . devil"—the sailor's eyes were narrowed, one last bit of defiance as he choked and hacked— "by—by—a—a shit-sack . . . *negro*."

The last word was accompanied by a fine misting of blood across his waistcoat. The heat beneath Nicholas's skin evaporated, leaving a perfect, cold diamond of fury in the center of his chest. He had been called far worse, been beaten for simply having been born on the wrong side of the blanket to a woman in chains. Perhaps it was the stark contrast of victory with defeat.

His life now held worth and value. On a ship, it mattered less what your origins were, and more what work you were willing to do; how hard you'd fight for the men around you. Nicholas had decided long ago to keep his eyes on the horizon of the future, rather than look over his shoulder at what he'd left behind.

Only—that expression the sailor wore. The way his snarl had curled the word into something hateful. Nicholas took a firm hold of the knife's hilt. He breathed in the sour stench of the man's breath as he leaned over his face.

"By your *better*, sir," he said, and drew the blade across the sailor's throat.

Nicholas had never been one to crow or luxuriate over another man's demise, but he watched as the last of the color left the sailor's face and the skin turned a waxy gray.

"That was a far kinder death than I'd have given him."

Captain Hall stood a short distance behind him, surveying the slowing fight with a filthy rag pressed against his forehead. When he pulled it away to get a better look at Nicholas, blood spurted from a gash over one thick brow.

Nicholas swallowed the stone that had formed in his throat. "Yes, well," he said. "I've never particularly enjoyed viewing a man's entrails."

The captain guffawed, and Nicholas cleaned the knife against his breeches as he made his way to the side of the towering man. He knew he was tall himself, broad in the shoulders, strong-bodied after years of hauling lines and cargo, but the captain had seemingly been carved from the rocky shores of Rhode Island.

Nicholas had been in awe of Captain Hall from the moment they met nearly a decade before—the Red Devil, other sailors had called him. Now, only his beard retained some of that original color. The grooves in the long planes of his face were set deeper by the years, yes, and several teeth and fingers had been sacrificed along the way, but Hall kept himself tidy, kept a tight ship, and made sure his crew were fed and well-paid. In their sphere of life, there was hardly better praise to be had.

The captain's eyes moved over Nicholas with a father's instinctive concern. He'd spent years trying to break Hall of the habit, but some things truly were impossible feats.

"Not like you to let someone get that close," Nicholas said, nodding at the cut on his forehead. "Need the surgeon?"

"And be forced to admit that one of this ship's cabin boys caught me unawares with a spoon as I went below? Wicked little bugger. I'd rather be boiled in oil."

Nicholas snorted. "Did you find the women?"

"Aye, they're in one of the officers' cabins in the stern. Safe and sound, the little doves," he said.

Relief bloomed through Nicholas, replacing his fury at the dying man's last words. Good.

"This job . . ." the captain began, for the fifth time that day. "I have to tell you, Nick, I'm grateful for the prize and its cargo, but I feel uneasy. I would rather you have nothing to do with the family. It seems like there's more to this than simply transport to New York."

Of course there was more to it; with this family, there always was. Ironwood's note had arrived a few days after the much-awaited Letter of Marque and Reprisal had come to Nicholas's employer, Lowe & Lowe Shipping, authorizing Hall's ship to act as a privateer and legally—at least in the colonies' view—hunt British ships. He'd had less than a week to consider the man's offer, to bring it to Hall and ask for his compliance in searching for this particular vessel and her passengers. They'd agreed to secrecy over the truth of their focused hunt, rather than draw any of the crew into Ironwood business. He'd been slow to send

52

his acceptance of Ironwood's terms for this job, all the while turning over the chances of it being a ploy to lure him back into Ironwood's nets for one last act of revenge.

But—it had been three years. They'd known precisely where to find him, having stranded him here themselves. Surely they would have come sooner if they'd wanted blood for blood?

He could live with a fair bit of uncertainty, and he could fight to protect himself if it came to that. But the simple facts were these: the job Ironwood offered was a good one, and the reward for its completion would help him achieve his life's aim far faster than simple privateering.

The neat, meticulously formed words had leapt off the page. *Bring the two women into New York City by the 21st of September. Do what you will with the ship and its cargo.*

He'd spent these three years in the employ of Lowe & Lowe, toiling on merchant vessels, overseeing shipments from the West Indies to the colonies until the outbreak of the war, all the while forcing himself to close off the part of his heart that stung deeply at any thought of Julian, of traveling. Nicholas had been hoping that Messieurs Lowe would reward him with his own privateer ship to captain, but he'd seen the uneasy way the old man and his son had surveyed him when Captain Hall first suggested it. He delivered results for them; he knew their hesitation couldn't be due to that. So then, it was merely him—the reality of the color of his skin—that made him unworthy. Their hesitation only renewed his interest in purchasing his own ship, one not beholden to any company.

As it was now, the Lowes would get the bulk of whatever payment the ship's cargo brought in, and the rest would be divided among the crew of the *Challenger*. It could be months before they found another prize. The ocean was wide and vast and the shipping companies were growing cleverer about avoiding privateers—perhaps this would be it for them, and Nicholas would be left to scrape together coins, scrimp and save, until he was dead in the heart and old in his bones. He hated the Ironwoods with the fury of a hurricane, but they owed him a debt for the time they'd stolen from him. And he intended to collect it.

"Did you survey the cargo?" Nicholas asked.

Hall sighed, recognizing the diversionary tactic. "A glance here and there."

A sailor exploded through the cloud of smoke in front of them, hollering and whooping, a cutlass brandished over his head. Nicholas whirled, his hand on his knife, but by the time he had it out, the captain had whipped out his pistol and fired.

"Sugar, rum, cotton, munitions for the ballast," Hall continued blissfully. The dead man slid away in a smear of blood. "I'm almost frightened of how well this has played out—you have your ladies, and we have a fair share of wealth coming to each of us. They've even got a bulkhead for us in the hold to detain the crew. Speaking of which, I've yet to see anyone I could reasonably believe would be the captain. Why don't you go find him so we can get the business of lowering their colors done with—" Hall broke off, distracted by something.

Nicholas had not seen such a look of unwelcome surprise on his captain's face since the time their former cook announced he had served the crew stewed rat instead of salted beef.

He followed the man's line of sight. There, between the sailors snarling at each other, a towheaded figure was emerging from below decks, rising through the curling smoke like Persephone returning from the underworld.

Nicholas winced as she slammed into the bare, scarred back of the master gunner, but she didn't scream, not even when Davies swung around, axe in hand, and made as if to gut her. It was *his* startled yelp that drew the attention of every man around them, damn his eyes—

It wasn't Sophia—he knew to expect another woman aside from her, but who was *this* . . . ?

"Poor darling has her feathers all ruffled," Captain Hall said at his back. Despite the wash of blood at his feet and the bodies strewn around him, his features went as soft as a kitten's. The old bastard couldn't help himself in the presence of young ladies, especially those in need of rescue. And this one was. Her white gown was torn at the hip—and bloodstained?

"She's hurt," Nicholas said sharply. "What the bloody hell is she doing?"

She spun in Nicholas's direction as if she had heard his words. He should have barreled forward and plucked her out of the mess of gore and violence, but it felt as though the whole deck, the whole ocean, gave a rolling shudder. Captain Hall knocked into him with a surprised grunt.

The girl backed away steadily as they advanced toward her, until finally she bumped into the bulwark lining the edge of the deck and had nowhere left to go. Her eyes darted around her before fixing on a nearby spear. Without a second thought, she swept it up from the deck, shouting, "Stay away from me!"

There was a sudden, almost painful tightening of his body as he caught sight of her face, her fierce expression as she swung the weapon back and forth in desperation. Hair thick and white-gold, generous brows, eyes with an almost feline tilt to them. A long nose, balancing out the generous curve of her lips. Awareness of her moved through him like slow, warm honey. She was, in a word—

No. None of that, now. Dangerous thoughts. But he could appreciate that she was, apparently, a fighter—though she seemed surprised herself at the fact, looking uneasily between the weapon in her hands and the two dozen men gaping at her. The last half-hearted scuffles had been abandoned in favor of dumb shock at her unexpected appearance. That was reasonable, he supposed. And now the effect of seeing her bloodied and fierce, like a queen on a battlefield, was rather singular. It spoke to his own blood, made it sing its secrets. She was . . .

A job. Nicholas shook his head, stomping out the blaze of heat that cut across his chest. *Payment owed for services rendered.*

A sharp, deafening *crack* broke through the faint hum in his ears; Nicholas swung his attention up, toward the aft of the ship. A section of the mizzenmast, the third mast of three, had finally snapped under its own weight, just as he'd feared it might.

And it slowed, time did. He let out a sound that was less a warning and more a terrified shout as the wood splintered and the sails collapsed in on themselves with a thwack and flutter. The lines supporting the mast snapped as if God himself had cut them, and the whole of it—the topgallant, the topmast, the rigging, the metal hardware—came crashing down over them.

Nicholas ran.

The sailors who dove to escape the mast's crushing weight weren't able to move far or fast enough to avoid the tangle of sails and rigging. Captain Hall roared out, *"The girl! Find the girl!"*

The men from both crews fell on the wreckage with their axes and swords, cutting it away, searching beneath it. Nicholas knew better. She'd been standing near where the mast smashed through the bulwark, but not in its path. The impact wouldn't have struck her directly, but knocked her back—

He leaned over the rail, searching the dark water between the hulls of the two ships, and—yes, there—a ring of white where something had fallen, struck the surface, and promptly sunk.

"Nick!" he heard the captain call, but he'd already shrugged out of his jacket and waistcoat and vaulted himself over the rail and into the sea.

THE ICY WATER DRANK HIM DEEP, ROBBING HIM OF THE BREATH he'd taken before the descent. Sunlight broke through the surface of the water, casting a warm glow about the wreckage and bodies sinking slowly to the ocean floor. He suspected the presence of sharks.

Still, there was plenty for the creatures to gorge on before they tasted his flavor. With that less-than-comforting thought, he dove deeper, his muscles afire from the stinging assault of cold water. Just before he sent up a small prayer for assistance, he saw her.

She must have exhausted all of her fight on deck; now the girl was as limp as seaweed caught in a current as she was dragged steadily down. He saw the problem immediately. Her legs and the gown were caught in netting, which in turn had wrapped itself around a heavy piece of the hull. Her arms floated up, as if still straining toward the surface.

Nicholas removed his knife and went to work sawing the net, her gown, anything but her skin. His chest felt tight enough to snap, burning with its need for air. The moment he had her free, he drew his arms around her and propelled them both up, kicking furiously with the last of his strength and sense.

They exploded up through the surface of the water, and he

greedily sucked in the first few gulps of briny air. He choked up some of the water he'd swallowed, stomach flipping with an unfamiliar panic. He brought a hand to one of her cheeks, still scissoring his legs to keep them afloat. A frisson of horror went down his spine when he felt the icy quality of her skin.

Hall's voice boomed above the others, calling down to him, "Nick! Grab the line!"

He caught the rope handily and went to work securing it around them. Despite the slither of dread in his guts, he spoke sternly to the girl.

"You will *not* die," he ordered her. "I expressly forbid it. Not on my ship, do you hear me?"

If he lost this girl, he'd lose everything.

"Heave ho, heave ho," he heard Hall order. "Almost there!"

Nicholas spread his hand out across her back to steady her as they came up level to the bulwark, and he turned to brace his feet against it. None of this made the least bit of sense to him—why had she run out? And this blood . . . was it even hers?

His shoulders were gripped by the solid force of half a dozen hands, and he and the girl were hauled onto the ship's deck.

Nicholas rolled just in time to avoid landing on top of her. The back of his skull bounced against the coarse wood with a sharp *crack*, blacking out his vision for one terrible instant.

"The surgeon's mate will look after her." Captain Hall's face swam in front of his.

"—is the lass dead?" someone asked.

Nicholas was trembling like a flag in a gale. He focused on the steady pattern of drawing in breaths and releasing them. Around him were the anxious, bedraggled faces of the sailors from both crews, all hovering about the girl with morbid interest. The men had forgotten their fighting with this spectacle, true, but his crew had *also* forgotten they were meant to be securing the other men in the ship's hold.

A movement distracted him from that thought. His eyes shifted to where a small figure in a navy coat was kneeling beside the girl, hands pressed firmly on her belly. Plain, crisp clothes; dark hair perfectly pulled back and collected at the base of his skull in a queue; a face like a child's—Nicholas mistrusted anyone who could stay so pristine on a ship, never mind in the midst of battle. It spoke of cowards.

"Easy, Nick," Hall said, helping him sit up, "it's only this ship's surgeon's mate."

"Where's Philips?" he demanded. "Or this ship's surgeon?"

"Philips went below to tend to the men there. Their surgeon is no longer in possession of the lower half of his body. I believe he is presently indisposed with the business of dying."

Nicholas shook his head, unwilling to accept that a child would be caring for her. "How long has he been out of strings? A year?"

Captain Hall raised a brow. "About as long as you, I'd wager."

He didn't like the liberty with which the surgeon's mate was cutting her gown and stays open—

"Couldn't be bothered to take off your shoes and stockings, I see," the captain continued, storm-gray eyes flashing with amusement. "You took off like the devil's hounds were on your heels."

Nicholas glowered at Hall, well aware of his sagging wet stockings and the ruined leather. "I didn't realize we are now in the habit of letting ladies drown."

His words were forgotten when Nicholas caught a movement out of the corner of his eye. He turned in time to see the surgeon's mate raise a fist and bring it down, hard, against her stomach.

"Sir!" Nicholas surged up off the deck, swaying on his feet. "You *dare*—?"

The girl coughed violently, her back twisting off the deck as she spat out the water in her lungs. Long, pale fingers curled against the deck and she took several panting breaths, eyes squeezed shut. Nicholas's eyes narrowed at where the surgeon's mate had placed a steadying hand on her bare shoulder.

No one spoke, not even Captain Hall, who seemed as startled as the rest of them to have her so suddenly returned to them from the land of the dead. Persephone, indeed.

"Ma'am," Nicholas managed to scratch out, with a curt bow. "Good afternoon."

Her eyelids fluttered as she collapsed onto her back again. Her hair, darker now that it was wet, clung to the curve of her skull. The sailors seemed to step in as one, leaning forward to peer down at her, and were rewarded with a wide-eyed gaze as pale blue as the sky above them.

"Um," she said hoarsely. "Hi?"

THREE

THERE WASN'T A PART OF ETTA THAT DIDN'T FEEL RAW and battered; the aching inside her skull did nothing to dampen the rank smell of blood and body odor, and something else that almost smelled like fireworks.

Looking from face to face—the knit caps, a crooked and fraying wig, a few wet eyes discreetly wiped against shoulders—her mind began the work of piecing it all together as if she were sight-reading a new piece of music. The notes became measures, and the measures phrases, until finally the whole melody drifted through her.

She was not in the museum. So, obviously, the rescue workers must have carried her out into the street, away from that strange explosion of noise and light. Her skin, hair, and dress were drenched through and through, because—because of the building's sprinklers, right?

And the costumes . . . maybe there had been some kind of play going on in a nearby building and they'd rushed out to help? Etta wasn't sure—what did firemen actually wear under their uniforms? *No, Etta,* she thought, *they* don't *wear loose white shirts, or buckle shoes, or hats straight out of* Masterpiece Theatre. So . . . a play. Theatrical production. They'd either been caught in the explosion . . . attack, whatever it had been, or had some very authentic makeup.

Mom? She tried to get her mouth around the word, but her throat felt like it had been scraped with a razor. *Alice.* Alice had been shot—Alice was—she was—

Dead.

That couldn't be right. That made *no sense.*

She brought a trembling hand up to rub the crustiness from her eyes, soothe the burn building behind her lashes. The sky was spread so wide over her, without a single building to block the view. Were they in the park? The smoke was still so overpowering, she couldn't pick up the familiar blend of the city's exhaust and the rancid-sweet smell of its festering garbage. No siren, no alarms, just . . . the creak of wood. The slap of water.

The bob and roll of the ground beneath her.

You're not in the Met.

Etta shook her head, trying to clear the thought, fight the panic.

You're not in New York.

She was confused by scenes she had imagined—the cramped room, the body, all the blood, the ear-splitting crack, falling—

"Ma'am," said a gravelly voice. "Good afternoon."

Etta craned her neck around, eyes watering against the harsh glare of sunlight. She couldn't see anything beyond a ring of bedraggled faces until two tall figures pushed to the front of the group. One, the older, middle-aged man, wore an olive-colored coat. His red hair, streaked with threads of white, was tied back at the base of his neck. He smiled, revealing mostly yellow teeth.

Something glinted in his eyes as he turned to look at the younger man next to him.

He was tall, even next to the giant beside him, his stance strong against the slight heave of the deck. He gave a little bow, his face disappearing—but Etta had seen it, and just that once was enough to lock it into her memory. The red-haired man's skin was pink across the bridge of his nose and cheeks, clearly sunburned and chapped, and the younger one's skin was a deep, sun-kissed brown. The overall effect was like he'd been lit inside by the warm glow of firelight.

From farther away, his face had struck Etta as being hard, impassive, cut from stone. In the instant before he straightened, though, the full weight of his gaze settled on her and she had a moment to study him, too—to see the small scars on the high planes of his cheekbones, the nicks and stubble on his square jaw, the evidence of a well-worn life. A ghost of a smile.

Etta realized, an awkward two seconds too late, that they were all waiting for some kind of response.

"Um," she managed to get out. "Hi?"

Some of the men shuffled, looking pleased. More looked confused.

"High?" one of them repeated, casting his gaze toward the sky.

Etta worked herself up onto her elbows, returning their startled looks with one of her own. Did all of them have this accent—vaguely British? The flow and curl of their words made her own sound harsh and grating.

Old-fashioned clothes. Old-fashioned accents. Old-fashioned ship?

Etta struggled to sit, and the men's attention shifted—from her face, down to—she sucked in a sharp, whistling breath, throwing her arms around herself. The gown was sliced down the center, and as the wet, heavy fabric dried, it was losing its cling.

The younger man tossed her a navy-blue coat. The wool rasped against her cold skin, and Etta had to fight the urge to bury her face in it, to disappear. It smelled the way she imagined the man would, like sweat, cedar, alcohol, and the sea itself.

"Madam, are you well?"

The young man sitting a short distance away from her was so slight, so unimposing compared to the others, that he'd simply faded into the background. He lifted his chin to peer at her through the round, almost laughably small wire glasses perched on his nose. The front of his odd pants were soaking wet, as were his knee-high socks and buckle shoes, and Etta had the faint, horrifying notion that she might have thrown up on him when she'd come to.

The young man's face steeled under her scrutiny; one small hand came up to stroke at the white cloth elaborately tied at his throat, the other to pat down his hair. Those were clean hands—perfectly manicured, which seemed at odds with the fact that they were on . . . on . . .

A ship.

With a pulse of fear, Etta leapt to her feet. The coat wasn't a barrier against their gazes, and it wouldn't be much of a shield against their weapons, but she felt better for having it close.

"Oh my God—" she choked out.

A ship. She'd seen it just before—before all of those sails had come crashing down and she'd been knocked clear into next Tuesday. Her back had slapped against the freezing water, ankle twisting down as she'd struggled to paddle up. All those years of swimming at the 92nd Street Y for nothing. Her fingers had been too frozen, her vision too blanketed with black, to untangle the netting.

It had hurt, so bad—her head, her chest, every part of her had felt like it was tearing apart with the need to breathe.

I drowned.

Etta looked from the young man with the wire glasses to the one who had spoken when she'd come to, the one with the dark, stern eyes. He watched her calmly, almost as if challenging her. The words registered almost as surely as if he'd taken one of his long fingers and stroked the letters into her skin.

Is this who you are?

He crossed his arms over his chest and leaned back, bracing himself against the roll of the ocean.

The ocean.

Not the Met.

Not New York City.

Not a piece of land in sight.

Just two tall wooden ships.

Just men in . . . costume. . . .

They were costumes. They *were.*

You know they're not. Etta tried to swallow, the memory of the concert ripping through her, tearing at her heart, her lungs. *Alice is dead. I . . . the Met . . . the girl . . .*

The older man with red hair sent the others out of the way, moving with long, efficient strides.

"She's well, and there's work to be done," he told the crew, motioning two burly-armed men forward. Both were missing patches of their beards and hair, as if they'd been singed off in clumps, and both were bare down to their waists. The impressive expanse of muscle was offset by the fact that Etta could smell them from a good ten feet away.

"Mr. Phelps, Mr. Billsworth, please escort this ship's crew down into the hold. And see that the carpenters begin their work posthaste."

"Aye, Captain."

These men . . . they'd been fighting, hadn't they? And not just fighting—killing one another.

The man said to bring them down into the hold, she thought. *They're being locked up.* Because . . . they were the enemy? Where the hell was she? How the hell had she gotten from the Met to a ship in the middle of nowhere?

"Now, sweetheart, come here," the man—the captain—said, beckoning her forward with a hand missing its last two fingers. Etta wasn't sure she trusted her instincts in that moment; the sight of him, bloodied and massive, made her chest clench. But there was nothing menacing about the way he was approaching her, or even a thread of threat woven through his words. She shook her head to clear that last thought before it made her do something reckless again, like let her guard down. If he thought he was going to grab her, he was going to get every last ounce of New York City she possessed. Etta swung her head around, searching for something sharp.

"Don't be afraid, sweetheart," he said, firmly, hand still outstretched. Soft eyes. Soft voice. Perfect for luring unsuspecting ingénues to their untimely deaths.

"I am not your *sweetheart!*" she snarled.

The man cleared his throat, a poor disguise for his laugh.

"We aren't scoundrels. Any man who attempts harm to you—who casts a single unwanted glance in your direction—will find himself eating barnacles off the keel."

In some strange way, she did believe him. If they'd wanted her dead, then fishing her out of the ocean and reviving her probably wasn't the most competent way of going about it.

Funny how it didn't make her feel any safer.

These people were strangers, and by the looks on their faces when she'd first appeared, they'd seemed just as surprised to see her as she was to see them. If anyone actually knew what was going on, and *where* she was, Etta knew her best and maybe only bet would be the girl she'd left below deck—the one who had pushed her through that strange door of glimmering air at the museum.

"Scoundrels?" Etta repeated in disbelief. "Are you supposed to be . . . pirates?"

The young man looked highly offended, but the red-haired man merely shrugged. "Aye, pirates. Legal ones, though I suppose His Majesty would beg to differ. That ship—" He pointed to the ship sitting alongside the one they stood on. Countless lines of rope and hooks connected the ships to one another. "She's a privateer outfitted in New London, Connecticut. The *Challenger*. We've captured this one," the man continued.

Right. Etta forced herself to nod. Of course.

The men who hadn't been sent to the hold were working now, scrambling around the deck like ants rebuilding their colony. Planks and beams of wood were being handed up from below, over from the other ship. Men disappeared below, still bloodied, and reappeared with bandages. Her stomach flipped and flipped and flipped, and she thought that there was a real chance she was going to tear the jacket apart at the seams just to do *something*. Something other than sit there and feel helpless.

You are not helpless. Being down wasn't the same as being out. She just needed to—find her bearings. Get her sea legs under her. Or whatever pirates said.

And now they were clearing the deck of . . .

Bodies. Say it, Etta. Bodies.

Alice. Did they have something to do with hurting her?

Killing her, a voice corrected at the back of her mind.

She swept her eyes back out over the water to avoid the grim efficiency of it, their twisted, stretched bodies—their pieces—being stitched up into linen bags by sailors with faces like stone. There wasn't a speck out on the far horizon. No land. No other ships. Just a sparkling blue that was darkening along with the sky. Just her, these ships, these men, and these bodies. The water and foam sloshing across the deck had turned a revolting shade of pink from the blood.

Etta barely made it to the rail in time to lean over it, stare into the dark water, and throw up. She closed her eyes, tried purging the images that were clinging to her mind like rosin on a bow. By the time she finished, she shook with exhaustion and more than a little embarrassment.

But she felt better for it. Clearer.

"Ma'am—"

Her shoes were long gone—if she'd ever been wearing them at all? Her heel slid against an edge of sharp metal, and she instantly seized on the idea of finally having a weapon. She stooped to pick it up. The many-pronged hook was nearly the size of her head and weighed twice as much—Etta barely got it in the air before it was trying to tumble out of her hands.

"Ma'am, please," the older man said, sparing a brief glance up at the heavens. "If I may, I would far prefer death by harpoon to death by grappling hook. Less of a mess for the men to clean up after, believe me."

"Perhaps you should take a moment to think through your course of actions." The younger man remained where he was, arms crossed over his broad chest again. Was he speaking to her?

That's when Etta noticed that he was as drenched as she was. *Idiot. You didn't get back up onto the ship by yourself.*

"I don't . . . You were the one that . . . saved me?" she asked.

"I should expect that's obvious," he said pointedly.

The older man turned back to him, blocking Etta's view of his expression. When he faced her again, he winked. "Don't mind him. He's allowed one day of good nature a year and he's already spent it."

The other man gave a curt nod, an abbreviated little bow, and said, "Nicholas Carter. Your servant, ma'am. This is Captain Nathaniel Hall. May we have the pleasure of knowing your name?"

Etta hesitated, looking between them again. Captain Hall clasped his hands behind his back, never once losing his pleasant smile.

The situation was so past the point of being strange, and Etta was still not totally sure she wasn't dreaming or having a nervous breakdown, that his question gave her pause.

Perhaps you should take a moment to think through your course of actions. The memory of Nicholas's words made her grip the coat again. She straightened slightly, making her decision.

Whatever this was, she needed to keep herself alive; and, at that moment, the best way to do it might be to cooperate.

"My name is—"

"Henrietta!" a voice called. "Where are you? *Henrietta?*"

"Henrietta?" Captain Hall repeated.

"Etta," she corrected, searching for the source of the shriek. "Etta Spencer."

The girl appeared in a cloud of rustling green fabric and stormy dark hair. An already pale face went chalk white, then green, as she braced herself and took in the scene. She took slow steps through the gore that hadn't yet been scrubbed away by the small boys with their buckets.

Her. Etta hadn't imagined her, either.

"Madam," the small young man with glasses said. "Has your stomach finally settled?"

Etta smelled the sick on her, saw the sheen of sweat coating her forehead and upper lip. The girl's bloodshot eyes locked on Etta.

"You had me so very worried!" she gasped out.

Etta had to throw her hands out to steady them both—and to keep her from getting too close. The girl was shorter than her, but her presence was made larger by the coiled hair piled on top of her head, now drooping off-center. Her dress's full skirt enveloped Etta's wet one, and the shade of ivy green only deepened the queasiness of her complexion.

I don't think so. Etta struggled out of the girl's grip and felt her nails dig into her hand. The girl's brown eyes were framed with full, dark brows, her lips set in a thin line—a smile that was as mocking as it was unforgiving.

The warning was clear: *Don't say another word.*

Etta struggled to hold on to her composure. She opened her mouth, with sharp, wild words already poised at the tip of her tongue, before she clamped it shut again.

Perhaps you should take a moment to think through your course of actions.

This girl knew what had happened. Where they were. Information would start and end with her, and the only way Etta was going to get it was if she shut her mouth and listened.

You know what happened. She pushed you. Etta exhaled loudly through her nose, turning to look out at the sea. She didn't trust herself not to give away her discomfort.

"Really," the girl said, keeping her voice light and airy, "you *must* not panic that way. I told you that everything would be perfectly fine! Surely these gentlemen mean us, as passengers, no harm."

"Battle can rattle even the steadiest of nerves," Captain Hall said. "Miss . . . ?"

"Oh—Sophia Iron—erm, Spencer." She gave a little curtsy. Etta watched without a speck of sympathy as the girl straightened and swayed, her eyes clenched shut, her fist pressed against her stomach. "And . . . this is . . . my sister."

She's seasick, Etta realized.

"Indeed?" There was a wry twist to Nicholas's mouth. "I can see the resemblance."

Etta was glad she looked back then, not because he deserved a laugh, but because she caught Sophia's reaction as she saw him for the first time. Her thin mask of pleasantness slipped into revulsion. It lasted only a moment, but the impression of it stamped itself into her memory.

Captain Hall gave Nicholas a wry look before turning to the

young man in glasses. "Perhaps you'd be so good as to tell us *your* name, as well as this ship's?"

"Oh! Certainly. This ship is the *Ardent*," he said. "I am Abraham Goode, the surgeon's mate, and now, sir, your most obedient servant."

"Looking to stay out of the hold, eh?" Captain Hall chuckled. "You'll serve the prize crew without complaint?"

"It would be my pleasure," Mr. Goode said bravely, setting his shoulders back in such a way that Etta caught Nicholas rolling his eyes.

"Where is Captain Millbrook?" Etta's "sister" asked, glancing around. "Are you now in possession of the ship?"

Her accent wasn't British. More like an old movie starlet's, with her careful cadences; so different than how she'd sounded at the Met.

"I'm sorry to say he's dead, ma'am." The diminutive man in glasses stepped forward from the rail, where he'd been hanging back. He had to raise his crystal-cut voice to be heard above the clanging from the men on deck.

Nicholas and Captain Hall exchanged a look.

"I suppose that makes your job easier," the older man said.

Nicholas shrugged, but his eyes drifted back to Etta. "Would you like to return to your cabin and rest? Today has been an ordeal, I know."

"Yes," Sophia said hurriedly, before Etta could speak. "A good course of action. May we continue to use the cabins near the great cabin?"

"Well, I certainly won't put either of you in the forecastle with the prize crew," Nicholas said. "That will be fine."

Etta turned toward him, surprised. So . . . he was in charge of this ship, not Captain Hall? Then that meant . . . Captain Hall led the other ship they'd mentioned, the *Challenger*, and they'd captured this one, installing Nicholas in command. The men that had been marched down into the hold must have been whatever was left of the original crew of this ship.

Sophia looped her arm through Etta's, drawing her attention back to her.

"I'm sorry for your loss," Mr. Goode said.

Etta must have looked as confused as she felt, because Sophia dug her ragged nails into her arm.

"Captain Millbrook was the young ladies' uncle," Goode said, scratching at his scalp. Sophia, as if suddenly remembering she needed to be devastated, dabbed at her eyes as the surgeon's mate continued, "He was escorting them back to England following the death of their father and the sale of their plantation in New Providence. We departed from Nassau a few days ago."

Nassau? New Providence? Why did she get the feeling they weren't talking about New York or Rhode Island?

"Ah, how terribly unfortunate," Captain Hall said, strangely unsympathetic.

"Forgive my rudeness, but I"—Sophia swallowed hard—"will take my sister below, and leave you to your work. Perhaps . . ." She swallowed again, squeezing her eyes shut as the winds picked up and batted at the ship. "Mr. Carter, you would be so good as to accompany us?"

Nicholas looked like he found the idea of pulling out his own fingernails more appealing.

"It would be my pleasure," he said stiffly.

Sophia smiled tightly and nodded, bidding Captain Hall and Mr. Goode a pleasant afternoon. Etta steadied her legs enough to trail behind her. Nicholas lifted the hatch's cover, a lattice of dark wood.

No, Etta thought as a flash cut through her memory of the body, the blood, the twisted face. *Don't make me go back down there. . . .*

Like she had a choice. Sophia put a hand on the small of her back and pushed her so hard, her foot nearly caught the hem of her dress.

"It's perfectly safe," Nicholas reassured Etta, holding out a hand. She focused on the warm pressure of his fingers closing around hers, not the sharpness of the descent, the smell of gunpowder and blood. The ladder wasn't a ladder so much as a set of steep, shallow stairs. Etta held the sopping fabric of her dress in one hand and kept the other on the rim of the hatch as long as she could for balance. Fabric pooled around her ankles, wet and itchy, as she took each step.

Etta managed to keep both her balance and her eyes open. Smoke hung in the air, heavy but no longer blinding. She got a better look at the long stretch of deck in front of her. Light was pouring through the square holes in the side of the ship, where men were rolling large cannons back into place and securing them with ropes. Etta couldn't make out what was at the other end of the space—canvas curtains were strung up to hide it from view.

Finally, Etta forced herself to look down, only to find that they'd moved the body. They'd rubbed every last trace of it away until there was only a faint discoloration on the wood. The repairs down here had begun immediately; the debris of battle had been brushed to the sides of the ship. Those men who weren't patching the walls were picking through the piles, tossing useless wood fragments and unsalvageable broken glass out through the gun ports to be swallowed by the waiting waves.

Etta stepped back against a wall, making room for the others to come down. Her heel glanced off something cold, drawing her attention down, and—there, on the ground, hugging the wall, was what looked like a small butter knife. It was in her hand before she'd realized she'd gone for it, and she pressed it deep into the folds of her skirt.

What are you doing? Etta asked herself. She gripped its slight weight, pressing her fingers against the etchings on the metal handle.

I'm protecting myself.

So she didn't know exactly how to use it—what was there to know, besides pointing the sharp end away from her? Etta focused on it, its shape, the way it warmed to her hand, with the intensity she channeled into attacking a piece of music. Only then did her breathing finally even out.

Sophia appeared next, stumbling down the last few steps, holding her stomach. A pair of leather shoes, water squelching out of them with each step, announced Nicholas's arrival. A pair like that would be ruined by salt water, Etta knew. She wouldn't allow herself to feel guilty about it.

"You must stay out of the forecastle," he said, seeing that Sophia's gaze had landed on the canvas curtains on the other end of the ship. "Unless it's to use the heads—the, ah, lavatory. It's the crew's space. You're welcome to take air whenever you wish, but only after we've finished refitting the ship, and only with an escort. And under no circumstances should you enter the hold where the other crew is being kept."

"We—" Sophia struggled with the word, pausing to collect herself. When she opened her eyes again, they burned in the darkness. "We won't have anything to do with you beyond what's required."

"I'd imagine not," said Nicholas crisply as he turned. "I will make your excuses at meals."

"You must love this," Sophia snapped. "How quickly the worm has come to try to inch its way back in. If I had known it'd be you, I'd *never* have agreed to this!"

They know one another, Etta realized. She looked between their faces—the obvious hatred on Sophia's, the careful impassivity on Nicholas's—and wondered how it was even possible.

"If you need something from the surgery or the galley," Nicholas continued, as if she hadn't spoken, "please let one of the boys know. They'll fetch it for you."

"Not playing the servant today, are you?" Sophia taunted.

At the rear of the ship where they stood were three doors. Nicholas opened the first one on the right, and Etta recognized the cramped space as the one she'd burst out of. Rather than let the two girls walk in, he glanced around, as if checking to make sure no one was in earshot. They were alone, save for the young sailor on his knees, carefully scrubbing the deck with a stone.

"It's my understanding," he said, his voice low, "that you knew a ship would be intercepting yours. Is that correct?"

Etta gaped at him. No, they *hadn't* known that. An hour ago—wait, how long had it been since they were in the museum?

"Grandfather is clearly losing his mind in his advanced years," Sophia said, "to have trusted *you.*"

"Perhaps it was desperation that forced him to appoint *you,*" Nicholas said. "I have been tasked with bringing you to New York, and as far as I am concerned, that is the beginning and end of our business." He glanced over their shoulders, toward the forecastle. "To avoid unnecessary questions, the other men should see this as nothing more than a regular prize we've captured. Do you take my meaning?"

New York? Etta thought. The two words teased out a tiny bit of hope from the tangled mess of the day.

"What would happen if the truth did slip out, I wonder?" Sophia asked, all sweetness. "What would the crew think of you, risking their lives for a reward they'll never see?"

Something about those words fractured the control over his temper that he'd clearly been wrestling to maintain. Nicholas's arm lashed out, his palm slapping against the wood beside her head. He had loomed over Sophia at his full height, but now he stooped to stare her directly in the eye. "Disparage me all you like, Miss Ironwood, spit out every vile curse you can think of at me—but if you threaten my livelihood again, know that there will be consequences."

Ironwood?

Sophia didn't so much as flinch. She brushed the threat away with a smirk, sickly green face and all. Nicholas shifted back, eyes flickering with a fire that seemed to burn to his core. In the silence that followed, with only the rhythm of the creaking bones of the great ship to mark time, Etta realized what she'd just witnessed, what the girl had found: a weapon to slice open old wounds.

If this was Sophia weak from seasickness, then she was mildly terrified of what the girl would be like at full steam.

Torn between letting the conversation continue, perhaps with more useful information, and watching them spar, Etta dug the dull edge of the knife against her thigh again, and breathed in the cold, briny air.

"We understand," Etta said finally. "Thank you."

It had the effect she'd hoped for, drawing Nicholas's attention back toward her.

He gave a curt nod. "I will have dinner sent to your cabins. Rest well, Miss Spencer."

Etta nodded, keeping her eyes on the toes that peeked out from beneath her dress. Nicholas moved toward the steps, and the air and smoke around them shifted, the skin at the back of her neck prickling with awareness as his eyes combed over her one last time.

When the sound of his feet on the stairs disappeared, Etta whirled to face the girl beside her. "What the *hell* is going on?"

Sophia sagged against the wall, the back of her hand pressed against her lips. At Etta's words, her face drew up. "Don't breathe another word until I say so, otherwise I will not be responsible for my actions."

Etta pushed the cabin door open again, and stepped inside with her fingers around the warm metal of the knife.

"Tell me who you are," she demanded. There was a small porthole window in the wall, but the light that filtered in was minimal. Sophia bent on unsteady legs to lift a metal lantern onto a small desk.

Etta shifted, trying to get some distance from the smell of vomit and Sophia's cold, assessing gaze. She wanted her back to the door—if this took an ugly turn, she could get herself out and lock Sophia in.

The girl sat heavily on the edge of the built-in bunk, drawing a bucket over to herself with her foot. "Damned ship, damned traitor, damned task—"

"Tell me!" Etta said. "How did we get here—and where is *here*? And who are those people?"

"I shouldn't tell you anything after that truly breathtaking display of stu—" Sophia heaved slightly. *"Stupidity."*

"You pushed me," Etta said, letting her words rage on. "You did something to me—you brought me here!"

"Of course I pushed you." Sophia sniffed. "You were as slow as a cow. We would have been there for ages, you crying all over yourself like a fool. I did us both a favor."

"Did you—" She could barely force the words out. "Did you shoot Alice? Was she trying to stop you from bringing me here?"

Etta's mind was frantically trying to connect why Alice would have been there, not in the auditorium, not with her mother in her office upstairs. She hadn't checked to see if she was carrying her purse—in any other circumstances she might have believed that someone hiding in the museum had tried to mug her. But it was too much of a coincidence. It was too simple of an explanation.

"Alice?" Sophia repeated, confused. "You mean the old bag? I have no idea who shot her—there were other Ironwood travelers there keeping an eye on our progress. And if it wasn't one of them, well, I wasn't going to stand around and let whoever it was get us, too."

Etta stared at her, a thousand thoughts spilling into questions. Sophia laughed at her stunned silence, and the last, frayed grip Etta had on her composure finally snapped.

She drew the knife up, her chest heaving, body trembling as she pressed it against the other girl's neck. Instinct overrode logic, compassion, patience. The ugliness that poured through her veins was unfamiliar and frightening.

What are you doing?

Sophia stared up at her, dark eyes widening just a fraction. Then she clucked her tongue impatiently and leaned forward into the blade, until a droplet of blood welled up at the tip.

Before Etta could stumble back, Sophia wrapped her hand around hers, pulling it back a fraction of a centimeter from her throat. Her skin would have been the envy of the moonlight, it was so pale and smooth. Her dark eyes burned with a wild kind of approval. Like Etta had passed an unspoken test.

Etta could feel Sophia's pulse flutter, light and warm, as the girl drew their hands toward her own throat again, skimming the exposed flesh.

"Here," she said, "right here. They'll bleed out like a stuck pig before they can squeal, and you'll be able to get away. Remember that."

Etta nodded, her throat too tight to speak as Sophia pried the knife out of her fingers and threw it hard enough for the tip to embed itself in the wall and stay there, shivering.

"They won't expect it from you," she continued, "and, fool that I am, I didn't either. Good for you. I *like* a fighter. But it won't do you much good against me."

"Says the girl who can't stop throwing up." Etta barely recognized herself in her anger, and she knew herself even less in her helplessness. It left her feeling the way she'd felt while drowning, watching the surface of the water grow darker by the second.

Sophia rose, picked up the silver pitcher from the desk, and poured it into a small porcelain basin, then splashed water on her face, her neck, her hands. When she finished, she gave it a look of ire. "I hate this century. It's so . . . rustic, don't you think?"

"What century?" Etta heard herself whisper.

"You really haven't done this before, have you? You truly had no idea. Remarkable." Sophia glanced up, lips twisting. "Guess."

She didn't want to say it out loud, but it was the only way to know. "Eighteenth?" she guessed, thinking of the costumes. "You brought me back to the eighteenth century?"

Desperation raised the pitch of her voice. *Tell me, tell me, just tell me—*

"No one brought you anywhere," said Sophia. "You traveled."

FOUR

TRAVELED. ETTA ROLLED THE WORD AROUND IN HER mind like clay, letting it take shape, smoothing it out, trying it again in different form. *Traveled.*

To *travel* was to imply some kind of choice; to cross a distance willingly, for a reason. Etta had followed that noise, the screams, because she'd wanted to prove to herself that she wasn't crazy, that there was a source, a reason for it. And it had led her . . .

To the stairwell.

The wall of shivering air.

Except, no . . . that wasn't the whole truth of it, not really. It had led her to Sophia, and *Sophia* had brought her to the stairwell, because . . .

"You were sent to bring me here," Etta said, putting that much together. "You pretended to be a violinist . . . you got yourself involved with the concert."

Sophia gave a little flick of her wrist. "Hand me that damp cloth over there, will you?"

Etta picked it out of the basin and threw it at her face, relishing the slap it made as it struck skin.

Sophia pushed herself up, her dress spilling out over the side of the narrow bunk. "Well you're in a mood, aren't you?"

Etta fought the urge to scream. "Can't imagine *why*."

The hammering and calls from above poured into the gap of silence.

After a while, Sophia spoke. "As amusing as it would be to watch, I can't let you flounder. If you slip and reveal yourself to the others, it'll be my neck waiting for the guillotine, not yours."

As she dragged a flimsy wooden chair over from the door, Etta asked, "What do you mean, exactly—*if I slip*?"

Sophia settled back. She was small enough to stretch her body out in the bunk without bending her knees. She folded the damp towel, draping it over her eyes and forehead. "It's exactly as I said. If you tell the men on this ship—or anyone else, for that matter—that you can travel through time, you damn us both by association." She lifted the cloth, her eyes narrowing. "Do you honestly mean to tell me that you know *nothing* about this? That your parents kept it from you?"

Etta looked down at her hands, studying the red, bruised skin on her knuckles. The questions hung between them like a strand of diamonds, blinding.

She looked up, an idea blazing through her disbelief. "If I answer a question, you have to answer one of mine."

Sophia rolled her eyes. "If you insist on playing games . . ."

"I don't know my father," Etta said. "I never have. He was someone my mom met only once, according to her. A fling. Now you tell me—why is that important?"

"I didn't specify your *father*." Sophia raised both brows. "The ability can be inherited from either parent."

Then . . .

Mom. Oh, God—Etta had to brace herself against the desk to keep upright, her full weight sagging against it as her legs turned to dust under her. *Mom.*

. . . you can't just pluck her off this path, not without consequences.

She's not ready for this. She doesn't have the right training, and there's no guarantee it'll go the right way for her—!

They hadn't been talking about the debut.

Confusion preyed on her thoughts, even as guilt locked her in its jaws. She'd said those things to Alice, those horrible things, because she thought her instructor was trying to hold her back.

She was trying to protect me. Her mom had wanted her to travel, to do this—and Alice hadn't. Was she one of them, too—a traveler? Rose had clearly let her in on their secret, even as she left Etta well out of it. How could they have known all of this, and never once mentioned it? Why would they put her in this position?

. . . you clearly don't know Etta if you're underestimating her like this. She can handle it.

Handle *what*?

Etta forced her jaw to set, to turn on Sophia with renewed suspicion. If her mother had wanted this to happen, she would have just *told* her to go with Sophia. The deafening feedback, Alice's death—none of that would have needed to happen.

It's her time.

A thought bloomed above the chaos in her mind. Rose and Alice clearly knew she *would* travel one day, and maybe they had always debated with each other about trying to stop it somehow, to protect her from this. That could be why they hadn't told her about what she could do—they were arguing about finally cluing her in.

Not soon enough, Etta thought, fighting to keep her breathing even. Not nearly soon enough.

Suddenly, she was terrified for her mom. Because if one of the time travelers—one of the Ironwoods watching them—had killed Alice without any hesitation in order to get to Etta, and Etta specifically, then who was to say they hadn't done the same to her mother if she, too, had tried to stop them?

Why had they come for her? Why did they want *her*?

"You are clever enough to figure it out, then," Sophia said. "The ability is inherited from one or both parents—usually one now, since our numbers have dwindled, and we've been forced to marry outside of our kind. There's a slimmer and slimmer chance of being born with it, but you clearly got it from your mother. Rose Linden."

Linden. Not Spencer. But why would she take a different last name—had she invented it on a whim, or did it really belong to Etta's father? How did he fit into this, if at all?

"Rather famous in our circles, I must say. She disappeared one day and caused quite the kerfuffle."

Sophia seemed to enjoy watching Etta's world unravel around her. It made Etta's hackles rise that this girl was lording the information over her, clearly hoping that she would beg for it.

She wouldn't. "Aren't you going to ask me another question?"

One corner of Sophia's mouth tilted up as Etta set her shoulders back.

"Do you know the name Cyrus Ironwood?" Sophia asked finally. "Does that mean anything to you?"

"That was two questions," Etta pointed out. "And, no to both. How do we travel and how does it work?"

Sophia groaned. "Christ! We spend years learning this—and now I have to give you a summary?"

"Yes," Etta said firmly.

"It's . . . a relationship of sorts, a special one that certain people have had with the timeline for thousands of years. There's no machine, if that's what you're thinking. It's more . . . natural than that. Grandfather doesn't like the word, but it's closer to what you think of as magic. Our ancestors had a unique ability to take advantage of tears in the fabric of time, pass through holes to emerge in a different era."

What was the most unbelievable part of that explanation? That the timeline could be "torn," or that she'd used the word *magic* with a straight face?

"They're like the natural crevices—fissures—you find around the world. The passages have always existed, and our families have always been able to find and use them. It's all rather simple, but do try to keep up." Sophia shifted, trying to get more comfortable. "A passage in medieval Paris could lead to one in, say, Egypt in the time of pharaohs. You step in as you would to any tunnel, passing back and forth between the entrances."

Etta nodded, trying to rub some feeling back into her freezing limbs, startled from her next question by a rogue thought. Sophia had said *our ancestors*. At first, Etta had taken it to mean Sophia's and her grandfather's, the Ironwoods—but were some of those faceless ancestors hers? The Lindens?

The thought filled the dark, dusty corner of her heart she'd closed off as a kid with a scorching, almost unbearable kind of hope. She'd never let herself *want* more people than the ones she already had; it felt too ungrateful for the amount of love her mom and Alice brought into her world. But . . . a family. One with roots, and dozens and dozens of branches by the sound of it—one of which she'd fallen from.

"There's another gown for you in the trunk in the other cabin," Sophia said, waving her hand. "God knows if you'll fit into *that* any better than what I squeezed you into."

The insult was shoved aside by the chill of sudden realization.

"Where are *my* things?" Etta asked. Her clothes—her mom's earrings—

"I burned your ugly dress when we came through," Sophia said. "It was ruined, anyway. The earrings you were wearing are in a pouch in there . . . somewhere."

The grip of panic eased. "You *swear* you didn't throw the earrings away?"

"I was tempted," Sophia said. "History wouldn't have missed one ghastly pair of earrings. But—the pearls were real. I thought perhaps you might need them one day. To sell."

Etta pulled back in surprise. To sell?

"Just go get the damned dress—undergarments, too. You'll find everything you need wrapped in brown parchment," Sophia said. "And hurry, will you? I have my next question."

Etta stood on stiff legs but stopped beside the door, listening. When she was satisfied no one was lingering nearby, she stepped out, ducking into an identical room. There was so little inside it—not even a desk—that she found the wooden trunk immediately and crouched in front of it. The heavy lid groaned as she heaved it up, and a lovely note of lavender rose with it.

There were satchels of it here and there, tucked inside the blanket at the top, even inside the leather shoes she set aside. The brown parcel was tied with rough string, cushioned at the bottom by another layer of blanket. There was little else inside the trunk: a bottle of what smelled like rosewater, a brush, and—she released the breath that was burning her lungs, and picked up the small velvet bag.

The earrings tumbled out onto her palm, and Etta lost it. The sob bubbled up from deep in her chest, ripping out of her so violently that her whole body shook. She pressed her forehead against her fist, felt the prick of the studs dig into her skin.

She shouldn't have left Sophia's cabin. She couldn't keep herself together without the pressure, the need to pretend. She didn't have to be brave now, or calm. There was nothing to prove.

Alice. *Oh my God. Alice.* She looked at her hands, as if expecting to see the traces of her instructor's blood. They'd killed her to get to Etta—why hadn't she stopped, listened to what Alice had tried to say to her in her mother's office? Why had Alice tried to stop any of this?

She needed to find a way to keep herself together, otherwise she was never going to get out of there. She was never going to find her way back to her own time.

Breathe, duck. Count it out with me. Three beats in, and three beats out . . .

Alice's voice drifted between the fractured pieces of her thoughts. She sucked the damp air deep into her lungs, focused on the way they expanded, and released the air slowly, the way she'd been taught. It had been so long since she'd been in the chokehold of panic and nerves, she'd forgotten how easy it was to slip into their grasp.

Close your eyes.
Listen only to the music.
Listen.

She was listening now, to the sounds of men singing above, to the pulse throbbing fast and untamed in her ears. It was instinct to lift her hands the way she did, to mime the shape of a violin out of nothing but air and play herself back to evenness. She stopped as soon as she knew what she was doing.

Etta breathed out heavily through her nose, rubbing a finger along the bridge.

Mom wanted me to travel. Not like this, she was sure, but one day. *She wanted me to know, to understand what I could do.* For the first time in her life, Etta realized she had finally stumbled onto her mother's secret heart—the core of who she was, why she guarded each and every memory of her past. Why she could close herself off so suddenly; why she drifted away into deep thought. In spite of everything else, Etta felt something inside her click into place. The icy knot their relationship had twisted into unraveled inside of her. She felt desperate with the need to find her, to make sure she was safe, to talk to her and really *know* her for the first time.

But none of that answered the question of why Rose had kept this a secret in the first place. The only travel she did now was between countries, across oceans; Etta felt certain of that. So why had she disappeared, as Sophia had claimed? And how many of her stories were actually true, not invented to lull a restless little girl to sleep?

I need to get back.

She'd woken up on this ship to find that all of her carefully conditioned composure had flown away, and what she'd been left with was raw instinct and will. She'd felt wild and unhinged at the time, but she'd proven to herself, if no one else, that she was willing to fight. Protect herself. Now she needed to use every ounce of her drive to survive at all costs; to channel her unwillingness to crack under pressure, and form a plan to get home.

Home . . . Her time. New York City.

Etta stuffed her feet into the tight shoes and slipped the earrings back on, pausing only to make sure they were secure. The slight weight of them would be a reminder of home, her mom, Alice, the debut . . .

Alice. Etta was a *time traveler*—could she get back to that moment when she'd fought with her mother and Alice? Could she use her ability to go back in time, leave the concert, and take Alice and her mother away with her?

Could she save Alice?

Etta had always known the direction her life was heading; she'd fought to stay on that path each and every time she picked up her violin. Her future was the stage, performances, recordings. . . . And yet, there had always been a tiny quake in the certainty of that vision. Opening the door even a crack into this was enough of a temptation for her imagination to rip it open and step inside. What would it be like, she wondered, to go wherever, *whenever* she wanted to?

To stand in the heart of a long-dead empire.

To cross continents and see the wonders of the world before they disappeared.

To sit in the audience in Vienna's Kärntnertortheater, listening to the debut of Beethoven's Ninth Symphony.

To beg a lesson from Bach in his years at Leipzig.

To save Alice.

What choice was there, other than to learn as much as she could, so she could get back to that moment in time? She had to put up with Sophia's smirks; with the sickening thought that she might be staring into the face of her instructor's murderer, or someone who'd had a direct hand in it.

I can make it, Etta thought, bending to pick up the parcel. *I can make it back.*

And she'd fight every step of the way if she had to.

SOPHIA WAS SITTING ON THE EDGE OF THE BED WHEN ETTA stepped back inside.

"Did you get lost?" she snapped, leaning her face over the bucket again. After the taste of fresh air, the smell of bile and vomit was enough to turn Etta's own stomach. "How is it, exactly, that you are perfectly fine and I—"

Etta turned away as Sophia heaved. She unwrapped the parcel, sliding the strings off, until she was left with a pile of linen, cotton, and silk. And something that looked suspiciously like a corset.

"What do I do with all of this?"

"Take off your soiled gown and see for yourself," Sophia sniped. "Start with the shift—the flimsy thing that looks like a nightgown. Next the stockings, which you'll need to secure with garters. And yes, you must wear them."

Someone had cut the front of her gown, and the corset-like garment beneath it, after pulling her out of the water. It was split nearly all the way down to where it met the dress's skirt. It should have been easy enough to pull off, but the wet strings of the corset had become tangled and knotted when she'd pulled Nicholas's jacket over her for cover. Once she had them loosened, it was easy enough to pull the pieces apart, drop them to the ground, and wiggle out of the remains of the sodden, bloodstained skirt.

You can do this.

Her mom's words floated through her mind. *Etta can handle this.*

She could. She would.

"What question did you decide on?" Etta asked, reaching behind her. The underskirts were the main thing dragging her down; there were two thick layers of wool tied together, separate from the dress. They slid down her legs, smacking against the ground. She braced one hand against the coarse wooden paneling on the wall and stepped out of them and the stockings. She was left standing in what looked like a long, thin cotton nightgown—with nothing else beneath it. Her face burned as she glanced over at Sophia.

"Change your shift and bring me the other stays. I'll lace you up again," Sophia said. "And again, yes, you need it. Twenty-first-century girls have no waists to speak of, apparently. The gown won't fit correctly otherwise."

Etta scowled. "Yes, Your Majesty."

"I rather like the sound of that, thank you," Sophia said. "No waist, but able to recognize her social betters. Perhaps I can work with you after all."

Etta rolled her eyes.

For whatever modesty it would give her, she turned her back on Sophia and tugged the shift over her head, replacing it with the clean, dry one. She threaded her arms through the sleeves, smoothing the fabric down when it caught and twisted at her knees.

Sophia stumbled ungracefully in the direction of her trunk. Etta caught a brief glimpse of more fabric before the other girl found what she was looking for—a long thin needle, carved from bone.

"Slide your arms through the straps of the stays," Sophia said. "These lace in the front, so you can do them yourself from now on."

"Great," Etta muttered. "Can't wait."

"Part of playing the part—of not being suspected—is dressing it," Sophia reminded her.

The needle, it turned out, was used for the stays' laces. Etta could smell the leather as Sophia worked the needle through eyelets on either side of the opening. The fabric was stiff, and the boning bit into her skin as Sophia pulled, tightened, pulled, and tightened again. Etta's posture changed, straightening, until she was sure she was at least three inches taller.

"Leave the laces in when you undress, only loosen them," she said, "and slide it off. You'll want to dress quickly on a ship of men."

"O . . . kay," Etta gasped out, tugging at the strings to loosen them. Sophia batted her hand away.

"You've ruined the nicer of the three gowns I bought you," she said. "But I suppose it hardly matters, seeing as we won't be dining with the crew. Both of these are in the *robe á l'anglaise* fashion."

"Translation?" Etta slipped another wool underskirt up to her hips and almost fainted at the sudden, sweet warmth of it.

"The bodices are closed, see? You won't need a stomacher to cover the stays." Sophia pressed the gown against her chest. "You forgot the stockings and garters. They're easier to do without the bulk of petticoats."

Etta blew out a sigh as she picked up the silky strips of fabric, bent to pull one up over her right leg, secured it with a ribbon just above the knee, and started on the left side. Sophia knew a considerable amount about this—but she clearly wasn't from the "rustic" eighteenth century.

"How old are you, exactly?" Sophia asked, returning to the bed again. "That's my next question."

"Seventeen," Etta said, pulling the gown over her head. "How old are you?"

"Seventeen," Sophia said. "And a half."

Of course. Etta fought the pathetic urge to point out that she still had her beat—she was only a few months shy of turning eighteen.

"Are you really good enough to play the violin professionally?"

Etta's fingers slipped against the ribbon that she was attempting to knot tightly enough to keep the stockings up, but loosely enough to keep blood flowing to her leg. She didn't have to give her the whole truth. "I think so."

"And your father—your future husband—" A swell of a wave passing under them sent Sophia falling back onto the bed. Once she was down, she stayed there.

"—your future husband," Sophia ground out, her face squeezed tight against another burst of nausea. "They would allow you to work? Even after you had children?"

Odd question. "Well, as I said, I don't know who my father is," Etta said. "But no one can or will tell me what to do with my life once I turn eighteen. At least, they can't force a decision on me."

Sophia watched her, eyes glassy. "Is that true?"

Etta knew what her next question should have been, but another one pressed itself onto her tongue. "What century are you from? I have two questions this round, by the way."

"I'm from every century," Sophia said, with a dismissive wave.

"My natural time, the year I was born, was 1910. Philadelphia. I haven't been back then since . . . forever."

"Where is the other opening of the passage located—the one that leads to the Met?"

Sophia burst out laughing. "As if I would ever tell you. As if it would actually matter if I *did*. Do you even know what ocean we're on?" She seemed to realize her mistake a second later. "That wasn't a question!"

"Yes it was, and yes I do. It's the Atlantic, isn't it?" Etta didn't need Sophia to respond to know she was right. "Is it—" She paused, trying to think of the right question. "How did we get on this ship?"

"We came through the passage. You were unconscious. I changed you into era-appropriate clothing and we both traveled to the docks to board this ship. It was the only one leaving out of—out of that particular port that could make Grandfather's requested arrival time. The issue was, this vessel was bound for England, so he hired that . . . that rat to capture it and bring it into port in New York, where he's waiting for us."

Those were far more answers than Etta ever could have hoped for. Sophia must have been getting tired to let so much slip.

"Can you wet this rag for me?" The other girl threw it. Etta caught it between two fingers, holding it out in front of her.

"Sure," she said, "and that was a question, by the way."

Sophia narrowed her eyes. "Damn you!"

"Why was I brought here?" Etta interrupted. "Why did you have to come get me?"

"Those are two different questions with two different answers," Sophia said. "To the former, I don't know. I'm not allowed to ask such things. To the latter, because I was told to."

"By who?"

"That's three, and a stupid one, seeing as I've already told you."

Etta swore. She had—*Grandfather*. Disgust coiled in her.

The question was small, quiet when it finally emerged from Sophia's pale lips. "When do women get the right to vote?"

Etta blinked, surprised again. Of all the things she could have asked . . . "You have passages to different eras, right? Do you seriously not know?"

"If you must know, before I was sent to fetch you, I hadn't been granted the privilege of traveling past a certain year," Sophia said irritably. "Answer the question, then—tell me if it's true—if what the moving picture box said was right about a woman running for president."

Moving picture box . . . the television?

This was getting more and more interesting. Sophia was a lot more curious than she'd originally given her credit for. She wasn't digging into Etta's past to find something to use against her—no, she'd wasted a question on this because she wanted to know the answer that badly.

"Yes, one's running, and with voting . . . maybe 1920?"

"Nineteen twenty," Sophia repeated. "Ten years."

Ten years from what—her birth year? Etta couldn't believe the explanation she'd given; that Sophia hadn't been given the "privilege" of traveling past a certain year. How could they stop her, when all the travelers had the whole of history at their fingertips?

That thought sparked another one.

"Can a traveler change history?" she asked.

"It's my turn," Sophia groused. "But, yes. Travelers have been known to accidentally make small changes with their own oversight and stupidity. It's quite easy to do if you're not careful. In most cases, it doesn't cause a big enough change to merit fixing. But changing something intentionally is against our rules and can result in years of being banned from traveling—or worse."

"I don't see how a small change couldn't turn into a big one," Etta pointed out.

"Sometimes it does, but sometimes nothing happens at all. It can be difficult to predict." Sophia crossed her arms over her chest, closing her eyes. "The best way to explain this is to think of the timeline as a kind of . . . constant, roaring stream. Its path is set, but we create ripples by jumping in and out. Time corrects itself the best it can to keep later events consistent. But if a small change snowballs into a much larger one, or if a traveler's actions are devastating enough, it can actually shift the flow of the timeline, thereby changing the shape of the future from that point on."

Etta leaned toward her. "What do you mean, the shape of the future?"

"What is education like in your time?" Sophia countered. "The moving picture box in my hotel made me believe it's common to attend with men."

"The *television*," Etta corrected, and gave a very impatient rundown of the educational system in America.

"All right, it's like this," Sophia said. "Big alterations, most of the time, take throwing an ungodly amount of money around and befriending the right, powerful people. Grandfather has done it a few times, of course, to secure our fortune and bring the other families in line."

"*What?*" Etta thundered. Her timeline wasn't the true timeline—her future was the one the old man had decided on?

"It's either a coordinated effort by multiple travelers, or the incredible luck of finding a linchpin moment in the timeline. Things like wars are harder, since they have so many moving pieces and it's like trying to hold back a tidal wave, but it is possible. It's far easier to change a city's skyline, create or ruin a company, back and fund laws that suit our business interests. Grandfather might have caused a few stock market crashes to ruin the fortunes of the other families, for instance, and those might have spiraled into something more, ah, historic."

Historic? What qualified as "historic"—the Great Depression?

"Again, it's not in practice anymore," Sophia continued. "We protect our timeline."

Your fortune and power, you mean, Etta thought. She was right—this family *was* ruthless, and she'd never been so grateful not to share blood with anyone in her life.

"What happens if the future *is* changed?" Etta leaned forward, resting her elbows on her knees.

Sophia sighed. "Tell me about travel in your era. What is it like on an aeroplane?"

Biting back her impatience, Etta told her, then waited for her answer, shifting uncomfortably on the hard seat.

Sophia folded her hands over her stomach as she stared up at the ceiling. "If someone did alter the past, and the consequences were large enough to shift the timeline, it would not erase you, a traveler outside of your natural era, from existence. You would go on, alive. It would, however, erase the world you know. You could return and find the circumstances of your life altered in such an enormous way, it would look unrecognizable to you. You wouldn't know the same people, live in the same home, and so on. You would be a refugee from your original, natural time. The moment the timeline shifts to a new one, what we call a *wrinkle* is created. Time will attempt to correct and realign itself the best it can by dragging you, the traveler, out of whatever era you're in and shoving you into the last common year between the old timeline and the new."

It made some sense to her that she wouldn't be erased from history by making a mistake. Erasing herself would also erase the initial mistake that caused it, making it impossible to have altered anything in the first place. But what Sophia was describing was terrifying. She could be returned to a time in which no one—not Alice, not Pierce, *no one*—would know her. It would void everything she'd accomplished with the violin, the name she'd worked so hard to establish.

"You're considering this, aren't you?" Sophia asked. "I can see it in your face. Before, you were afraid. Now you're curious."

"It doesn't matter if I'm curious," Etta said. "I'm going home."

"You won't be going back until Grandfather allows it, and if he's demanding your presence, he must have a good reason for it. I'd like to know what that is."

Etta forced her shoulders to relax. "You and me both."

"Unlace me," said Sophia. I'd like to rest now."

But this game isn't over. And her last question . . . Etta had spent so much of her life sorting through critiques and assessments of her playing, she felt fairly confident in her ability to pick out the truth from an exaggeration, a preference, or a lie. What Sophia said had been the truth, but not the whole truth.

"So now you won't return the favor?" Sophia huffed. "I knew I should have brought a maid."

Etta pushed herself up as the ship began to rock. Sophia turned green again as Etta's nimble fingers worked down the row of tiny buttons.

The fabric, some kind of damask, was warm and damp from the girl's sweat; the stays were heavy with it, the shift beneath translucent and reeking sourly. In spite of everything, an aching kind of sympathy made Etta turn and retrieve a fresh one from the nearby trunk. In the instant before she looked away, Etta saw the deep, angry grooves the corset had left behind in the girl's skin. Sophia let out a small sigh of relief as she slipped into the fresh undergarment. If they were in agreement over one thing, it was the not-so-insignificant fact that this wasn't a stellar era for women.

"How are we supposed to move in these?" Etta said, tossing the stays onto the desk.

". . . They don't expect women to do much of anything," Sophia said. "Well," she added, "at least not women of any station. I'm sure the peasants of this era are glad for some support when they're hunched over cleaning their homes, or doing whatever it is peasants do. Makes running and fighting bloody hard, though."

Etta rubbed her forehead, not sure where to start with that.

"For now, your role here is wallpaper," Sophia said. "Decoration. Until we get to New York. And then it'll be whatever Grandfather asks of you."

Etta recoiled at the thought. If her mom had been here, the mere idea would have sent her on a tirade that blistered ears and scorched hearts across the entire ocean. *Wallpaper. Decoration.* Her whole life and person, whittled down to nothing.

"I don't accept that," Etta said. "I'm neither of those things. And, for the record, neither are you."

At that, Sophia's expression changed, and the softness of exhaustion was pulled back by keen interest. "You've been spoilt, you know. You and your voting, your schooling, your independence . . . it's been wasted on you."

Etta bristled, as Sophia clearly wanted. Like any girl, she still felt the echoes from earlier eras of repression. She'd been raised by a mother who'd fought hard to get a wage she deserved, to have access to education when she lacked every advantage, to travel on her own terms. The idea that she was being asked—that she was *expected* to simply play along—made the blood throb in her veins. She was already in the damn stays. Wasn't that enough?

"Why stay here, if you can go anywhere in time?" Etta asked. "You can come back with me—I mean, travel forward again. Or go into the past and try to alter the laws—"

Sophia let out a single, flat laugh. "I've no choice. This is the year all travelers are forced to travel from, where our family is currently based. Grandfather chooses, and we follow. Regardless of where and when we're born, we all meet there. We all offer our services to the head of the family. We play the roles each era demands of us, and we do not meddle with laws or society. At least not anymore."

Wasn't that convenient, thinking that this was some kind of *role*? That they were playing *parts*, like this was all one great big play and they'd been cast as the leads? It was an easy way to wash their hands of responsibility for *fixing* things, to sit back as wars were waged and people were oppressed. Etta was protective of her future, the life she'd known; but the idea of doing nothing when there was the power to act made her uncomfortable, and more than that, angry.

"What's the purpose of traveling, then?" Etta demanded,

impatient with all of these non-answers. "If you won't try to fix anything, make the world a better place, why bother traveling?"

"To serve Grandfather's will," Sophia said, sounding tired by it all. "Protect the family's interests. To tour what an era has to offer and enjoy it."

Wonderful. They had the rarest, most bewildering power in the world, and how did her family choose to use this incredible gift? To line their pockets with cash and go sightseeing.

"That's it?" Etta sputtered. "Seriously?"

"We protect our timeline. We defend it from attacks by enemies of our family—remnants of the other three traveling families that refused to be absorbed into our own."

"You do have a choice, you know," Etta told her after a moment. "There is *always* a choice. You know where the passage is to my time. You could choose to leave. But you don't. So what's really keeping you here, other than loyalty and fear?"

"Are you calling me a coward?" Sophia asked, her words chipped from ice.

The other girl had this power, too. So what was keeping her in check, Etta wondered, when clearly she wanted so much more than what her family was offering?

"I'm saying, you're smart. You want something better. So take back the control of your life and *go*."

And you can take me back with you. Etta wove her hands together again in her lap, watching for the shift in the other girl's expression; it wasn't exactly manipulation, per se, but an offer to ally herself. If she could convince Sophia she *did* deserve better than what the past had to offer, then the girl might bring her back to the passage they'd come through. Together, they could figure out how to get off this ship. Etta was almost positive, with some creative lying on both their parts, that her mom would be willing to help the girl get back on her feet.

Sophia shut her eyes and shook her head. When she opened them again, Etta felt scorched by the fury in them.

"Save your breath," Sophia hissed. "Our life entails order. It requires rules, and the act of *blending in* to ensure our survival. You don't understand, Etta. There are less than a hundred travelers alive now. We are already dying out, without the risk of being captured or killed in an unforgiving era. We all observe the norms of the era, no matter how it might affect us."

"Tell yourself that, if it makes you feel better about it," Etta said.

Sophia rolled her eyes. "Could you imagine what kind of abuse we'd suffer if the right people found a way to force us into their service?"

Etta didn't have to imagine anything. She saw the flicker of horror on the girl's face.

"We protect ourselves by playing roles fit for the year we're in."

"What do you mean?" Etta asked.

"I mean exactly that—the future *you* know. Before Grandfather united the families, they were constantly trying to destroy each other's natural timelines. There was no stability. Now there is. So cling to your rights, your beliefs, your *future*—but know that none of them will help you here. You haven't been forced to survive in the same way as the centuries of women who came before you. You know nothing of the impossibly small weapons we must use to carve out knowledge and power."

The many scattered scraps and pages of Sophia's life began to assemble themselves in Etta's mind. She felt them drawing together, saw the rigidity of the spine that held together someone seething, boiling with so much spite and cunning. Sophia's own small weapon was finding other people's vulnerabilities, chipping away at their fears and desires until they were exposed like raw nerves. What kind of life had her family given Sophia to make her so desperate for more, to force her to sharpen this skill?

Sophia's voice was growing rougher the longer she spoke. "Now that our game is at an end, allow me to be perfectly clear. Society is always the same, regardless of the era. There are rules and standards, with seemingly no purpose. It's a hateful, elaborate charade, equal parts flirtation and perceived naïveté. To men, we have the minds of children. And so you will not make eye contact with any man on this ship. You will eat slowly, carefully, and little; and, if not with me in my cabin, then alone. You will not leave your cabin unless I am there to accompany you. And you will do us both the favor and act the part of a mute, unless you have been asked a direct question and I am not there to answer it. And you will not, under any conditions, speak or associate with Carter beyond his capacity as our servant."

Anger whipped fast and hot against her pulse; she was tired of Sophia acting as if every other living soul was beneath her. "Nicholas isn't our servant."

Sophia pushed herself up onto her elbows and repeated, *"Nicholas?"*

Etta realized her mistake a moment too late—even she knew that, in this time, it wasn't proper to address anyone you weren't close to, or related to, by their given name, least of all a person of the opposite sex.

"Mr. Carter," she corrected herself. "You know what I mean. Don't you dare treat him like—"

"Watch yourself," Sophia cut in. "I know what you're thinking, the conclusion you've just drawn, but know this: my mistrust is of a very personal nature. I have seen the rotten edges of his soul, and I know him for the deceitful swine he is." There was no mockery, nothing false in her voice. "Stay away from him."

Etta rose, gathering up her wet clothing to hide the way her hands shook.

I'm not wrong . . . I'm not. She'd bet on the person who had jumped into the ocean to save her, not the one who'd trapped her in the past against her will. Any day, any century.

"Unlike you," she said when she reached the door, "I'll make my own decisions."

But as Etta gave in to the urge to look back over her shoulder, to see if her words had landed the way she'd hoped, Sophia was already on her back again, eyes closed.

"Go on," Sophia said as the door creaked open. *"Try."*

ETTA STEPPED INTO THE HALLWAY, SHUTTING THE DOOR. SHE leaned back against it, searching for the rhythm of the repairs happening on the deck above her, the voices drifting up from beneath her feet. A song of work, one that spoke of labor and skill. The notes floated through her ears, arranging themselves to match the tempo and drive—

Stop it, she thought, fingers tightening on the fabric in her arms.

A breeze escaped through the open hatch, and brushed by her on its way toward the forecastle at the other end of the ship. The curtains there were gone now, and she could make out hammocks, plus a small area where a few men sat scraping food off metal plates. One turned, and the whole left side of his face was covered with a blood-soaked bandage. She turned back to the other cabin door, ready to be alone.

Who's the coward now?

She draped the damp gown and underpinnings over her own built-in bunk to finish drying. She brushed at the thin crust of white salt clinging to the stiffening fabric before turning her attention to Nicholas's jacket.

Mr. Carter's jacket.

Something in her snapped. Why was she staying here—because Sophia had ordered her to? She could go up on deck if she liked. She could escape the smell of sickness, the cramped confines of the cabin, take in the fresh sea air and look into the distance. She'd make her own choices in all of this, no matter what Sophia said.

Only . . . Etta deflated the moment her fingers brushed the handle. *He* had asked them to stay below while the ship was repaired—and to stay out of the forecastle. It didn't matter that the request must be partially powered by his desire to keep Sophia away from him. While she wouldn't take orders from the other girl, Etta couldn't bring herself to ignore Nicholas's wishes. Plus, the deck had been littered not only with bodies, but weapons, and shards of metal and glass. Until they cleared it completely, it wasn't safe, and she wasn't about to get in the way of their work.

How do I do this without her? Think, think, think. . . .

Etta breathed in the calming scent of soap and cedar as she sat on the edge of her bunk, and realized with surprise that she was still clutching the jacket. Her hands were still wrapped in its warmth, at odds with the toes freezing in her shoes. With as delicate a touch as she could manage, she polished the line of brass buttons that ran down the front, and draped the large expanse of the jacket over her legs to smooth out the creases she'd left in the fabric.

Her fingers brushed a small line of raised stitching, where someone had mended a tear just below the shoulder. She wondered what had made it—an accident? Carelessness? A weapon?

Ask him. The words rose again and again until she couldn't ignore them. *Ask him for help.* They had a common enemy; maybe he wouldn't be so willing to do Sophia's bidding when it came down to it.

Nicholas—*Mr. Carter*—disliked Sophia, but would that be enough to compel him to put her back . . . where? She still didn't know the location of the passage she'd come through to get here. But—she sat up straighter, the idea racing from her head to her heart. The crew in the hold—*they* would know where they'd sailed from, wouldn't they? Everyone on this ship was bound to know where she and Sophia had boarded from.

I have seen the rotten edges of his soul.

I know him for the deceitful swine he is.

Etta shook her head. The crew members were the key, both the ones working above and the ones below. If they got to know her, knew that she'd essentially been kidnapped, would they help her get away from Sophia? Would they be willing to bring her back?

She could figure out a way to play the perfect eighteenth-century girl, on her own terms. It would just be a matter of convincing the crew to like her.

Which, given her track record of friends . . . might actually be the most difficult part of this. She had acquaintances on the competition circuit, but she knew more about their technical skills as violinists than about their personal lives. And then there had been Pierce.

Etta's throat felt thick as something lodged in the base of it. The familiar sting of tears, the pressure behind her eyes—thinking of Pierce now only made her think of Alice.

I'm going to save her.

Her death wasn't a conclusion. It wasn't the end.

Etta blanked the thoughts out of her mind by sheer force of will and stood, setting the jacket beside the gown. Her hands itched with the need to be busy, to play the violin until her head emptied and she sank into music. Instead, she dug through the layers of blankets in the trunk, feeling for the silver hairbrush she'd seen somewhere at the bottom.

The bristles felt like they were made of some other, stiffer kind of hair. She examined the fine detailing of leaves and flowers on the silver back, surprised that Sophia had included something so beautiful and nice for her to use—not, say, a small rake that would tear out her hair by the roots.

By the time she'd worked one stroke through the nest of knots, Etta wasn't so sure a rake would have been less painful. She worked with agonizing care, biting her lip to keep from crying. The hair spray she'd shellacked on before the concert hadn't been washed out by the salt water, but had only hardened. It might have struck her as sort of impressive, if her scalp hadn't been on fire, and what hair she could work through the brush hadn't been standing straight out like a stretched cotton ball. Both the pitcher and the basin in this cabin were empty, and Etta was too proud to steal some water, even if Sophia was asleep.

There was a faint scratch and knock at the door. She held her breath and stayed quiet, hoping whoever it was would assume she was asleep. Instead, after another knock, the door cracked open, and a small face peered inside.

A young boy, the one she'd seen on his hands and knees scrubbing the deck, kept his face turned down, his hands folded in front of him. "Oh! I hate to trouble ye, but—"

His face was an explosion of freckles against pale pink skin, topped off by gorgeous red hair that seemed wasted on a boy. His eyes were a bright, clear blue, and as he looked up, they popped out wide.

Etta had the sudden painful realization that, while her hands had stopped working and returned to her lap, the brush had not made the journey with them. It dangled from the side of her head.

"Miss!" he gasped. "You didn't—terribly sorry, I only—I just need the captain's, that is, Mr. Carter's jacket?"

With as much dignity as she could muster, Etta pointed to the bunk. "It's just over there. Tell him I'm sorry I kept it so long."

The whole time she'd been using it as a security blanket, it hadn't even occurred to her that he might not have another one.

Idiot. She was embarrassed by her own rudeness.

The boy scampered and plucked the jacket up, all scrawny limbs and big ears. She turned back to her work, trying to disentangle the brush without ripping out any more of her hair. The creak of the door hinges never came.

"Don't ye have any pomatum, miss?" he blurted out. "Looks painful the way 'tis." Then, going white in the face with fear, added, "Apologies—"

"No, it's all right," Etta said, thinking quickly. "I don't have any . . . pomatum. Or water. Could you possibly get them for me?"

Nicholas had said to use the boys if they needed anything. . . . Etta wasn't sure what the expected behavior was here, but the

109

boy didn't seem troubled or even wary of the request. In fact, he bounced into action. "S'all right, miss, I'll be back. I'll give the jacket to another boy to brush, and bring some fresh water for ye. Me mum taught me how to do her hair right and proper, like a lady—" He caught himself on the next breath, steadying himself so he stood straight, thin shoulders back. Looking at him now, Etta guessed he couldn't be more than twelve, maybe thirteen. "If you be needing the help, miss?"

She did need help, all right—both the kind he was offering and the kind she had just realized he could provide. Sophia had warned her not to be too familiar with anyone on the ship—anyone in this era, really—but now she had a justified excuse for keeping him around, wringing what information she needed out of him. Etta pressed her lips together to keep from smiling, hiding the excitement rippling through her. "I'm Etta Spencer—what's your name?"

"Jack, Miss Spencer." He gave a little bow.

True to his word, he did return—with a pitcher of warm water, a rag, and a canister of something that smelled wonderfully spicy and sent a cramp of hunger through her empty stomach.

Jack was serious about his business; when Etta tried to help him rinse and towel her hair off, he gave her a stern look. She bit her lip to keep from smiling and let him go about his work stoically, applying the spicy mixture—the pomatum, she guessed. A few minutes into being groomed like a delicate lapdog, Etta put her plan into play.

"Jack, are you a member of the prize crew? Or one of the *Ardent*'s boys?"

He puffed out his chest as he announced, "Prize crew, miss,

and one of the best at that. Captain Hall keeps us all trained right and proper."

Perfect. Exactly what she'd hoped for. "Could you tell me about the men?"

Jack pulled back, giving her an incredulous look. "Well . . . they drool and snore and fart like any other man, I promise ye."

She bit her lip to keep from laughing. "No, I mean . . . how about their names? Where they come from? What they do when they're not working. I've *always* been so curious about that."

Always, as in, the last ten minutes.

Still Jack hesitated, brow creased, as if he were puzzling out the propriety of it all. Etta brushed aside the guilt and gave the boy the most manipulative smile of her life, adding, "I'm only asking because I trust your opinion above everyone else's."

Jack seemed to enjoy this.

"All right. Suppose we'd best start with Mr. Carter," Jack said, finally.

Yes, Etta thought, *let's.*

"He's a right fine seaman, and I like him fine. Kind. Teaches me letters when he isn't barking at the other men, which he don't have to do, understand? Reads to me sometimes when I brings him in his breakfast. Reads so much, I don't see how he don't get bored with all them words." Jack made a face. "He's the prize master. He'll bring the ship into the prize courts and get our earnings. I know he don't like turtle soup much. Always makes a face when I serve it to him. He's from . . . well, I don't rightly know. Captain Hall raised him, though. Is that what you meant, miss?"

Etta nodded. "Exactly what I meant."

Jack went through the roster of the prize crew, noting how

much he liked each man, which ones burped most often after he served them, which ones snored, the ones who had perished in horrifically brutal ways during the boarding. It shifted naturally into chatting about the work above, his excitement during the boarding, how some of the boys from this ship, the *Ardent*, had agreed to work for Mr. Carter but they didn't much like Jack yet. She was so distracted by his torrent of words, she missed the fact that he was guiding the brush through her hair easily now, top to bottom, top to bottom, until it felt silky and only a bit damp to the touch.

"How d'ye like it fashioned?" he asked her, gesturing to her hair.

"I'll just braid it," Etta began. "Thank you for your help—"

"I can do that, miss," Jack said.

"You can?"

"A sailor who can't braid s'no sailor t'all," he proclaimed. "Learnt to marry and braid the lines and ropes first thing."

"Marry them?" Etta asked, glancing up at him under a curtain of her hair. He'd been appalled by her sitting on the floor, but it was the only way for him to stand over her to do his work.

"Aye, splice and bind the ends of two ropes together so that they're one. Join 'em together, like."

She wondered if that's where the word had come from, why you *married* someone when you joined your life to theirs. How strange; casting something she thought she knew in a different light, tracing its unexpected origins back. Here was one small, unexpected benefit to time travel: at least she was learning something. Something she would only be able to use in trivia games, but still.

"—the devil are you, Jack Winstead?" a voice called.

Jack shot over to the door and pulled it open.

"Christ, lad! Were you hiding in there? The new cook's a beast, but he won't eat you—"

Etta pushed herself to her feet. The man at the door was younger than she'd expected, given the deep baritone of his voice—she recognized it, though, as the one that had been booming out over the others, issuing commands, even singing. His dirty-blond hair was tied back at the nape of his neck, giving her a nice view of his round, open face and a stitched-up cut running along one cheek. He had the wide shoulders and rounded chest of a pigeon, but moved to snatch Jack's collar like a hawk.

"I'm so sorry, it's my fault for keeping him," Etta said, feeling almost frantic. He wouldn't hurt the boy, would he?

The other man looked up, releasing Jack. "Oh, beg your pardon, Miss Spencer. If he was assisting you, it's all right."

Jack turned back to her, eyes wide.

"He was," Etta confirmed.

The man looked down at him. "Cook's been calling your name for the past quarter hour. Go on, look lively, lad."

He tore out of the room, only to have the man catch him by the collar and drag him back. Jack did his quick version of a bow. "Pleasant evenin' to ye, miss!"

"We'll teach that one manners yet," the man said with a faint trace of exasperation, "though I seem to be lacking them myself. I'm Davy Chase, first mate of the prize crew."

Etta wasn't sure what to do with herself as he drew his heels together and gave her yet another bow—curtsy? Nod? She ran through what Jack had given her about him. *Likes: music, ale, dock wenches. Dislikes: cabin boys who don't follow orders, winters in New England, tea.* Most interesting, however, was the fact that he'd been raised—fostered, really—by Captain Hall and his late wife, alongside Nicholas.

"Are you well? You gave us quite the fright," he continued.

"Better now, thank you," she said carefully, pleased she had managed to sound calm and collected. Maybe this would get easier, or at least more comfortable, with practice?

"I see your sister is still poorly—rather, I smelt as much as I passed her cabin. That's a poor stomach for you." He looked like he was fighting a small smile, and in that moment, Etta decided she liked him. "I've had the cook make a broth that should help settle her some. We'll get her in shape to sail again soon."

The sooner Sophia recovered, the sooner Etta would be back under the girl's watchful eye. Etta needed all the time she could to win the crew over, and to turn the ship around, back to whatever port it had sailed from. Back, hopefully, to the passage leading to New York in her time.

"And you? Will you be joining us for dinner this evening?"

Etta opened her mouth to decline—exhaustion had made even her bones feel heavy, and she needed to practice speaking in their formal way before she trusted herself to hold a full conversation—but her stomach answered for her with a loud, rumbling groan.

Etta's face flamed as she fumbled for an apology, but his warm brown eyes only lit up in delight.

"I believe I have my answer," he said, and held out his arm.

FIVE

Mr. Edward Wren had clearly never let the truth stand in the way of a good story.

Nicholas sat back against his chair, fighting the urge to knock a fist against the table and move the conversation—by force, if necessary—past Wren's staggering tale of past valor. As far as Nicholas was concerned, half-truths only added up to a whole lie.

Glancing around the table, he gauged each diner's reaction. From his prize crew, the men who had boarded the *Ardent* with him and assumed control of it, was Trevors the bosun, deep into his cups, his teeth stained with port. The man had actually nodded off, clutching a stomach distended from eating his own weight in lobscouse and buttered parsnips. To his right was another surviving officer from the *Ardent*'s crew: Heath, the sailing master. The older gentleman's right ear was bandaged beneath a flop of a wig, and he spent the entirety of the dinner turning in his chair to try to hear what was being said by Miss Henrietta Spencer, who inhaled her meal with a wolfish enthusiasm that Nicholas found himself appreciating.

Henrietta Ironwood? he wondered. The old man's letter had been vague—there hadn't been an indication either way—but she seemed to lack the venom that pumped through the family's heart. It was entirely possible, however, that she was the kind to nestle close before sinking her fangs in for the kill.

His eyes shifted to her right, where the newly appointed surgeon and all-around milksop, Goode, was focused on cutting his food into bites small enough for a chick.

"Miss Spencer, you haven't touched a bite of the lobscouse. I can't recommend it enough," Heath blurted out, nearly shouting over Wren's quieter tones. Nicholas had been in his position before—the agonizing ringing and temporary deafness of coming too close to cannon fire—and couldn't fault the older man for his booming voice. "It's Cook's specialty."

Knowing that they'd be eating hard biscuits and turtle soup every night if he let one of the prize crew take control of the galley, Nicholas had reluctantly agreed to let the *Ardent's* cook stay in his position after meeting him. The man had all but shackled himself to the stove, stoic and grim, as he offered up a pastry as proof of his skill. He kept his appearance well enough, with a trim dark beard and hair queued neatly. More importantly, "Cook" had tolerated *his* presence on the ship, having clearly lived through any number of boardings in his time.

"It's made from salted beef that Cook hangs over the side of the ship, until it freshens," Goode explained. "The stew is merely beef, potatoes, onions, and a little pepper if he has it."

Henrietta—no, Etta—no, *Miss Spencer*—favored Jack, one of the cabin boys, with a small smile as he sprang forward to spoon the stew into her bowl.

They watched as she took a careful bite, compressing her lips at the taste, swallowing hard. She managed to choke out a single word: "Delicious."

"There's a good girl," Chase said with a chuckle.

As fair-haired as an angel and as big as a bear, his friend, the first mate for the remainder of their journey, was a study in contradictions. An open, round face, perpetually tinged with pink, displayed his irrepressible good nature. He had been one of the few to sneakily thumb away his tears of relief when Miss Spencer had awoken. Moments later, he'd been back at work, assisting the others in patching the hull and singing bawdy songs in the highest register he could manage. And tonight, following the dinner's conclusion and the final watch, he'd be in his hammock, darning his and the crew's stockings with exquisite care.

On the deck, however, Chase was as formidable as a mountain; there was no quarter for shirking duties or disrespect, not without fear of the cat-o'-nine-tails or a fist sailing toward your soft parts. Usually, a good pint or glass of wine was enough to put Chase in high spirits, but Nicholas was almost relieved that the other man looked as surly as he himself felt. Maybe he wasn't the only one exhausted by this whole ordeal.

Wren smiled fondly at Etta—*Miss Spencer*—and gestured to his bowl, still full from the first serving. "I don't like it much myself. The curse of having a refined palate, I suppose. But, I swear to you, I would have eaten this every day rather than starve on the island with the others—"

Bloody hell, would there be no mercy from this?

By some unfortunate act of God, Wren was another surviving officer of the *Ardent*, which unfortunately granted him the privilege of attending meals in the captain's cabin, outside of where he and the other men were being kept in the hold.

Nicholas took a steadying breath of the savory, salty smell of the lobscouse and allowed Jack to refill his bowl when he emptied it. The boy's hands shook slightly from nerves. This was his first voyage, and Nicholas remembered the feeling well.

"You're doing a fine job," he murmured to the boy. "Well done."

Jack straightened up, setting his shoulders back. He struggled to keep the smile off his face as he moved to serve Chase. When he arrived at Wren's side, the man broke off his story only long enough to give the boy the full brunt of his condescension.

"Have you gone deaf as well? I said I wasn't fond of it." Wren glanced at Nicholas. "Your charity knows no limit. Employing half-wits and simpletons?"

A growl curled in Chase's throat at the same moment that the spoon in Jack's hand "slipped" from his fingers and landed with a wet thump in Wren's lap.

"You damned—!"

Nicholas's body tensed as the other man raised his hand. The impertinence would be dealt with, but not like this—for, whatever weaknesses other men might accuse him of, Nicholas would never condone striking a child, even to discipline him. "Mr. Wren—"

He wasn't quite sure how she moved as quickly as she did in those heavy skirts, but Etta was suddenly standing over Wren, settling a hand on his shoulder.

"Oh no," Etta said loudly. "How clumsy, Jack! You'd better apologize."

Chase yanked Jack out of Wren's reach as the man glanced at Etta, distracted for a moment from his anger.

"Sorry," Jack mumbled. Chase gave him a little shake and the boy added, *"Sir."*

"It's all right, isn't it? Accidents happen," Etta continued soothingly, picking up Wren's displaced napkin. "There you go—"

She turned slightly as she reclaimed her seat, meeting Nicholas's gaze evenly. Well. That was a masterful manipulation of the moment. He tilted his head in acknowledgment. *Well played.*

Etta tilted hers right back, cocking an eyebrow as if to ask, *And where were you?* He bit back an unwelcome grin at the challenge.

"The bugger did it on purpose," Wren insisted.

Etta continued, "Now, what were you saying about the island and food . . . ?"

As Wren was, mystifyingly, an officer, he was granted a measure of respect by the able-bodied seamen of *both* crews, including the ship's boys. There were standards of how a captured crew was to be treated, and the truth was, Jack would need to be disciplined for his actions. There was no way to avoid it without stepping on the exasperating decorum of it all, but Miss Spencer . . .

He turned to find Chase watching her with brows raised. She'd blown out the flame before the fire could catch.

Now, however, Miss Spencer seemed to devour each of Wren's words like bites of a second supper. Ironwood had trained her well. Nicholas would need to watch her to ensure that he himself wasn't being played—or perhaps the better strategy was to stop watching her altogether.

The candlelight was doing fascinating things to both the silk of her gown and the color in her cheeks. She struggled to lift her fork to her mouth, clearly in discomfort from the fit of her gown. Perhaps that, too, explained the breathy way she laughed and laughed at Wren's inane jokes.

Where was the little lioness, he wondered, roaming the decks with her hair down and floating like a cloud around her? The one who'd looked ready and willing to do violence to two men twice her size—with a grappling hook, no less? She'd gone into the cabin wild, burning, and come out as cool and pale as a pearl. If she'd coifed her hair and powdered it, he might have been convinced he was watching someone from his own century.

Beside her, Edward Wren was the pride of bloody England with his beautiful manners and charm. Nicholas had made a dispassionate assessment of him when the *Ardent's* first mate was brought up from the hold, and had found him lacking in everything but pretty manners. The look on his face when Hall had introduced Nicholas as the master of the ship . . .

His fingers closed around the silver knife, gripping it until his breath was steady. Disbelief. Disgust. Worse, even, than Sophia's open malice.

They'd made their introductions just as Captain Hall and the *Challenger* were readying to sail. Not a single word had passed between them after the captain left; they'd merely studied one another, Wren taking stock of him the way he would a horse he was considering purchasing. Nicholas returned the favor now.

Dark hair, dark eyes. Heroically bruised and bloodied, naturally. Wren was a great deal shorter than Nicholas, but walked with his chest puffed out and his chin raised, as if he was always on his way to meet the king.

"Watch that one," Captain Hall had muttered as he returned to the *Challenger* to continue their hunt. "Both eyes open, Nick. He'll make as if to cut your throat from the front as another knife slices clean through your back. You won't see his hands move."

"A charming image." Nicholas laughed, but the older man was grave.

"I know his type. More wind than a tempest, and more pride than Lucifer himself."

Nicholas wished he could have convinced the captain to stay. But Hall, floating on the wave of victory, was already eager for another prize—and, no doubt, to have Nicholas make a quick journey of it back to New London.

Captain Hall had clasped his shoulder and pounded his back, light eyes sparkling as the sunset turned the sky a warm rose. "I know you're ready for this and more. Finish your business with the family and meet us back in port."

A pure thrill moved from his scalp down his spine, warming him to the core. *I am ready.* He wanted his own command the way the dying wanted their next breath; it was just a matter, as always, of money. Of outrunning the ghost in his past that seemed to haunt him at every turn.

Nick! Help me, help me—!

He breathed in deeply through his nose, his fingers twisting in the tablecloth as if caught in a memory of their own.

The past was past. Now he needed to see the young ladies safely delivered into the hands of Cyrus Ironwood, and escape whole and preferably unscathed.

By the time he was finished with that task, finished with that family for once and all, Chase and the others would already have the *Ardent* in the hands of the Lowes' agent, who'd then bring her and her cargo to the prize courts for a ruling.

A crucial part of that process was the testimony of the ranking officer of the captured vessel. He couldn't stab his fork into Wren's eye—well, he supposed he could. The man only needed his mouth to serve as witness to the courts that the vessel had been fairly won. Did *every* nicety need to be observed?

His stomach soured again as Miss Spencer gave a pretty little gasp of dismay. Wren, brave Mr. Wren, consoled her by saying, "Do not fret, my dear. I have stitched up more than one wound myself. This was, however, the first time I had ever seen my own entrails."

Nicholas scoffed. If a man could see his own entrails, he could *also* see the hand of God swooping down to take him to his eternal reward. There was no living with a wound like that. He had seen enough proof to drive that fact home, even if his guest had not.

Guest. A dark, humorless laugh welled up inside him. Hostage, really, but why use the true term when you could be *polite*? If there was one thing Nicholas loathed more than almost anything else, it was this. Behaving, even to an enemy, with hollow civility and false flatteries. He preferred to be direct in his dislike, and if that did not make him a gentleman from society's mold—well, then so be it.

"—the ship was tossed onto the reef by the swells . . . there was simply nothing we could do other than hold on to her as she was wrecked. Those of us that survived, who made it to the sandbank, crawled ashore. We lived as savages for a week, foraging for food, hunting wild boar, creating shelters from palm leaves and whatever dry wood we could find, searching day and night for water. There was only a single knife between us—a blessing, I think, for we were so out of our minds, we might have killed each other in murderous rage had there been more."

"A cryin' pity that would have been," Chase grumbled, jabbing his spoon into the stew. Nicholas cleared his throat.

Chase's green eyes slid over to meet his, and he raised his glass. The prize crew was, by Hall's design, filled with sailors who had known Nicholas for years. Davy Chase had known him the longest.

He and Chase had been brought aboard Captain Hall's old ship, the *Lady Anne*, to serve as cabin boys—just weeks before the *Lady Anne* was torn apart at the seams by a squall. Both they and the captain had been pressed into temporary service in His Majesty's Navy by the very same ship that rescued them from the waves.

Wren told his story in hushed tones, his voice rising and falling with each imagined danger. Having survived his own ordeal at age eleven, living through two days and nights of starvation, thirst, and fear of death from exposure in the rough winter waters, Nicholas found himself growing steadily more impatient. Hall had kept him and Chase alert and distracted by relating stories about his travels as a young man in the West Indies—his favorite dock doxies; a past storm when the water, the masts, the deck, had been lit by strange blue flame; the small hoard of old Spanish bullion he'd all but tripped over, running from the British Regulars through Tortola.

The experience wasn't something Nicholas spoke of now. It wasn't something he enjoyed *thinking* about. His lips had cracked and bled, burning at all hours from the salt water, and there were times even now when he imagined he could still feel the splinters beneath his nails from the section of the bulwark he had clung to. His vision had gone dark at the start of the third day, and panic had choked him, until Captain Hall had swum to his side and held him afloat by force. The rescue had only been the beginning of another nightmare.

Something ugly in Nicholas stirred when the first mate put an all-too-forward hand on Etta's bare wrist. Something made him want to promptly remove the whole arm from the man's body.

She is a job.

She is a means to an end.

But she was also not Wren's.

"Mr. Wren," he interrupted. The resulting silence cracked over the cabin like a whip. "Perhaps you'd be so good as to clarify one point in your story?"

The other man's face twisted into a smirk. "Of course. What troubles you?"

Wren's first mistake had been to assume that those around him had never sailed through the Virgin Islands.

"You mentioned that the island where you ran aground was about two leagues from Tortola, did you not? Just northeast of Peter Island?"

Chase's chair creaked as he shifted his weight.

Wren's own smile slipped for a moment, but he said, "Yes, I believe I did."

"I thought, surely, that you must be referring to Dead Chest Island," Nicholas began, wondering if he looked half as diabolical as he felt.

"I am," Wren said, a slight flush creeping over his face. "I wasn't aware you were familiar with it."

That much was obvious.

"I think you'd be hard-pressed to find a sailor who hasn't heard of it, sir," Nicholas said. "That *is* the island where Blackbeard set his fifteen sailors ashore with only cutlasses and a bottle of rum between them in retaliation for their mutiny, correct?"

"That is correct," Chase confirmed happily. "They tried swimming to Peter Island, but drowned. That's why they call that stretch of sand 'Deadman's Beach,' of course, owing to the bodies that washed ashore."

Etta leaned forward, unexpected interest sparking in her eyes at this delightfully gruesome detail. "Really?"

"Truly. But that's the trouble, you see," Nicholas said, turning back to Wren, whose smile seemed frozen. "Having seen Dead Chest myself, I'm afraid it doesn't match your description. It's an outcropping of rocks, with no fresh water, no vegetation, and certainly no wild boars for you to hunt."

His spoon scraped against the bottom of his bowl. When he dared to look up again, Etta was watching him, biting her bottom lip. Her eyes sparkled with laughter, and he felt a small bundle of warmth tuck away inside of his chest in response.

Wren busied himself with the task of refilling both his and Etta's glasses with claret. Perhaps it was the awkwardness, or the fact that Wren seemed to be steaming enough to curl a wig, but Etta drank the dark wine in a single gulp, and sang, in a charmingly tipsy way, "Fifteen men on the dead man's chest! Yo-ho-ho and a bottle of rum!"

Nicholas blinked. Silverware clinked as it was set down on plates. Chairs creaked as the men around her shifted, turning toward her. Etta blanched, looking down at her lap, as if her skirt would offer up some kind of excuse.

"Where did you hear such an extraordinary song?" Wren asked.

The question instantly sobered her, dousing the flush of laughter from her cheeks. She sat up as straight as a mainmast in her seat, pushing her wineglass away, and steeled her expression to try to hide the flash of regret and panic he saw in her eyes. Nicholas wished she would look up, to see how easily mended this was. If Sophia was not here to mop up her spills, he would gladly take on the challenge.

"Perhaps from Captain Hall? He has a charming repertoire of songs," he suggested.

Chase gave him a narrow look. "That's not one I've heard before. Is there more to it?"

125

"It was in a book I read with my mother," she said vaguely. "We used to read adventure stories before bed. I don't remember the rest. Excuse me for being, ah, so rude."

"Rude? Nonsense. What a delightful voice you have!" Wren said. "Do you have any other musical ability, Miss Spencer? Perhaps you'll treat us to a song later on?"

Grateful for that shift in subject, aren't you, weasel? Nicholas thought.

"I—no, well—" She looked to the ceiling for rescue, more panicked than before. "I play the violin."

"The violin? That's most irregular," Wren said. "I suppose I'm out of touch with the training you ladies receive. Are there many instruments of quality in the West Indies?"

Etta straightened and repeated, "The West Indies?"

A horrible suspicion snaked through Nicholas's mind. Was there a possibility that she didn't know the location of whatever passage she had come through? But then, wouldn't that mean . . .

She's not here of her own free will.

Anger flashed through him at the thought, and he brought one boot down against the rug, as if to stomp it out.

It does not matter. Your concern is bringing her to the old man.

But he knew the feeling of being caught in the Ironwoods' net. He knew it very well indeed.

"Ah! If I remember correctly, there's a violin somewhere around here. . . ." Goode said, glancing around the cabin. Aside from the shelves of warped book spines, a sturdy desk, and the berth for sleeping, there wasn't all that much to observe.

"Perhaps Nicholas will be so good as to search for it, so that we might hear you play tomorrow?" Wren said.

"*Mister* Carter," Chase bit out.

"Curse my clumsy tongue," Wren said, raising a glass in a mocking salute.

Nicholas raised his own. "Thankfully, you have a sparkling imagination to make up for it."

His lips tight, Wren returned his attention to Etta, who was toying with a spoon. "I must say, I'm highly affronted that the captain kept such lovely young ladies from us. Though I suppose I can see why he would want to shield the crew from such radiant beauty."

Nicholas choked on his next sip of claret. Etta flushed from her cheeks down to the slope of— He returned his eyes back to his plate, gripping his knees beneath the table.

"I meant to ask about that very thing," Chase said to her. "The others only knew there were passengers because these two gentlemen were moved to the bosun's and carpenter's cabins in the bow. They were as startled as the *Challenger*'s crew to see you."

"My sister, as you know," Etta said carefully, "is not well. We were confined to the cabin because of that."

"Why did you not ask for the surgeon? Both Mr. Farthing and I would have been glad to have been of assistance," Goode said.

Nicholas registered the girl's expression. Her silence was telling.

"Likely because a surgeon would try to fix with a saw what water and broth could easily soothe," he said.

"I resent that implication, sir. There have been advances in medicine, and having studied—"

"I can hardly credit the two of you as sisters," Chase said, pushing the hair off his forehead. "You're so markedly different in appearance and accent."

Nicholas kicked his foot beneath the table. A drunken Chase was a blunt Chase.

"That observation is hardly polite," Wren said coolly.

"I only meant to ask if they've different mothers, is all," Chase groused. "My apologies, Miss Spencer, if offense was taken."

"That's all right," Etta said weakly.

"And the late captain was your uncle?"

Where the devil are you going with this? Nicholas thought, studying his old friend.

"He was indeed, Mr. Chase," Mr. Goode said, venturing into the conversation again with a disapproving look. "Related to Miss Sophia's mother, their father's first wife. Correct me if I misunderstood his story, Miss Spencer, but I take it to understand your father and his second wife, your mother, had a fine plantation on Nassau before they lately passed away. Miss Sophia was bringing her sister back with her to England."

"Yes," Etta said quickly. "That's exactly right."

This was beyond belief. Ironwood had actually seen to it that an elaborate history was created to explain the differences between the girls. If he had to guess, the old man had bribed the captain to pose as their uncle, so they would have an escort and protection on this journey, as the rules of the era dictated.

"It's regrettable," Wren interrupted to regain Etta's attention, "that your voyage was so rudely interrupted. Will you be able to get word to the family waiting for you in England that you were forced to alter your destination? My God, what if they think you've been lost at sea? Imagine their devastation."

He was looking at Etta, but clearly speaking to Nicholas.

"Rest assured, sir," Nicholas said with a patience he did not know he possessed, "they will be able to write to their family once we are in port. They will be well cared for until we can find them safe passage home. There's bound to be a Royal Navy ship or a

British Army encampment near enough to Connecticut willing to assist them."

"Ah, yes. I long to hear how this little skirmish is shaping up. How long before Washington surrenders? Let's place our bets, gentlemen." Wren's fingers drummed against the table. "Perhaps another month? I've heard Howe has his eyes set on New York. *That* would be a terrible blow to your army's efforts, would it not? The loss of such a vital port and city?"

"They certainly aren't *my* efforts," Nicholas said, an uneasiness creeping up on him. "I have no investment in this war beyond what ships it brings to the water that we can capture."

"Really?" Etta asked. "But I thought this crew was American?"

"Well, Americans were Englishmen until a few months ago," Chase said. "Some on our crew still consider themselves to be. But the *Challenger* sails under a Letter of Marque from the Continental Congress, and we're authorized to prey only on British ships, so I suppose that seals our allegiance."

"A lot of good those papers will do for you if you come across the Royal Navy," Wren said. "Traitors are worse than murderers in the eyes of the king. A length of rope will be your reward."

"Please, sir," Chase begged, holding up a hand. "I've enough of a headache without a bloody recitation of 'Rule, Britannia.'"

Wren's look was withering. "I only meant, *Mister* Carter, it strikes me as odd you wouldn't want to join your Congress's fledgling navy. Surely there's some fortune to be found in legitimacy over piracy? Perhaps some . . . honor?"

Chase snorted. "A fraction of what we'll take on board a privateer. And rest assured, this *is* a legal endeavor—much to your own misfortune."

Nicholas raised his own glass, but recognized the glint in Wren's eyes. The name belied his true nature—this was an osprey across from him, one that was wheeling in circles, waiting to dive.

"I don't understand," Etta said, looking uneasily around the table. "Why is it odd? It's his choice to stay out of the American navy, isn't it?"

It was the opening the other man had been hoping for.

"Why, on his *brethren's* behalf," Wren said, his smile all teeth. "Surely all this commotion about *freedom* and *liberty* has stirred some memories of the chains of his past. Though I've also heard that, unlike the British, there have been no offers of freedom in exchange for military service for the slaves of the colonies."

Hall had told him once that if Nicholas allowed his dislike of every man who insulted him to sharpen into hatred, he'd only end up cutting himself. But truly, did Wren think pointing out the obvious would somehow discredit Nicholas in the eyes of the others? That it would undermine his authority?

You may have this, Wren was saying, *this moment, this ship, but you'll never be anything other than what men like me decide you are.*

Never. Never again would he allow any other man to define him, set his course.

Chase shot to his feet so fast that his chair toppled backwards. His blood rushed the other way, straight to his face. "Sir, I'd call you out if—"

Nicholas put a hand on his friend's shoulder, stood to retrieve his chair, and promptly guided him back into it. "Remember that there's a lady present, my friend."

The very same one who looked perfectly horrified. What a *wonderful* meal this was turning out to be. And to think, there'd likely be about ten other variations of it as they sailed north toward New York.

Nicholas refilled his friend's glass with more claret, hoping it would settle his temper instead of stoking it.

"Are you speaking of Dunmore's Proclamation in Virginia last year?" he said, ignoring Wren's smug expression. "In which slaves of rebels would earn their freedom by escaping and fighting for the British army? The Continental Congress has, in fact, encouraged the Virginians to dispute the ruling, and they have since driven the governor out. I can't credit your implication that all slaves will be free at the end of this exercise, either. The king is well aware of how much the colonies rely on enslaved labor to produce the goods he enjoys. He means only to punish his wayward children by taking away their tools. Empty their pockets for a time. Nothing is likely to change."

Wren turned his glass on the table. Nicholas met the man's eyes, trying to keep the loathing from his own.

"In truth," Nicholas said, "I simply cannot abide the hypocrisy of fighting for a man who supposedly embodies the ideals of freedom, while at home, dozens of slaves work his land."

Not to mention any number of military expeditions that this man had fumbled in his youth, and how he had never been deemed worthy of a commission in the British Army. He admired the man's tenacity, but the moment he'd learned the colonies would actually *win* the war, he could have been knocked over by a feather.

"You mean Washington?" Etta asked, startled.

Nicholas nodded. "You should also know, Mr. Wren, that I am a freeman, and that will never change."

"How diverting!" Heath offered loudly, only to deflate when he saw the faces around him.

Nicholas watched as a cabin boy brought in some sort of pudding for dessert.

"Perhaps it *will* change," Wren said as his pudding was placed in front of him, "should the colonies break away, and the landowners in the South seize control of the new government. They will be in the position to create their own Eden. Isn't it fair to say that slavery has been a boon to Africans? At the very least, it breaks them of their laziness and their barbaric violence—brings them into God's flock. The work they do is fit for their capacities."

Ah, yes. Here it was, a hundred years' worth of justifications for the wrongful enslavement of human beings, gathered into a tidy, single breath of hot air. These sweeping lies about the minds of Africans, the denial of every opportunity to advance themselves by reading and writing and *thinking*, kept them not only in physical chains, but insidious, invisible ones as well.

It didn't matter that none of it was true. That Nicholas himself stood as evidence of it. What mattered was that these beliefs had swept through the souls of everyone else like a plague. He couldn't see the end of it. Even a hundred years in the future, he knew, the roots still had not been fully pulled up from society. Wherever, *whenever* he went, the color of his skin set the boundaries of what he could achieve, and there was very little—if any—recourse for finding a way around it.

Etta's palms were pressed flat against the table, and she was breathing hard in an obvious attempt to master her . . . anger? She was angry? On *his* behalf?

If Wren had spared her a glance, he might have thought

twice before adding, "I suppose you owe your faculties to . . . your father, perhaps? Forgive me if I've made incorrect assumptions about your parentage."

"You have not, Mr. Wren," Nicholas said, wondering why he had ever resisted the urge to lodge his fork in the man's eye. "To your point, though, I suppose we are all born with deficits. In your case, in manners."

He understood this now for what it really was—punishment, for having made the other man feel like a fool. First with the seizure of the *Ardent*, and tonight, revealing his lies. This knowledge in itself was enough to settle him somewhat; the pettiness of it stripped some of the pain as these old wounds were sliced open.

Wren swayed in his seat, the full effect of the claret seeming to strike him all at once. His words became slippery at the edges, slurred slightly, as his eyes gleamed, giving his anger a darker edge. "What was it that Voltaire supposedly said? Your race is a species of men, as different from ours as a breed of bulldogs is to terriers?"

"Mr. Wren!" Etta began, scarlet in the face.

"Having actually read the Voltaire in question, I can confirm the quote is, *as different from ours as the breed of spaniels is from that of greyhounds*," Nicholas said coldly. "Interesting, though, that in the end we're all just dogs."

"Perhaps," Wren said, leaning forward in his seat. "But not all of us are mutts without pedigree."

Etta stood at the same moment as Chase, only she was the one close enough to land a slap on the officer's face. The crack of flesh on flesh stunned Nicholas, who'd leapt up to restrain his friend from lunging across the table.

"And these are the actions of a lady?" Wren sputtered.

"Aye," Chase said approvingly. "And a damn fine one at that."

"Can you actually hear the words coming out of your mouth?" she demanded, pieces of her hair falling out of its braid as she threw an arm out toward the door. "You need to leave the table— *right now.*"

Wren's eyes narrowed at her tone. Nicholas didn't like the way the man was looking her over, as if preparing to strike. Strike *her.*

Nicholas's fingers pressed against the knife he'd set on his plate.

"I beg your pardon, madam," Wren said, "if I've caused you any offense."

"You *know* I'm not the one you offended!" she said, trembling with anger. "I think it's time for you to leave."

Wren folded his hands together and rested them on his chest. "I haven't eaten my pudding yet."

"Oh my God, you are *despicable!*" Etta snarled.

"Careful, madam, blasphemy is still a sin—"

Even if Nicholas had been the gambling sort, he never would have wagered a single coin on her next words being "Then I guess I'll see you in hell!"

The look of outrage on her face would have sent even Nicholas flying to the other end of the ship; he wondered, not for the first time, *when* she was from. What era had produced such a fearsome, magnificent temper? But Wren stayed precisely where he was, the smug arse, and it was Etta who left the room in a whirl of skirts.

Chase craned his neck around. "That one, I like."

Nicholas waited, but didn't hear the telltale slam of a second door . . . meaning, she hadn't gone back into her cabin. "*That one* is up on the deck. Alone."

He implicitly trusted his crew, but no lady of this era was allowed to wander in these circumstances unescorted, and there were plenty of ways for her to be injured, never mind tossed overboard in a swell. Moreover, he was a little frightened that she had set out to find another grappling hook.

He stood, turning back to his friend. "See to it that Mr. Wren is returned to the hold. And, sir," he said, returning his gaze to the weasel, who was contently eating beside a shocked Goode, "you will not be dining with us for the duration of our journey. Call my character into question as you like, but if it reaches my ears that you've attempted to besmirch Miss Spencer and her reputation, you will find yourself without a tongue to enjoy your future meals."

It was a relief to be free from the warm, muggy air inside the cabin; what with the wine, and the upset in his stomach, he'd felt like he was being slowly drawn into an unwilling sleep. The dark autumn air brushed his skin sweetly, a balm to the heat trapped beneath it.

She'd walked only a short distance along the starboard side on the quarterdeck, and was standing at the rail. The wind pressed back against her gown, molding it further to her shape. The full moon cast her in ivory light, stretching its hand out over the water in a trail leading to the horizon. If not for her pose, the arms crossed over her chest as she surveyed the dark sea churning around her, she might have been one of the great masters' statues, brought to life.

And in a thousand different ways, she was just as entirely out of his reach.

SIX

DAMN, DAMN, DAMN . . .

Etta scrubbed the cold, salty water from her eyes and cheeks with one hand, and clawed at the front of the dress with the other. She couldn't dislodge the ball of panic that had settled just under her ribs; the stays were squeezing so tightly that her spine ached each time she took a shallow breath. Worse, though, was the throbbing sting in the palm of her right hand. An unwelcome reminder of how badly she'd blown dinner.

If—*when*—word got back to Sophia that, one, she'd gone to dinner, and two, had made a mess of it, Etta would be lucky if the girl let her go to the head unsupervised to relieve herself. Wandering the ship and winning over the crew? Out of the question entirely.

Everything had been fine—or mostly fine—through the first hour. Mr. Wren—no, just Wren, he didn't deserve any better—had droned on until his dinner grew cold in front of him, sucking up whatever energy she had left. Despite the worldly airs he put on, Etta didn't think Wren—or *Edward*, whatever name he'd tried to whisper in her ear—was all that older than herself, or even Nicholas.

She pressed a hand to her mouth. *Nicholas.*

Every ounce of Etta beat back against the thought, but there was no way around the truth: Sophia had been right. Etta really had no idea what it was like to live during a time where you had no legal or societal protections in place. All she'd learned from that dinner was how very helpless you were to other people's perceptions.

Nicholas didn't need her to fight his battles for him. He'd been doing a masterful job of handling Wren, turning each remark back on the other man—proving, without directly stating so, what an absolute idiot he was. He never gave in to the anger that the other man was obviously trying to stir up.

Etta hated the tired resignation she'd seen in his face as Wren had exposed his own ignorance and hatred, the obvious expectation of it. And *then* Wren had the nerve to look around the table, like he was waiting for the rest of them to agree.

The anger that had flooded her veins was so pure, she thought it must have turned her blood to acid. You could read a hundred books about the attitudes and beliefs of the past, but the impact of witnessing this casual, ignorant cruelty firsthand was like having a bucket of ice upended over your head. It forced Etta to see that the centuries padding this time and hers, along with simple privilege, had protected her from the true ugliness of it. People *believed* this trash, and they were spreading it around like it was nothing. Like they weren't even talking about humans.

Etta braced her arms against the rail, looking out over the dark water. The peak of each ruffling wave caught the moonlight, turning them a sparkling silver. A symphony of sounds moved around her. The slap of the water against the ship's curved sides, the fluttering of the huge sails overhead, the thump of something deep below—a rudder, maybe? She'd found the creaking wood unnerving at first, wondered if there was a chance the ship might just split apart at the seams, but now it reminded her of the way her old prewar apartment settled and resettled into its bones every day.

You messed up.

She *couldn't* make mistakes. Not when Alice's life was at stake.

She laced her fingers together, resting her forehead against them. Was she going to have to apologize for hitting him? Cough up the words from some numb place inside herself, and hope she didn't throw up in the process? *I won't do it, I won't, I won't, I won't*—she squeezed her eyes shut.

"Look at you, a regular Jack Tar."

She turned at the smoky, deep voice. The sight of Nicholas cutting a path through the dark finally popped the bubble of panic. She counted the steps between them, and he finally stopped to consider her, running a hand over his closely cropped hair. He searched her face as if wondering how to start.

Etta wasn't the least bit ashamed of studying him back, but she was sure she wouldn't get much from it. Nicholas seemed to guard his expression so carefully, protecting the privacy of his thoughts.

Etta shifted her eyes away from his face. She'd been right before—it was his only jacket. He wore it now, brushed clean. The fit had swallowed her, but was perfect over his white shirt, emphasizing the broad span of his shoulders. His pants hugged his legs as he crossed that last distance between them. Nicholas was tall, his muscles compact and lean; everything about him seemed efficient, from the way he spoke to the way he moved with steady, easy grace, shifting with the sea.

His presence was larger-than-life, bigger even than his physical body. As he stood beside her, Etta felt as warm as if he'd spread his coat over her again, wrapped her up in it.

"You've got steady legs," he explained finally, turning his eyes up. "You'll be a seasoned sailor by the time we reach port."

"I don't know about that," Etta said, following his gaze along the large, central mast, to—was that a man, working on the long beam the sail was hung from? Earlier, she'd seen the men climbing up and down the ropes like spiders sharing a web, but none had gone this high—high enough that she couldn't make out the man's face. He was a pale blur against a quilt of stars. It was dizzying just to look at him.

"Is he going to be able to get down?" Etta asked, and realized that she was clutching his arm. He went absolutely still at the same moment she did, inhaling softly. The wool was rough against her fingertips, and the sensation lingered even after she let go and stepped back.

"He'll be fine," Nicholas said gently. "Most of us have been climbing the rigging since we were boys. The wind's picking up, so Marsden is reefing the sails—reducing their size to keep the ship stable."

She nodded, fiddling with the edge of her sleeves, trying to ease some of the tightness there. He'd said it so casually, the way Etta might tell someone she used to climb trees in Central Park.

Nicholas crossed his arms over his chest again, turning his face into the breeze, his eyes shut.

"I really hate that I ruined dinner," she said quietly. "But I'm never going to be sorry about what I did. He was out of line and wrong."

His lips twitched. "Alas, that meal was doomed from the moment they laid out the plates. And rest assured, you are among company that deals in considerable physical violence. A good effort is always appreciated."

"I've never slapped anyone before," she admitted.

"How did you find the experience?"

"It would have been *more* satisfying if he'd gone flying out of his seat like I imagined," she said. "I wanted to do it the whole night, but . . . I'm worried that what I did is going to cause more problems for you."

Nicholas looked at her in what Etta thought might be utter amazement. Too late, it hit her that this *also* wasn't something a young woman in this time would say.

She rushed on, explaining, "He was trying so hard to bait you. I don't know what the next level of that is, but whatever it is, I'm worried he'll find another way of taking it out on you."

"Well, he certainly won't be taking it out on *you*," Nicholas said, his voice harsh. "Not if he values his skin. I'd take entirely too much pleasure from personally stripping it with the cat-o'-nine-tails."

The violence in the words was a promise.

"Are you sure you can't just . . . maroon him on a remote island with a bottle of rum?" Etta asked, only half kidding. "Make him walk the plank straight into a shark's mouth?"

"Maroon him? *Walk the plank?*" To her surprise, he actually laughed. It felt like a reward to hear it. "Why, Miss Spencer, I believe there's a pirate's heart in you. I wish Captain Hall had stayed, if only so he could have told you some of his stories over dinner."

"Too bad," she agreed, relieved that a small bit of the tension had finally eased. "Do you know any good ones?"

"I'm not as good in the telling as he is," Nicholas said. "Perhaps you'd be interested in hearing the charming tale of pirates who disemboweled and cut out the heart of a British officer, soaked it in spirits, and ate it?"

Her jaw dropped. "Spirits? As in, alcohol? Was that supposed to make it taste better?"

"I'd imagine few things could improve the experience," he said. "But anything is possible with enough rum and courage, I suppose."

This exchange was so beyond the stilted, polite dinner conversation that it felt almost like a trap. Etta remembered Sophia's warnings, but it was such a relief to talk to someone who wasn't trying to outthink her, or lord information over her. She relaxed her hold on the railing and laughed.

"How do you stand it?" she heard herself ask.

He turned to her, brows raised. "I'm not sure I know what you're asking."

"The rules . . ." She crossed her arms over her chest, letting the rise and fall of the ship anchor her to the moment. A part of her knew this was a dangerous train of thought to bring up with him, but another part of her, the one still a little clouded from the wine, didn't seem to care. "There are so many of them, aren't there? Rules on what we are and aren't allowed to talk about. Where we can talk. There's probably even a rule that says we're not supposed to be talking without someone else here, isn't there?"

"Believe me, pirate, we've already traveled so far past what's deemed appropriate that I'm not sure we'll ever manage to find our way back."

"I don't have a problem with that if you don't," she said hopefully. If this got back to Sophia, what were the chances she'd be locked in her cabin and fed only scraps of salted beef slipped beneath the door?

Nicholas's interest only seemed to sharpen. "And what would your *sister* say about that?"

Oh—damn. She scrambled for an explanation, feeling the heat wash up her throat the longer it took. "I wasn't raised the way Sophia was. . . . I'm still learning what's expected of me. And clearly not doing the best job."

He seemed confused by this. "Not raised the way . . . you mean to say . . ."

What could she possibly that would make sense here, worked through an eighteenth-century filter? "This family . . . I didn't know that Sophia even existed, that any of them did, until they came and *took* me. They interrupted my life, and now I have to play by their rules and do whatever they ask, and it doesn't matter what I want or how I feel. It's not my choice."

Nicholas turned again, resting his arms against the railing; he had locked his thoughts away so deeply inside of his mind that Etta couldn't begin to guess at them. His expression gave nothing away as he said, "So you would rather return to Nassau than continue to New York?"

Nassau! That was the second time it had been mentioned. So not Nassau County in New York, which meant . . . the Bahamas. "Is that an option? Can you bring me back?"

"No," he said flatly, extinguishing that tiny flare of hope. "My payment depends on delivering you to New York."

Of course.

"Unless you're in fear for your life—"

"What if I am?" she interrupted. "If it were up to me, I'd take one of those small boats and row myself back to shore."

"Don't be a fool." His whole body went rigid beside hers. "Aside from the fact that it would take you days before you spotted land, you wouldn't know the first thing about navigation, nor would you have enough water or food to sustain you."

"So you'd keep me here against my will—"

"Know this, pirate," he said, his hands gripping the railing, "you are my passenger, and I will be damned before I let any harm come to you."

She was unsure how to respond to the fervor of those words. "Another rule?" she managed finally.

"A promise. If I see that you're in danger from Ironwood, I will help you escape myself. But should you try to leave on your own, know that I will go to the ends of the earth to bring you back."

She felt color begin to creep up her throat, her cheeks, at the intensity of his words. "You'd risk not getting your payment?"

"Don't be ridiculous. We'll escape *after* I get my payment." He shook his head, but Etta caught the hint of teasing in his tone. "Really, Miss Spencer. You ought to surrender your colors for that."

"Do pirates ever surrender?" she asked. "I thought they only went down in blazes of glory."

"Only the bad ones," he said, one corner of his mouth kicked up. "The rest live long enough for another war and go legitimate."

She managed a small smile. "I'll keep that in mind."

"You're right," he said, studying the small scars scattered over the back of his hand. "About the rules—they go largely unspoken and without explanation."

At first, watching the men at their game had been almost funny—it was so ridiculous to hear such devastatingly polite words delivered with such obvious hatred. And then, with Wren, it had suddenly become sinister—a way to do serious harm while still fitting inside that mold of acceptability.

Sophia had described it as a game, but Etta disagreed. In that first hour, the ceremonial flow of introductions, conversation, seating, had made her feel like they were part of a small orchestra. Written into every piece of music were strict rules on how to deliver the notes, how to keep the pacing, and a hundred other aspects that added up to the sound and movement that the composer had intended. There wasn't much room to be playful, to reinterpret pieces; that's why Etta always tried to flood her performances with some kind of emotion, to set them apart from what was expected. The most critical judges always seemed to be looking for perfect execution over inspiration, or even passion.

But both the game and orchestra metaphors were flawed. They implied that everyone was a willing participant, but the truth was, she doubted that anyone was really eager to participate in the charade of society aside from the people who created and benefited from the rules.

"I choose to exist outside of it whenever possible," Nicholas said slowly, as if unsure whether he wanted to continue. His voice dropped, and Etta had to lean closer to him to listen. "This—having to dine with the captured officers—is a rare exception. I have no problem paying respects to the men I sail with, because I admire and appreciate them. But you're right, the falseness is tiresome. And worse, deceitful."

"It seems like one of the benefits of being out here," she said, gesturing to the water, "should be the ability to make your own rules."

"Well, in all truth, there are more rules to follow on a ship, and they tend to be far stricter. You might have plucked young Jack from danger after the spoon fiasco, but everyone in the cabin knows he'll be disciplined for behaving that way toward an officer."

"Disciplined how?" Etta asked sharply. "He's just a boy—"

"You don't have the luxury of being 'just a boy' when you sail," Nicholas said, not callously. "He is a member of a crew. Our rules and hierarchy add up to survival, and there's a logic and purpose to it all in maintaining order, even in the most desperate situations. The punishments for breaking them are as severe as they are because failing to fulfill your role affects everyone."

Etta set her jaw, taking a step back from him. He'd mentioned using a kind of whip earlier, and the thought of it snapping down on the boy's bare back, the thought of him trying to take it stoically under the eyes of the crew, for doing something that everyone at that table wished they could do . . .

"Miss Spencer, I only meant his rations will be docked," he said quietly. "Don't trouble yourself. He must learn discipline, but it was hardly a capital offense."

There was a softness to the words that she hadn't expected. "Were you ever . . . disciplined?"

He nodded, rubbing a thumb over his bottom lip. Etta watched its path as it skimmed over the generous curve until she remembered she wasn't supposed to be watching at all.

Focus. Home. The pearl was cool between her fingers as she rolled her left earring back and forth. For a moment she felt a strange prickling sensation just below it, like someone was watching the stretch of skin where her exposed neck met her shoulder. But when she looked up again, there was no one else nearby, and Nicholas had fixed his eyes on the moon.

"When I was about his age, certainly," he said. "I had a devil of a temper then, and it took every ounce of Hall's restraint to keep from smothering me out of exasperation. I thanked him for it in the end, since he gave me the opportunity to be a part of his crew. I prefer the candor of this life, that we're forced to cut out things that don't truly matter—qualities that matter far more to landlubbers. Here, what defines me first and foremost is my work, my capabilities, just the same as Jack. And unless you've been pressed onto a navy ship, a man's there by choice."

Nicholas didn't come right out and say it, but she had a feeling these "qualities" directly related to the color of his skin.

"You really didn't wish to leave Nassau?" he said quietly, apparently coming to some conclusion of his own.

"No, I didn't." The understatement of this particular century. Etta blew out a sigh, pulling the length of her braid over her shoulder. The wind had picked up, as promised, and was whipping the loose strands around in a flurry.

"I'm sure the unfortunate travel companion doesn't help matters."

"Companion," she said with a dry laugh. He was avoiding her name.

Nicholas closed his eyes for a beat, and when they opened he had clearly made a decision. "Sophia Ironwood would gladly cut the limbs from my body, pickle them, and throw them in a trough for the pigs. She would rather perish than admit we come from the same stock, let alone that we have anything in common beyond a mutual distaste for each other."

The words caught her across the face like a spray of seawater, a cold slap of realization.

We come from the same stock.

Family.

As in . . .

She stepped back, studying his profile, and he refused to meet her gaze.

Of course. *Of course*—why hadn't she seen that possibility before?

I have seen the rotten edges of his soul.

I know him for the deceitful swine he is.

Would Sophia have said something so virulent about someone she barely knew? And he'd mentioned Ironwood—Sophia's "grandfather"—any number of times, with more knowledge behind the word than a casual business acquaintance. Sophia knew him because he was one of them.

A traveler.

But . . . he was here, taking each shift in the wind and water as if he'd been born on a ship. If he'd been sailing since he was a child, then when—?

Etta took another full step back away from him, stunned.

"She truly told you nothing," Nicholas said, his voice flat. "I cannot say I'm surprised."

"You . . ." Etta struggled to bring her fractured thoughts back in line. "You weren't going to tell me either, were you? Do you have *any* idea what I've been through? How much better I would have felt at that dinner table, knowing I had a real ally? God, no wonder you kept stepping in when I messed up. You *had* to."

"Of course I stepped in to assist you," Nicholas said, seeming almost confused. "It is against our laws—and against better judgment—to allow our secret to be revealed. You should know this well by now."

And just like that, she knew that her plan would never work. Even if she could win the rest of the crew over, they wouldn't go against his wishes. She wasn't going to be able to grind his resistance down with reason or charm—not that she was all that certain she even *had* anything resembling charm. Nicholas wasn't just a hired acquaintance orbiting around the periphery of the Ironwood family's galaxy; he was part of their system. He was one of them.

"Your training—" he began.

"What training?" she cried, letting her temper fly again. "I didn't even know I could time travel until Sophia pushed me through a . . . through a passage, or whatever you call it!"

"*Pushed* you?" He spun back toward her, eyes flashing. "You mean to tell me you've never traveled before now?"

"Try: never traveled, never heard the name Ironwood, and possibly never going back to my home. They aren't even *my* family—they *killed* someone I loved to get to me!"

He swore viciously under his breath, turning his back on her for a moment. "You didn't even know you possessed the ability? Your traveler's sickness must have been unbearable. No wonder no one on the crew saw you—you must have been unconscious for days."

Traveler's sickness?

No—she couldn't get distracted, not about this.

"Don't act like you weren't in on this," Etta said. "You and Sophia—"

"No!" he said sharply, drawing her toward him, walking them both backward. She realized, as the world suddenly took shape around her again, that Wren and Chase had left the cabin, and were now moving steadily toward the hatch to the lower deck. "Don't put me in league with her. Ironwood's request said nothing of this. I assumed he was calling you and Sophia back to assign you to some task. I don't make a habit of abductions, Miss Spencer."

"You mean, aside from stealing other people's ships and holding their crews hostage?"

His brows rose, and he actually looked like he might smile. That settled her, but only somewhat.

"His letter didn't explain anything else?" she asked. "Nothing about why he wants to see me?"

"No. I was to intercept the *Ardent* and bring you and Sophia to New York City by September twenty-first. Christ," he muttered, rubbing the back of his neck. "The first time *I* traveled, I attacked an automobile with an umbrella and nearly pissed myself in terror. So when I say you are taking this well, I hope you'll believe me."

Etta couldn't begin to picture him looking frightened.

"I wish you'd told me," she said quietly. "You *are* an Ironwood, aren't you? Sophia mentioned other families, but . . ."

"I wish I could say I wasn't," he said, disgust curling his upper lip. "I don't associate with them, not anymore. This is purely a matter of business to me. I don't travel, I don't obey Ironwood, I live my life free from all that. And when the transaction is complete, they'll be cut out of my life for as long as I can keep it."

What was she missing here, then? If he hated the Ironwoods so much he was practically spitting as he talked about them, why agree to work for them? And if he could travel anywhere, to any time, why stay in one so openly hostile to him?

Based on what Jack had told her, Nicholas and Chase had been raised by Hall from the time they were boys, and Nicholas had said he'd been sailing from that age. So when had he done his traveling?

I don't travel, I don't obey Ironwood, I live my life free from all that.

And why had he stopped?

Etta could feel him pulling back, retreating not only into his mind, but instinctively stepping back in the direction of the captain's cabin.

"Knowing what they're like . . . you still won't bring me back home?" she asked. "Do you know where the passage is that Sophia brought me through? Is it in Nassau?"

"This ship sailed out of Nassau, so it's a likely conclusion to draw, but . . ." He shook his head. "I was never given a list of the passages and their locations. What year are you from, precisely?"

She told him, and it was worth it alone for the expression of complete wonder that transformed his face.

"I was told there wasn't a passage that opened beyond the Second World War. That is the commonly held belief. Of course, I do know there are many ancient passages that are uncharted, their destinations unknown. Perhaps yours is one of them. What family do you belong to?"

"Linden," she said. "According to Sophia."

She'd caught him by surprise again. "Linden? Are you certain?"

"She could be lying, I guess, but she did mention my mom, Rose." Etta stole a glance at his face. "Do you recognize the name?"

He blew out a long breath from his nose, unable to look at her face. "Who in our small world hasn't heard of Rose Linden? She's the only traveler to successfully outwit Ironwood. Stole something of his and disappeared without a trace. My God, what are you then, ransom? Why wouldn't he have just taken her if he found the two of you? Is she still alive?"

Etta nodded, latching onto this small piece of information. "What else do you know about her? Anything?"

"Only that she left a broken heart in her wake—Augustus Ironwood, Cyrus's son and heir, spent *years* searching for her.

Went nearly mad with it." Nicholas shook his head, and when he spoke again, there was a blaze of promise in his words. "I'll ensure that you get back to your time. If you are bait, or if he intends to use you to threaten Rose, then we'll leave at our first opportunity and search for the passage ourselves."

Disappointment sliced through her. *If*. She hated that word now. *If* and only *if* she was in true danger, he'd help her. Of course he wasn't going to turn around out of pity—in the first place, he didn't know where to bring her; in the second, he was earning good money for this job. But . . . as stupid and small as it made her feel, she had hoped. She'd read something in his hesitation.

Her stomach gave a firm, desperate little twist.

"You said someone was killed," he began. "Who was it?"

The first words that floated to her lips were a lie; she hated herself for it, for wanting to give in to the easy simplicity of a fake story, rather than peel off the bandage and bleed every messy feeling and thought about the violin all over again. But she liked this honesty between them—it felt like something real and solid, strong enough to tie herself to, when there were so many lies and secrets trying to pull her in every direction at once.

"You've been through a trial," he said quietly when she'd finished explaining. "I'm sorry for it. I was about to ask if you'd like me to find the violin that Mr. Goode mentioned—if it might be a comfort to you."

She felt sick at the thought, shaking her head. "The opposite. I can't . . . I can barely stand the thought of playing right now. Not until I get her back."

He opened his mouth to say something, then promptly shut it, shaking his head.

"What?" Etta asked.

"You mean to save your instructor? Alice?" he asked. "Change the past?"

"I know how it looks, but she was innocent—she didn't deserve to die, and not—not because of me."

He let out a heavy sigh, with a kind of pity that turned her stomach again. Etta lifted her hand off the rail as the wind kicked up and the ship tipped down to the right. The soles of her shoes were too soft, too slippery, and she felt one foot slide out from under her—

An arm banded around her waist, pulling her feet back to the deck and to the solid, warm anchor of Nicholas. Her face was pressed against his shoulder, her fingernails digging into, twisting, the back of his jacket. All she could hear was her own breath grating against the silence; all she could feel was the jackhammer beat of a heart hidden beneath layers of fabric and warmth.

Etta stepped back, trying to think of some way to break her awareness of the hand pressed firmly to the small of her back. He beat her to it.

"Careful," he breathed out, glancing down at the polished black leather of his shoes. "I've only the one pair left."

"Still at it?"

Etta couldn't say which of them was more startled at the sound of Chase's voice.

"Next watch starts soon; best to get the lady back to her cabin." He stood a short distance away from them at the edge of the hatch, arms crossed over his chest. It was too dark to make out his expression, but he didn't move until Nicholas took a generous step away from her, his hands suddenly clasped together in a knot behind his back.

"Time to retire, Miss Spencer," said Nicholas. "I'll escort you to your cabin."

He didn't take her arm or offer a hand. Nicholas kept a careful distance after that, his hands still hidden behind his back.

Now she understood how the *Ardent*'s crew had felt as they were led down into the belly of the ship, unsure of when—or even if—they'd be allowed to take in the sun, the stars, the sky. She hadn't appreciated the conversation for the small slice of freedom it was. Between Sophia and the crew, would the two of them ever be able to speak openly again before they reached New York?

His thoughts mirrored hers, apparently.

"Ten days to Long Island," said Nicholas. "Perhaps fewer if the wind is in our favor. I'm glad we had the chance to speak now, as I doubt Miss Ironwood will let you out of her sight once her stomach settles."

Etta paused outside her door, and he paused at the captain's cabin, just across the way.

"Can I ask you one thing?" Etta whispered.

He nodded, his eyes shining with the light from a nearby lantern. She took in a deep breath, inhaling the scent of salt and wax, and considered her words.

"If you can travel anywhere . . . to any time, for the most part," she began, "why do you stay *here*? In an era where there are men like Wren, who treat you that way?"

"You presume I have a choice," he said. "Good night, Miss Spencer. Rest well."

With that he disappeared into his cabin, shutting the door firmly behind him.

SEVEN

SOMEWHERE AT THE END OF A LONG LINE OF HAZY gray days, Nicholas woke at the first touch of shell-pink morning light, the devil's own hammers at work inside his skull. Bloody rum. Bloody dead captain hiding the bloody bottle in a place Nicholas could bloody well find in a moment he needed to numb his nerves. Good ideas had in the dark, he thought with a groan, were generally best left there.

The call of sighted land was repeated as he rubbed his face. His legs were the last part of him to realize that sleep was over, prickling painfully as he shifted. He swore as his knees connected with solid wood—his berth.

He slid along the berth's padding until he was sitting with his back against solid wood, his legs mostly stretched out in front of him. Above him, the ship's replacement bell sounded, signaling the morning watch. Nicholas swallowed to ease the dryness of his mouth and stared up at the low ceiling overhead, listening to the footsteps and calls above him on the deck.

Land meant their ten-day voyage back to the colonies was

over. In a matter of hours, he would come face-to-face with the man who'd attempted to destroy him.

He unfolded his long legs, stretching, and clenched his teeth against the cold air swirling around him. He dressed quickly, and had nearly finished shaving when Jack brought in his coffee and porridge. Chase appeared just as the boy was on his way out, filling the doorway with his broad shoulders and a storm cloud of anxiety.

"It's an hour to Oyster Bay," he said, shutting the door behind him. "Tell me once and for all that you're certain about this madness."

Rather than risk bringing the young ladies into New York Harbor on a captured British merchantman, Nicholas had made preparations with Ironwood to bring them ashore near Oyster Bay, off of Long Island Sound, where they would be met by a carriage. Nicholas remembered enough of this conflict's future to know that, by this day, the twenty-first of September, the British would already be in control of the city and its harbor. Wren had been right about this: if caught with a captured British ship, he and his prize crew would be tried as pirates, and—worse yet—traitors.

"I'm certain," Nicholas said, straightening his jacket. "Do you foresee any problems bringing the *Ardent* into New London without me?"

"I think we'll manage the feat, but how*ever* will I keep a dry eye knowing you're gone?" Chase said dryly.

It had been his sole condition—that the *Ardent*, its captured cargo, and his crew be kept well out of the way of trouble, and brought directly to the Lowes in Connecticut. Cyrus Ironwood, however, had demanded that Nicholas escort the girls into Manhattan, where he had taken up temporary residence. He had refused to meet them out on Long Island, or even in Connecticut, where they might have avoided the British altogether. As always, the sun rose and set on Ironwood's expectations, and any complications in bringing Sophia and Etta to him would be up to Nicholas to solve.

They had less than a day now to meet Cyrus Ironwood's firm arrival deadline; there simply wasn't *time* for complications, not with so much pay at stake.

"Will you see to it that our two passengers are ready to depart?" Nicholas asked. "I'd like to make one last inspection of the ship and crew."

"Miss Etta Spencer has been up for nearly two hours," Chase said with a chuckle. "Said she sensed we were close and was too eager to sleep. *Sensed* it! Personally, I think she saw one last opportunity for some freedom from her sister."

As Nicholas suspected, Sophia had taken a turn for the better and was alert enough to terrorize her "sister" with her constant, domineering presence for the rest of the voyage. Nicholas had given up counting the number of times he had come across Etta hiding somewhere in the galley or forecastle, playing a game of cards with Jack and the other boys, only to have Sophia swoop down in a swirl of silk and linen and snatch her away. In all of ten days, he'd managed to steal only four words. It left his stomach sour and his mind ill at ease.

He glanced back at the table, and at the violin and bow resting atop the pile of charts. He'd found it the night after the fateful dinner, stowed inside a cabinet, and had left it out in the hope . . . on the off chance she might change her mind and seek it out.

Chase cleared his throat. "Before you make for shore, if I may be so bold, my dear friend—"

"You may not, but you will," Nicholas replied.

"I know you've struggled to find a moment alone, and perhaps I should not have interrupted that first night, but I should hope it's as obvious to you that the girl has paid special mind to you—"

"She's a charming creature, and she's interested in the business of sailing," Nicholas said quickly. "She has paid *special mind* to everyone present, yourself included—"

"I'm not finished," Chase cut him off. "I was not implying anything improper. I wanted to ask if you remembered Hall's wife, Anne—what he said of her?"

"I only remember what happened when she passed," he lied. A long year, in which they had chased Hall from tavern to tavern and hadn't spent a single day on a ship. He'd had no idea a man so large and powerful, who'd fought and survived a thousand battles, could be broken into so many pieces when his lady took ill.

"Liar," Chase said, not unkindly. "He said he'd never remarry, because he'd never find another lady that fit so neatly at his side. He called her his equal in spirit."

Nicholas's hands smoothed over his sleeves, trying to formulate his argument. Anne had been one of the sweetest ladies the world was ever likely to see. She'd cared for both of the boys as if they were her own, and had never questioned the way Hall had brought them home, one at a time, like the strays they were. She was the pearl to the captain's rough, wild reef.

He couldn't let his friend finish. Put the hopeful thought into the world. It would grow into something that would only crush him in the end. "She's not for me."

157

"I think she is," Chase insisted. "Yet you can't see it."

"What I see is that there's no future there, even if the lady were amenable." The words were sour in his mouth. "What do you expect, for me to marry her? The match is forbidden by law."

"You've never let expectations rule your life before. Why start with something as important as this?"

Nicholas didn't want to puzzle it out and arrive at the conclusion he'd feared all along. It was better to stand aside from it, not to invest any more precious thought in the matter. Besides, it assumed too much . . . like the feelings of the lady in question.

"Fine," Chase said gruffly. "I'll tell the others that you've laid no claim."

Nicholas's eyes narrowed. "What the devil do you mean?"

"Half the men worship at her feet; the other half have already proposed marriage, including young Jack, who has sworn to his dear 'miss' that he'll be true if she'll only wait a few more years for him."

"Unrepentant rascal." A rumbling irritation rolled through him as he reached down, running a finger along the violin's curved body. "Have they been untoward?"

"Not in the least," Chase laughed. "They like her fine, though—enough to want her to stay."

And for that reason alone, Nicholas was grateful that this short voyage was at an end.

HIS REMAINING TIME ON THE *ARDENT* ESCAPED HIM LIKE WIND passing through his fingers. Much sooner than he might have liked, Nicholas found himself surveying the emerald tufts of distant trees along the shoreline. They faded in and out of his sight with the slow rolling fog, giving him the uneasy sense that the pale, misty air was breathing around his shoulders. The scent of damp earth wove itself through the smell of the sea, settling heavy in his lungs.

Etta wore a gown of deep blue, and the color reminded him of midnight, the winter seas, as if it had been meant specifically to draw his eye, to speak to the devil in him. He stood beside Chase on the deck, watching as the crew passed her around to say their farewells. It was near impossible to fight against the pull of her tide, but he forced himself to, turning to face his friend more fully.

"I'll meet you in port in a week's time," he said. "Make sure the agent is fully apprised of the fact that Wren is hostile. Likely he won't cooperate in dealings with the prize court."

"Understood," Chase said, clasping his shoulder. "Send word if you're delayed."

"I won't be," Nicholas said. His friend's look told him Chase wasn't nearly as confident.

The jolly boat, one of the ship's small rowboats, was lowered; Nicholas would have preferred the stability of a longboat, as well as the help of the additional hands required to man it, but this would suit them fine—it wasn't so long of a distance for him to row alone, and both had transferred their few possessions to bags he'd sewn from excess sail, rather than haul their trunks.

Once Nicholas was situated, the girls began their careful descent into the jolly boat. Sophia looked ready to spit on him should he try to help, but he did reach up and grip Etta by the waist as she stepped down, bracing his legs against the pitch and bob of the boat. He felt where she had held on to his shoulders long after he sat down and picked up the oars.

Nicholas looked back up to wave a farewell to the crew just as Chase leaned down and whispered something in Jack's ear.

The boy brightened, whispered something back, and jumped up onto the rail.

"How 'bout a kiss, hey?" Jack shouted down.

Etta laughed and obliged, blowing a kiss. With one last dry look up to a guffawing Chase, Nicholas drew the oars back and began the first long stroke. A good burn coursed through his stiff muscles as he eased into the steady motion. He kept his mouth shut as he rowed, even as Sophia grumbled, "Can't you go any faster?"

The mist began to burn away as the sun rose higher. Birds called from where they hovered above the water, and he didn't mind in the slightest when the sweat soaked through his shirt, not when there was fresh, cool air in his lungs. Sophia closed her eyes, drumming her fingers against the sack in her lap impatiently. Etta fixed on a point past Nicholas's shoulder. He craned his neck and followed her gaze toward the dark outline of the trees lining this deserted stretch of beach.

Nicholas had read Cyrus Ironwood's description of the meeting spot to Flitch, and they'd worked to match it to the coastal charts and maps. But he didn't feel confident they'd done a good job until Etta said, "I think I see a light."

Nicholas saw it now, too. A lantern cast a faint glow into the gloom that clung to the rocky beach, and as they grew closer, the dark form behind it took shape. Nicholas drew the oars in, letting the tide do the bulk of the work, until the bottom of the jolly boat struck sand. He jumped out, splashed into the cold water, and dragged the boat ashore.

Before he could reach in to steady her as she stepped out, to warn her about the strange hollow feeling that crawled up your legs as they settled themselves to the stillness of land, Sophia had jumped out and crumpled on the loose sand.

It was manners, the legacy of the saintly Anne Hall, that made Nicholas reach down and offer her a hand. The expression on Sophia's face, the flush of embarrassment, made her look like the young woman she was, not the wasp she insisted on being. For a moment, he might have even detected what Julian had once found appealing.

But then he saw her remember who he was.

What he had done.

Her face went as hard as flint, and her fingers curled in the sand as if she might throw a handful of it into his eyes. When she stood again, it was by her own strength.

Etta placed a hand on his shoulder to steady herself as she stepped out of the belly of the boat. Together they watched Sophia stagger toward the waiting coach and driver.

He ought to tell her that there were yet more rules about touching, about the propriety this century demanded.

But . . . perhaps not yet.

"If you can believe it, that's actually an improvement in her mood," Etta whispered. "This morning she threw half of her trunk at me when I came in to wake her up."

"Ah, the Ironwood charm," Nicholas said. "I suppose she then made you pick it all up for her as well?"

"Actually, I threw the water from the basin on her to cool her off." A dark look passed over Etta's face as they watched the carriage rock with the force of Sophia's entry. "Should have grabbed the chamber pot instead."

He barked out a sharp, surprised laugh.

"Thank you for showing that measure of restraint," he said, still struggling with his smile. "I wish I could say that you'll have a more welcome reception when you meet Cyrus Ironwood. But be warned—if he scents fear in you, he'll take particular delight in tearing you to pieces."

Etta set her shoulders back, starting ahead of him up the hill.

"Well, you'll have nothing to be afraid of," she told him, a little smile on her face. "Because I'll be with you."

Nicholas shut his eyes, and took in one last breath of the sea-kissed air.

If only that would be enough.

NEW YORK CITY
1776

EIGHT

THE SMOKE ROSE TO GREET THEM MILES BEFORE THEY reached the Brooklyn Ferry.

"What is that?" Etta asked Nicholas. "Some kind of battle?"

He seemed just as perplexed as she was, following her gaze out of the window to where black plumes were streaming into the darkening sky.

"That's your cue," Etta told Sophia. "Any time you want to elaborate on what that terrifying thing in the distance is, that would be great."

Sophia studied her fingernails.

"Withholding information endangers all of us," Nicholas reminded her. "I can't protect you if I don't know what's ahead."

She dropped her hands back into her lap with a look of exasperation. "Fine. It's the fire—it's been burning since this morning. The 'Great Fire of New York.' You would know that, if you'd actually paid attention to any of your training."

"If I'd *received* any training aside from how not to be killed, how to avoid sharing our secret, and how Julian wanted his cravat tied, I might have been able to retain it," he fired back.

In the midst of the thunderous charge sparking between them, Etta blinked, trying to remember if she'd ever read or learned about this.

"What caught fire?" she asked. To kick up *that* much smoke, it would have to be enormous.

"The entire west side of the city," Sophia said, after another dragging silence. "From what I remember, it broke out this morning—the twenty-first of September. It's probably burned through the quarter by now."

Not for the first time, Etta thought about how strange it must be for the Ironwoods to live outside of the normal flow of time, to know everything that came before them and nearly everything that would happen, up to a certain point, after. It must have made it much easier to invest their money, choose their homes, and pick their battles for the benefit of the family. "What started it?"

"It depends on who you ask—the British seem to think it was one of Washington's spies. That some mongrel set it when the army was forced to flee the city." Nearly everything seemed to be made of wood in this time period—all it would take was a single spark. Etta rubbed at her forehead, glancing at Nicholas. He'd untied his neck cloth and let it hang over his shoulders, his shirt parted at the front to reveal a span of warm skin. His clothes were well-worn, rumpled from days of work and travel, and he seemed unbothered by it even as Sophia fussed with her gown and beat the road dust from the skirt. She had patted on more perfume of some kind, but Etta focused on the scent of him—it was cool breezes and sunshine and rum.

While Sophia's anxiety was manifesting in the way she kept folding and unfolding her hands in her lap, and in the impatient jumping of her legs under her skirt, Nicholas seemed to be retreating inside himself. The worry she'd seen on his face when they'd come ashore felt very different from this; there had been some anger knotted into his exasperation for Ironwood, when he'd warned her. His finger was currently worrying his upper lip; his gaze was cast out over the landscape rolling by, but he didn't seem to be focusing on any one thing.

Etta thought that Nicholas could likely count the things that unnerved him on one hand, maybe even one finger. He could manage Sophia, and he seemed prepared for Ironwood; so, then, what was left to put such ice in his expression?

Rather than sit in the unbearable silence of not knowing, she asked, "Did you get to see New York before the fire?"

Idiot question. She *knew* he'd been to New York; that he'd even lived there for a time. Jack had told her as much during her fact-finding mission.

It was amazing how small you could feel when someone wouldn't so much as *look* at you. For a second, Etta was sure he wasn't going to answer at all, just keep his gaze fixed out of the window. Then, she got a single word: "Once."

"What did you think of it?" Etta pressed, focusing on her irritation, so she wouldn't have to acknowledge the creeping feeling of being hurt.

"Filthy."

To her surprise, Sophia said, "The only point on which we agree. They throw the slop and garbage out into the streets hoping the animals and vermin will eat it, and whatever's left washes out to the rivers with the rain. You can smell the city for miles before it comes into view. Fire smoke will only improve it."

Here was the truth about the past, as Etta was coming to realize: it was startlingly quiet at times, the pace of life moved slower than a crawl, and the smell of the people and places was actually unbelievable. Her nose still hadn't adjusted to it.

By the time they rolled to a stop, and the carriage rocked as the driver stepped off his perch to open their door, Etta would have tried splitting her skull open against the ground to relieve the pressure of her headache. Sophia stumbled out on unsteady legs behind her, using her shoulders for support. Nicholas brought up the rear, handing over a small bag of what looked like money to the driver, who went to tend to his horses.

Smoke clogged the air, a steady breeze carrying it across the bobbing water of the East River. Etta could taste it now at the back of her throat. Buried beneath the overpowering smell of charred wood was a rotting sweetness and hot manure, but Etta wasn't sure if it was coming from the burning garbage or the smell of the soldiers moving around her.

The first time she'd seen the pops of vivid scarlet scattered across the rolling green landscape of Long Island, she was shocked. She recognized the famous red coats at once—the uniforms the British soldiers wore as they made their way through the towns, patrolled the roads, stopped and read the papers the driver handed them at each checkpoint.

Up close, Etta could see the careful white-and-gold detailing on the lapels, the shine of the buttons running down the cream-colored vests they wore underneath. Most of their breeches and stockings were splattered with dust from the road, and each wore a different version of the same exhaustion as they milled around the ferry landing, ushering crowds to and from the flat barges, away from the burning New York City.

"—would burn it to the ground before they'd let us have it, would they?"

"—deliberate, the fire's taken it all from Broad Way to the Hudson, going north and west and taking the only decent taverns with it—"

Etta turned as two soldiers strode around her, heads bent closely together. Seeing her, they both nodded politely and went on their way with nothing more than, "Evenin', ma'am." The faces beneath the black hats were surprisingly young—why was she always assuming everyone in the past was so much older than she was? In the whole course of history, war had always fallen on the shoulders of the young.

After some negotiation, the ferryman agreed to make one last trip over the river before night fell and he was due home. Sophia charged forward like a gunshot, practically pushing her way onto the low, flat boat. A hand appeared in the corner of Etta's eye—Nicholas, offering to help her step down. After his earlier aloofness, Etta didn't feel much like validating his chivalry, and instead fixed her gaze on the forest of masts and sails drifting along the river.

The nonexistent skyline of this Manhattan made it impossible to figure out exactly where they were; somehow, not even being able to orient herself in the city she'd grown up in made something twist sharply deep inside her. The distance from the very tip of the island, what she knew as Battery Park, the view of it . . . She closed her eyes, picturing Brooklyn Bridge stretching over her head, the fanned-out cables, the sturdy stone arches. But when she opened her eyes again, there were no glossy-windowed skyscrapers scratching at the violet evening sky. The smoke wasn't drifting around the faces of luxury high-rise apartments. None of the buildings seemed taller than a few stories.

Two ferrymen moved them along the river using what looked

like long oars, splashing and thudding—nothing like the mechanical roar of the modern ferries' motor engines. It was so quiet without the highways, the traffic. Etta looked up, waiting to see a plane cross the sky overhead.

This isn't New York, she thought, *this isn't my home, this can't be it*—

Do not cry, she ordered herself. *Don't you dare. . . .* It wouldn't do anything except draw more unwanted attention to the fact that she was out of place.

Nicholas stood nearby, leaning against the ferry in his usual pose—arms crossed over his chest, face devoid of almost any emotion. She didn't understand how one person could guard their thoughts and feelings as fiercely as he did.

"Are you talking to me again?" she asked.

"I was born here, in 1757." His eyes shut briefly, but Etta saw something move in them. "Initially, it wasn't . . . pleasant."

Etta waited for him to continue.

Nicholas swallowed hard. "Captain Hall, whom you met briefly . . . he and his wife had a little house near the commons. After he purchased my freedom, I went to live with them, and my life was vastly improved."

Purchased my freedom. The pain lanced through her, hot and jagged, chased by confusion.

"You mean . . ." Etta began. "You were born into the Ironwoods, but they—"

Anger choked the rest of the words from her throat. Nicholas shrugged.

He *shrugged.*

"I wasn't legitimate, nor was I wanted. A child takes on the status of its mother in this time period. My mother was their property; therefore, so was I." Nicholas glanced at her. "They didn't know that I'd inherited their . . . gift . . . until later, after I'd already lived for a time with Hall and his wife."

"You grew up with Chase too, right?" she asked. Seeing a flicker of surprise, she added, "He told me a little about it a few days ago, while we were walking on the deck—that Mrs. Hall told the captain he wasn't allowed to take either of you out to sea until she taught you to read and write."

At that, he actually smiled. "She was a lady of uncommon kindness and bold spirit. Once we lost her, there was no reason to come back here, aside from occasional business."

"How did Hall find you?" Etta asked. "Why did the Ironwoods . . ." She couldn't bring herself to say *sell you* without wanting to vomit.

Nicholas lowered his voice. "You know, I presume, that the ability has become rarer as the family has moved forward, yes?"

Etta nodded.

"Hall is a more distant relation to the Ironwoods—in fact, *he* was taken in to the Ironwoods when Ironwood finished off *his* family, the Hemlocks, and brought the survivors into line," Nicholas explained. "But he isn't as you and I are; he's what we call a 'guardian.' They cannot travel, and are stationary in their natural times. But they watch the entrances to the passages to ensure the safety of the travelers, and take note of all comings and goings. They also do other work for the family—see to their financial interests and property in various eras, relay messages between the centuries."

Etta's eyes widened. "How in the world do they do that?"

"If they precede us, they leave letters in various family vaults which are checked by other guardians. If they follow this era, the letters are brought back by a designated traveler. Hall himself was required to oversee the transportation and sale of sugar from one of their plantations in the Caribbean from 1750 until just recently."

She was missing a piece of this. "Had you met Hall before you went to live with him?"

He shook his head. "Ironwood decided to have the old family house on Queen Street sold, along with its possessions. My mother was purchased outright with another house slave, and claimed I ran away. She left me hiding in a cupboard, and hoped I'd be able to escape and live a life of freedom. I would never have agreed if I'd known what was truly happening."

Etta was about to ask what had become of his mother, but he barreled on quickly.

"Hall found me when they came to inspect the house before the purchasers arrived. I was half-dead from hunger, filthy as a stray pup—my mother had told me to stay put and keep silent, and I was much better at following orders then." Nicholas gave her a wry smile. "He carried me out. Made sure my freedom was legal. It was years before Ironwood came back to that era and learned of me. I trained and traveled for a time on Ironwood's behalf, but no more. I'll not leave the sea or my true family again."

Etta forced herself to move past the thought of him as a young boy, hiding in the dark for days. "What will you do after you finish your business with Ironwood?"

He shifted, absently reaching up to rub at his shoulder. "I

need to meet Chase and the others to see to my responsibilities as prize master. Captain Hall will be back in port before the month's end, and we'll sail again soon after."

Of course he had responsibilities. That was his life—it had just so happened to overlap with hers for a few days. Why did Etta feel so anxious at the thought of him walking away? "Is it safe to travel? Will you be all right?" she asked.

"Don't worry about me, Miss Spencer," he said as they bumped up against the other ferry landing. "I always manage."

"You could call me Etta," she said, smiling. "I'd like that."

There was a crack in that calm mask—a flash. Etta's eyes read it as anger, but instinct registered something worse: a painful kind of shock, as if she'd knocked him off the ferry and into the cold river.

"You—" he began, his gaze shifting up to the sky, a small, pained smile on his face. Etta couldn't look away, not at Sophia, who was calling her name, not at the sails cutting through the blooming dark. He let out a quiet laugh, sounding almost dismayed, his hands pressed hard against his sides. "There are times, Miss Spencer, you defeat me utterly."

Before she could process those words, he'd moved to the front of the ferry, to assist the other men in securing it. And when it came time to disembark, only Sophia was waiting for her.

"Was he bothering you? Thank God he'll be gone soon enough," she said, loud enough for all of the city to hear.

"No!" Etta said quickly. "Not at all."

Still, Sophia eyed Nicholas as he strode in front of them, blowing past a cluster of women with bright eyes and rouged cheeks. They were nearly spilling out of their low-cut dresses.

"Looking for a place to sleep, love?" one asked, trailing after him. "'Ope the fire didn't get your pretty house. I've got a spot that's warm—"

"I'm spoken for," he said, gently removing her hand from his shoulder. "Have a nice night, ladies."

Spoken for? Etta watched his back, the stretch and bunch of the muscles as he moved.

Sophia then let out a strangled gasp and swore a blue streak as she stepped directly into a pile of fresh horse droppings. Etta's stomach actually cringed at the way the smell tangled with the smoke. "Of all the rotten luck!"

It was nearly pitch-black by the time Nicholas found Ironwood's carriage in the chaos of the fire refugees—they were staying, in Sophia's words, at a "mean little tavern" called the Dove outside of the city proper—outside what Etta knew in her time was the financial district. Cyrus Ironwood had thrown enough money around to convince the proprietor to let his family's rooms in the attic for three nights, while they and their servants slept in the cellar.

"Why not just buy a real house in the city?" Etta said, thinking of Nicholas's story. Clearly, the family could afford it.

"Grandfather is making inquiries about available property," Sophia explained, her voice strained. "He's decided to subject us to this era for the foreseeable future, so he'll need more permanent accommodations. For now, he requires us at the Dove, so that is where we'll go."

"Not looking forward to all that 'rustic' living?" Etta asked, arching a brow.

Their path ran along what the driver had called the Old Post Road. Etta had recognized the names of streets when they were in

174

the thick of this version of Manhattan—Wall Street, Broad Way. But once they were past the commons—a green park crowded with fire refugees, their rescued possessions, and all the soldiers trying to keep them in line—the city turned to farmland.

Empty.

Rolling.

Farmland.

Etta shook her head in amazement.

"I know," Sophia murmured dreamily. "It tempts one to buy up a few parcels and hold on to them for a few centuries."

In the city—*her* city—you got used to moving in the shadows of giant buildings during the day, and sacrificing your view of the stars to light pollution. But out here, the sky was naked, untouched, revealing all of its thousands of glittering lights; there was nothing to see beyond occasional houses, some small, some grand. Etta heard the bleating of sheep and whinnying of horses, the quiet bubbling of what sounded like streams. She missed the rapid pulse of life at home; the way the heat rose off the cement, the sunlight's reflection in endless glass windows, the crowds; the constant drone of traffic, alarms, trains.

This will be over soon, she reminded herself.

Hopefully.

The tension that wrapped around her stomach spread through her veins like spiderwebs, too sticky to dislodge completely. Etta tried to picture what this "Grandfather" would look like, what he would think of her, but she'd only had Sophia's and Nicholas's descriptions to go on; together they had painted a rather vivid image in her mind of a man with a bloody sword, guided by a shriveled lump of ash and ice for a heart, in possession of actual fangs and claws.

Breathe, she thought a bit desperately, *breathe.* What else could she do? Whatever information she might squeeze out of him would only help her to get away, to figure out how to get back to Alice.

The Dove Tavern was farther uptown than she'd expected. She spent most of the ride trying to use the position of the East River to figure out where they were on the island—toward the east, but still close to the center—maybe what she knew as Lexington, or Third Avenue?

"What is that?" she asked, leaning forward to get a better look at the constellation of small campfires on the ground up ahead.

Nicholas leaned closer to see, his warm arm pressing against hers. "The Royal Artillery Park, if I had to guess."

The guess was a good one. As they drew closer, the torches and lanterns in the camp blazed; the evidence of war gleamed. Beyond the impressive row of cannons were lines of wagons, carts, stables, white tents. What plain buildings Etta saw were flanked by the few trees that hadn't been hacked to pieces for firewood and stacked nearby.

The Dove stood directly across from the park, hugging the dirt road. The candles in its windows warmed its plain wooden face, and it looked more like a large colonial house to Etta's eyes than a tavern. A two-story house, in fact, not including the attic, and one that seemed to lean ever so slightly to the right. Someone had tried to add a bit of charm with red paint on the shutters. A wooden sign hung over the street, swaying as Sophia passed it. In the dark, the soaring bird carved onto it looked more like a crow than a dove.

"Come along," Sophia said, after the driver had lifted her down from the carriage.

Etta trailed behind her, trapped between the thorns of antici-pation and trepidation; no matter which way her heart swung, she felt stung by the intensity of the feeling. Her own lingering excitement at being brought into the fold of this secret history sickened her, twisting her insides so much more than the dread of what Ironwood really wanted from her.

This is it.

She could go home.

This is it.

Find a way to save Alice.

This is it.

Etta just needed to breathe.

Nicholas stepped up beside her, gazing up at the tavern's windows. It was dark, but the light from the lanterns reflected warmly against his skin. Etta looked away quickly; she knew he could read her anxious expression as easily as she had read his, and she couldn't stand the thought of him seeing her weak and out of her depth again.

"The only way out is through," he said.

Etta nodded, squaring her shoulders.

The noise from the tavern burst out onto the road like a tan-gled chord as a patron, a soldier who'd only managed to get one arm through his uniform coat, staggered out. He patted at his wig, swinging around unsteadily to stare first at Sophia, then Etta.

"Hullo, girls. . . ." he began softly.

Etta stepped back, bumping into a solid warmth. Nicholas's hands closed lightly around her elbows, and she was lifted that last step up past the soldier, to the door.

"Good night, sir," Nicholas said firmly. When he opened the door, he released the muggy air trapped inside.

"Don't look at them," he said. Etta barely heard him over the roar of conversation. It was minutes past midnight, but there were more than enough soldiers and common men circling the tables, hauling themselves up out of their seats to stagger toward the bar. She sucked in a deep breath; the air was flavored with wax from the dripping candles, sour body odor, and the hoppy tinge of ale.

The skirt of her dress caught on something, yanking Etta hard enough to stumble into Nicholas again. She reached down to unhook it, and jumped when her hand brushed warm, damp flesh. Nicholas let out a sharp breath and reached down to push away the meaty hand. The soldier seemed to be sweating out every ounce of alcohol that went into him; his shirt was drenched at the pits and all along his back.

"Keep going," Nicholas murmured. Etta tried to turn back, to cut the man with a glare, but Nicholas guided her toward the stairs at the back of the room.

"I could have handled that," Etta muttered.

"I know," he said, his breath on her skin. "I did him an undeserved favor. But if you demand blood, I'll give him a scar to remember on my way out."

The words rocketed through her. Etta turned so quickly on the bottom step, and the bulk of her gown threw her so off-balance, that he had to reach up to steady her. The weight and warmth of his hands bled through the gown, the stays, the shift, but she hardly noticed. They were finally standing eye to eye.

He quirked a brow in response.

"You're leaving tonight?" Etta asked.

"For Connecticut? No, not until the morning. But I'll need to find an inn."

"You can't stay here?"

His expression softened, and Etta could have sworn, just for an instant, his grip on her tightened. "No, Miss Spencer. I cannot."

"Come *on*, Etta," Sophia called. "He doesn't like to be kept waiting."

Etta didn't budge. Softly, Nicholas asked, "Do you really believe I'd take my leave of you without so much as a good-bye? If nothing else, I gave you my word that I would take you away from here if you were in danger."

"Promise?" Etta whispered.

"Always."

The stairs creaked under their combined weight, and were so narrow that Etta was tempted to turn to the side and walk up that way. Nicholas had to bend at the waist to avoid bashing his head against the low-hanging ceiling.

Etta glanced at the second floor as they passed it, trying to spy through the cracks in the doors that had been left partially open. They must have been private rooms—there were fewer men up here, with their uniforms in better shape than the ones she'd seen below.

Based on Sophia's description, she'd been expecting the walls to be falling down around their ears, the furniture and rugs to be moving around the halls on the backs of a sea of rodents. Instead it seemed tidy, if cramped and a little bleak.

It was even plainer on the third level. There were three doors to choose from. Sophia smoothed her hair, then her dress, and moved to the one on the far left, where a man armed with a rifle was standing guard. Nicholas measured him with a single look.

Before Etta could knock, a ringing voice called, *"Enter."*

Etta, Sophia, and Nicholas followed the voice. This room

was as bare as the hall, but practically stifling with the heat from the fireplace. With the exception of a four-poster bed with a side table, a trunk, and a porcelain chamber pot, the only other occupant was a wing-backed chair. A man was in it, positioned directly in front of a roaring fire.

He didn't stand as they came in; merely absorbed each of them with a single look. Etta heard Sophia swallow hard. The old man raised his right hand expectantly, and she practically tripped in her rush to step forward and kiss the gold ring on it.

"Hello, Grandfather. You look well."

"And you smell like a horse's arse."

Etta let out a shocked laugh and his sharp gaze swung toward her, choking the sound off with a single tilt of his head.

His face was round like Sophia's, his features bold, despite the drag of age. His hooded eyelids hung over icy blue eyes; the corners of his mouth were naturally tipped down, giving him a look of tired apathy, like he could hardly abide their presence. He adjusted the blue silk damask robe he'd tossed over his shirt and breeches.

That single look ripped Etta open faster than any razor.

He turned to Sophia. "You're dismissed."

She jumped as if he'd shoved her in the direction of the door. "But—"

"You question me?" he asked calmly.

Sophia sealed her lips and turned to look at Nicholas.

"He stays," the old man said firmly, with an impatient wave. "My God, child, I'll die of old age before you ever reach the door."

Etta saw the way Sophia took in a deep breath, set her shoulders back, and moved with practiced grace on her way out—and she understood something about the other girl, truly understood it for the first time. Sophia wanted *in*, when she was only ever being sent *out*.

"Step fully into the light," the old man ordered when the door was shut. He set the book in his lap on the floor.

Nicholas stood with his hands clasped behind his back, fingers curled into fists. When she stepped forward, so did he, remaining a small step in front of her.

"I'm Etta," she said, trying to fill the agonizing silence that followed. The longer she went without any sort of response, the more she had to fight the way her feet naturally wanted to turn toward the door. In all of her experiences of stage fright, each crippling attack of performance anxiety, she'd never felt so smothered by pure dread. With the heat of the fire at her back, and hours of travel behind her, she felt a pressure start to build just beneath her lungs.

Why was she just standing here? Why wasn't she yelling, telling him what she really thought of the way he'd forced her to come here without any explanation? She could have been *home*, but here she was, because *he* wanted her, and he wasn't doing a damn thing other than a passable impression of a gargoyle. And this was the same man who had kept both Nicholas and his mother enslaved—who thought it was fine to sacrifice their freedom in the name of *playing a role* and *blending in*.

"You're late, Samuel."

Maybe it was only a trick of the light, but Etta could have sworn Nicholas stiffened.

"My name is Nicholas now, as you've known for years. And I don't see how you've reached that conclusion."

"I wanted them here by the twenty-first. And yet here we are, ten past the first hour of the twenty-second. Your pay will be docked accordingly."

Etta's blood steamed. "That's—"

"My man of business is downstairs. I expect you remember him? Of course, he'll know you by your true name. *Nicholas!* My word. Perhaps you should have chosen the name Charlemagne when you decided to remake yourself. You certainly strode in here like an emperor."

Was the old man mocking Nicholas? For choosing a name that he liked and wanted, rather than the one given to him? What a vicious way to remind him of what he had been.

I can handle this. She clung to her mom's voice, the words, that trace of belief. If nothing else, she wouldn't flinch under the old man's steely gaze. She would make her mom proud.

"Tell me why I'm here," she said coldly.

"Why do you think you're here?" he asked, cocking one thin silver brow. A lion, staring down a common house cat.

"I think your plan is to hold me hostage," she said. "To get back at my mom."

Cyrus let out a deep laugh. "Do you? How would you feel if it was quite the opposite?"

Etta's gaze shot back toward him, disbelief twining with terror as the old man retrieved a small, glossy photograph from the front pocket of his silk robe. Her dread was so paralyzing, she almost couldn't lift an arm to take it from him.

Her mother's face, partially obscured by a gag, glared back at her. If she'd looked frightened, rather than furious, some part of Etta might have been able to believe it was someone else they'd found to impersonate her. But no—Rose was still wearing the dress she'd worn at the Met. The room around her was dark, but Etta recognized their living room all the same. An arm reached into the photo with a copy of the *New York Times*, dated the day after the concert.

All she could see was Alice's face as her eyes slid shut that last time.

All she could feel was Alice's blood as it dried on her hands.

"Because of her, you owe this family—our kind—a debt," the old man said. "And you will do exactly as I say, or she will take her last breath and you will never, ever leave this godforsaken time."

NINE

THE SHOCK SNAPPED, LEAVING ONLY A POOL OF ANGER in the pit of her stomach. Etta lunged toward Cyrus, only to be caught around the waist by Nicholas and hauled backward, still struggling. "You *bastard*—!"

"Miss Spencer—" Nicholas's arms tightened, trying to hold her still. *"Etta!"*

At the pleading note in his tone, she stopped struggling, sagging against the tight band of his arms. Cyrus stood, studying her face more closely as he circled around them.

"I thought, actually, that you might be an Ironwood—that Augustus had made another folly—but I see now I'm wrong. You don't bear our stamp at all. Who *is* your father?"

"As if I'd *ever* tell you," she snarled back.

He gave a dismissive wave, moving to a trunk near the bed. "It hardly matters, seeing as it's clearly not Ironwood, Jacaranda, or Hemlock."

Sophia had said there were three other families who could travel, Linden included. But she and Nicholas had both also

184

said that the other families were gone now, or had been forcibly merged into the Ironwood clan.

"Your mother was the last living traveler of the Linden line, until we learned of you."

Cyrus found what he was looking for in the depths of the trunk and pulled it out. He held it out for her to take, and only then did Nicholas release his hold on her.

It was a small leather-bound book, embossed with the initials RCL and a gorgeous golden tree. Etta found her eyes tracing the shape of it over and over, the slight curve of the trunk, the branches that stretched and twined until they disappeared into the heavy, full body of leaves. The roots of the gold tree were similarly interwoven, the thin lines weaving in and out of each other's paths.

"You don't recognize it, do you?" Ironwood said, clearly amused by this. "Your mother and her grandfather, Benjamin Linden, were so blasted proud of their heritage. It's your family's sigil."

"Each house has a tree sigil," Nicholas said quietly when she looked up for confirmation. He nodded at the chest, its lid emblazoned with a magnificent, strong-armed tree, its thick branches so low that they seemed to rise directly from the ground.

Her grandfather. Her mother *had* told her she'd been raised by her grandfather. So then . . . everything *wasn't* a lie? Just a carefully crafted truth?

"We crossed paths with Rose, sightseeing in Renaissance Italy—it seemed quite the happy accident at the time, as her grandfather had recently passed, and she found herself alone," he continued, something accusing in his gaze. "I'd made the necessary arrangements to bring her into our family, to marry Augustus and rescue her from a life alone, but your mother disappeared seventeen years ago, and we've been searching for her ever since."

Her hands clenched around the book until she couldn't resist opening it. She flipped the cover open, scanning the neat notations—all in her mother's handwriting. It felt like opening a random door and finding her waiting there.

Victorian London. Rome in the fifth century. Egypt in the early twentieth. There must have been a hundred different places listed, all with small journal entries, like *Saw the Queen as she and the Prince rode past us on their way to Buckingham Palace* and *The camel nearly ate Gus's hair, ripped it from his scalp like grass* and *My God, if I never see another big-bellied man wrapped in a toga . . .*

"Travelers keep journals," Nicholas explained in a low voice, "noting the times and dates of when they move through the passages, to avoid crossing paths with themselves by accident."

Etta nodded, her fingers pressed tight against the leather, but her mind spun. What did that mean, *crossing paths with yourself*? Why would they need to avoid it?

"Stand up straight, child—you'll give yourself a hunchback before you're even an adult. My God."

Instead, Etta began to pace.

Her mother *went missing*? Or ran away?

The realization ripped her down the center. Her mother *had* run away. She'd run away from an overbearing foster father. One who'd tried to control her life.

Etta turned, studying the old man from under her lashes. The remaining members of the other family lines had been adopted into the Ironwood clan. What if that's what her mom had really meant? If, after her grandfather died, she'd been forced to become an Ironwood?

"I, too, looked for her." Cyrus turned, pulling a leather satchel up from the floor. He thumbed through the bag, finally plucking out a piece of parchment and thrusting it at Etta. She took the parchment and carefully unfolded it. Inside, the handwriting was unfamiliar.

January 2, Our Year 1099

Gus,

I'm about to make my report to Father, and yes, gladly receive the punishment, but I've been battling my conscience over whether or not to tell you this. You've kept a brave face about it, but I know it's been a considerable source of pain for you over the years. Surely knowing is better than living the rest of your life with the uncertainty hanging over you? These are the questions I've sat with for days now.

Earlier this week, I found a passage near to where I was staying in Nassau, and well, chap, the truth of it is that I was bored and more than a little resentful at being called back again to 1776. Why must I follow every absurd lead in his never-ending quest to find this blasted obsession of his? So I heard it, and I went—and you can imagine my surprise when the passage put me out well past 1946, into what looked to be some kind of museum. I'll spare you the rather vulgar actions of the people around me and say that, upon checking a newspaper, I realized I was in Manhattan in 2015.

Yes. You read that correctly. It was an absolute crush of humanity all around, and the amount of building that's been done to the island is startling. You'll see for yourself soon, I believe.

But here is where I hesitate again. Will you hate me for this? I can't be sure, knowing how one sight of her in Paris tormented you for years. Gus, I read through the newspaper, trying to get a sense of what was happening in the world— better to butter up the old man with it, right? But in one section I saw a photo that nearly stopped my breath, because I thought, with all certainty, it was of our Rosie.

Instead, it was a girl named Henrietta Spencer—she's a violin virtuoso, and the article was about a competition she'd just won in Russia. I skimmed it to the end and sure enough, there was mention of a mother—a Rose Spencer.

The technology of this time is remarkable, but I haven't the space here to tell you of it. A librarian at the city's public library helped me search for more information on something called— the InterWeb, maybe? No, InterNet. In any case, it was easy enough to continue on my own, and I felt I owed it to you to chase this down the rabbit hole. The earliest record I could find of them was a police report on October 5, 1998, stating that a young woman, a Rose Spencer, along with her three-month-old, had been picked up for theft in some sort of department store. In it, Rose said she was new to the city and was hoping to contact a friend.

I hope I haven't upset you, brother. I know you've built yourself a life, and you've Amelia and Julian to content yourself with. But I also hope that this helps you put it all to rest, and eases your bedeviled mind. Both Rosie and her daughter seem well enough, and despite the pain she's caused this family, I felt content to see them settled.

—Virgil

"Virgil was my other son, gone shortly after this letter was sent," Cyrus explained, snatching it back out of her numb fingers. "Augustus a year later, when his ship sank in the seventeenth century."

Nicholas swung his gaze back to the old man, an edge to his voice. "Enough of this. Tell her straight what you need of her."

Cyrus leaned back, giving him a long look. "I could not use Rose, therefore my task falls upon Miss Linden—"

"*Spencer,*" she corrected sharply.

"*Linden,*" he practically roared, "and damn you for it. I need you to steal back what was stolen from me by your mother."

That put a stop to the scalding words she was about to fling onto him. "Excuse me?"

"Don't play deaf, I haven't the patience for it. I meant precisely what I said earlier. If you continue to be uncooperative, I'll resume the search for it myself, and you'll be left here. I'm sure you saw the women as you came off the ferry, the ones who linger by the docks?"

Nicholas growled, "You *dare* imply—"

"I imply nothing. I mean precisely what I say. That will be your own recourse for survival. What, without any skills or knowledge or protector in this time, will you do otherwise?"

So, her choices were to prostitute herself to others, or to serve him? "I know where the passage is." Roughly. "All I need is to get back to Nassau—"

"I would bury the passage before I'd ever let you through it again, child, so think twice before you spite me. Let's play a game, shall we? Close your eyes and try to envision a scenario in which you could possibly get to the island before my men. What funds would you use? What friends do you have here who would help you?" Cyrus asked, his voice light, like he was speaking to a child. "And what would prevent us from coming to claim you again?"

Nicholas would help me. Etta risked a glance over to him, feeling the air vibrate around the two of them with unspoken fury.

"What would prevent us from killing your mother?"

She sat back on her heels, defeat rising up in her like a wave of nausea. When she spoke, her words were sharp enough to draw Nicholas a step closer to her side. Etta wondered if he was worried he'd need to grab her again to keep her from clawing the old man's face. "You already have one life on your hands. Are you really so evil that you'd kill another woman?"

"Another woman?" he asked, brows rising. "My agents didn't report a casualty, though they were authorized to . . . shall we say, use force and their best judgment."

Fury blazed in her. "She was *innocent*. She was a defenseless, elderly woman!"

Cyrus shrugged one shoulder. "Then she was already at the end of her life. Don't waste tears on this woman. Most don't get such a full life. My son, for instance. My grandson. I'm far more concerned with the blood your *mother* has on her hands. By our old traveler laws, I'd be more than justified in killing *you* to end this feud. Be grateful I've chosen the high road."

Etta was so stunned, so tackled by disbelief, her next words flew out of her mind. Clearly seeing this, Cyrus continued as if she hadn't spoken at all.

"After the passage was discovered, I sent numerous agents to your filthy, crowded city to conduct their investigations. When it became clear Rose had borne a child, and one that might possibly be gifted, arrangements were made to put you directly in a position to travel," Ironwood continued, lacing his fingers together over his chest. "My agents bestowed a rather sizable donation on my behalf to the museum that employs your mother. They suggested that the museum might invite you to perform—of course, anything is possible when money is being passed beneath the table."

She felt her lip curl into a snarl, but she forced herself to stay silent, too afraid of crossing that line between cooperative and uncooperative.

"It occurred to me that perhaps your mother didn't realize the passage was there—that she hadn't heard it. Or perhaps you didn't carry the ability. And so Sophia was sent, to see if you could hear the passage, and if so, bring you through it."

Hear. He knew she'd heard *something.* But Etta had been inside the museum any number of times, and that night was the first time she'd ever heard that booming call.

"How very thoughtless of Rose to not explain this." Cyrus seemed to read her thoughts before she did. "Our ancestors, those who created the passages a thousand years ago, were of purer blood than those of us today. It became necessary to . . . mingle . . . our bloodlines with common ones in order to survive. The ability to hear and see the passages *naturally* has faded. We rely on resonance."

Cyrus slid a harmonica out of a velvet sack in his satchel. Putting his lips to the mouthpiece, he released a powerful burst of air, playing three simultaneous notes.

Before he'd pulled the harmonica away, Etta heard it—the shuddering, distant scream. She pulled back instinctively, reaching out to grab something, anything, until her hand found the fireplace mantelpiece. The noise pounded like a second heartbeat in her head.

"The passages resonate with the chord of G major," Cyrus said.

Etta rubbed her forehead, trying to dislodge the knot of pain behind her temple, the blazing wildfire of sound trapped there. The Largo from Sonata no. 3 . . . the one chosen for her . . . that contained those three notes—G, B, and D—only a few seconds into the piece.

She'd called to the passage with her violin, and it had called back.

"How *curious*," Cyrus began. There was a cane leaning against the left arm of the chair, and he took it in hand as he rose to his feet, thudding toward her in three beats of sound. "How very curious that your mother kept this from you."

"How *curious* that she ran away from *you*," she said sarcastically. "I can't imagine why."

His hand lashed out, gripping her chin, stilling her. The pressure of his grip, combined with her own shock, made her arms go limp at her side. He was taller than Etta was, but otherwise built with the solid stockiness of a bulldog—and his quiet cruelty took a very different form when he was towering over her. For a half second, with the fire scorching her back, she honestly thought he'd push her into it.

"Stop this," Nicholas said sharply, thrusting an arm between them.

A small protest, but it did something. The blue flame of his eyes shifted from Etta to Nicholas, and she felt his hand relax, slide down the length of her neck before settling there like a collar—a noose.

"Your mother ingratiated herself to my family as we searched for an item of value that once belonged to my ancestors. She played the part of the sad, sorry orphan, gathered what information she needed from us, and stole it from under our noses. Decades of searching, wasted."

I have never stolen anything in my life.

Her mother had only just said those words to her—when Etta had joked about her stealing the earrings. She'd seemed almost devastated by an accusation that hadn't been an accusation at all.

No matter how bad things got, or how much I wanted something.

Nicholas straightened, his expression sharpening as something came together for him. "You're speaking of the astrolabe—you mean to imply that *Rose Linden* is the traveler who stole it?"

"I *imply* nothing. It is a statement of fact, one you were not privy to in your position." Cyrus blew a sharp breath out from his nose. "I'd heard various reports of eras and places where she'd hidden it, but it all added up to nothing but further loss." He turned back to her. "The search to reclaim this object has cost me two sons and a grandson, all three of my direct heirs."

"Then maybe," Etta bit out, "you should have stopped looking for it while you were still ahead, and left me out of this!"

He removed his hand from her and pulled it back, as if to strike her. Nicholas stepped farther between them, his shoulder blocking her view of the old man. "Enough. Don't pretend as if you've actually been mourning them. I seem to recall you referring to Julian as a *gnat* on more than one occasion. You didn't shed a single tear when he died."

Something occurred to Etta. If Augustus and Virgil were his sons, and Julian was his grandson . . . where did Nicholas fit into the family tree?

"Did Sophia search their possessions while she was in that time period?" Nicholas asked. "How do you know it's not there?"

"Rose knows better than to keep it with her. She will have guaranteed that finding her does not mean finding the astrolabe—she always was a spiteful creature, even after everything I'd done for her," Cyrus continued. "She claimed it belonged to the Linden family, but nothing could be further from the truth."

Someone tried to pull a fast one on me once, and I've never forgotten what that felt like. I almost lost something of your great-granddad's.

Etta forced herself to stay as still as possible, terrified of giving these thoughts away, too.

"One of my agents conducted a thorough search of their abode a few months ago," Cyrus said. "If such a place may even be called that. By his description, it was a closet."

"Your agent . . ." Etta felt the blood leave her face, drain slowly from her heart, until it seemed to stop beating all together. "Your agent broke into our apartment and went through our things?"

"And several safe-deposit boxes he traced all over Manhattan. He returned with a peculiar letter that was of great interest to me, and I sent him and the others back to continue their investigation of you."

A peculiar letter? Etta's brows furrowed. What did that mean?

The old man continued, "They were to assist Sophia if necessary in prompting your travel, as well as restrain your mother." He touched his pocket, where he'd returned the photograph of her mom. "They await my command as to what to do with her. Do you understand?"

Etta forced herself to give a curt nod. "What's so special about this astrolabe that you couldn't just find yourself another one?"

Etta only knew what an astrolabe was from her many tours through the Met with Alice and Rose. Larger than a compass, the instruments had been used in ancient and medieval times for astronomical, astrological, topographical calculations—even to tell time. The lowermost layer, the one that cupped the smaller round plates that moved inside, was divided into the hours of the days and degrees of arc. The plates were etched with latitudes, altitudes, even parts of the celestial sphere.

But apparently this one also had another purpose.

"It can examine a passage and inform the bearer of the destination and time period on the other side by reading its vibrations," Cyrus said. "And whether or not the passage is stable enough to enter without collapsing."

She turned to Nicholas, looking for confirmation. He kept his gaze on the snapping, shuddering fire as he explained. "When a traveler dies, a surge of . . . power . . . is released. The nearest passage is rendered unstable by it, and will often close. But if it collapses while you're traveling through it, you could be tossed out to a random time, or be trapped in the passage forever."

Etta felt a shudder work over her skin.

"There are hundreds of passages we use, but there are many more uncharted ones. Our numbers, as travelers, are dwindling," Cyrus continued. "Every time I send a traveler through, I risk him or her never returning—stumbling onto a battlefield, being caught unawares in the wild, or by the ruling authority. Can your little mind possibly fathom the importance of finding the astrolabe to save them from that fate? Allow me to put this plainly: our numbers grow fewer and fewer. Think of all of those travelers who are . . . *stranded* . . . in the future, who do not know what it is they can do and who they are meant to serve. Their family requires their assistance, and, by blood or by conquest, they owe me their allegiance."

The prickling started at the base of Etta's spine and worked its way up over her scalp. Is that what this was really about? Her mother had taken it to save future travelers from being under his thumb?

If I found it . . . and if I handed it over . . .

Rose had wanted to protect the travelers, but if Etta knew her mother, it was more than that—lineage could be hidden, names changed, people relocated, until they were lost to the records of time.

"Wouldn't giving it to you change my future?" Etta asked, the thought suddenly occurring to her. "Or erase it completely?"

He raised his brows, as if surprised she'd even know to ask. "Your future will be preserved. The investments I've made over the centuries depend on it. I merely mean to protect and find my own kin."

"Then why not convince Rose to tell you, and leave Miss Spencer out of this?" Nicholas asked. "Trade her daughter for the location?"

"Don't be stupid, boy," Cyrus said. "The woman would die before giving the location up, and, in the process, lie and send members of this family off to every dangerous hell on this earth to retrieve it. We cannot sustain such losses. Therefore, this Miss Linden is the perfect candidate for retrieval—she is a blank slate. And, should she perish, she will have at least deciphered this for us to use."

A folded sheet of notebook paper emerged from the same pocket of his robe, and he handed it to Etta with a look of keen interest. "My agent uncovered this in your home. I believe there's a manner of reading it that's . . . peculiar . . . to your family, and that the clues themselves pertain to the Lindens. I've only been able to pull a single thread from it."

The letter itself, which began with *Dear Etta, my sweet little star,* was . . . gibberish. The phrases themselves made sense, were complete thoughts, like *The trees look lovely today.* But that was followed up by *Ask yourself if unknown gods exist.* There was no meaning behind the words, no sense to the composition of it.

With a sickening jolt, Etta knew exactly what she was looking at—she knew exactly how to read this letter, because her mom had been coding letters and messages for her this way for *years.* There was no second sheet to layer over it—sometimes her mom didn't have time to cut out the shape, in which case, she'd use the clue in the first few lines. . . .

Dear Etta, my sweet little star . . .

While that was a nice sentiment, her mother had never called her something so sentimental in her entire life. Which meant, then, tracing a star over the letter would reveal the full message.

She wrote this for me.

Only her.

Etta can handle this.

Etta kept her eyes on the page until she was sure she wouldn't give herself away. Cyrus had managed to extract one meaningful phrase from the jumble of words, but the rest of it was lost to him. He didn't know there was a key to bring the nonsense together, tie it together into the message buried beneath. Tracing a star over the letter would give her the rest of the phrases she'd need. It was only bad luck that he'd been able to pull *any* line out of it and recognize its connection to the Lindens.

She wants me to find the astrolabe.

She doesn't want anyone else to.

This was what she'd meant when she said it was Etta's time, wasn't it? Rose didn't just know she would travel back in time at one point, she knew she would one day travel back for *this purpose*, and if Etta had to guess, because Ironwood had willed it.

"As you can see, this was written *for* you to find. The fourth line down," he said. There was a single phrase underlined, the words spread across one line, where, if Etta had to guess, the widest part of the star would be. "*Tell tyrants, to you, their allegiance they owe*—that is the one that interests me."

"What about it?" she asked, all innocence.

"It's a famous song in this period about the execution of Nathan Hale, the American spy," Cyrus explained. "After a time, I finally placed where I had heard the phrase."

Nathan Hale—the *I only regret that I have but one life to lose for my country* Nathan Hale? He had been an American spy caught behind enemy lines during the Revolution, and was hanged for it.

"I'd prefer you *not* reveal—" Nicholas began.

"How positively adorable that you think I care a whit for your preferences," Cyrus snapped. "I recognized it, in fact, because Benjamin Linden was annoyingly fond of singing it when he was deep into his cups. Surely it couldn't be a coincidence, given its connection to her only family. But imagine my surprise when I discovered that history didn't have a record of the exact site of his execution. I had to make my way here to determine it for myself, and, lo, there was a previously unknown passage waiting just across the way. It is my belief that there are clues within this letter that will lead from one passage to another, connecting in a trail that culminates at the correct location and era where the astrolabe may be found."

In other words, each clue pointed to the location of a passage that would need to be taken in order to find it. Sort of like . . .

connecting flights, in order to arrive at a desired destination. Only she needed to find the right planes.

Etta forced herself to swallow, to keep her expression neutral, as she ran her fingers over her mother's journal. Ironwood caught the movement, and pulled the journal out of her hands, tucking it back under his arm.

"Tomorrow is Hale's execution," Cyrus said. "We've had to wait months and come to 1776 Manhattan ourselves to search for the exact spot, as history remained uncertain about the actual location of the event. As you've hopefully ascertained, the hanging will take place across the way, in the Royal Artillery Park."

The passage was still moaning, still screaming, but the wind seemed to be carrying the sound away until all that remained was a faint drumming.

"You're not going to do anything about it?" Etta asked. "Try to save him?"

Cyrus burst out laughing. "Interfere? Change the timeline? I think not. The fool got himself caught, out of uniform, behind enemy lines. His death is on his head."

The attitude was disgusting.

"You'll decipher this letter before you set off to hunt for the astrolabe. We may even be able to prepare you with the right clothing and mannerisms before you begin."

Nicholas straightened. "A few hours of tutelage won't do anything for her."

That pricked Etta's pride. Wasn't she handling this all fairly well, given the circumstances? And, not to be competitive about this, but if *he* could master the ins and outs of traveling, then so could she.

He must have read the fire in her expression, because Nicholas's eyes widened slightly. "I only meant—"

"She'll be fine," Cyrus interrupted. "I've waited long enough. Here are my terms, Miss Linden. Decipher this letter and the clues it contains about where to find the necessary passages to connect through; travel through them; and bring the astrolabe back to me. Then your mother will be freed, and you'll be returned to your home."

Etta held his gaze for as long as she could stand it. Exhaustion bled into her, and the weight of her thoughts began to feel like too much to carry. She worked through the necessary points as quickly as she could:

Cyrus would not reveal the location of the passage back to the Met, and her time, if she didn't do as he asked. And maybe not even then. Which might mean never saving Alice's life.

Nicholas would not necessarily take her back, as her life was not technically in danger.

Her mother had lied to her, reshaping the truth, omitting huge chunks of the rest, inserting little riddles and clues into her life for Etta to maybe piece together one day as she tried to fend for herself. Which, wonderful parenting right there. And all to . . . to keep this astrolabe in the family? To give it another protector who would find it and hide it again if any other traveler should stumble upon it? Then why not *train* her, *prepare* her for this—so it wasn't—so it wasn't so *overwhelming*—so *impossible*—

No wonder Alice had argued she wasn't ready—she *wasn't*. But her mom believed she could do this, and she wasn't about to let either of them down. Etta closed her eyes, breathing in deeply through her nose until her heart calmed to a steady roll of thunder in her ears.

Home.

Alice.

Mom.

And, soon enough, her debut. All of those things, waiting for her.

Was there a way to rewrite Alice's fate? To make sure her mother was safe—to not give the old man what he wanted, but still save her life?

"You cannot be considering this. . . ." Nicholas said incredulously. "Think, Miss Spencer. This is no simple task he's asking of you."

"I do not recall asking you to weigh in with your opinion," Cyrus thundered.

"What is there to consider?" Etta asked coldly, looking directly at the old man. "You'll kill her if I don't bring it back, won't you?"

He smirked. "With pleasure. You should know that you'll need to return no later than September thirtieth. If not, the deal is void."

The thirtieth? As in . . . nine days away? No—eight.

"That's not nearly enough time!" Nicholas cried. "Julian and I spent *years* searching. What does it matter if it takes her eighteen days instead of eight? What's a few more days when you have the whole of time at your fingertips?"

"My reasons are my own," Cyrus said. "She will return by the thirtieth or she will lose everything."

Etta folded her hands in front of her, choking off the supply of blood to her fingers. Being made to work for the man who'd hurt her mother, who'd invaded their lives and stolen Alice's . . . Etta felt sick.

What do I do?

The answer came to her, ruthless and simple, a blade that sliced through her doubts: find the astrolabe, use it to find the passage in Nassau, and go find her mother. All without Cyrus Ironwood catching on to what she was doing. She and Rose could go back and save Alice, and then disappear—

And what kind of life would that be? One without a spotlight, playing the violin professionally; everything she'd worked for would be sacrificed, to stay hidden.

But if Alice and her mom were safe, it would be worth it.

"I'll do it," Etta said, pushing through the uneasiness; then, with a desperate hope Cyrus wouldn't sniff out the lie, added, "It might take me some time to figure out how she coded the letter. I'll need more than tonight."

She'd need less than two minutes, but that wasn't for him to know, was it?

Nicholas shook his head, muttering something beneath his breath as he swung away from her, bracing an arm against the fireplace's mantelpiece.

"Excellent," Cyrus said, clapping his hands together. "You may keep the original copy to decipher, and you will resume in the morning. You and Sophia will share the room beside mine."

Etta didn't fight her grimace. After the electric, hissing fury she'd seen on the girl's face when she'd been sent out, sleeping on the roof during a thunderstorm would be safer. Realizing she'd been dismissed, she turned toward the door.

"Miss Linden?" Cyrus called, just as her hand gripped the knob. "Know that I have a copy of that letter, should you try to destroy it. Know, too, that it is unwise to test me."

"I understand," said Etta.

But I'm not afraid of you.

The noise from the tavern floated up to her on a cloud of tobacco smoke, leather, and wet dog; just before she closed the door, she took one final look at Nicholas's profile as he stared into the glowing fire, despondent.

That would have to be enough. As soon as the tavern cleared out and its occupants wound themselves down to sleep, she would follow the lingering rattle of the passage to its entrance, the way she had in the Met. For the first time in days, she felt in control of her life again, not just an unwilling passenger at someone else's mercy.

A hand latched onto her arm, wheeling her around. The man posted on guard raised a single black brow as Sophia hauled her the last few steps toward the next door down the hall. Once inside, she shut it gently behind them and went to stand beside the wall separating the bedchamber from the old man's.

Cyrus Ironwood had drained what last bit of patience she had, and exhaustion was making her head throb as she surveyed the cramped room. This, again? Maybe this was the old man's real punishment for what her mom had done: keeping her trapped in confined quarters with a furious Sophia, forced to listen to all of her rantings without strangling her. The frustration that choked her was so real, she felt her hands curl over the back of a frail-looking chair, and seriously considered smashing it against the nearby wall.

"What are you even *doing*?" she asked, but Sophia only held up a hand and pressed her ear to the wall.

"I can't hear them," she said quietly. "So, hopefully they won't hear us."

She sat down on the bed in a flounce of skirts, seething. "The *nerve* of them, making me look like a fool—shutting me out, after *I* was the one who retrieved you. How dare they keep this from me!"

"From *you*?" Etta asked pointedly.

"Yes, from *me*," she said, tearing the pins out of her hair. A trunk had been left in the room, filled to the brim with cloth, glass bottles, and a silver brush. Sophia yanked the latter through her loose hair, tearing at it fiercely.

The old man was as pleasant as an enraged cat; if Etta had been in Sophia's shoes, she would have welcomed the opportunity to spend as little time with him as possible. The man had forced Sophia to serve him, had basically barred her from going to any year that might have gifted a woman with a few real rights. Etta had to wonder how much better Sophia's life might be if she wasn't under Grandfather Dearest's unyielding thumb.

"Why did you even want to be in there?" Etta asked. "If it bothered you that much that he didn't tell you why he wanted me, couldn't you have argued to stay?"

Sophia scoffed. "No one fights with Grandfather. Just ask the other families. They'll tell you firsthand what you get for ignoring his wishes."

Etta considered the situation, moving slowly to sit beside her. The girl was fuming, blowing out one harsh breath after another, and Etta couldn't tell her anger from her humiliation.

"Tell me exactly what they said," Sophia demanded.

Etta did, mostly. She kept the coded letter from her mother pressed against her gown's heavy skirts, out of the other girl's sight.

"The astrolabe?" Sophia repeated with disbelief. "He's still looking for it after everything that happened?"

"Do you know anything else about it?" Etta asked carefully.

Sophia let out a humorless little laugh. "Of course not. Why would they tell *me* anything about it? You'll have to ask your friend, *Mr. Carter*. He and Julian were sent out to look for it four years ago."

The mysterious "Julian" again.

"Cyrus's grandson, right?" Etta pressed.

"He's . . ." Sophia began. "He's dead. He was the heir after his father got himself drowned and his uncle managed to shoot himself in a hunting accident."

She ran a hand back through her thick, dark hair, her doll-like face bleak and empty. "He was my intended."

Intended. As in . . . "You were engaged?"

Despite everything, Etta felt a flush of sympathy. She fumbled for a way to cool her emotions, regain some of the distance she felt toward the other girl.

"From the time we were children," Sophia said. "It was a perfect match. Do you know how rare it is for travelers to be able to marry each other? It was only because I was born to a distant cousin. It was my—"

"Your what?" Etta prompted. The way Sophia said it, barely catching herself, made her wonder if maybe the other girl *did* want to talk about this—if there was no one else she could discuss it with.

"My father was *no one* in this family," Sophia said, raking a hand through the ends of her hair. "A distant cousin of Grandfather's who forced himself on some unsuspecting harlot and came back for seconds, only to find the woman dead and me all alone. He drank himself to death a few years later, and only Grandfather was willing to raise me. Said he couldn't allow a true traveler to slip through the cracks. Most people only have one shadow, but I feel as though I have two. My past trails me every day, every second, and I can't shake it off. Marrying Julian might have finally stopped the whispers from the other travelers. It might have finally earned me a measure of respect."

Marrying up was the only way that any number of women in history had escaped their pasts and whatever stations they'd been born into. They couldn't work to improve their lives the way men did, and live by their own means. It was grossly unfair to them—and it was especially unfair that Sophia, someone who should have had a future, access to opportunities, was trapped inside of this cage the family had thrown over her.

Etta finally released her last trace of anger and pressed a hand to her forehead, trying to process this. Sophia pushed herself up onto her feet and began to tug at the strings of her stays and gown.

After a moment, Etta stood to help her. "If you *are* related to the old man, and there are so few travelers left, why aren't you Cyrus's heir?"

Sophia rolled her eyes. "Because an infant born a few months ago, who's so distantly related to Grandfather as to only share a drop of blood—somehow that child is more eligible, simply by virtue of having been born a *boy*. Little Marcus Ironwood is the heir. For now. I'll have to wait until he's old enough for everyone to discern whether he's a traveler or a guardian. If it's the latter— well, perhaps Grandfather will be desperate enough to reconsider the rule."

"That's ridiculous," Etta said. The idea of Sophia leading the family and subjecting them to her will was mildly terrifying, but she could hardly be worse than the old man. She was ambitious, and Etta still wasn't convinced she had been an innocent party to

Alice's death, but Sophia shouldn't have been denied simply for being a girl. No woman should.

"That's—" Sophia cut herself off, surprised. "You agree? It's simply the way it's done, and has been done forever, but the older cousins renounced their claim by marrying outside of Grandfather's wishes. I'm the only one of my generation tied closely enough to his bloodline to have a true claim, and I'm certainly the only traveler left alive who's been under his direct tutelage."

"Maybe it is really time for a change, then," Etta said. "Can you make your case?"

"Women are not allowed to attend the family meetings, so how can I? How can I get Grandfather to see what's been in front of him all along?" Sophia shook her head. "How do you fight against a mountain? How do you move it when you don't even have a shovel?"

"Maybe you don't have to move it," Etta said, folding the gown over the lid of the trunk. "Maybe you have to climb it."

Sophia studied her, her face still flushed from the heat of her words. "I don't know if there ever will be a better choice than Julian. He was . . . he was perfect."

"No one is perfect. Not even *you*."

The other girl snorted, climbing into bed and shifting so she faced the far wall—making room for Etta. After a moment's hesitation, Etta climbed in after her, scooting as far as she could to the edge without falling off. The mattress felt strange, like it'd been stuffed with straw—it smelled that way, too. The frame creaked, but there was another sound beneath it—the ropes supporting the mattress. They scraped against each other, and sounded like the lines had on the ship when the men were adjusting the sails. Her mind shifted back to Nicholas, wondering where he'd sleep.

Sophia leaned over her, blowing out the candle on the bedside table. The smoke trailed out into the darkness like a silver chain.

"Was Augustus Nicholas's father?" Etta whispered into the night.

"Yes." The whole bed shifted as Sophia turned over. The silence stretched out for a few beats, punctuated only by her sigh. "I don't know much about this, truthfully—most of it is gossip. But Augustus was madly, madly in love with Rose. Your mother. Everyone knew it, just like they all knew that he wasn't the same after she disappeared. He was . . . troubled."

What had the letter said? *But I also hope that this helps you put it all to rest, and eases your bedeviled mind.*

"He spent *years* searching for her, even after Grandfather tried to force him to stop. Eventually he had to do his duty and provide an heir, so he married, and Julian came into the picture. But Augustus was . . . not pleasant. Never faithful. Never loving. An absolute beast. He took what he wanted from whomever he wanted. Do you understand?"

Etta understood.

Nicholas's mother had been the family's slave, and Augustus had assaulted her, abused her, and in the end had never freed her. Etta's fury sprouted a new head, this one with knives for teeth. She thought, just then, that she could tear down the walls of the inn with only her bare hands.

"Julian wasn't like that," Sophia continued softly. "Not at all. He was kind."

"Did you love him?" Etta asked. There was a careful reservation in Sophia's voice when she spoke about him; either the grief was still too new and intense to touch, or there hadn't been a great, smoldering kind of love between them.

"I was . . . content," Sophia said. *He* deserved to live, not the bastard. It's Nicholas's fault Julian died, you know, and he readily admits it—like that could somehow absolve him of some of the guilt. They never should have taken that path through the Himalayas, not in the rainy season. He was there to take care of Julian, to see to his needs, keep him from harm; to sacrifice his life, if need be. He should have forced them to turn around and take a different route."

Etta turned over to face her, almost too afraid to ask. Nicholas had stopped traveling for a reason. He'd implied he was trapped in this era, and she had a feeling she was on the verge of finding out why. "What happened?"

"They were going to search the Taktsang Palphug Monastery for something Grandfather wanted—"

The astrolabe? Etta wondered. Nicholas hadn't seemed surprised to hear of it. . . .

"The monastery is high in the mountains, built into a cliff with sheer walls. If you believe the rat's story, there was a storm, and Julian slipped and fell. How could they have been standing so close to one another, and Nicholas not have been able to catch him?"

"Oh my God," Etta whispered.

Sophia turned to face the wall, the column of her spine rigid. "One brother lived, one brother died. And if you ask me, he did it on purpose."

Etta felt her jaw set as she hugged her arms over her stomach. "Why would he ever do that? Julian was his half brother—and more than that, Nicholas is honorable—"

"What good is honor when greed eats away at its foundations?" Sophia continued. "You're right, though; it all comes down to the blood they shared between them. With Julian out of the picture, he had the next best claim. He is in Grandfather's direct bloodline."

"No," Etta whispered, closing her eyes at the image. Not him. The thought ate away at her picture of him, dissolving it completely. He was her anchor here, the one reliable person who she could count on for the truth, for *decency*. She couldn't let Sophia take that away from her, too; not until she'd heard Nicholas's side of this. "No way. . . ."

"And you know what the truly sad thing is, Etta?" Sophia whispered. "If he'd asked, if he'd put his case forward, Grandfather would have considered it. I know he would have. Because being born a bastard in this family is still preferable to being born a girl."

"Leave, Sophia," Etta urged. "Run away if you have to—if there's really nothing you can do to fix things in this family, get out the way my mom did, and start over!"

It was a long while before the answer drifted back to her.

"If I'm not an Ironwood, then I am no one," Sophia said in a thin voice. "And I have *nothing*."

"That's not true," Etta said, shocked by the defeat in the girl's voice.

But only the passage answered back, in a rolling murmur, a growling whisper of lies—one that spoke of freedom, of discovery, of reclaiming what was lost, but delivered only a cage of lies and disappointment.

TEN

NICHOLAS CAST HIS GAZE TOWARD THE FIRE, WATCHING the dance of light. He'd felt the weight of Etta's eyes on him, but had kept still until the door shut behind her, and he heard the wet rattle of Cyrus's breath as he moved toward the bedside table to light a candle. Nicholas watched the steady movement of his fingers as they ran over the gold frame of a small, oval-shaped portrait he'd seen many times before.

His first wife, Minerva. Not his second, the sorry shrew of a woman who'd borne him two sons and died in the process of giving him yet another. Not Augustus, nor Virgil, whom he clearly had no desire to honor even in memory—not even Julian, who'd done everything the man had ever asked of him, superbly and without question. A love match by all accounts, and with another traveler.

For Cyrus, there was only Minerva, with her golden hair, green eyes, and uncommon beauty—a true Helen of Troy. When they'd wed, Cyrus had been at the center of a conspiracy to control the travelers' fates.

He had hidden her, but it had not saved her in the end. And

when Cyrus's rival, Roman Jacaranda, murdered the woman, the four families had been flung into all-out war, and the last vestiges of the man's humanity were torn away. Julian had told him stories of the old man's vengeful rampage, harrowing tales of how he'd outmaneuvered all of his enemies, until he alone had become the Grand Master, ruling over all of their descendants.

None of it would bring Minerva back. His rivals had been strategic, choosing a rare year to which no passage led, so that Cyrus could not return to her hiding place and intervene. He could not travel to the years leading up to it to wait out the days, not without crossing paths with himself; nor could he warn anyone, or even himself, in sufficient time without altering his future control of the other families.

And, Nicholas thought, that was really all one had to know about the man. He wouldn't shatter the sanctity of his rules, and he would not compromise his position or riches, not even for a woman whose memory continued to haunt him. Cyrus Ironwood's heart had hardened into flint, capable only of being sparked into fiery anger. It allowed him to scheme without mercy—to steal a young woman from her home, thrust her into a decades-long search that amounted to little more than madness.

"You cannot be serious with this request," Nicholas ground out. Fighting the urge to clench his jaw, he added, "She could lose her life. You're asking her to take a number of enormous risks, with only your word that she'll be returned to her home."

Etta of the twenty-first century. Etta of the distant, unforeseeable future. Etta with the pirate heart. This astrolabe had already cost three lives, and now he was demanding that she sacrifice hers, as well?

Cyrus eyed him. "Has she proven herself to be spectacularly

unsuited to this task? She has the motivation and the means to see this through, and she won't run the risk of crossing paths with herself, unlike almost every other traveler. I hardly require more, beyond her discretion about our family, and that is easily maintained by notifying the guardians across time to watch for her appearances, to note her arrivals and departures through the passages."

Etta would think she was working independently, none the wiser that the old man was like the mythical Argus, eyes scattered across the whole body of time. Would it be better or worse, he wondered, for Rose to have used other uncharted and unknown passages aside from the one across the road in the Royal Artillery Park? She would be able to travel without the interference of guardians stationed nearby to watch the passages, but if something were to happen—if she were to become hurt, or worse—who could help her?

"This is a task for your family—"

"Our family," Cyrus corrected.

This was a man who had hit him across the face so many times when he was a child that Nicholas had learned to listen for his voice and avoid his path entirely. Of course, the spineless sop had never raised a hand to Augustus, his monster of a son, even as he terrorized everyone around him with his maliciousness.

"Julian was all you had in life, and, still, you sent him to his death—"

Cyrus slammed his fist down on the table, and Nicholas jumped at the bang. "I gave him to you to protect—I live with the consequences of your failure every day."

Hardly. Nicholas's bitterness turned inward, until it frosted his heart. He often dreamt of it: the last look of trust on Julian's face before the glove slipped off his hand and he fell through the curtain of rain to the rocks below; the bursts of light reflected in the white haze; the cracking boom from the nearby passage, as it absorbed the surge of power that marked the end of a traveler's life. He dreamt of it in rushes of panic and ice, just as he thought Cyrus must only dream in fire and blood.

The last time he'd stood before this man, he'd been weak with hunger and exhaustion, burdened by guilt. He'd been made to stand there for hours and report what had happened. Julian's death collapsed the passage they had taken to Bhutan, forcing Nicholas to use his brother's rambling travel journal to find another passage in that year to use, and connect to another one, and then another, until he finally found his way back to the year the old man was residing in. It had taken months, and, even if he'd had the strength left in him, Nicholas hadn't had the heart to stop the words and fists that knocked him around until he was mute and suffocating on his apologies.

He wouldn't be silent again.

"Miss Spencer is my passenger. I'm honor-bound to ensure her safety."

"You're honor-bound to me," Cyrus reminded him, "and me alone."

"I answer to no one but myself," Nicholas said sharply.

This man would not take him in again. A snake could shed its skin, but never change its colors.

The old man studied him, resting his hands on his knees.

"When I heard the rumors that you possessed our ability—when I tracked you and Hall to the docks all those years ago—do you know what my first thought was upon seeing you?"

Nicholas stiffened.

"I thought you had the bearing of an Ironwood, for all that you were a knob-kneed stick of a thing. I was impressed by how quickly you agreed to be trained and work beside Julian."

It was the greatest shame of Nicholas's life that he had given in to the wonder of what Ironwood had offered. Adventure beyond reckoning. Status beyond imagination. And . . . "You promised me compensation, and information on who had purchased my mother," he said flatly. "You provided neither in the end."

Four years of his life, wasted. And when he'd been exiled to this—his natural time—as punishment for failing Cyrus and allowing Julian to die, he'd been cut to the bone with a second blow. By the time he'd discovered what had become of her on his own, his mother had died of fever—alone, among strangers—as he and Julian had merrily drunk themselves into a stupor in 1921 New Orleans, chasing another fruitless lead for the astrolabe.

The lingering call of the passage filled the silence between them, a low murmur beneath the fire's snaps and pops.

"I warn you," Nicholas said, "if you attempt to do the same to me now—deny me that which I've earned for bringing the ladies here—I'll kill you where you stand, and gladly be hanged for it."

Cyrus gave him an approving look that did little more than make his guts roll.

"Your job is not yet finished, Samuel," he said.

"My name is Nicholas." It was the name he'd chosen for himself as a child when the Halls had presented him with the opportunity to redraft his life into something of his own making. It was a name the old man had refused to use, even when he'd brought Nicholas back into the family years ago to serve Julian.

Nicholas, the patron saint of sailors, repentant thieves, children—all of the things he was and could be. The name made him feel more than protected. It made him feel like he could be a protector.

Naturally, the Ironwoods saw it as yet another way that he had failed.

Cyrus inclined his head. "You've pleased me thus far. I would like to raise the stakes some, if you are amenable?"

Something about the words caught him, held him in place for an instant, before he managed to shake himself free.

"Our business is concluded," Nicholas said firmly. "I will meet with your man of business downstairs."

And figure out a way to untangle Etta from this.

"That sum is hardly enough for you to buy your own ship," Cyrus said. "Oh, yes, I am well aware of the reason you accepted this task. There's no need for surprise. I am pleased with your vision. Your acumen. You remind me of myself."

Nicholas felt as though he'd overturned a bucket of boiling tar on his head. "I assure you—you and I are nothing alike."

Cyrus waved his hand again. "You're entirely right. I cannot send the child alone. Not only is she likely to give herself away and be killed, she is her mother's daughter. Wily and cunning—I looked into her eyes and saw Rose Linden staring back. I won't be taken for a fool twice."

Nicholas wondered if he'd also seen the flicker of recognition in Etta's eyes as the girl had looked over the letter. He'd sensed the rebellion rising in her, even as she'd agreed.

"In addition to the original settlement, I will relinquish total control of my plantation holdings to you in this era, to do with as you please," Cyrus said. "Free the slaves, sell the land, or continue it as it stands. You'll fund not just a single ship, but a whole fleet of them."

Nicholas's whole body went tight, but he couldn't identify the source of the feeling. Was it hope or terror?

"Why would you do such a thing? Sophia said that you had decided to stay in this era—that you were looking to purchase property," he said. The Ironwoods earned income from several centuries, made investments, owned shares in lucrative companies. He knew this was merely a drop in the ocean of their wealth, but it came too freely offered. There would be shackles attached.

"Sophia is not privy to my thoughts. I have no desire to stay in this era beyond waiting for the astrolabe to be brought back to me," Cyrus said, surprising him with an actual explanation.

Nicholas hesitated a moment before nodding for him to continue.

"In exchange for what I've offered, you will accompany the girl on her search. That girl has too much of her mother in her. She *will* try to abscond with it at some point. I will need you to ensure that she doesn't reveal herself as a traveler, or meddle with the timeline, and see that the astrolabe is returned to me—all without revealing my conditions to the girl. Should she become aware of our agreement, our contract will be destroyed, and I personally guarantee that you will never set foot on a dock again. Not in America, not in Europe, not in the Indies."

Nicholas felt the cold sweat collect along his spine, and tried to tamp down his desperate longing. He could picture being on the other side of this so clearly, and was struck by the profound power of finally being in the position to free the family's slaves, of finally being granted reparations. This offer would open the door to nearly everything he desired. Money was power; he could demand respect, and spite those who would not freely give it.

But he could not help seeing Julian's face. He could not banish the searing agony of that moment as it played out again behind his eyes. Yet again, he was being cast in the role of servant, put in a position to fail. Yet again, he owed something to someone who—

Julian's face was gone, replaced by Etta's, pale with terror. The image seared his heart.

Not again. He could not survive it.

"I realize, of course, that you are not a blank slate," the old man continued. "You will need to ingratiate yourself to her, earn her trust wholly, so she confides in you about the location of the astrolabe once she has ascertained its location. If you are separated from her, you will return to me immediately and we will proceed accordingly."

And leave her alone, to be lost, harmed, or taken, as she continued on without him in the meantime? The thought pricked his pride, stoked his fear.

Nicholas had promised her protection, vowed to get her away from Ironwood should the need arise; there was no question now that her life was in danger. But . . . perhaps he could reconcile his hopes with that promise. Keeping Etta safe meant not only shielding her from harm, but also preventing her from crossing Ironwood. Once they found the blasted thing, he could be the one to ensure the old man kept his vow. Nicholas could deliver her back to the passage in Nassau, wherever it might be.

What else was there to do? Give up the future within his reach for someone who, in time, would only be a memory? He had lived nearly his whole life for others—wasn't it time to live for himself, secure his future?

He owed it to himself. What's more . . . he owed it to *Julian* to finish what they'd begun, so his death wouldn't be for nothing.

I am the one who truly owes a debt to them—not her. He'd stolen Julian. He could give the old man this, and then he'd never need to see his wicked face again.

Cyrus watched him carefully. "I see the indecision on your face," he continued. "If it makes the offer more palatable, I will lift the ban on your traveling. Your exile here in your natural time will end. You will be free to go wherever, *whenever*, you like."

Nicholas recoiled instinctively, but caught himself. "My exile is payment for the debt I owe for Julian's life. I have no desire to return to traveling."

It was the truth, and it made him uneasy that the man had even offered. Ironwood had raged when he'd returned, weak and wounded and without Julian, and he'd understood his fury; felt, even now, that he deserved it. Not for depriving the man of his last direct heir, but for depriving the world of the only decent soul in the family. Now all would be forgiven, as if it were nothing? As if Julian were nothing?

Nicholas had all but toasted the news that the man who had fathered him had drowned before Cyrus could come to find him; but he'd languished for years now over Julian's death, battering himself at every turn. He tortured himself with that one question: why travel at all if nothing could be changed? Why travel if he could not save Julian, if he could not so much as warn himself not to go down that path—to stay away from Ironwood? The futility was devastating, and always would be.

Nicholas had worked hard to earn back the trust of Chase

and Hall after abandoning them for false promises and hollow revelations. Hall had done everything in his power to dissuade him from leaving with Ironwood, and Nicholas had waved away his every concern like a fool.

"Why the thirtieth?" he asked again. "What is so important about that date?"

"It is merely a deadline," Cyrus said, "to hold the girl accountable."

The old man never did *anything* without a reason. There was something important here that he was withholding, but the man's chosen currency was secrets. Nicholas wasn't sure he was willing to trade to find out what this one was.

"Say yes, Nicholas," Cyrus coaxed, holding out a hand.

Did it matter so much? Nicholas saw the future he'd built during all of these years, and it was resting in the old man's calloused palm. He only had to agree. A few words to seal that fate . . .

Perhaps they were more alike than he'd care to admit.

"I need this in writing—a proper contract," Nicholas heard himself say.

The old man's eyes lit up. "I've already taken care of it. There's a copy for you to keep."

The contract was waiting in his trunk, along with a ballpoint pen for signing. It had been so long since Nicholas had used one of them, the weight felt unfamiliar in his hands as he brought the metal tip to the parchment. He felt sick to his stomach reading through the terms. The old man had known he'd be weak enough to give in—should he have put up more of a fight? Were there better terms to be had?

"Good man," Cyrus said, taking one copy and folding it neatly into thirds, and held out his hand. Nicholas gave it a brief, firm shake, and felt the burn of it as if he'd taken the devil's hand, still warm from the fires of hell. Cyrus continued. "You'll leave tomorrow with the girl, just as soon as she has deciphered the next clue."

Nicholas nodded, a stone lodged in his throat.

Forgive me, Mother, he thought, taking his leave as quickly as possible. *I will do what I must.*

He was not doing this to take up the Ironwood name, to stay within a family that had never wanted him in the first place. He was not doing this to take up the life of a traveler again, or to see beyond the horizon of his natural years. He was not doing this for a girl who would never truly belong to him. He was doing this for his future. For Julian's memory.

He would master his feelings.

He would see this arrangement through.

And he would close this chapter once and for all.

NICHOLAS WALKED.

For miles, heading nowhere in particular, he walked for what felt like hours, trying to force his legs to grow reacquainted with the steadiness of land. He carried only his freedom papers in his coat pocket and the money Ironwood's man had provided for bringing Sophia and Etta to New York—neither of which he was foolish enough to leave behind at the tavern. He passed the time under an unusually cloudless sky, as night edged into the earliest morning hours and the world slowly began to lighten around him. And when those thoughts wove into a long, dangerous rumination on the color of Etta's eyes in comparison to that same faint blue, he turned his mind back to another unwelcome task: mentally composing his letter to Chase. *Dear friend, you were right.*

I'll be very late seemed too short, and would give his friend far too much to crow about; but *I must venture through time with the pirate queen* would be met with confusion, and fear for Nicholas's mind.

I've further business to attend to here in New York. I'll be in New London by the start of November. That was better.

He felt a pang at the thought of the others sailing without him. *But you'll be sailing on your own ship soon enough,* he thought. What would Hall think of him, knowing he'd thrown in his lot with Ironwood again? Nicholas couldn't imagine better business partners than Chase and Hall—perhaps they would come to see reason once they took a look at the plantations' ledgers?

The road rose and fell beneath him, riddled with puddles of stale, festering water and sun-roasted mounds of animal droppings, as he passed fields of crops and country homes. It remained empty as he turned back in the direction of the Dove and the Royal Artillery Park.

He knew a hanging would take place within hours. A spy had been caught behind enemy lines, and this was the natural outcome; it was a testament to how rattled he was by Ironwood that he felt the old, foolish guilt come creeping into his heart. A man was set to die, and none of them had done a thing to stop it. If he knew them at all, both Cyrus and Sophia would take in the execution as spectators, and add it to the tally of noteworthy events they'd witnessed.

If Nicholas had not looked up from the mud, he might have missed the distant, dark streak that crossed the road as it blazed a path toward the Royal Artillery Park. A swirl of sapphire fabric, long gold hair braided like a rope down her back—

He took off at a run, cursing. Veering off the road, he followed the tracks that led into a cluster of nearby trees, behind what must have been the officers' quarters. The air smelled of wet animals, gunpowder, men—all evidence of the camp nearby.

"Miss Spencer!" he hissed into the silence. The river rose up before him, a glimmering line of blue waiting to be lit by the sun. Where had she gone? Had it been a trick of the mind?

No—he found the trail of footprints again. Ironwood had been right after all; Etta was attempting to trick him, in this case by leaving under the cover of night without his knowledge. No doubt in possession of the actual meaning of her mother's letter as well.

As he pushed forward, a crackle of power snapped against his skin. He knew that sensation. The passage was no longer singing in his ears, but there was a powerful hum below the quiet chatter of birds: a faint burning hiss that reminded him of the moment after a flash of lightning appeared over the sea. Of the rare white-blue lights that sometimes danced upon the masts and sails.

The entrance to the passage was a glimmering wall ahead, just at the edge of where the land met the river. It was still rippling, as if someone had only just passed through it.

"Bloody fool," he breathed out, rubbing a hand over his head to force down the fear. For a moment, he was at a loss as to how to proceed. There wasn't time to go back to the tavern to collect the rest of his belongings. She could fully escape, or, worse, be injured or killed in the time it took him to return to the Dove and tell Ironwood what had happened.

Nicholas shook his head. The old man had given him explicit instructions to gain the girl's trust and return with the astrolabe by any means, both of which seemed impossible if he were to fetch her back. She would doubt his motivations when he needed her full confidence. And he couldn't predict what punishment Ironwood might levy on her, her mother, or both, for this.

He had signed Ironwood's contract, and both he and Ironwood knew his punishment for failure; Nicholas would have to trust that the old man would recognize the truth of what had likely happened when he woke in a few hours to find them both gone. Besides, in the end, all that mattered to the old man was that they returned with the astrolabe in hand. What was it that Julian had always said? *Better to ask forgiveness than permission.*

His brother was still on his mind as he took a deep breath and walked steadily toward the passage, trying to quell his wariness as he approached. How long had it been since he'd felt a passage enclose his skin, his bones, crush the air from his lungs? Longer than a year. Long enough to force him to take a deep, steadying breath.

Come on, Nick. Julian's voice rose on the breeze at his back. *We've a journey to make.*

And, with one last breath of his world, he stepped through, surrendering himself to the pressure and the devastating blackness as time bent around him.

LONDON
1940

ELEVEN

ETTA CRASHED DOWN INTO AWARENESS IN A SYMPHONY of shattered glass, hearing it break a split second before she felt the shards slicing through her skin. Pain stole her breath and turned the world to sand around her. Just when she was sure she'd managed to get a grip on her surroundings, the images and sensations drained to nothingness again. Her body throbbed as she fought against unconsciousness. The lingering pressure from the passage didn't ease, not even when she threw up.

Now she knew why she couldn't remember what had happened with Sophia—how she had traveled to the ship after arriving through the passage.

Don't—she clung to the word, forcing her burning eyes open—*don't pass out. . . .*

Etta was caught in between charred beams and what looked like a blown-out window frame, her body cradled in it like a doll that had been dropped from above. Carefully she shifted, twisting until her feet touched the ground. Fabric tore—her right sleeve separated at the shoulder—and in the instant before her knees collapsed under her and the world blacked out again, an unnatural chill crept under her skin and turned her blood to ice. Her cheek struck the cement, and she felt nothing at all.

IT WAS THE WARMTH SHE NOTICED FIRST; THE GENTLE PRESSURE of the touch. Her legs and back ached as they came awake, but the pain on the right side of her face was scalding, raw. The air smelled of smoke—fire—but also . . . Through her lashes, she saw a dark head bent over her, cleaning dirt and blood away from her right hand. Nicholas's face was drawn, stricken, as he worked, and Etta's throat tightened as he carefully brought her hand up to his mouth as if to kiss it, his warm breath fanning over her skin. Instead, he shook his head and carefully set her hand down to rest on her stomach. In spite of the pain rattling around inside of her, the lingering pulse of the nearby passage, Etta let herself feel a pang of regret.

And then she remembered.

Panicked, Etta tried moving her legs, shifting to get them under her. If he was here, then . . . she hadn't gotten away. Ironwood would know she'd tried to slip out of their deal. And her mom . . .

He's going to kill her.

She shouldn't have left—she should have been more careful. What was the point of any of this if Cyrus turned around and killed her mom while Etta was centuries and continents away from protecting her?

I had to take the risk—I had to get ahead of him, to beat his deadline.

But when she closed her eyes, her mind was already imagining it, already seeing her mother's lifeless eyes staring back at her.

This was better. Leaving without his permission had to be

safer for her mother than waiting and ultimately running out of time. The air seemed to tick around her, counting down.

"Miss Spencer?" Nicholas said, his voice loud in her ears. "Can you hear me?"

Etta forced her eyes open all the way, taking in his face, the remnants of a broken ceiling, and the blue sky beyond. Unsure of what to say, she tried, "Hi?"

The relief in his face flashed to irritation. "Do you realize you could have been killed—or worse? What the devil were you thinking? Or were you not thinking at all?"

Irritation burned through Etta. "Mind your own . . . business."

Need to move . . . need to find it . . . need to get to Mom . . .

But her legs were still not cooperating.

"I ought to throttle you for this," he continued. "Is anything hurting other than your cheek and hand? I've cleaned your cuts as best I could—"

She shook her head. Aside from those things, she was fine. Mostly. "Dizzy."

He sucked in a sharp breath. "That is traveler's sickness. It'll ease with every passage. For now, I'm afraid you'll have to bear it."

"H-horrible—" Etta tried to get her hands beneath her, to push, so she was at least sitting up. Aside from the anger she felt radiating off him, Nicholas seemed completely unaffected.

She twisted away from his hands as he reached out to help her, and scooted back through the dust and debris until her back hit a wall. A cool expression slid over his face, and she was suddenly pinned by guilt. If it were possible, Etta felt worse than before.

"You were attempting to run," he said, stating the obvious. "Incredibly foolish. Do you honestly believe Ironwood's reach is limited to the eighteenth century? If nothing else, have a care for your mother! If he sees you crossing him this way, he *will* kill her."

"I left a note with—with Sophia, saying I needed to leave now, because of the deadline. . . ." Etta shook her head. She'd written it by moonlight, and waited only long enough to be sure the man on guard outside their door was asleep. "I can't run out of time." *And I don't necessarily want Ironwood to be able to follow me.* "You don't understand—"

She'd known it was a risk; that she was maybe naïvely banking on the chance that Ironwood would not punish her mother if she left without his permission in order to, as she'd written in the note, "make your deadline." Etta had a feeling the old man had ways of tracking her progress across time. She needed a little bit of a head start to find her footing and avoid anyone tailing her to report back on her movements—which passages she'd used. Unfortunately, she hadn't factored in traveler's sickness.

Or Nicholas.

"Explain it to me!" he said, his voice a harsh, deadly quiet. "Explain to me why you'd risk her life—why you'd risk *your* life—leaving without any supplies or preparation! I didn't take you for an idiot!"

She clenched her jaw, glaring back at him. Her arm was filled with pins and needles as the blood rushed to it, but she lifted it all the same, searching the ground for the bag of things she'd "borrowed" from the trunk in Sophia's room.

It looked like they were in some sort of hallway—only, maybe *hallway* wasn't the right word. The vaulted stone ceiling was broken up by shattered skylights and long hanging lanterns. There were shops inside here—she saw battered chairs, shoes that had been blown out of storefronts. The second-story windows above each gold-and-black store entrance looked like they had been thrown open all at once.

"There," she said, pointing to the leather bag a short distance away. "I didn't c-come un-unprepared."

What had happened here? It looked like a bomb had gone off; everything looked damp, like the people here had only just put out an enormous fire. *Where am I?* she thought, panic gnawing holes in her core. She heard distant voices, clipped English accents, too faint to decipher.

Nicholas sorted through the bag. "A pair of sewing scissors, a harmonica engraved with Sophia's initials, a small mirror, a few pieces of gold, your mother's letter, a—"

Etta smirked.

"—a lady's support garment, an apple, and a revolver," he finished, closing the bag again. Sophia hadn't had a truly modern "support garment," but the one Etta had found in the trunk was as close to it as she was going to get.

"What else would I need?" she asked innocently.

"Water? Maps? A list of known passages? Era-appropriate clothing? Ammunition for said revolver? Do you even know how to use the weapon?"

Well, he had her there. "If you try to bring me back, I'll—"

"You'll what, Miss Spencer?" Nicholas said, crouching down in front of her. "You'll glare at me?"

Etta's hand closed around a nearby shard of glass, holding it out in front of her. Nicholas's expression changed; his eyes darkened, drawn first to the makeshift weapon, then to her face. She refused to wilt under the pressure of his gaze, and stared back as defiantly as she could, with one of her cheeks swollen to twice its size.

He broke first, his face softening. He sat down on a nearby piece of rubble and took out a folded handkerchief. "You've cut yourself again, pirate."

After a moment, Etta set the piece of glass down and let him hold the warm cloth against her palm, staring at the way his large hand cupped hers. Her chest grew tight as she searched for the right words.

"Why didn't you tell me?" he asked quietly. "You made me promise not to leave without a word. You couldn't have done the same for me?"

"Sorry." She hadn't thought of that. The knife of guilt wedged in her stomach was gripped by fear, and given another twist. "I didn't want to waste another second, not when he could hurt Mom, kill her. I think Ironwood knows better than to hurt her until I come back with the astrolabe. If he did hurt her, then I'd really have nothing to lose, right?"

Nicholas nodded. "He has other ways of hurting you."

"But not motivating me. And—" Etta hesitated, unsure of whether or not to tell him the other motivation that burned inside of her. "I told you about Alice—I need to finish this, get back to her."

Nicholas sat back on his heels, glancing up at what they could see of the sky. His usual move, she realized, to try to collect his thoughts. Hide his expression. "Etta, you can't save her."

"Of course I can," she insisted, but her heart sped up at the expression on his face: the guilt, the sympathy. "I just have to travel back—"

"And change the past?" he finished. "Alter the timeline?"

Etta set her jaw. "I don't care about that—I *don't*! Ironwood

ALEXANDRA BRACKEN

has been changing the past for years, and I can't even save *one* life?"

"No, Etta, listen to me," Nicholas said quickly. "What you're speaking of isn't a matter of morality. It's an impossibility."

She pulled back against the wall, away from him, away from his words.

"Didn't Sophia tell you this? You can't cross paths with yourself—you cannot exist twice in the same place, at the same time. Time itself won't allow it; you'd be bounced back out of the passage before you could move through it," Nicholas said, keeping his voice low. "That's why travelers keep journals, to remember the dates and years they've already been to."

Etta felt like he'd thrown a bucket of ice water over her. Her chest clenched painfully—so she wouldn't be able to use the passage to get back to that moment before Alice was shot? Never mind that—she wouldn't even be able to go to any month or year before that and warn her it would happen. All because some past version of herself was already there.

"Didn't she explain that the passages connect *years*, not days?" Nicholas pressed.

"What do you mean?" Etta whispered.

His expression softened. "I see. So she didn't. Even if you could find another traveler to use that passage to save her, you would need to wait a year in order to do so. It's easiest to think of each year as a tiny stream, all flowing parallel to one another, all moving in one direction, even as we jump between them. We left Manhattan on the twenty-second of September, 1776. We arrived here on the twenty-second of September, whatever year this might be. Do you understand?"

Etta nodded, unable to speak for several long moments. *There has to be another way.* It couldn't end like this. Alice couldn't die—not for her.

Mom will know what to do.

"Blank slate . . ." she said slowly. "That's what Ironwood meant when he called me that. It wasn't because I didn't know anything, but that I haven't been anywhere. The chances of me crossing paths with myself are slim. Right?"

He nodded, touching her elbow. "You do understand, don't you?"

She lifted her chin. "I understand there's always another option, another way, if you look hard enough for it."

He let out a faint laugh, closing his eyes. "I thought you might say something like that."

"Wait—" Etta said, another thought suddenly occurring to her. "Oh my God—won't Ironwood be after *you* for traveling?"

After what had happened to his half brother, Nicholas had been banned—exiled, he'd said—and she didn't think this would go unnoticed.

"My fear for you outweighs my fear of him," he said simply. "And I told you, didn't I? If you left, I'd follow you."

But should you try to leave on your own, know that I will go to the ends of the earth to bring you back. The words echoed between them, unspoken. A cloud of ash filtered down from above. Without thinking, Etta reached up and brushed the flakes away from his hair. He closed his eyes, bowing his head, leaning into the touch just enough to make her hand tremble.

"You know what the letter says—the one your mother wrote. And you don't trust me. . . ." he began. "You see me as one of them, don't you?"

"No!" she said quickly. It was true that he'd agreed to work for Cyrus, to bring her to New York, but he stood apart from them, didn't he? He'd been badly wronged by them, hadn't he? She didn't want to get him tangled any deeper in the family, or give them another reason to make his life miserable.

"You do," he said. "After everything I've told you?"

Etta dropped her head back against the wall. He could take her apart with a single look, couldn't he? But she wanted to tell him this; she wanted him to understand that she wasn't just being a reckless idiot. She wanted him to be on her side.

She needed what he knew about the Ironwoods. About traveling. But how mercenary did that make her, to see if he'd come with her—and then leave him to deal with the fallout?

"Can I trust you?" Etta asked. "Will you trust me?"

Nicholas gave a curt nod.

She took a deep breath.

"I *do* know how to read the letter," she admitted. "And I think the old man's lying, or at least not giving us the full truth."

His lips parted, the only slip in his mask. She'd surprised him. "What brought you to that conclusion?" Nicholas asked.

"My mom isn't a thief," Etta said. "I don't care what he says. I think this thing, the astrolabe, it belonged to the Lindens." *Her* family—the one that had been whittled down to her and her mother alone. "They, or at least my mom, felt responsible for protecting it."

"It might have truly belonged to them," Nicholas conceded after mulling this over. "My understanding from Julian is that there was an astrolabe for each of the four families—Ironwood, Jacaranda, Linden, and Hemlock—but three were lost, or destroyed outright, a century ago. Ironwood feels that because he is the Grand Master of all of these families, they all belong to him, regardless of the original owner."

Etta nodded, wondering what else had been stolen from her family—what heirlooms, secrets, and history had been absorbed into the Ironwood clan. Maybe her mom would be able to tell her.

Maybe they could reclaim some of that together.

After you somehow outsmart the old man, save your mom, save Alice, and perform at the debut next month.

"And this letter—she must have known something was going to happen, otherwise why write it?" Etta said.

Nicholas braced his arms on his knees. "Well, you can ask her once we have the astrolabe back in Ironwood's hands and he frees her."

Etta blinked. "You want to come with me?"

She saw a flash of sharp emotion pass quickly over his face, but couldn't decode it. He glanced away. After a moment, Nicholas scoffed. "As if I'd ever feel comfortable letting you attempt this without any kind of aid—I can see in your face that you're unhappy, but I trained for years to be able to travel. You've only just begun. It's not weakness to require help, or a protector."

"I don't need a protector," Etta said. "I need a partner."

Nicholas's gaze had been skimming the destruction around them, over the glimmering wall of air that was the entrance to the passage, but at her words, he met her eyes. His lips parted, as if the idea had startled him. "What are . . . the terms of this?"

Didn't you travel with Julian? she wanted to ask. But . . . Sophia had called him little more than Julian's servant, a kind of valet; and, while Etta had initially taken it as the girl being cruel and dismissive, she now had the evidence right in front of her. Her heart cracked and cracked again—at the role they'd thrust him into, at how he'd assumed it would be the same with her.

"We watch each other's backs," she said. "You call me Etta. And we don't keep secrets." Except, of course, that she'd never give the astrolabe to Ironwood if she could help it. "And—"

"We continue our mutual disdain of Ironwood?"

She grinned, even as doubt began to cloud her thoughts.

What if returning it is the only way he won't punish Nicholas for this?

She couldn't think about that now. It was a question for when, and if, they actually found the astrolabe. But accepting his help had consequences. He would be risking the old man's wrath.

As if he'd leaned over and peered into her thoughts, he said quietly, "It's my choice. What I do, I decide for myself."

"All right." Whatever invisible string had been tied so tightly around her heart loosened. "Before we find out where we're going, do you have any idea where we are?"

He climbed to his knees, giving her a dry look. "I was rather distracted by you lying in a pool of your own blood."

"There isn't a *pool*," she protested, rubbing at her swelling cheek. He reached over, as if it were the most natural thing in the world, and pulled her hand away to hold.

"Don't fuss with it," he said. He ran a featherlight finger over the scrape. She didn't breathe until he let his hand fall away.

"Now you've the look of a real pirate," he told her, with a small, quiet smile. "But I'll need to purchase clothing and supplies. Will you be all right if I leave you here for a few moments? I won't be long, I promise."

Etta opened the bag she'd hastily packed, and rooted around

inside of it until her hands closed on the small velvet sack of gold. She handed it to him. "My mom might not be a thief, but I don't particularly care if I am."

"Seems like just payment," he agreed, weighing it in his palm, "considering what they've done to you."

He set off into the wreckage of stone and storefronts around them. Etta watched him turn, and caught his eye as he glanced one last time over his shoulder. She gave him an exasperated wave to move him on, and the laugh that echoed back settled in her like a sip of warm tea.

She looked around again, struggling up onto her feet. The wall behind was enough of a support to lean against as she stepped through the piles of glass and wet, scorched wood. The signs were in English, and by the smell and scene, she could at least guess that there'd been some kind of fire.

Etta stepped back to where she'd been before and tucked herself against the wall, out of sight. Every now and then she heard a voice or the soft growl of an engine, and leaned forward to peer down the long hallway at the streets on either side. A bright red bus rolled by, followed by two young women in skirt suits and little hats pinned in place. Etta was painfully aware of her eighteenth-century gown, and the stays squeezing her ribs.

England, she thought, half-amazed. London, if she had to guess. And the fashion . . . 1950s? Or—

No.

She took in the demolished walls, the evidence of fire, the uniformed men passing by the opposite end of the hallway.

Wartime London.

World War II.

Nicholas confirmed it when he returned, with clothing for her tucked beneath his arm. He'd changed into a crisp button-down shirt and trousers, and traded his shoes for oxfords. She could only imagine how he might have explained the breeches, stockings, and jacket he'd been strolling around in.

"I wasn't entirely sure of the size. . . ." he began, his eyes on the ground as he passed a cornflower-blue dress and smart matching jacket into her hands. Etta studied the dress—V-neck, modest length, short sleeves—and ran her fingers along the lace detailing she had just noticed.

"It's beautiful, thank you," she said. And also generously loose in the waist; but it came with a belt that would allow her to tighten it if necessary. "How was it out there?"

Nicholas stared at her as she struggled to blindly unbutton her dress until Etta, flushing, finally cleared her throat. He startled and spun on his heel, giving her a little bit of privacy, as she got enough of the buttons undone to pull the dress over her head.

"Men are working to clear the wreckage from last night's attack—they're searching for survivors still," he said. "I overheard them saying they would move to this area soon, so we need to proceed with some haste."

Etta thought so too, but it wasn't helping her get her stays unknotted any faster. Her hands throbbed from where they'd been scraped raw by her fall, and she could not get her fingers to stop shaking.

"I'm sorry," she muttered, "I need help—"

Nicholas glanced at her, then immediately turned back to face the wall. Etta felt a blush moving up over her face and chest. Stays and a nearly see-through shift. She could have at least crossed her arms over her chest.

He took in a pained breath and turned around. She studied the quick, sure movements of his calloused hands as he worked, forcing her arms to stay down at her side until the laces finally gave. His broad shoulders closed out the rest of the world; Nicholas stood close enough that she could have leaned forward, pressed her face against the space between his neck and shoulders—she could have—and, for a moment, she felt she might be trapped in the heavy grip of her own want if she didn't. His pulse fluttered in his neck, and she couldn't take her eyes away from it.

"There," he murmured, though his fingers lingered on the loose laces a moment longer, his thumbs skimming along the upper edges of the stays, ghosting against the fabric of her shift. Etta held herself completely still, too afraid to lean forward into the touch; too afraid to move, or do anything that might end it.

The dizziness was back. She felt the warm breath of his sigh fan against her collarbone, an instant before he stepped away. He kept his gaze down as he said, in a voice like warm honey, "Sailors. Good with knots."

It wasn't until he turned back around to let her finish that Etta's mind cleared again enough to remember the scissors she'd taken and stowed in her bag, for this exact reason.

The dress he'd chosen fit her well enough, but Etta would have to make do with the lace-up leather boots she'd taken from Sophia, and just ignore their pinching until there was a better option. She reached up, touching her earrings to make sure they were still there.

"Okay," she said, smoothing her hair back over her shoulder. "How's this look?"

As he stared, she reminded herself very firmly that he was

staring at the hideously bruised lump jutting out of one side of her face, and only the hideously bruised lump.

After a moment he said, "You'll do, pirate. Now, tell me what your mother's letter truly says."

As he balled up the gown, rolling the fabric up into a tidier bundle, Etta retrieved the letter and pen that had rolled to the bottom of the bag. Using the wall, she sketched the outline of a star over the face of the letter, studying the flow of words that were contained inside of its shape. Nicholas stepped closer, reading over her shoulder. Around them, the morning was picking up in pace, bursting with voices and the smell of fire and gasoline; but they were tucked inside a quiet pocket, a passage of their own.

"*Rise and enter the lair, where the darkness gives you your stripes. Tell tyrants, to you, their allegiance they owe,*" Etta read, running a finger beneath the words within the star. "*Seek out the unknown gods whose ears were deaf to lecture. Stand on the shoulders of memory. Bring a coin to the widowed queen. Remember, the truth is in the telling, and an ending must be final.*"

"My God," he said, with a hint of delight. "How did you know to do this?"

With as little explanation as possible, she told him about the secret messages her mother had hidden in her violin case, and in her suitcase when she traveled.

"She wanted you to be able to read it," he said, practically glowing with excitement. "She thought that someday you might have to find the astrolabe. Do you understand any of the clues?"

Etta shook her head, scanning the words over and over again, wondering if she'd been wrong—if it was meant to be another shape. The words didn't make any sense.

"If we assume this is a list of instructions, directions, then I believe we can ignore the first clue," Nicholas said, taking the letter from her. "The second, *Tell tyrants, to you, their allegiance they owe,* refers to the place where Nathan Hale was killed—the passage we came through—meaning the next one is likely relevant to us now: *Seek out the unknown gods whose ears were deaf to lecture.* Does that stir anything in your memory?"

Helplessness tugged at her as she shook her head, and she felt her hope start to fray. How were they going to figure out multiple clues like this in seven days?

"What do 'unknown gods' have to do with London during the Second World War? Are they people? A certain faith? The last clue tied the location of the passage to one man's death." And the clue had used a song that her great-grandfather was fond of belting out now and then. Would this one relate to her family in a similar way—be as personal?

Something nagged at her as she thought back to the Dove, the Artillery Park, but she brushed it aside as Nicholas said, "Lecture . . . lecture, lecture, lecture . . ."

He spun toward her so quickly, he almost knocked her back a step. His eyes lit up, making the planes of his face seem almost boyish. "Is it possible it's referring to St. Paul's Areopagus sermon?"

Etta returned his eager expression with a blank one.

"Heathen!" Nicholas teased. "Acts 17:16–34. The Apostle Paul gave a sermon—a lecture, in fact, as it was against Greek law to preach about a foreign deity—in Athens, at the Areopagus."

"I'll take your word for it."

He chuckled, absently brushing a featherlight finger along her chin. He didn't seem to realize he'd done it, but every inch of Etta's skin was sparking with awareness.

"The Areopagus is the rocky area below the Acropolis. It served as the city's high court of appeals in ancient times," he explained, and Etta felt both impressed at his knowledge and terribly inadequate in the face of it. "I've read of it. Captain Hall saw himself as a philosopher as much as a seaman—he was educated at Harvard, if you can believe it—and kept any number of treatises around in the hope that Chase or I would stumble upon them one day. And Mrs. Hall was rather stringent in our biblical education."

"I wish I could say the same," Etta muttered. The only service she'd attended inside of a church had been the funeral of Oskar, Alice's husband. Considering the role of religion in the eighteenth century, the depth of Nicholas's knowledge shouldn't have surprised her. She found herself leaning toward him, something sparking and warming at the center of her chest as she reappraised him in light of this. For the first time, Etta was truly grateful he had followed her through the passage.

"The sermon is something to the effect of, 'Ye men of Athens, I perceive that in all things ye are too superstitious. For as I passed by, and beheld your devotions, I found an altar with this inscription: *To the Unknown God.*' The sermon was centered on his distress at seeing the Athenians worshiping false idols—the Greek pantheon of gods."

"And the connection between London and Ancient Greece is . . . ?" Etta prompted, hoping he'd have the answer, since she didn't.

"Architecture, law, statues, and art," he offered. "I'd imagine that it's a place or thing you have a personal connection with. Have you visited this city before?"

Etta nodded. Any number of times. She, her mom, and Alice had flown back to visit, spent summers in rented flats to escape the sweltering heat of New York. Alice had grown up in London, and . . . well, she'd always been told her mother had as well, though that seemed up for debate now. The truth and fiction in her stories had started to bleed together, damaging them, like a waterlogged painting.

During their holidays, they'd rented any number of flats, but remembering them now, none of them stood out from the others. They'd walked all over the city, visiting the parks, the house Alice had grown up in—they'd gone to the theater, museums—

"Oh!" she said. It felt like the thought reached up and slapped her in the face. She turned to Nicholas, almost giddy that she could finally explain something he might not know. "This idea is crazy, but . . . London—the British Museum—has a ton of artifacts from ancient Greece, doesn't it? The most famous set were removed—or looted, depending on who you're talking to—from the Parthenon by a British lord, Elgin, who brought them back here and sold them to the British government for the museum. It's a whole legal mess."

Etta rocked back onto her heels, looking up at the clouds and smoke trailing overhead. "I might be reaching here, but the Acropolis, and the Parthenon, are so close to the Areopagus, it feels like they're linked. It's been a while since I visited that room of the museum, and I can't exactly remember what the Elgin Marbles depict—some kind of battle, I think. But there are statues of men and women . . ."

"Go on," Nicholas urged.

"I was trying to figure out the 'deaf ears' part, thinking of real, living people, but what if it's talking about the statues themselves? They can't hear or see or feel."

"Do you recall ever hearing any strange noises while in their proximity?" he asked.

She shook her head.

"Based on the way your mother used the clue about Nathan Hale's execution, it's likely the passage is in the museum, near where those statues are housed. The British Museum of my time is likely quite different than the one you know; I've never been granted access to it, nor was I ever given the full record of where all of the known passages are located—I'm a bit lost as to what to suggest."

Frustration pooled in the pit of her stomach, rising with each passing moment. Nicholas watched her, waiting. "I don't know—are we overthinking this? Should it be something simpler? More obvious?"

He stooped slightly to look her in the eye. "It's all right. Perhaps it would help to think aloud? Anything, however small, might help us. . . ."

She nodded. He could help her clarify her thoughts, and might catch something buried in the words. "Mom works for a museum, but in New York. There's been a lot of renewed debate recently about whether or not the Elgin Marbles should be returned to Greece—it's been all over the press. The British Museum is just the British Museum, you know? Or, well, I guess you don't. Yet. But . . . Alice used to give us her own special tours. Her father was a curator. She told me the whole story about how they came to be in the museum's collection."

"Alice . . . your instructor?" he clarified.

Her throat was suddenly too tight to speak. Nicholas merely nodded again, as if he'd somehow put all of the pieces together.

With a small, tentative smile, he asked, "Shall we go, then?"

With the image of Alice still too close to the front of her mind, and exhaustion stretching every emotion, Etta didn't trust her voice. She nodded, accepting his arm when he offered it. It didn't even occur to her that her hands were cold until she placed one into his. Despite everything, Etta felt anticipation fizzing through her veins, prickling across her nerves. The scene around them sank through her, became real. Nicholas gave her a knowing look.

"It's just . . . unbelievable that we're here," she told him. "All of this . . ."

It was beautiful, and strange, and unnatural, and she couldn't help it—she wanted to explore what was around her. To see it for herself, the world unfolding as it was—not the edited versions presented in films and books.

"Under other, less dire, circumstances," he said, "might you be glad to see this?"

It felt like a betrayal to her anger at the Ironwoods to give the *yes* that was in her heart, even with the way he'd couched the question. "I don't know. Let's see how we do, and then I'll answer that."

Let's see if I can find the astrolabe and my mother, and set my life straight again.

Nicholas slung the leather bag over his other shoulder, letting it slap against his hip as they navigated the maze of debris. He stopped suddenly, craning his neck around. Etta followed his gaze to where gold letters gleamed high above the entrance archway. The contrast between them and the battered ruins of the structure made the hair rise on the back of her arms.

"Burlington Arcade," he read.

She knew this place—she'd been here once, years ago, for a performance. Alice had walked her through the long enclosed shopping center with all of its glittering stores. They'd found Christmas presents for Rose.

"I think I know where we are," she said. "Roughly."

Rough was a good way to describe what they saw as they stepped out of the ruined arcade and onto the street. She'd known to expect destruction—she'd seen pictures, heard Alice and Oskar describe it with a raw pain that lingered decades later. What Etta hadn't expected was that so many Londoners would be out and about in suits, dresses, and heels, carefully picking their way through the piles of debris that had blown out of storefronts, deftly avoiding the craters that had collapsed in whole sections, the surface of the street torn away to reveal the pipes beneath.

Clouds passed over the sun, spotting the ground with shadows. Etta watched Nicholas as they made their way down a succession of connecting streets, heading east. He was drifting to the left, pulling away, until her hand slipped off his sleeve. The nausea and wooziness from the traveler's sickness had passed, but she felt disoriented all over again, in a very different way. Though Nicholas stayed only a step ahead of her, she felt the distance build between them until she felt suddenly alone.

Every now and then Nicholas caught sight of something new—a bicycle, a window display, a police officer in uniform, a traffic light—and it would drag his attention away. Etta could tell he didn't want to have to ask her to explain—there was some part of him that was enjoying the process of figuring it out himself— but he was curious.

"Have you been here before?" she asked finally. "Here-here?"

He shook his head, answering quietly, "I only went as far as 1925, and that was in New Orleans."

Compared to the quiet of the eighteenth century, twentieth-century London practically roared around them. A car beeped and sped past them, and Etta felt a hand clamp over her wrist. Nicholas flew back against the nearby shop, and Etta stumbled after him.

A nearby shopkeeper was writing BUSINESS AS USUAL on a piece of wood in the shattered front window of his store, and looked up at the sudden movement in alarm. Etta sent the man a reassuring smile before turning back to the man next to her.

The breath tore in and out of Nicholas, his nostrils flaring as the car rolled to a rattling stop nearby.

After a moment he explained, "They're . . . louder than I recall. Faster."

She nodded. "They probably are."

"And," Nicholas said, his voice lowering as he looked down at her, "you have them in your time, as well?"

"Yeah, even better ones. Faster, quieter—they use less energy, some have built-in navigational systems—" Okay, too much detail. His eyes had widened at the words *less energy*, and she knew she'd lost him. "Everything changes, when given enough time."

He worked his jaw back and forth. "Everything?"

It might have been the way he was studying her mouth, or how his hands seemed to be lightly tracing the folds of her dress's skirt without even being fully aware of it, but the trickle of confusion roared into a jagged, painful understanding.

Oh, she thought, throat thick. *Oh . . .*

"Do you want me to tell you?" she asked him. "Do you really want to know what my time is like?"

If he did plan on returning home and never traveling again, he would never benefit from any progress—never see it for himself. It would drive anyone crazy, knowing what was out of reach of his natural lifetime.

Finally, Nicholas shook his head. "I'd rather discover it for myself."

She could protect him in the meantime, at least. "You covered for me on the ship. The least I can do is return the favor now, the best I can."

His smile turned rueful. "This 'partners' business is a rather novel concept for me . . . but I appreciate that."

Etta wanted to ask him about Julian, but she also couldn't let him drift away into a pool of terrible memories. She stepped back out onto what little was left of the sidewalk, cupping her hands over her eyes to shade them from the sunlight. "Well, I officially have no idea where we are."

His jaw actually dropped. "Did I not say we needed a map . . . ?"

She wasn't about to let him win that argument. "Hold on— just a second."

"Hold on to *what?*" he called after Etta as she walked away.

The shopkeeper she'd seen a moment before had ducked back into his store, and was now sweeping out the powdery dust and ash that had blown in from the street. She leaned in through the doorway.

"Hello," she said. "I'm sorry to bother you, but I'm wondering if you could help me?"

The man leaned against the handle of his broom, the severe features of his face softening as he returned her smile. Behind him was a long wooden counter, with shelf upon shelf of dark bottles marked with paper labels. Some kind of pharmacy.

"An American?" he ventured. "Not the best time for a visit, I'm afraid. Unless you're the first in a new wave of defenses? Are the Yanks finally jumping in?"

Probably he was joking, but there was a tremor in his voice as he said it, a vulnerability peering through the "business as usual" façade.

"Not yet," she said, trying to keep her voice cheerful. "I think it'll be a while. . . ."

And only after we're directly attacked. But she couldn't tell him that.

Etta felt it then for the first time—the fragility of the past. It was an eerie sensation to be in this shop, with its thousands of glass objects packed in so closely around her, and know that one slight misstep on her part could send them smashing to the ground. Etta doubted that telling this stranger about America's entry into the war, if she presented it as a guess, would be enough to change anything in the timeline. But she wasn't willing to bet that one small change wouldn't send the future she'd known crashing down around her, shattered.

The man knelt to sweep the dust into a bin. "A waiting game, I expect. What can I help you with?"

Out of the corner of her eye, she saw Nicholas watching through the blown-out window frame. "I'm wondering if you could point me in the direction of the British Museum?"

His gray brows rose. "All you've got to do is continue east on this road. Make a left on Dean Street and a right onto Oxford Street, which'll turn into Great Russell Street for you. Doing a bit of sightseeing, then?"

"Yes—I just wasn't sure if I was headed the right way. Thank you so much, you've been a great help."

She had already turned to the door when the man let out a faint laugh. "Miss—come back, miss—I should've told you straightaway. Can't resist a bit of teasing now and then, especially in times like these."

Uh-oh. That tiny bit of excitement was instantly scrubbed out.

"You can go to the museum, but I'm afraid there'll be nothing to see," he said. "They took out everything valuable last summer, and it's been closed ever since."

THE BRITISH MUSEUM WAS CLOSED.

She should have believed the shopkeeper, but it seemed impossible that they could have come all that way only to be met with locked, towering black gates. The somber stone building, with columns and reliefs inspired by ancient times, seemed to fade away the longer they stood there. It taunted them.

And just to put the last nail in the coffin of possibility, Etta took the harmonica out of the bag at Nicholas's side—the harmonica she'd stolen out of Sophia's trunk, seemingly identical to the one Cyrus had used to find the passage in New York—and blew a quick, hard burst of air into it. She strained her ears, trying to lean through the bars of the gate, like that could somehow help her hear a sound that wasn't there.

"Nothing," Nicholas said.

"Nothing," she agreed, placing the instrument back in the bag and cinching it shut with more force than was probably necessary. "Even if the statues themselves were removed, I think I was still hoping the passage would be with them."

"Perhaps we underestimated your mother," he said. "I can't imagine she would have made it so easy for anyone to find."

"A World War isn't enough of a hurdle?" Etta asked, rubbing her hand over her face. "Okay, okay . . . we just have to think this through. . . ."

"I do have an idea, but I'm afraid it's terrible," Nicholas said, surveying the lock on the gate and giving it another hard tug.

"A bad idea is better than no idea," Etta said.

"I'm glad you feel that way, because this is an exquisitely bad one." He turned toward her. "We can go around the back of the museum and I can lift you over the gate. You can then slip into the museum and hold any guards or curators inside hostage, until they give up the information about the location of the statues."

"Hold them hostage?" she repeated.

"Don't you know? That's how real pirates like Blackbeard made most of their money. He ransomed whole cities," he said. "I'll even teach you how to use the revolver."

Despite herself, Etta smiled. "I really appreciate the faith you have in my criminal abilities. But even if I find someone in there, I doubt they'll be good for anything other than calling the police to pick me up. It seems like the kind of information people would do anything to protect."

He leaned against one of the black bars. "Would they really have taken out a whole hoard of valuable items?"

She gestured to the streets around them—the pockets of rubble, the burned-out husks of buildings that were missing entire sections. "If they thought there was a chance that they might be destroyed or looted, then yes. I know you said you don't really want to know about these things, but—Germany invades France and occupies Paris for most of the war. France does the same thing with the paintings and sculptures at the Louvre—the curators and volunteers bring them out to different hiding spots in the countryside, which saves them in the end."

"When I first learned of this war, I believed Julian was trying to make a joke of me," he admitted.

She nodded. "Well, it's a good thing the museum thought ahead. One bomb, and thousands of years of art and culture could have been lost."

A humming buzz overhead drew their gaze. Two planes— fighter planes, by the looks of them—made a pass, their long shadows sweeping over them. Nicholas stiffened beside her, and before she could ask what was wrong, he was already chasing them down the sidewalk, his gaze fixed on them with a wonder that made Etta's chest ache. She stayed close on his heels, drinking in his wide eyes, the faint smile, until finally the planes disappeared into the horizon.

"Flying," Nicholas muttered under his breath, as if still in disbelief. "It shouldn't surprise me that men continue to think of grand new ways to kill one another, and with greater precision, but . . ." He shook his head. "If we take this to mean the statues aren't here, is it worth finding them? Or is it a matter of taking another look at the clue and coming up with a better guess?"

"I felt so good about this," Etta said, sounding as stubborn as she felt. "I think we're on the right track. This is just a little setback. We'll figure it out."

Nicholas snorted. "Little?"

Etta turned back, studying the spread of steps leading up to the entrance of the museum. It was eerie to see it so deserted.

Clouds of pigeons and birds ambled around the courtyard like they were wishing each other a pleasant afternoon. *What are you trying to tell me, Mom? Is there something I'm supposed to see here?*

"Hey, this ship hasn't sunk yet," she said, tearing her gaze away from the museum. "We may have one sail, but we're still going."

Another laugh. "I appreciate the metaphor you chose on my behalf. I'm not sure how you can keep this . . . sensibility about you. I suppose when you're worried, that's when I'll know we're in real danger—"

Etta had seen the young, stylish couple making their way down the sidewalk toward them, the woman's coat a bright pop of red against the charred surroundings. The man's face was hidden beneath the rim of his hat, but he tilted his face up as they approached. Nicholas stepped closer to the gate to let them pass. The man assessed him coolly, before muttering something to the woman at his side as they passed by.

"Can we leave this place, please?" Nicholas said, teeth clenched. "If there's nothing here, I think that we should go."

But . . . he'd just been talking about hopping the fence. "What's wrong?"

"Nothing," he said. "Please, let's leave."

She looked around, trying to find the source of his concern, but aside from a few men and women standing on the other side of the street, she couldn't see anything that should have triggered that kind of reaction—aside from the obvious discomfort of being in a strange place, in a stranger time.

"All right," she said, putting a hand on his back. He tore away from the touch, and every inch of Etta's skin stung with embarrassment.

Etta trailed behind him as he walked back in the direction they'd come from. She didn't really think he had a destination in mind; he barely looked up, except to acknowledge the flow of traffic. It wasn't until she got caught on the opposite sidewalk, waiting for a stream of cars to pass, that he finally stopped and whirled around.

And as sharp as his anger had been, his relief was soft, palpable, as he waited for her. Etta hurried to his side, but he still didn't move; his throat worked as he swallowed.

"You don't have to explain," she said. "Everything about this is hard."

"It's not that," he said, his whole face tight with strain as he eyed the street. "It's only . . . you resign yourself to a certain invisibility, when . . . when you look as I do. I didn't expect the opposite to be true in this time, and I find I don't like the attention. The looks."

You idiot, Etta told herself. What a privilege it was to never feel like you had to take stock of your surroundings, or gauge everyone's reactions to the color of your skin. Of course he felt uncomfortable. *Of course.* And if he'd never been to this time before, he wouldn't be able to predict people's reactions.

"I don't mean to be so . . . irritable," he muttered. When he looked at her again, his eyes weren't as wild as they'd been before. "But I cannot be what I'm not."

"I wouldn't want you to be anyone but yourself. I'm glad you told me," Etta said. "I want to understand how you feel."

Something she said made him pull back again. He opened his mouth and Etta knew what was coming, the way he would try to wedge more space between them.

"Miss—"

"Don't you dare call me Miss Spencer," she warned. "It kills me when you act like we aren't even friends."

"We *aren't* friends," he said, and she couldn't help it—she flinched. One of them had clearly misunderstood whatever was between them. Apparently, it had been her.

Etta charged away from him down the sidewalk. He caught up to her in three long strides and took her arm in his hand, forcing her to stop. She couldn't bring herself to look up; she only waited for Nicholas to speak.

"I forget myself with you," he said roughly. "I forget the rules. I forget every other living soul in this world. Do you understand?"

We are not friends.

Because, to him, they were . . .

Her heart threw itself at her rib cage, hard enough that, for a moment, she couldn't breathe. "I don't care about rules or anyone else. People are awful—they're idiots—and if they try to hurt you, I won't need the revolver. I care about you, and all I ask is that you try not to make me feel like an idiot for it. You're supposed to . . ." She clenched her hands to keep from gripping his shoulders. "You're my partner."

Etta risked a glance up, meeting his eyes. That same flush crept up her throat, washing over her cheeks. Her hands hovered above the warm, smooth skin of his strong forearms, and for a moment she wondered what it would be like to touch him there, to ease some softness into the rigid lines.

Stop it. She knew herself well enough to know that if she kept looking, if she leaned forward like she wanted to, rocked up onto her toes, and he pulled away again . . . this *partner* thing would get very complicated, very quickly. And Etta couldn't think of that now. She couldn't think of his jawline, the scars and nicks in his skin, his lips as they parted, the way the fabric of his shirt would feel between her fingers. . . .

Home, she reminded herself, even as her own skin came alive, prickling and sensitive to the cool autumn air.

"Okay," she said, crossing her arms over her chest, looking back in the direction of the museum. "Glad that's settled. Back to business."

Nicholas raised a brow. "Hardly, but I take your point."

The afternoon was creeping on, and they needed every hour of the day. She didn't want to try to imagine where they would have to sleep if they were caught here another day, and she also didn't want to think about how easy it would have been to find out the statues' location by plugging it into a search engine. Or even just asking Alice, who had always given the Internet a run for its money in her breadth of knowledge and speed of recall.

The thought of Alice gripped her, pinned her in place with a weight she couldn't fully shake off. *Think, think, think.* . . . She should know this. She must know it—she'd felt something looking past the gates to the solemn museum, a flutter of awareness. . . .

But when Etta closed her eyes, trying to picture the empty courtyard, what she saw wasn't the deserted steps or daunting locks. Instead, she was on her back, on the couch in her living room at home, looking up at her mother's paintings on the wall. The third one down, square in the middle, was of this very same scene. Birds scattering as a younger Alice walked through them.

The answer seemed to drift down from the sky like a lone feather, landing right on top of her head.

No, she thought, *no . . .*

It couldn't be that simple.

The clue was most likely about the Elgin Marbles, as they'd

thought. But to find them, to find the passage, she'd need to do what she and her mother always did when they needed something explained: ask Alice.

Alice, who had grown up in London during the war.

Alice, whose father was a curator at the British Museum.

Alice, who had shown them the house she'd grown up in at least three times.

She turned toward Nicholas, trying to steel herself to tell him without going to pieces, but his gaze was fixed across the street, where a man in a trench coat and hat stood leaning against a gleaming mailbox. There was a folded newspaper in his hands, but he didn't seem to be reading it.

"What's wrong?" she whispered, watching Nicholas's shoulders grow rigid.

"Start walking," he said, voice low. "We need to keep moving."

"I know where we have to go," she told him. "Just follow me."

Etta wasn't sure when she noticed it, when the suspicion curling at her neck like a stray strand of hair became strong enough to force her to look back over her shoulder. The man with the trench coat was matching their pace. A woman in a rich brown suit drifted in and out of sight, but always reappeared.

Nicholas nodded, giving her the last confirmation. They were being followed.

Etta took in the street around them, searching for a place where they could talk, when a burst of familiar red caught her eye. Without stopping to explain herself, she lifted an arm and waved, flagging the bus down.

"Etta—"

The driver waved back in acknowledgment as she rushed

to his window. The scrape of Nicholas's hurried steps trailed behind her.

"What is this madness?" he asked, his teeth gritted.

The window rattled open. "Entrance's at the rear—" the driver began.

"Does this bus cut through Kensington?" Etta asked.

The bus driver was an older gentleman, his belly almost large enough to touch the wheel. But he had an open face and a friendly smile. "It does indeed, love. I've got no official stops, though. The conductor will be able to tell you how much you owe. You just give me a smile and a wave and I'll let you off."

The entrance to the bus was open, at the vehicle's right rear. Etta hauled herself up using the pole, and, after an uneasy look, Nicholas followed.

Etta should have pulled him into the nearest seat and just sat. Instead, she tried to move them toward the front, where the driver would have a better view of her, and she would have a better view of the road. But she'd forgotten that while she had seventeen years of bus-riding experience, Nicholas had none. The moment the bus pulled back into traffic, he swayed drunkenly, nearly taking out a little boy and an older woman with a bag of groceries.

"Excuse us," she said, gripping his arm and dragging him upright. She nodded to the supports hanging from the ceiling. "Grab those—just go slow."

Getting to the front of the bus was a sluggish, lurching process, even for someone used to the heaving decks of ships. Nicholas collapsed onto the seat, a river of sweat working its way down the side of his face. One hand clenched the back of the seat, the other her knee.

"My God," he shouted over the roar of the engine. "What is that smell?"

A man in uniform, likely the conductor the driver had mentioned, came down the stairs from the upper level. He had a kind of rack hanging around his neck, with small, brightly colored tickets held in place by small springs. "That would be the petrol, lad."

Nicholas gave Etta a look of utter betrayal. "Will we suffocate before we arrive?"

The conductor shook his head, laughing. Etta forced herself to laugh, too, flashing Nicholas a warning look. But he'd clearly recognized his mistake—he pressed a hand to his forehead and sighed at his own slip. "Destination?"

"Kensington," said Etta.

"Two pennies each."

To her surprise, Nicholas dug into his bag and turned over what looked to be actual copper coins, not the gold she'd expected to barter with. The man dutifully dispensed their tickets and moved on to the other new passengers.

"Exchanged the gold and some of my payment," he explained. "We've enough to get by."

"But that was your payment for bringing Sophia and me to New York," she said, guilt slicing through her.

He waved a hand, dismissing this. "Focus your concern on the guardians who've already managed to track us here."

"The man with the newspaper was definitely a guardian?" she pressed, somehow already knowing the answer. "Are you sure?"

"I've never been to this year," he said in a low voice. "I haven't met the Ironwood guardians who call it their home, but what other reason could he and that woman—the one in the brown suit, did you see her? What reason could they have for tracking us?"

It seemed so unfair that Ironwood's guardians had already found them. Etta sighed, leaning her forehead against the seat in front of them. So much for getting ahead and keeping her movements and travels quiet from the old man.

He leaned forward to rest his elbows on his knees, and dragged his hands back over his closely cropped hair. "He has guardians watching every known passage. They likely were following us for longer than we even realized. They have to be Ironwood's."

Her brain had been so cluttered with shock, and foggy from traveler's sickness, that she hadn't even thought about Cyrus's reaction to finding them gone. "How much trouble are we in?" Etta asked quietly.

"Unfortunately, if Ironwood wants us brought in for acting without his permission, a world of it. We'll be held in one of the Ironwood properties in this time to await the old man and whatever punishment he decides to mete out—and he isn't renowned for his forgiveness." Nicholas let a rough smile break through the tension on his face. "Fortunately, however, he doesn't yet know we pirates are damned hard to capture."

THE LAST TIME ETTA HAD SEEN THE HOUSE WAS FIVE YEARS AGO, over seventy years in the future.

It had been freezing; the kind of day that switched from rain to sleet every other second, where water seemed to be coming at you from all sides. The last time she'd seen this flat-roofed, three-story beige brick house—this green door with its gold lion-shaped knocker—had been through a rental car window. Etta had been tired and annoyed and cold, pretending to be asleep to end the tour a little faster.

She could have smacked twelve-year-old Etta, because the longer they stood in front of the house's gate, the less sure she was that they'd found the right one. She was definitely not sure that she wanted to ring the bell, at any rate.

"You said you'd been here before," Nicholas reminded her. "If your instincts are telling you this is the place, I believe it."

If her mother and Alice had brought her here three times, then they wanted her to remember it. How to find it.

But Alice . . .

"Will you be all right?" he asked quietly. "I can speak to her if it feels unbearable."

The house faced Kensington Square, a short walk south from the palace and gardens. The neighborhood was quiet, beautiful— nearly untouched by war. The midafternoon sun disappeared as the sky grayed over with clouds, but the trees in the park stood out in flaming contrast, all gold and red. Men worked nearby, pulling up some of the fences and railings, collecting them in piles to be carted away. Here and there were small gardens—including one in front of the green door.

Etta shook her head. She was grateful for the offer, but if he was right, and she really couldn't save Alice, then . . . *This is my last chance to see her.* The thought broke something wide open in her.

Nicholas opened the gate and gestured for her to enter. Etta set her shoulders back, stomach flipping between excitement and dread. Then she lifted the knocker and pounded out three sharp knocks.

For a terrible second, Etta thought no one was home. She leaned forward, her ear against the wood, when she heard a girl cry, "Just a moment!" and the sound of feet on the stairs. Etta stepped back. Something scraped—the peephole cover, maybe? She glanced at Nicholas, who stood at the base of the steps with one hand on his bag. There was an audible gasp, a cry, as the door flew open.

"Rosie? But what are you doing—"

Etta drank down the sight of her in one long gulp.

The girl's long, auburn hair was loose around her shoulders, her face shaded by a green felt hat. The collar of her grayish-green dress had been unbuttoned down to the spot where a white patch was placed over the pocket on her chest, its red letters reading WVS CIVIL DEFENCE.

She was so young. Unbelievably young. Alice had freckles, a whole galaxy of them spread across her nose and cheekbones. Etta had seen pictures . . . but . . . but this Alice hadn't yet lost the baby fat from her round face. It was her eyes that Etta instantly recognized—that pale gray she knew so well. Etta's whole body seemed to seize, her voice too thick to speak, and she had to cross her arms over her chest to keep from throwing them around her.

"You're not Rose," said Alice slowly, gripping the door as if prepared to slam it shut.

"No," Etta said, reaching out to keep the door open. "I'm not."

TWELVE

"I haven't any tea to offer you, but there's no milk or sugar for it anyway. Rationing and such. Very sorry."

Alice led them into the front parlor of the house, motioning for Nicholas and Etta to sit on a stiff, overstuffed Victorian couch. She disappeared for a moment, but rather than let her vanish completely, Etta leaned into the hall to track her progress. She returned with glasses of water and a few crackers.

"Everything all right?" Alice asked her.

Etta forced her eyes away from her and onto the painting hanging over the fireplace—an impressionist's take on a field of red poppies—and let a smile curve across her lips. It was like seeing another old friend. The thing had traveled, complete in its ornate gold frame, across the Atlantic to Alice and Oskar's apartment on the Upper East Side. But that wouldn't take place for another ten years.

Sheet music was piled neatly on top of a closed piano, and tucked beneath its gleaming wooden body was a small music stand and a violin case—Alice's violin case—containing the violin that Etta would, decades later, hold and practice on for hours every single day. She'd forgotten this, that the war had forced Alice's lessons to come to a halt; she'd only begun playing professionally in her twenties, after she grew restless with London.

"You'll have to excuse me for being rude," Alice said, sitting in a leather chair across from her. "But I've got to be off to my shift in a few minutes."

"That's okay," Etta said, her voice thick with the need to cry. All those things she'd said to her at the Met before the concert . . .

Some things never changed; including, apparently, the way Alice's face softened in sympathy.

"I just have a few questions," Etta continued. "If that's okay with you?"

"About Rosie?" she asked, studying Etta as closely as Etta was studying her. "I'm afraid you're out of luck. I haven't seen her in years."

Etta shifted uncomfortably in her seat at Alice's firm tone. Up until now, Etta had been convinced the coolness she'd detected from her had been mere wary politeness. Now she recognized it for what it was: outright suspicion. Etta's appearance, so close to her mother's, must have caught Alice completely off guard at the door.

She's not going to tell us anything. Did she actually *know* anything at this point in time?

"Were you . . . are you close to her?" Etta asked.

"Hardly," Alice said, and Etta knew it had to be a lie, just based on how she'd opened the door. "We went to school together until the professor—her grandfather—passed. She disappeared on and off, ran with a certain crowd, but she stayed with us occasionally. As I said before, I haven't seen her in years."

Etta shifted in her seat, drawing a look of concern from

Nicholas, who'd been studying his water for the entire duration of the conversation, as if he couldn't quite believe there wasn't dirt swimming in it.

"I don't mean to be rude," Alice said again, this time with more steel in her tone, "but who are you, and why are you here?"

Might as well have it out than keep burning time. "My name is Etta. I'm her daughter."

Nicholas sprayed the water he'd just taken a sip of, subsequently pounding his chest and choking on what he'd managed to swallow. He spun toward her in disbelief.

"Daughter?" Alice said, her voice changing completely. She was practically chirping. "That's wonderful! My goodness. You look so much alike it's startling. I should have known. Etta—is that short for something? What century were you born in? It's *so* confusing to meet out of order, you know."

A flood of confusing, conflicting emotions—anger, excitement, hope, frustration—swept through Etta, and it took her a second to catch her breath and process this.

"Henrietta," Etta said. "And this is Nicholas Carter."

"Your servant, ma'am," Nicholas said with a nod. He put a steadying hand on Etta's shoulder and kept her firmly in place. Etta was grateful, as she felt she was about to float up out of her skin.

"But, darling, who's your father?" Alice asked. "Henrietta . . . is it . . . is it possibly Henry?"

Etta felt the world bottom out for the second time in less than a minute. "Henry?" she whispered.

"Etta doesn't know her father," Nicholas explained. "I'm afraid the situation is rather complicated."

He did the best that he could to explain what had brought

them both to her doorstep—a far better job than Etta would have managed with the thousands of thoughts rattling around her head. She watched Alice's expression transform again, from horror to amazement to something that looked like genuine fear.

"Then you're like us?" Etta asked. "I'm not even sure where to start with my questions."

"I wish!" Alice let out a faint laugh, looking as overcome as Etta felt. "Professor Linden—your great-grandfather—was cousin to my father, a great friend and mentor. Neither he nor I inherited the ability from the Linden side of our family."

"A guardian, then?" Nicholas confirmed.

Etta sat back, stunned. In her heart, Alice had always been the grandmother she'd never had. Love had been enough to sustain that feeling, even knowing there wasn't a drop of shared blood between them. But apparently they were from the same family; distantly, maybe, but both Lindens all the same.

Alice had aged like anyone else. And when Etta's mother had escaped Ironwood, Alice had gone to find her. Etta felt the tears prick her eyes again, swamped with the now-familiar guilt, the frustration of knowing the truth too late.

Alice protected us. She was a guardian in every sense of the word.

"They had quite the little game going," Alice continued. "The professor would 'happen upon' some relic and use my father to bring it into the museum. It was very hush-hush, of course." She lifted a chain from under her plain uniform dress, showing them the coin hanging from it. "Rose brought this back from a holiday in Greece. Greece before Christ."

"How did she end up with the Ironwoods?" Nicholas asked.

"The professor worked very hard to keep her away from the

other families, especially them," Alice explained. "I'm sure you know, but they were at war with one another over who should be making the laws for the families—and then it was all about revenge for the natural times that were rewritten and the loved ones murdered. The professor always said that the traveler lines were on the verge of destroying themselves. As the last two living Lindens, they simply hid, rather than take sides. Once Ironwood's control over traveling was secured, and the professor passed away . . . Rose spent some time with a group that banded together to travel. They called themselves refugees?"

Nicholas set his empty glass down on the side table with a bit too much force. "Refugees, you said?"

Alice nodded.

"I've heard of a group like that," Nicholas explained, giving Etta a sidelong glance. "Refugees, to us, are people who, after the timeline is changed, find themselves without a home to return to. I might have been prevented from leaving my time—exiled to it—but they lost their natural times. The years they were born to, the ones they had grown and thrived in, were lost."

"Sophia mentioned that," Etta said. "That when the timeline changes and a traveler's natural time is affected by a big enough shift, they don't cease to exist, but everything and everyone they'd known might be lost."

"Precisely. It happened constantly during the war between the families. The timeline became so unstable, so unpredictable, that many began to fear what might happen if it continued. Some of the remnants from the Jacaranda and Hemlock families eventually came to Ironwood and pledged their service and allegiance. But there was a group that dogged him for years, trying to sabotage his business holdings and retaliate on behalf of their dead loved ones . . . *Thorns.* That's what Ironwood calls them. They're constantly trying to create snags in the timeline that will restore their futures. That's a dangerous group for your mother to have aligned with."

"The old man made it sound like she'd purposefully infiltrated the family and manipulated them. . . ." Etta trailed off, looking at him. "Is it possible that they were also trying to find the astrolabe and knew he wanted it, or that he was on its trail?"

"That's a logical assumption." Nicholas rubbed at his chin. "Perhaps they know where it's hidden, too? Only . . . it seems the sort of thing they'd wish to use."

The thought settled between the three of them, as heavy as a thundercloud. Etta braced herself for thunder, for the lightning bolt of dread.

"It's been a pleasure to meet you, but . . ." Alice stood suddenly, gathering up the water glasses. "I'm sorry, I've really got to be going."

Etta studied the girl, recognizing the evasion for what it was. "What do you know about the astrolabe?"

"Nothing," Alice said, keeping her back to them. "I'm sorry. I don't know anything about it."

Not yet, not yet, please not yet. Etta felt almost desperate with panic. *You can't go yet.*

"I'm just trying to get back to *Rosie,*" she tried. "I think this is the only way. If I find the astrolabe, I'll find her. Please . . . whatever you know, however small, could help us."

"You may be her daughter, but it feels like such . . . like such a betrayal," Alice said, her voice small. "She didn't want anyone to find it, least of all the Ironwoods."

"Why?" Etta asked. Nicholas crossed and uncrossed his legs,

as if suddenly unable to settle himself in a comfortable position. "At least tell me that."

"She thought—God forgive me, she thought they'd use it for their own ends. That they'd damage the world irrevocably for their own gain," Alice said. "It's a family heirloom. It *did* belong to us, for whatever that's worth, and we debated for years over what to do with it—to let it remain where the professor's father hid it, or to move it. It was supposed to stay lost, but then Ironwood, somehow, started to get close. Rose didn't remove it from its original hiding spot until he'd nearly found it. She and the professor should have just destroyed it, but they couldn't bring themselves to do it. History is too important to them."

Alice set the small porcelain figurine of a tiger she'd been fussing with back down on the fireplace mantelpiece, continuing. "Ironwood thought she'd be stupid enough to trick and use; and now I suppose he's trying the same with you."

Etta shook her head. "I won't let him have it. I'm just trying to get home, back to her, and—back to you."

She turned slowly. "Me?"

"Yes," Etta said, standing up and crossing the room. "She travels to the future, and you're there to help both her and me. You live in New York. There's a really handsome Polish violinist in your future—"

Alice held up her hands, stopping her. "Don't tell me any more. I mean it. I can see in your face that there's something you want to tell me, but you can't—I might not be able to alter the timeline, but *you* can, just by *telling* me. And I'm starting to find this story rather convenient."

Etta looked around the room again, trying to find some proof that she knew Alice—the future Alice. Her eyes landed on the painting. "I know you bought this painting while you were walking along the Seine. You bought it because someone wrote a beautiful poem in French on the back. And I know your father loathes it, and you actually bolted it to the wall to keep him from taking it down."

Alice reached up, pressing her fingers against the bottom of the frame. It didn't budge. She turned back to them, shaking her head. "I want to help you, but . . . she's protected me for so long, I feel that it's my turn to do the same."

It was so Alice. This woman had guarded them over the years like a lioness defending her cubs. It made Etta want to hug her that much more, even as Nicholas tensed beside her, frustration plain on his face.

"I'm not interested in changing the future—her future," Etta said. "For one thing, it would completely change my life. There is no way I'm letting Ironwood have access to my time, either."

The couch squeaked as Nicholas stood and made his way to the window. He crossed his arms over his chest and surveyed the people passing on the sidewalk below.

"All right," Alice said, wringing her hands red. "I don't know anything about where it is. I'm sorry, but . . . I suppose . . . I suppose it wouldn't hurt to tell you that it's the last of four. Long ago, each family had one. Three of them were either lost or destroyed by rivals in the other families."

So, it was exactly as Nicholas—and Julian—had thought.

"This one is the last of its kind," Alice said, "which is a blessing, considering what it's capable of."

"Reading passages, you mean?" Etta clarified.

Alice blinked. "No. *Creating* passages."

"Creating them?" Etta asked, looking back toward Nicholas

271

just as his gaze shot over to hers. Her own shock was reflected on his face. That couldn't be right—

"Yes," Alice said, eyes wide as she realized neither of them knew this. "My impression is that many of the passages are becoming unstable or collapsing because of traveler deaths, and—well, old age. As Rose explained it, what Ironwood and his rivals—the Thorns, as you called them—what they want is to gain access to years that have been closed to them, and affect events there. Whoever controls the astrolabe could potentially control the whole of time."

Oh my God, thought Etta. No wonder Ironwood had been willing to sacrifice his sons and grandson in the search for it. This was the ultimate prize. The trump card of travelers. If his control wasn't already complete, it would be once he had it in hand. All people, in all ages, could be affected by whatever Ironwood had planned.

Did this mean that the passages weren't a natural phenomenon that travelers had found and tentatively stepped through centuries ago? They'd been made by the ancestors of these families for their personal use? No wonder there were years without passages, and that so many passages were uncharted; they must have predated when the families began to record the destinations, or they had simply been forgotten altogether.

Or, some passages were secret, created for one particular family's use alone.

"How do the Thorns fit into this?" Nicholas asked.

The notes of the symphony of lives, desires, and revenge suddenly swelled into a chorus of generations, blasting through Etta's mind. She already knew the answer to his question. "They're united in wanting to create passages to the past, to return to what they all see as the original timeline, to restore the centuries and years that orphaned them when Ironwood began to bend the timeline to suit his needs."

Which wouldn't be the future she had grown up in: days in the park, lessons with Alice, tea with her mom . . . For a moment, Etta wasn't sure which was more terrifying: if Ironwood moved forward into the future, or if the Thorns interfered with the past.

"And those who were lost to them," Alice added. "To save them."

The way I want to save you. Etta pressed her fingers against her mouth, trying to seal in the whirlwind of sudden uncertainty whipping through her. *How is what I want to do any different than what they want to do? Why does Alice deserve to live more than their loved ones?*

No—she couldn't think about it. Alice deserved to live. She didn't deserve to die, not the way she had.

"They wouldn't dare," Nicholas said. She could tell he was trying to avoid looking at her, even as he added, "We cannot save the dead. We cannot even warn them, should we cross paths with them."

"Only if you follow the rules," Alice pointed out. "The rules Ironwood established when he rose to power. He destroyed everything, including our way of life."

More secrets. More to agonize over. More reasons to find the astrolabe as soon as they possibly could. Etta rubbed at the spot between her eyes that had begun to pound in time with her heart. *Just keep going.* Stopping to think about this too hard would only keep her locked in a cycle of doubt, and she couldn't afford to be overwhelmed just then. She needed to take things as they came. Her plan would stay the same: Find the astrolabe. Save her mom. Save Alice. Escape Ironwood if they had to.

"I wish it could be the way it was, back when the families flourished and balanced out each other's powers," Alice said. "The professor and my father used to talk about it very wistfully. Each family had a proper role, and they alternated them every few decades to ensure no family undermined another and the timeline remained stable."

"What kind of roles?" Etta asked, curious.

"Record-keepers, financiers, and shifters—that last one entailed correcting any changes to the timeline and checking on the stability of the passages themselves," Alice explained. "And, of course, one family would hold trials and enforce punishments for breaking the rules—the enforcers."

"That was ages ago," Nicholas said dismissively. "Corruption unraveled it rather neatly. My understanding is that it only worked well for a few hundred years, back when the 'families' were still mere alliances and clans."

"Alliances?" Etta repeated. "What do you mean?"

"Did your mother never tell you about our own history?" Alice asked.

She shook her head, trying to beat back the frustration. "It's . . . complicated."

"Ah, well," Alice said. "No bother. While it's generally accepted we all come from a common ancestor with the ability, the families today originally existed as alliances between many separate families that united together under banners—the trees we now use as our family names—against their rivals and enemies. That was another time of huge conflict; everyone was trying to claim centuries and territories to control. It was mostly resolved through treaties and the establishment of the system of roles and laws. You can still see the evidence of how widespread their numbers used to be in the diversity within the remaining members of the families today."

Nicholas flicked his gaze back onto the street below. He shifted again, and now all Etta could see was the long curve of his spine, the strong width of his shoulders, and his left fingers as they tapped against the muscle of his right arm.

"Enough history; it hardly matters now. Ask her the question that brought us here," he said, a note of impatience in his voice.

Etta turned to Alice with an apologetic look, but she didn't seem bothered.

"Mom left me a series of clues to find it," she said. "In a coded letter."

"A letter that can only be read when a key—a symbol—is placed over it, showing which words are meant to be read?" Alice said with a knowing smile. "We all used to exchange messages that way."

Etta felt the hair rise on her arms. It was a connection, how-ever thin, to a larger family she'd never known. "We think the next riddle—the clue—is meant to lead us to a passage near the Elgin Marbles, but we're not sure where to find them in this year. I thought you might know, since your father works for the museum . . . ?"

"Can you answer one thing for me first?" Alice said. "How did you know to come to this house? Did you look up the address? Ask around?"

"I didn't need to," Etta said. "You and Mom brought me by a few times. You said it was very special—that it was important for me to see where you'd grown up."

Alice sighed, sounding almost relieved. "Then both of us wanted you to be able to find me. That's good. They—we, I mean, we must have known something like this might happen."

The fact was cemented in her now. None of this was a coincidence. Alice, her Alice in the future, had met Etta in the past. She'd known her as nearly an adult before she'd ever met the small wisp of a girl clutching her child-size violin. This was the reason she and Rose had fought—because Alice knew Etta would come here, because she'd already lived through it.

The thought of their inevitability in each other's lives burrowed deep into her heart, past the hardened shell she'd put up to keep herself together.

"The museum and government have taken the Marbles underground," Alice said. "They're tucked away in the Underground, in the tunnel between the Aldwych and Holborn stations. It's not exactly near where I report to work, but I can at least point you in the right direction."

"Will we have access to the tunnel?" Etta asked.

"Both stations are being used as shelters during the air raids," Alice explained. "You'll need to find an opportunity when the stations aren't being watched by police, but you should be able to climb down from the platform and walk through the tunnel. The Marbles will be in crates, but they're obvious enough by their size."

Etta nodded, processing this.

"Is there a back entrance out of your home?" Nicholas asked suddenly, drawing the curtain shut in front of him.

"Well, yes," Alice said, rising slowly. "Why?"

"Two gentlemen in the street are watching this house," he said. "Unless they're interested in painting it, I think it's a fair assumption that we've been found."

THROUGH THE BACK DOOR, THROUGH THE BACK GARDEN, through a gate that opened out onto a street. Etta had one second to celebrate their narrow escape, when the man she'd seen before—the one with the fedora and newspaper—appeared at the other end of the street.

"I know him," Alice said, grabbing her wrist.

"One of Ironwood's?" Etta asked.

She shook her head. "No . . . I don't think so. Rosie left me photos to identify them. This one's definitely come round looking for her before, though."

Not an Ironwood guardian . . . then who the hell was he?

The girls struggled to keep pace with Nicholas's longer strides. He kept one hand buried deep in his bag—if Etta had to guess, it was on the revolver inside. Whether or not he'd actually bought ammunition was anyone's guess, but Etta had a feeling that the answer was—

She slammed into something, and felt herself ripped away from Alice's grip. One of Etta's feet caught the other and she landed hard on her bottom, her scraped hands singing in agony. When the spots of black cleared from her eyes, Etta saw a woman, the one in the brown suit, reeling and clutching her nose. Just past her shoulder, Nicholas wheeled around, his face blank with horror.

A pair of hands scooped Etta up by the elbows, hauling her back before she could get her feet beneath her. The smell of cologne and sweat flooded her nose, and she threw her head back, trying to hit some soft, fleshy part of him.

"Rose," the man gasped out, "Rose, damn you—"

Rose?

A pale fist flew past her face, landing on the man's jaw. Alice's face was glowing red with fury as she shook her hand out, but it was Nicholas who charged past her and tackled the man to the ground. Etta finally had a look at him: horn-rimmed glasses, a mussed tweed suit. It was a different man than the one who'd carried the paper. Younger.

"I'm not—" he gasped as Nicholas hauled him up with a snarl and launched a fist into his face. "Not—"

Not what? Etta looked to Alice for an answer, but the girl only shrugged and shoved aside the woman in brown, who was still moaning in pain.

"Come on, Carter!" Alice called. "Keep moving!"

He didn't move, except to raise his fist again.

"Nicholas!" Etta called. "Come on!"

He finally shook himself out of his anger's grip, dropped the battered man back onto the sidewalk, and ran to catch up to them.

"Are you all right?" He tried to reach over, but Etta only ran harder, toward the crowds gathering in front of them and the cars honking to get through.

No time. Just run. Run.

Her breath burned inside her chest as they pushed through the busy city, dodging through street after street of homes and shops until, after nearly twenty minutes, they reached their destination. Over their heads was a rainbow array of glowing advertising signs and lights—LEMON HART, BP, SCHWEPPES—and, at the center of a traffic circle, a statue of Eros watched the slow crawl of double-decker buses and police cars. Even without the

278

modern billboards, Etta recognized the intersection. They'd run the whole way to Piccadilly Circus, and her blisters and cramping legs and feet were proof of it.

Alice looked around, her face pink and gleaming with sweat despite the chill in the air. "I can't take you all the way there, I'm sorry—I can't miss my shift. There are people depending on me. I wish I could—"

Etta swallowed the small, selfish pang of desperation to keep Alice close, and said, "That's okay. Thank you for getting us this far. Is the Underground station much farther?"

"It's another twenty-minute walk from here," Alice said. "I can give you money for a taxi—"

"It'll be easier to lose them on foot," Nicholas said. "Thank you. Where do we go from here?"

Using the back of her mother's letter and a ballpoint pen, Etta had Alice quickly write out the remainder of the instructions. *Head east as the road turns from Piccadilly Circus to Swiss Court, to Cranbourn Street to Carrick, up King Street past St. Paul's Cathedral, back down to Russell, right on Catherine Street once you pass the Royal Opera House. . . .* All at once, Etta missed her phone and satellites and the luxury of never having to feel lost.

"Be safe," Alice said, throwing her arms around her.

The faint anxiety that prickled over Etta's skin sparked into paralyzing dread. *No time. No time for this, but—*

"We must go. . . ." she heard Nicholas say gently, in warning.

She pulled back with a bone-deep reluctance, an aching hollowness at the pit of her stomach. *What you're speaking of isn't a matter of morality. It's an impossibility.*

What would change—what *could* change if she warned Alice now? The thought gnawed on her; it would be a small ripple, wouldn't it? A small change in an enormous sea of moments. If she couldn't travel back to her time and pull Alice to safety without crossing paths with herself, she could at least do this. She could rewrite that moment, the pale terror of her instructor's face, the blood. . . .

"Alice—"

"No, no, none of that," Alice interrupted. "No tears, no secrets. I want the life I'm meant to have, Etta. It's as simple as that. My father always says that the way to truly live is to do so without expectation or fear hanging over you, affecting your choices—and that's bloody hard to do with you travelers coming and going. I want to know you the way you know me one day. I want to play my violin, make my mistakes, fall in love, live in as many different cities as I can. . . . Would you really take that from me?"

Etta couldn't breathe; her hands were curling and uncurling at her side, and she was trembling with the effort to keep from sobbing. She glanced at Nicholas, who had turned his head to survey the crowd and was politely pretending he wasn't listening. Finally she shook her head.

"We're called 'guardians' because we're meant to take care of *you* lot, as you take care of our world. And Etta, don't forget—the truly remarkable thing about your life is that you're not bound to live it straight forward like the rest of us. You can come see me for a visit anytime. It's like how the song goes: *I'll be seeing you, in all the old familiar places.* . . ."

Etta pulled back, half-stunned to hear those words again. She watched Alice wave and step into the rush of bodies around them, until even the flash of her bright hair dimmed and disappeared completely.

"—Etta? Are you all right?" She didn't realize Nicholas was

speaking to her until he reached over, brushing a thumb over her unhurt cheek.

"She said that before . . . the last time I saw her, just before . . ." Before she died. She needed to say it. She needed to *accept* it, because it was clear to her now, so agonizingly clear, that Alice remembered this meeting. She knew Etta would try to tell her about what would happen to her, and she, in her very Alice way, wanted to let her know what she had said in the past was true. She didn't want to know. She didn't want to change the life she'd lived with Etta up to that point.

But Alice had loved her enough to still fight to keep her from having to travel, or at least travel without knowing the truth. Maybe that's why her mom had been so firmly against telling Etta; she could be unsentimental when Alice and Etta couldn't.

"She doesn't want me to save her." Etta wiped at her eyes, surprised to feel the wet tracks of tears dripping down off her chin. "Sorry . . . I'm just . . . a little overwhelmed. And tired."

All I wanted was to save you. What was she even going back to now? Was there a point to performing in any kind of debut, having any kind of career, if Alice couldn't see it?

She knew Alice had been in what Rose called the "twilight years" of her life—she'd lived a long time, and even as a young student, Etta had understood that she wouldn't be around forever. But she couldn't reconcile herself with this. She couldn't understand how any of this was fair.

I'll see her again, she thought. *Not in my time, and maybe not even soon, but one day . . .*

"There's nothing to apologize for. We'll rest as soon as it's safe, but we do need to keep moving," Nicholas said.

Etta nodded and followed.

The line of his body was rigid, poised to strike. Sharp, cutting dark eyes assessed each person who passed them. Now and then he rubbed at the broken skin on his bruised knuckles, and she knew that while she was thinking about Alice, his thoughts were locked on what had happened behind the house. She reached over to brush her fingers over the back of his hand, trying to break him out of what looked like a vicious cycle of thoughts. They'd already lost a day trying to solve this clue; they couldn't waste a second more on regrets.

Etta began walking faster, nearly at a jog, but he kept up easily with his long strides. Sweeping her gaze around the street, she tried to identify the source of the uneasiness rippling down the back of her neck.

"What do you think the man who grabbed me was going to say—he wasn't a *what*?" she asked. "An enemy? An Ironwood?"

"If Miss . . . Alice . . . is right, and he's not an Ironwood, then it's likely he's a Thorn," Nicholas said slowly. "Equally dangerous, considering they want the astrolabe as well."

Rose. The man had called her Rose.

"He used my mom's name," she said. "That man had clearly seen her before if he mistook me for her."

He gave one of his curt nods. "Alice implied that your mother was tied to the Thorns at one point or another."

Etta frowned. Something about all of this was rubbing her the wrong way, brushing up like sandpaper against her attempts to puzzle this out. Her mother had *wanted* her to travel; she'd known it was inevitable. Etta was beginning to think the "consequences" Rose had referenced in her fight with Alice had to do with trying to change the timeline by keeping Etta from going. So why would Rose join a group that wanted to use the astrolabe for itself—and would stop Etta from getting it? Had she pulled the same kind of con on the Thorns as she had on the Ironwoods?

Rose could be cold, guarded, but Etta hadn't realized before now that her mother could also be *ruthless*. It gave her hope that, if her mom really did believe she could handle this, she recognized there was fight in Etta, too.

They were going to have a *long* conversation when Etta found her. Starting with why she hadn't just destroyed the astrolabe in the first place, and saved everyone the grief.

The sun was setting, and the mood of the city was shifting into something that made her stomach churn. Heavy curtains were being drawn behind windows, and cardboard was being placed in the flat windows of storefronts. The streetlamps remained off. The crowds of people began to disperse, breaking off in clusters and heading up the side streets, jumping in whatever bus or taxi was passing by. It was like the city had sucked in one last, enormous gasp and was holding its breath. Etta felt as though she were walking along a crack that was threatening to cave in on itself.

"I thought they had . . . elect—electricity?" Nicholas said quietly. The leather satchel at his side bounced between them, but every now and then the back of his hand would brush hers and break the rhythm of her pulse.

"They do," Etta whispered back, glancing back at the milky pink of the sunset. Was this part of the "rationing" Alice had mentioned, or was this some kind of power blackout?

They passed Leicester Square; couples dressed up in furs and hats were loitering outside of the theaters, sharing cigarettes as if it were any other day in any other year.

Almost there, almost there . . .

"May I ask you something?" Nicholas said into the darkness gathering around them. A midnight blue clung to the air, that last gasp of afterlight before nightfall. Without any illumination, Etta's other senses came into sharp focus. The smell of gasoline and smoke. The sound of their footsteps. The dryness of her mouth as she tried to swallow.

"You can ask me anything," she told him.

"What will you do when you find the astrolabe," he asked, his voice reserved, careful, "knowing what it truly does?"

Etta didn't want to lie. "Whatever it takes to save my mom. My future."

"Are there any circumstances in which you'd give it to the old man?" he continued.

What a strange question—was that some kind of test?

She raised an eyebrow. "Would you?"

His lips parted, but just as quickly, he turned his gaze up toward the sky as it bruised under the night.

"I can only imagine what he'd do with access to more of the future," Etta continued. "It's how badly he wants it, and how far my mom had to go to protect it, that scares me. It definitely makes me second-guess giving it to him. Nothing about the old man makes me *want* to play nice."

"But isn't it the easier solution—give it to him, and get your life back? Your mother? Perform at your concert?" he asked, his voice strained.

"What's *left* of my life at this point, you mean. Whatever parts of it he hasn't torpedoed." Etta didn't want to continue down this line of conversation, not when her own thoughts were still too frustratingly tangled. Her mom was safe for now, and would be, so long as she could get to the astrolabe before Ironwood's deadline.

He gave her a helpless look. "'Torpedoed'?"

"An underwater missile that . . . You know what?" she said with a faint laugh. "I'll explain later. I'm not so sure it wouldn't be a good idea to torpedo the stupid astrolabe and just be done with this."

"That would be unwise. The whole business of getting home could be made considerably easier by creating a passage, rather than sailing to the one in Nassau," Nicholas said. "I hope you'll take this as the compliment it is, but I imagine Ironwood will be eager to see you and your mother as quickly as possible. He might even create one for you."

"We are talking about Cyrus Ironwood, right?" Etta said, brows raised at this little fantasy. "The one who told me he was going to leave me so destitute I was going to have to resort to prostitution?"

Nicholas groaned. "*We* will create one for you and your mother, then."

"If we can figure out how to use it," she pointed out. The thought made her feel tired all over again. In truth, at that moment, all she really wanted were two things: her mother and a hot shower. And toothpaste. Three things. The last should have been easy enough to find, and maybe it would have been, if every store they passed hadn't been closed for the day.

"Can I ask *you* a question?" she said, eyes sliding up his profile.

He inclined his head, granting permission, but she saw his hands bunch into fists at his side. "I suppose it's only fair."

"What are you going to do with the money you got from

Ironwood?" she asked. "The money you got for bringing me and Sophia to New York?"

His shoulders slumped as he exhaled. "I would dearly love to hear your guess."

"You're going to buy a ship," she said instantly.

"Yes—did Chase tell you that as well?" Nicholas's gaze swung out to take in the sight of St. Paul's Cathedral, its ornate dome looming between the shadowed buildings surrounding it.

"No," she said. "It just seemed right. That's where I see you."

Standing under the blaze of the sun, the wind teasing and pulling at his shirt and jacket, the water rolling out beneath them—*him*, she corrected, rolling out beneath *him*—like a sparkling carpet.

Nicholas stopped, his arm brushing hers again as he stepped in front of her, looking down in what she thought might have been genuine amazement. "You could read me so easily?"

She smiled, flicking at his chest in a teasing way to keep from doing something else that would embarrass her and likely startle him. "You were so good at it, and you loved it. I could see it in your face—what is it?"

His gaze was so heavy, it felt like he had dropped his hands onto her shoulders, and was holding on for dear life.

"Etta . . ." he began, his voice a rasp. "You . . ."

There was a movement just behind him, brown and black and white and gray—three men booking it down the street. The men from before—the one in tweed was pulling something out of his pocket—*Thorns*—charging directly at them—small, silver—

Gun.

Etta shoved Nicholas, hard, into the brick wall beside them.

286

He stared back, dazed, just as a bullet screamed by, slicing the air between them.

"Run!" Etta said, grabbing his wrist. *"Run!"*

He tried to wheel back around, to see, but she dragged him forward, feeling his pulse jump beneath her fingers.

"Turn here!" he said. "We've—"

The sound was like an inherited memory; she couldn't remember ever having heard it before, but recognized it instantly for the way it seemed to slice through her, striking the marrow of her bones. The revving wail was spinning out of the silence, louder and louder, as the buildings picked up the sound of the sirens and volleyed it between them.

"What the devil is that?" Nicholas said, spinning around, trying to locate the source.

"Air raid sirens," Etta said, shooting a look back over her shoulder. The men were slowing at the warning of the approaching attack, as if unsure whether or not to keep going. No—Etta's breath left her in a rush—to *aim.*

The man out in front fired; the bullet went wide, striking the brick wall behind them. A splatter of dust and debris exploded into her hair, scratching the back of her neck.

"Stop, damn you!" one of them called. "Don't make us shoot you!"

"Hell and damnation," Nicholas forced out between gritted teeth. Etta was too furious with herself to speak. Why hadn't she even thought about this? She should have pushed to leave Alice's earlier; they should have taken a taxi; anything to get them to the Aldwych station and the passage hidden inside of it as soon as possible. This was the *Blitz*, for God's sake. Alice had *told* her a

hundred times growing up that there had been bombings nearly every night.

"What do we do?" he shouted.

A distant, loud drone choked the words right out of her, made her look up through the clouds for planes.

"We have to go underground!" she said. This Alice had said the Underground stations were being used as shelters—if they could get to Aldwych—if they could run ahead of the attack, they could reach the passage *tonight*—

But if the bombing began before then, in this area of the city, they'd be dead before they realized what hit them.

The Thorns seemed to be having a similar debate. She caught fragments of their conversation—"Go back!" "Follow—" "—*not dying*—"

They'd passed a shelter in Leicester Square and had seen the tube stop nearby, but Etta didn't want them to go back, not when they could get out of London tonight. The Thorns seemed to be hoping they would bail, ditch the streets for cover, and Etta had the unsettling feeling of being caught in a deadly game of chicken. Ending up in the same shelter as them would only get her and Nicholas caught again in Ironwood's web. She needed them to take the nearest shelter, and she needed to get her and Nicholas the hell out of London.

This was war, this was real, and they were going to die if she didn't make a decision right now.

"Let's double back," Nicholas said. "That square had shelter—"

"No," Etta said, "we can make it to the Aldwych station!"

"No—the other one is closer!" he shouted over the sirens. "We can cut a path around them if we have to!"

I am getting us out of here.

I am getting us out of here.

I am getting myself home.

She grabbed his hand tightly in hers and dragged him forward. Nicholas tried to pull her back around, but Etta wouldn't turn. "We can make it! We can't lead them to the passage—Ironwood can't know which one we take! We have to lose them!"

We. They had to do it together, or not at all.

"Damn you—" he swore, but when she started running, he did too.

It sounded like thunder from a late summer storm—the kind that used to rattle her and her mom's apartment windows, a boom that cracked over the city and echoed against the glass-and-steel structures. The whistling alone made her eardrums feel as if they were about to split; the high whines fell eerily silent before each tremendous, deafening crash. Her skin prickled, feeling as if it was about to peel away.

Etta would never complain about the sound of the passage now, not ever again. Not after hearing this.

Nicholas craned his neck up to watch the shapes ripping through the night sky. It looked as though a thousand black bugs were being released from each plane, all streaming down to the city around them. The eager curiosity she'd seen earlier on his face had vanished.

Etta turned—the street was empty behind them. "They're gone!"

She pushed her legs harder until she felt her ankle turn on a piece of rubble. But Etta didn't stop, and neither did Nicholas. He looped her arm around his neck and carried her forward as they turned onto Catherine Street.

"It's at the end of the—road—" she gasped out.

"I see others, they're going the same way—" he said, the words rumbling in his chest, echoing the planes' thunder. "We're almost there."

Families, couples, policemen were all converging in front of a building with a redbrick façade. A white banner ran along the top, over the arch of windows: first, PICCADILLY RLY, then the smaller lettering below: ALDWYCH STATION.

She let out a sharp "Yes!" at the same moment that Nicholas shuddered and said, "Thank God."

A man in a dark police uniform stood at the entrance, waving everyone in. They dodged the clothes, bedding, toys, and suitcases that had been dropped in the panicked flight down, and joined the flow of bodies. Just before they were swallowed into the horde, Nicholas shifted her arm, wrapping it around his waist instead. His other arm fixed across her shoulders, drawing her closer, squeezing them between the dozens of people around them who were all quietly trying to fight their way down an endless series of stairs.

"How far underground are we?" Nicholas asked, eyeing the pale lights running along the ceiling.

"Very far," Etta said, hoping the words were more reassuring than they felt. The pounding hadn't stopped; it was only muffled. The world flickered around them as the electricity was tested by the bombing. Sweat poured down her back, and Etta couldn't stop shaking, even as they broke off from some of the others and headed for the eastern track, as Alice had instructed.

Some part of Etta had hoped that they would be able to just walk to the very end of the platform, jump down onto the track, and slip away into the tunnel. No hassle, no fuss, no questions.

But as they came down the last steps and rounded the corner, she could see they had a problem.

That problem being the hundreds of others who had already beaten them down there. Londoners had spread out across the platform, even nestling down on the track. The press of humanity filled the air with a damp, sticky warmth. Many of the men and women had taken off their coats and jackets and hung them up along the walls. Someone had even engineered a kind of clothesline at the entrance to the actual track tunnel.

They couldn't spend the night here—they couldn't lose that bit of time when the old man's deadline was edging closer by the second.

Nicholas's arm tightened around her again as they were gently pushed forward by the people behind them.

"Damn," he swore softly. "Which way did we need to go?"

She pointed to the other end of the track, where rows upon rows of people were curled up on blankets or gathered in circles of friends and families. Many were talking quietly, or trying to entertain the few little kids she saw with toys or books, but most remained close to silent, their faces stoic.

Etta had to hand it to them; they were calm. They seemed almost resigned to this, like it was one great bother, instead of a terrible way to die.

"All right, we'll wait. We can be patient." If Nicholas was aware of the eyes that were tracking their progress along the platform, he didn't show it. They navigated through the crowd until they found an empty space near the end of the platform, under a sign advertising the Paramount Theatre's showing of something called *I Was an Adventuress* staring someone named Zorina.

Nicholas took off the bag and his jacket as Etta lowered herself down onto the patch of concrete, leaning back against the curved wall. She drew her legs up to her chest and hugged them there, hard enough for her knees to crack.

Calm down, she thought, *calm down.*

But the bombing hadn't stopped, and Etta could almost see how, if one was dropped in just the wrong place overhead, it would mean game over. Not just for her and Nicholas, but for the hundreds of people packed around them like sleeves of wafers.

Nicholas rummaged through the bag, producing their lone apple. Etta wasn't hungry, though she hadn't eaten since they'd left New York. Her stomach had turned to stone, throbbing in time with the muscles that still burned from the run.

Nicholas glanced at her, concern dragging down the corners of his mouth. "I should have found us water. I'm sorry, Etta."

"We'll be fine," she whispered. They'd find some once they went through the next passage.

"I have to say," he muttered, leaning back, "I am harboring some incredible ill will toward this mother of yours."

Etta wasn't feeling so fond of her at that precise moment either, even as she was terrified for her; her mind was constantly looping back to that photograph, the way she'd been tied up, the kind of men that were holding her.

"Well," Etta said weakly, "she's always told me a good challenge builds character."

"Then we'll have an excess of it," he said dryly.

Conditions on the platform were so tight that they sat shoulder to shoulder, hip to hip, leg to leg. Etta was glad for the solid presence of him, that she could lean into him, now that her nerves seemed poised to sweep her into a full-blown panic attack. She crossed her legs, letting the cool cement press into the exposed skin. None of Oskar's breathing tricks seemed to be working, not when all hell was raining down on the street above. The woman to her right quietly prayed.

How many hours would they have to sit down here, hoping? It was the twenty-second of September. That only left them with eight more days to find the astrolabe *and* get back, and they still had no idea how to decipher the other clues.

Her breath hitched as panic began to creep into her system. How was Nicholas so calm—so steady, like he'd been through this all before?

Maybe he had, in a way. The bombing didn't sound all that different than the pounding cannonade from the ships, the small explosions of each gun. She wanted to ask him, but she couldn't speak, afraid that admitting anything might open the floodgates in her. Everyone was holding it together. She could, too.

I wish I could play.

Etta craved the distraction, the absolute focus of playing. If she couldn't feel the weight of the instrument in her hands, then she could at least imagine; she closed her eyes and called the music to her. The phantom press of strings against her fingers filled her, for the first time since Alice had died, with a sense of familiar joy—not the disgust and humiliation she'd felt when she thought about her performance, or the shattering anger and grief at wondering what had happened to Alice's body—if she and her mother would even make it in time for the funeral.

For lack of anything better to use, she took her left forearm into her right hand, closing her eyes. She could pretend, just for a few seconds, that her wrist was the neck, her veins the strings. She imagined the bow gliding across her skin, focused on the movement of it.

Bach. Bach demanded her concentration. Bach would take her out of this moment.

"What are you doing?" Nicholas asked.

"Playing," she said, not caring how ridiculous it must look and sound to him. "Distracting myself."

A man, stretched out on his stomach in front of them, lifted his face up out of his book and glanced their way curiously.

It was perfectly strange timing that a high, clear note broke the odd spell of calm in the station just then. Down toward the center of the platform, an older man had brought out a violin and was working the instrument in slow, mellow song. She recognized it—it wasn't a classical composition but something that had come scratching out of Oskar's old record player.

The sound bloomed around them, like a flower unfurling one petal at a time, carrying across the walls of white tiles with their patterns of black crosses. A passing police officer tilted his hat toward the man. Etta sat up, straining to see him over the heads between them.

She had, however, no trouble seeing the young couple that was dancing in their few feet of allotted space. The man's arm was locked around her waist, and he took her hand in his. The woman laughed, looking around them nervously, but followed his slow, rocking movements, resting her head against his shoulder.

Nicholas watched them, entranced. Etta thought for sure he'd say something about how scandalous it was for them to be dancing so close together.

"That's beautiful," she said.

He turned to her. "Would you like me to go take that violin for you? I'd gladly fight whatever angry mob rises up if it might make you smile."

Her heart just about burst at that.

Be brave. "I would only want to play for you."

He turned slowly, as if taking the time to assemble some sort of expression or response. But she didn't want there to be any mistake, any way for him to dismiss or misunderstand her words. If she was wrong, and he wanted nothing more between them, she would pull back. But now . . . now she just wanted to be brave. Her hand came to rest on top of his, and despite all of his obvious strength, the shields he threw up to protect the privacy of his mind, she felt his fingers slide through hers.

The lights flickered again, sending her attention, and her heart, shooting upward. The banging was loud, like hands slamming down directly on top of them. A boy started wailing, and the sound moved like a wave through the other kids. The dancers stopped dancing, but the older gentleman didn't stop playing until the lights blinked out completely, leaving them in pitch black.

Etta couldn't stop shivering. She bit the inside of her mouth and drew blood. The darkness seemed to shudder and rock around them, and whatever terror she'd managed to bottle up broke free.

I don't want to die down here.

I don't want to disappear.

I have to get home.

Mom.

Mom is going to die, and it's my fault—

Hot tears rolled down her cheeks, and she hiccupped as she tried to take in air.

"Etta," Nicholas said, close to her ear. He shifted, drawing her closer. She pressed her face against the slope of skin between his neck and shoulder, and felt a hand weave through her hair, pulling it back from where strands were sticking to her wet cheeks.

"Shhh, Etta, we're safe," he said. "The battle's ours, pirate. They'll strike their colors, and it will pass."

She breathed in the sea salt that always seemed to cling to his skin, no matter how far from the ocean he was. Her mind felt foggy, her face raw, as his hand slipped away from her face and glided down her arm. With an aching tenderness, he laced his fingers through hers and brought them to his other arm, resting upturned in his lap.

He'd rolled the sleeve up, and she felt a shock of hot skin against her fingertips as he pressed her hand there. "Play me something."

"What?" Etta whispered.

"Something that'll lift us out of here."

His fingers unhooked from hers, following that same path up her arm, and then back down it again. The feeling was so distracting, so good, so sweet against her clammy skin. She didn't choose a piece from her repertoire; Etta gave herself over to the notes that started streaming through her mind, rising from somewhere deep inside of her.

The melody of her heart had no name; it was quick, and light. It rolled with the waves, falling as the breath left his chest, rising as he inhaled. It was the rain sliding down the glass; the fog spreading its fingers over the water. The creaking of a ship's great body. The secrets whispered by the wind, and the unseen life that moved below.

It was the flame of one last candle.

Nicholas's arm was a map of hard muscles and delicate sinews, heartbreakingly perfect. She wondered if he could hear her humming the piece against his skin over the droning roars overhead. Maybe. His free hand skimmed up her skin, leaving a trail of sparks in its wake.

With the world blacked out around them, she could catalog all of her other senses, capture this moment in the warm darkness forever. He brushed back the loose hair across her forehead, his breath hitching as she turned her face up. Soft lips found her cheek, the corner of her lips, her jaw, and she knew it had to be the same for him, that they'd never been so aware of another person in their entire lives.

She released his arm, and he drew it up around her, guiding both of them down so they were on their sides, their heads cushioned by the bag, his jacket drawn over them. Etta understood that here, in the darkness, they'd found a place beyond rules; a place that hung somewhere between the past and the future. This was a single moment of possibility.

The clattering of the attack from above faded as he rested his forehead against hers, his thumb lightly stroking a bruise on her cheek. She traced his face—the straight nose, the high, proud cheekbones, the full curve of his lips. His hand caught her there, taking it in his own; he pressed a hard, almost despairing kiss to it.

But when she tilted her face up, half-desperate with longing, her blood racing, Nicholas pulled back; and although Etta could feel him beside her, his heart pounding, his ragged breath, it was as if he had disappeared into the thundering dark.

THIRTEEN

THE BATTLE EXPLODED AROUND HIM WITH A FEROCITY that left him gasping.

Nicholas had kept an eye on the horizon to the west, where steel clouds had begun to swirl as if God himself was stirring the pot. The skies around him were cast in shades of darkness that left his guts coiled in anticipation. He turned, poised to begin the process of readying the ship to weather the storm, and—

The crew was gone.

Every last one of them.

Chase's name tore out of his throat as he ran toward the bow of the ship, the sound of his footsteps lost to the shrieking winds. The sails snapped and fluttered above him in warning. A movement caught his eye—there was someone on his ship after all. His back was turned, but there was no mistaking the dark curls rising on each brutal breeze, the steady stance, the hands clasped behind his back.

"Julian?" he called. But—by God, how was he alive? Had he

survived the fall? They needed to get back to port, back to New York—

The other ship appeared like a ghost, gliding through the misty, shadowed waters around them. He had less than a moment to suck in a shocked breath before she fired a broadside.

Nicholas felt the ship tear apart beneath him as if it were his own skin, his own bones shattered into a thousand jagged fragments.

"Julian!" he screamed as the fire and debris exploded around him, trapping him in a blaze of suffocating fire, a swarm of splinters. And all the while, the cannonade never slowed, never stopped. The intensity burned the hair from his face, left him with nothing but scalding white behind his eyelids. He let out a hoarse cry as he was knocked off his feet; the ship dipped sharply to the right, a terrifying slant that could only mean one thing—she was taking on water, and he would drown. Blind, burned, alone.

And then, the silence.

It was the suddenness of it that finally woke Nicholas from heavy, dream-laced sleep, dragging him up by the scruff of his neck into awareness. Exhaustion clung to his mind like a barnacle, unable to let logic in. Pure, unyielding panic rushed in like a sweeping wave, forcing him to roll away from the soft warmth he'd been curled around. The white tiles—the hundreds of brown, blue, red, black lumps of blankets around him—people—

Nicholas sat straight up, pressing his back into the wall behind him. He scrubbed his fists against his eyes, trying to slow the embarrassing way his heart was pounding in his chest.

You know where you are.

He did.

London. Twentieth century. War.

This was a . . . transportation tunnel. For a . . . "train." The Underground.

Nicholas blew out a sigh, wiping the crust of sleep from his eyes. The overhead lights flickered like candle flames dancing in the breeze. He cocked his head, listening to the strange sound they produced—somewhere between a hum and a frantic clicking, like the cicadas in the southern colonies.

Electricity. It had been so long since he'd had the privilege of it, and even when he had, he had never seen the abundance of this era. Julian had been the one to introduce him to it, the one who'd chuckled as Nicholas investigated his first lightbulb. Nicholas had managed to push the memory of his half brother to the very edge of his thoughts for years, where the regret could not infect his hope for the future. But traveling and Julian were inexorably tied together. Julian was the sole reason he'd gone through the passages at all. At first he'd thought that he was there to ensure that Ironwood's remaining rivals could not touch him—that he was a protector, a role in which he could take immense pride. In actuality, he'd found himself attending to his brother's clothing, doing the washing and mending as if he were a valet. He saw to Julian's mercurial needs and managed his wild, swinging moods. Even as a traveler, he had been a servant. A slave to Ironwood's will.

I don't need a protector, the girl had said. *I need a partner.*

The past few hours had proven that she did, in fact, need a protector; but . . . *partner.* That was something he had never thought to hope for.

He spent another moment collecting his nerves before looking back down at the girl sleeping beside him. The air in his lungs and nose was tinged with the smell of roses, as though he'd spent hours with his face buried in her mass of unruly blond hair. Before he could think about why it was unwise, ruminate on what a blackguard he was for taking advantage of the girl in the darkness, he reached over and gently brushed that same hair back from her face.

In some ways, each time he looked at her, it was as if he was seeing her for the first time on the deck of the *Ardent*. The symptoms of this sickness were unmistakable: the sharp dive of his heart as it dropped, recovering a moment too late; the tightness in his chest; the way his fingers seemed to curl instinctively, as if wondering how it would feel to weave them in her hair. He knew lust—he'd been consumed by its burn too many times—but Nicholas knew the ways to appease it, how to avoid the tangle of attachment, to leave content and calm and ready to return to the ship.

As he'd held her last night, he had genuinely believed the result would be the same. Touching her would answer his lingering doubts about whether her skin could possibly be as soft as he imagined. Giving in to the pounding need in his head to comfort her would be acceptable, just this once, when they could not be seen or judged for it. . . .

Instead, each second he spent breathing her breath, running his hands along her face, fighting the temptation of her lips . . . it only fed the burn in his chest. He wanted to believe that he had done it because she'd needed comfort, or at least distraction. He wanted to believe it was because being a stranger to this time had left him feeling unsettled. He wanted to believe that their lives could have ended at any moment, and there had been only this one chance left.

But the truth was, Nicholas had held her because he wanted

to. He hadn't thought about her reputation, or what anyone else might have cared to think. He'd taken what he wanted, and to hell with everyone else.

Nicholas felt a rueful smile spread across his face. And a curse be on him for it, because now he knew her. She'd shown him her mind, and she'd opened up her heart, and now he knew the taste of her tears.

And he was wrecked.

He clung to his willpower the way a man clings to battered remains of flotsam; it was hard enough to stay afloat, to remind himself of the important facts that remained, when she was so soft and warm and alive in his hands.

Could he kiss her, knowing that he was on the verge of betraying her and ensuring that the astrolabe got back to Ironwood?

Could he kiss her, knowing that she must return to her time and he must remain in his? The vilification they would face if she were to come with him back to his time, and they were made to deal with the cruel laws of the colonies . . .

Could he kiss her, knowing she might not burn the same way he did?

From the moment he had been exiled, Nicholas had used the dream of owning a ship as ballast to weather the storm of guilt and anger and devastation. He had learned, again, to swallow the limitations of his era's society, even if he never fully accepted them. Traveling with her had stirred up thoughts inside of him that he had been so very careful not to touch; it gave him ideas of a dangerous nature. What would life be like, if he did not return to his time? If, rather than return the astrolabe to Ironwood, they spent their lives like pilgrims, moving through lands and centuries until they found one in which they could be safe, one that suited their needs? When two people didn't belong to the era they were in, did they have to follow anyone's expectations besides their own?

Except, of course, she's desperate to save her mother and go home.

And he was as desperate to see his own ambitions through. It was nothing more than a thought that had gone rogue, spiraled out of his control. What Nicholas wanted was his ship—multiple ones at that; to live a life without restraints; and to be rid of his family and their scheming forever.

And surely, Etta would not be safe under any circumstances if he didn't bring the astrolabe to Ironwood, would she? Not truly. Perhaps one day she might see this, and come to terms with his deception.

It was all too easy to be carried off by wild, baseless theories. The old man merely wanted to expand his flock. Find more servants. And, while their departure through the passage had been sudden and unexpected, he did not doubt that all would be forgiven—so long as he gave Ironwood what he wanted.

But there had been a moment, as Alice and Etta had dissected Ironwood's possible intentions, when the confession had nearly tumbled off his tongue.

You could keep her. The words slithered through his mind, bringing a host of images with them that filled his heart with a savage kind of joy. When had it become his policy to give up his prizes? When had Nicholas ever given up a treasure that was rightfully won?

We were made for each other.

Once the thought was there, it clung to him like a second skin, near impossible to scrub away. Because no, of course they weren't. They were two ships sailing in opposite directions, having met for a short time in the middle of the voyage, and he could no sooner "keep her" than capture the wind. Nor would he insult her by trying, let alone think it was possible. When the time came, they would continue on as they had before. She would be with her family, safe; he would have his ship, be in full control of his fate, the only thing he'd ever truly wanted for himself.

This would be a mild disappointment in an otherwise successful life.

He would not surrender to the disaster of loving her.

In time, the pain would pass.

But . . . he would regret the loss. The simplicity. Neither of them had to work for the other's regard, nor did they make the other feel as if they had to. It struck him as very peculiar, given his somewhat limited exposure to future centuries, that this girl fit so well beside him; that they understood each other so very well. Life had shown him that there were only two ways he could gain something: through the kindness and pity of others, or by taking it through sheer force of will. Why had this arrived in such a different manner?

He looked around him again, at the spread of sleeping families, husbands and wives, friends . . . how uncomplicated they made it seem. The couple that had danced together hours before—how freely they could hold and touch one another, live in a moment they created.

Enough, he ordered himself. *This is a job. She is my companion in it.* The stakes were too high for either of them to be distracted by feelings.

Nicholas searched for the uniformed man he'd seen walking along the edge of the raised platform the night before, and found him asleep on the steps they'd used to come down. Here and there were patches of space scattered among the sleeping Londoners—some must have left at the end of the air raid and gone to whatever was left of their homes.

He heaved himself up into a crouch, trying to avoid thinking about the city's destruction. The inhuman sounds of the flying machines and the shelling hadn't been half as terrible as the thought of what might have happened if they hadn't run as fast as they did; if the firestorm had been dropped on top of them.

They needed to leave this era. Quickly. The guardians of this time would be up and searching for them by now.

He reached over, his finger hesitating a moment before stroking Etta's cheek to wake her. She shifted, stretching her legs out, and drew his jacket over her with a soft sigh. Nicholas put a hand on her shoulder and shook it until her eyes blinked open. She stared, all warm and rumpled by sleep, and his reason for waking her almost flew out of his head.

"What are you . . . ?" she mumbled.

He held a finger up to his lips as he stood, sliding the leather bag over his shoulder. Etta took the hand he offered to pull herself up off the ground, swaying. Holding her steady, Nicholas wrapped his jacket over her shoulders. It was only after they started to make their way along the edge of the track, skirting the sleeping Londoners, that he realized he was still holding her hand.

Nicholas gestured toward the other end of the raised platform, and Etta nodded—he was headed the right way, then. Good. Once he lost sight of the sky, it felt impossible to tell north from south, east from west. He found the experience of being underground about as pleasant as being blown to bits, like the ship in his dream. There was something unnatural about not being able to feel the sunlight on your skin in the morning.

The platform ended abruptly; he was forced to release Etta's hand and jump down onto the tracks. His shoes butted up against the raised metal beams running along the ground. Etta sat on the edge of the strange cold, gray, stone ledge and slid down into the dark with him, careful to avoid the clusters of families packed between the tracks. Determination and focus sharpened Etta's features in the glow of the lights. She turned toward the dark tunnel and led the way.

The air smelled vaguely of fire; his frown deepened, a new uneasiness stirring in him. He kept close to Etta, forcing her to slow her pace. When he turned, there was a man leaning over the platform, peering down the tunnel. At first, he thought the man had skin darker than his own, but the truth came like a swift blow: the man's face was stained with soot, but his features were recognizable. He'd shot at them the night before as they'd run toward the station. How the bloody hell had he found them already?

"One of the Thorns," he said. "We need to move faster—"

"I see something," she said. There was a light up ahead, a break in the tunnel. "It must be the next station. We're getting close."

Without breaking his stride, Nicholas reached into the bag and pulled out the harmonica. He put the instrument to his lips and blew softly.

The note was nothing but a faint gasp of sound. In return, they were showered with such clapping thunder and monstrous shrieks that Etta instinctively pulled back against him, trying to escape it. They had come up just short of what had to be the Elgin Marbles. Indeed, he saw the top of a white chiseled head over its wooden shelter, the lifeless eyes tracking their path through the thick darkness.

"Stop!" the man cried.

Never.

"There! Right there." She pointed toward the wall, where the air seemed to ripple in the darkness. The rattling screams reached a fevered state, making the blood pound inside of his head as he crossed through first, Etta at his back.

The momentum launched him out through the gate at the other end of the passage. He felt his breath catch, the hammering pulse of his heart. The world dissolved into pure darkness, the squeeze of air around him popping the bones in his stiff back. And, as quickly as he had leapt into it, Nicholas was spat out through the other side.

BIRDS AND INSECTS SCREECHED FROM THEIR PERCHES IN THE FLESHY green trees and brush around him. There was always a moment of blindness as his eyes adjusted to being inundated with light. He pressed his face against the wet earth, trying to clear the fog in his mind. No sooner had he started to get up, when a weight crashed into his back and sent him sprawling down into the mud again.

"Sorry!" Etta gasped, rolling off him. "Oww—"

He sat up, his vision swinging back toward the passage's entrance. When it became clear that the other man wasn't about to follow them through—that if he was indeed a Thorn, he was a guardian, rather than a traveler—Nicholas began to look beyond it. Jungle—a vast, thick shield of green and brown around him.

The air was heavy with the contradictory scents of rotting vegetation and floral blooms, lit green by the screen of bright leaves and tangle of thin branches overhead.

"Are you all right?" he asked, the words scratching out of his dry throat. "Etta?"

She was flat on her back, the sky-blue dress splattered with mud. Before he could stop himself, he began to pluck the long, green leaves out of her hair, flicking them away as the girl groaned, shaking madly.

"You're all right," he told her. "Look at me, just for a moment— just a moment, pirate."

It had taken him at least five trips through the passages during his training before he'd worked the last of the traveler's sickness out of his system. He knew too well how she was feeling: the weakness, the way every sound was battering her skull, the blood that was turning to ice in her veins. Etta opened her eyes, but they were unfocused. A soft sigh escaped her lips, and her eyelids fluttered shut.

" 'S fine," she said. "Just . . . need . . . moment."

They didn't have a moment, and they wouldn't, until he figured out where the passage had brought them and whether more guardians were near. The man in London would report what he'd seen to any nearby traveler, and he or she would be sent to follow them. They'd need to find the next passage immediately, and be gone before they could be tracked again.

Nicholas would bring Ironwood his damned astrolabe, but he wished to do it on his own terms, and keep Etta well out of Ironwood's grasp. He needed to keep her from sensing that this journey would have a very different end than the one she imagined.

He looked down at her grimacing face, and swallowed the burn of bile in his throat.

After another look around to ensure there was no one nearby, and that the only immediate threats were hunger and dehydration, Nicholas gathered her up into his arms and began to walk.

There was no trail, no evidence of human touch. He strained his ears, trying to hear above the rattle and buzz of the insects, and—*there*—he heard what he hoped was the sound of rushing water.

Etta's weight felt good and solid in his arms; but the feel of her in his arms, Nicholas thought with some uneasiness, was getting a bit too familiar. He stepped over the powerful arm of a root jutting up out of the soft soil. He let the branches blocking their way do what they would to his neck and face, and did the best he could to shield Etta.

"Where . . . ?" she asked, already coming around. He fought a smile. The next time would be easier on her, then.

"Not entirely sure, to tell you the truth," he said.

"Put me down," she said. "I can walk, I promise."

His hands tightened around her waist, her legs. The air had grown warm, and he knew he must smell worse than whatever ungodly rotting stench the jungle was belching out, but reluctance tugged at him even as he set her down on her feet.

She can look after herself. Etta knew herself well enough to know what she could and couldn't fight through.

But that, of course, didn't preclude him wanting to take care of her.

Etta looked around, taking in the knot of green foliage, the way the canopy shielded them from the sun's glare. "Well . . . this is different."

He snorted. "Come, let's see what we can find in the way of water and food."

His ears hadn't failed him—there *was* a stream nearby, and it moved quickly enough for him to feel mildly comfortable drinking it. Whenever he and Julian had tried to survive in the wild, they'd carried packs stuffed with supplies. Pots for boiling water and cooking. Blankets for freezing nights. There had been matches to start fires, hooks and lines for fishing. It had been Hall who'd taught him how to survive with none of these things.

He had a small knife he'd carried with him from New York. That would have to be enough.

"Wait here a moment," he said, gesturing toward a stone on the bank of the stream. "I'll be right back. Shout if you see or hear anything."

She nodded, distracted by something in the distance. He walked back the way they had come, veering right when he saw a tower of pale green out of the corner of his eye. Bananas—none of them ripe, but food all the same. He sent up a prayer of gratitude to whoever might be listening as he began to pull them from the tree and stow them in the bag. The most pressing issue now was finding some kind of container in which to boil water, and locating wood and brush that were dry enough to strike up a fire.

He ran a hand along the spine of a downed tree, considering. Using his knife, he cut away a section of it and brushed off the dirt and insects. The tree was mostly hollowed out inside, and if he carved it right, it could be used as a small bowl.

Nicholas stripped off his wilted shirt, surprised to find it was already damp with sweat as he stowed it in his bag. The air had taken on the quality of the swamps down south in the colonies, pregnant with the potential for a raging storm. Perhaps they wouldn't need to boil water at all, only catch it.

His knife chipped and cut away at the tree, and Nicholas lost himself in the good feeling of accomplishment, stopping only to relieve himself in the privacy of the leaves and eat half of a banana. He felt better for all of it, and knew she would too, once he gave her something to fill her stomach.

But when he returned to the small stream, Etta was nowhere to be found.

Disappeared.

He closed his eyes, which was a mistake. All he saw was Julian's face, how he'd looked just as he was swallowed by mist and distance.

"Etta?" he called, his voice cracking. "Etta!"

Gone. Had she slipped somewhere? Fallen? Drowned? Panic flared in him, white-hot, leaving him dizzy with it. He charged around the clearing, straining his ears for any hint of her footsteps, any sign of her.

He had a feeling Etta hadn't shown him whatever her true intentions were with the astrolabe—how she wanted to confront Ironwood—but she wouldn't have just *left*, would she? Gone on ahead?

She did it before, a cruel part of his mind whispered, *in New York. . . .*

The brush behind him rustled and Etta stumbled back out, eyes wide. "What is it? What's wrong?"

For a moment, the residual terror was enough to choke him, make his heart start pounding in his chest. Her hair was mussed, and there was a streak of dirt across her cheek that matched the bruise and scratch on the other. She straightened the skirt of her dress, and he had a sense of why she had momentarily disappeared.

"I—" he managed to get out. "I told you to stay put!"

Her brow furrowed at his anger, as if she couldn't possibly understand why wandering off in the middle of a jungle could be dangerous.

"You agreed!" he said, feeling ludicrous, but a fire was blazing in his chest that he couldn't seem to put out.

"Okay," she said slowly, "I'm sorry—"

"You're sorry?" Nicholas knew he should accept it, that he should move on to the business of starting a fire, but he couldn't bring himself to move past the fear just yet. "What if something had happened? How would I have found you? When I ask you to do something, please endeavor to *listen* to me!"

She rose to her full height, and for the first time he noticed that she'd removed her jacket and was cradling something in it—a severed head—

Of a statue. His heart settled back into its rightful place as he took in its serene smile. It made a perfect counterpoint to the look of irritation on her face as she set it down. "I was *going* to say, I think I know where we are, but since you clearly know everything, I'll let you figure it out for yourself."

Etta stormed along the stream; Nicholas waited for her to come back and laugh after a moment, so the band of tightness around his chest would fray enough for him to breathe again. Only she didn't, of course. She tripped, but caught herself handily, against—was that a stone wall?

It was. More than that, there were steps, and more statues that had been knocked over or absorbed into the thick bodies of trees. Most of these stone figures bore a similar face to the one Etta had found, but some had been left with no features at all. Time, and the forces of the jungle, had worn them away.

The thunder that shattered the jungle brought her up short, made her press her hands to her ears. The insects and birds became almost frantic, the latter launching themselves from the trees at the first small drops of rain.

"Oh my God," Etta gasped, turning to look back at him. Her arm was outstretched, pointing at something orange and white a short distance away, half-hidden by foliage.

Nicholas's eyes were fixed only on what was at her feet, and watched as its head rose up out of the mud behind her, scales glinting and slick as its hood flattened out. She must have stepped right on it and been none the wiser.

"Don't. Move." Terror thrummed inside of him, fast and desperate, as another burst of thunder exploded over their heads. Etta started to step back, turning to look at him, and the snake bobbed in the air, poised to strike. "Don't move!"

He didn't trust his aim with the knife just then; any slip, any gust of wind, and the blade would be in her leg and not in the damned snake. Before he could question himself, the revolver was in his hand, the snake lashed forward, and he fired.

ANGKOR
1685

FOURTEEN

THERE WAS A SMALL EXPLOSION BEHIND ETTA, AN instant before heat seared the back of her left calf and she was thrown forward onto her hands and knees. She looked up in time to see the tiger's tail flash as it turned and ran deeper into the trees. Her ears were ringing, aching, as she turned around and saw the head of a cobra staring up at her, a short distance away from the long, coiled muscle of its body. Both the head and the body were still moving.

Etta stared at it, unable to so much as feel the rain that suddenly burst down, shaking the leaves, pounding the mud.

Nicholas stood a few feet back, the revolver still in his hand, looking as if he'd been the one shot, not the snake.

Etta reached down, touching her left calf muscle and coming away with blood. She stared at it long enough that the rain began to wash it away, long enough for Nicholas to snap out of his own shock. He rushed forward, kicking the snake aside.

"Did it bite you?" He took her leg in his hand, trying to see for himself, and she was right—he was shaking. "Etta! Did it bite you?"

317

No; but on its path to the snake, the bullet had grazed her skin, cutting close enough to leave a red, angry mark. She had been that close to getting bitten, and she hadn't had any idea.

"Christ," he said, pressing his hand against it. He tore the sleeve off the jacket she'd been carrying and dug through the bag for the scissors. As gently as he could, he dabbed the blood away and wrapped her leg with another, cleaner strip of fabric.

But where is the tiger? Etta wondered. When she'd spotted it, at first she had felt surprised and delighted. Its luminous eyes had tracked their progress forward with keen interest. Only then had she realized that there was no barrier between them.

Nicholas's hands were smoothing down her wet hair, and kept moving over her shoulders, down her arms, and back up again to cup her face. He slowly came into focus, and she realized he'd been speaking to her this whole time.

"Can you stand?" he asked her. The ground had turned into a river of mud beneath them, and she was eager to get out of it. She nodded, accepting his help up, and gingerly tested whether or not she could bear to put weight on her leg. Her hands stayed on his bare shoulders as she looked up into his face.

"All right?" he asked, his voice still sounding odd to her ears. Etta nodded again. Standing was easy; speaking was not. "Do you want to walk?"

She nodded, hugging her arms to her chest.

Nicholas nudged them forward, but a thought spun in Etta's mind, and she tugged him back. "Wait—we should take it—"

"It?" he repeated. "The snake?"

"Yeah." Etta shook off the last bit of shock blanketing her mind. "What if . . . what if we need to eat it? Shouldn't we take it with us?" Thinking about this further, she added, "Maybe not the head, though."

Flanked by a curtain of green that glowed vibrantly, even in the silver overcast light, with rain pouring down over his face, his shoulders, the scars that crisscrossed over his chest, Nicholas blinked and started to laugh. He tilted his head back, catching the rain across his face; and when he finally leaned down to kiss her, the sweetness of it lingered on his lips.

It seemed to end before it even began. He pulled back, looking equally abashed and afraid, studying her face. Her hands itched to smooth the lines of worry away from his forehead, from around his beautiful, dark eyes. But he wasn't the type to like being soothed—she knew that—and she also knew that this concern was more than just stupid eighteenth-century propriety. They were beyond that now.

She set her shoulders back, meeting his gaze with a challenge. "You call that a kiss?"

One corner of his mouth quirked up. "We haven't the time for a proper one, pirate. Now tell me, where precisely are we?"

AT SOME POINT BETWEEN THE TIME WHEN NICHOLAS HAD LEFT to . . . to do whatever it was that required him to be shirtless . . . and her finding the Buddha statue's decapitated head, a suspicion had begun to take root in the back of her mind. And as she'd walked, glimpsing the dark peaks of the temple in the distance, she'd had a single moment of relief at having been right before the anger began to pump through her again.

New York.

London.

And now, Cambodia.

It was too much to be a coincidence. She'd taken out the letter, rereading the first clue they'd been able to ignore, as it came before the passage in New York: *Rise and enter the lair, where the darkness gives you your stripes.* It must mean the Taktsang Palphug Monastery in Bhutan, called the Tiger's Lair or the Tiger's Nest, where her mother claimed to have gone into one of the caves to meditate on what to do with her life. Which now seemed, in a word, unlikely.

Her mother had told her how to decipher the letter. She'd told her any number of times, under the guise of bedtime stories, about her life and adventures—she'd even painted the scenes, hanging them on the wall of the living room in the correct order, which made Etta feel like an idiot for not making the connection right away. Each clue had been carefully disguised to hide the reality of her life as a traveler; each was hiding in plain sight.

Now Etta was sure that the painting of the British Museum hadn't been meant to lead her to the museum, but to the painting's other subject: Alice. And Etta was willing to bet that, if she double-checked, she'd find that her mother's supposed first apartment in the city, the one she'd painted to show a glimpse of the lights of Midtown East through one of the windows, was in the same location as the Dove Tavern.

Are you listening, Etta?

Etta, are you paying attention?

Let me tell you a story. . . .

Rose had planted the seeds, watered them again and again by repeating the stories over the years. She *had* given Etta what she needed to find the astrolabe; Etta only had to make the connection.

Etta had never been to the Tiger's Nest, let alone Bhutan, but she knew someone beside her mother who had.

She and Nicholas walked side by side, her eyes trained on the ground, his on the path in front of them, until more of the dark stones and statues rose out of the foliage and marked their path forward. From her mother's apparently half-true stories, Etta knew that both cities—Angkor Wat, and their present location, Angkor Thom—had, in her time, been largely cleared of the jungle's ever-reaching overgrowth to allow for tourists to explore the spread of temples and structures. But whatever year or era they were in, it was clear it was after it had been abandoned by the Khmer Empire, but before it had come to the attention of Western civilization.

"We'll need to swim," Nicholas said, the first words he'd uttered in nearly an hour. They'd come upon what Etta thought might have been part of the moat that surrounded the remains of the grand city. The moat had naturally filled up with earth and wildlife over the years, but with the rain lashing down around them, the water level was high enough that they couldn't wade their way across.

"No, my mom talked about some kind of a bridge . . . at the southern gate, I think," Etta said. She doubted it looked anything like the modern causeway that existed in her era, but it was worth finding, to avoid whatever was living in the moat.

To fill the silence and stop thinking about the way the rain made the trees rattle like angry snakes, Etta asked, "Where did you travel with Julian?"

"Here and there."

All right. Julian was still off-limits, and she wouldn't press him, not when it was clearly still painful. But Etta was incredibly curious about that sliver of time in his life.

321

"I think you were close to getting on the right trail to the astrolabe," she told him. "I'm not sure if you were in the right year, but I'm almost positive the first clue refers to the Tiger's Nest. And that's where Julian died, right?"

Nicholas ran a hand back over his short hair and nodded.

Etta's fingers twisted around one another. "It's my mom's fault, isn't it? Everything. You traveling with him, his death . . ."

"I can forgive your mother for doing what she believed to be right, even if her methods were questionable and a damned pain," he said, "but if we trace the blame back to its roots, there's only Ironwood at fault."

Always Ironwood.

"I'm not sure where or how to begin," he said, holding a branch out of her way. Nicholas searched for the words. "Julian and I were sent to Bhutan because the old man had found records that a monk once sighted a young blond woman in one of the meditation caves—one who never emerged from it again. We thought for certain it would be another fruitless trip. Over the years, the search took us everywhere from Mexico to India, to what I think you'd know as Alaska . . . ?"

Etta nodded.

"It's not . . . it's not such an easy thing to discuss," he said, his low voice drowned out for a moment by the cracking of thunder. "For a time, I was blind to the real role I was playing. I told myself I wasn't there as Julian's servant, but as a brother; a friend and protector. I think he did see me as a confidant, but . . . I'm afraid I've too much pride. The realization that I was actually there to play valet festered in me. Made me resent him. Just before he died, I told him that I didn't want to travel any longer—I wanted out of the trap of servitude again. Ironwood had promised me status if I returned to the arms of the family—promised me wonder, adventure, all the things that sound exciting to a boy of fourteen. But I was never given freedom. I was issued orders. I did not receive the full training, or the locations of all of the passages, you see—I wonder now if Ironwood feared I'd escape through them and somehow disappear."

She did see. Cyrus was a masterful manipulator. He would probably have promised to lasso the moon and bring it down to Nicholas in order to get him to travel with Julian.

"I wanted to make those choices again. Build my own life, feel like I was at its helm again—the way I only felt with the Halls, when I sailed with the captain."

"What did Julian say when you told him you wanted out?" she asked.

Nicholas was silent a long while. "He told me there was a contract I'd signed, and not a single drop of shared blood would compel any of the Ironwoods to break it. He said it was my purpose, one way or another; that it was the order of things. *Terribly sorry, old chap,* and all of that. I don't believe he had a black heart in him; he'd only been poisoned with these justifications like all the rest of them."

Etta itched to take his hand, but by the way his shoulders were bunched, she wasn't sure he wanted to be touched.

"I realized my mistake. I had been planning to slip away from the family once we returned to the eighteenth century, to fall back into place in my own natural timeline, and I thought I might be able to, after we returned from . . ." He trailed off again. "Does Sophia still believe I let him fall?"

Etta winced, giving him his answer. "I told her that was impossible."

"Is it?" he said, brushing a branch out of the way, "I don't blame her. The whole family must have known I was desperate to escape my contract of service. Exile is a rather neat, if extreme, method of accomplishing just that. I've . . . I've even wondered if something in me let him fall, knowing what the consequences would be."

She shook her head. "No. And, for what it's worth, Sophia does recognize it was an accident."

"But she does blame me," he finished. "I blame myself. And I'm the fool, because in spite of everything, he was my brother. I never saw him as anything less, or cared for him less than Chase, who is my brother in everything but blood. And it clearly wasn't the same for him."

She tried to remember what Sophia had said—that Julian had insisted he and everyone else should think of Nicholas as his brother—but words must have meant very little when he clearly hadn't demonstrated any of those feelings.

"That doesn't make you a fool," Etta huffed, wiping her sopping wet hair out of her face. "You deserve to be loved and treated with respect."

If he heard her, Nicholas didn't acknowledge it. He turned his face up to the rain for a moment, then continued forward in silence.

"I should have saved him," he said after a long while. "When I came back to find that you'd gone . . . it brought me back to that moment on the mountain. It . . . *gripped* me and wouldn't let me go, even after I saw that you were all right."

A panic attack? she wondered. Or an echo of a terrible memory. That would explain the overreaction.

"All that's left in the end is the certainty that I *can't* protect you from every small thing, and it's difficult to accept," he said. "But I am truly very sorry for the things I said."

"It drives me crazy to be treated like a child," she told him. "I know that wasn't your intention, and I know things are different in your time, but almost nothing gets my temper going faster."

He nodded. "I know. It was irrational."

Etta shrugged. "I'm no stranger to irrational thoughts, believe me. I spent the better half of my life secretly convinced I was a mistake my mom regretted bringing into the world, and that's why she was so distant. Hardhearted and impossible to please. But I know it's not true—when I was younger, she was . . . very different. And she's given me everything I've ever needed." Except, of course, for the truth about traveling. Etta looked over at him, meeting Nicholas's gaze. "I've never told anyone that before. I'm not sure I've even let myself put that feeling into words before, even in my own head."

"And now that you know the truth—" he began.

Etta, who had been navigating through pockets of sinking mud and rivulets of water, caught a flash of bright color out of the corner of her eye. Without warning, she crouched and tugged him down with her.

Nicholas landed on his knees with a surprised grunt. Etta's attention sharpened, focusing on a point in front of them, as she rose slightly to peer over the brush. They'd been walking along the edge of the moat, following the walls of the city the best they could, even as the jungle did such an excellent job of disguising it. But now Etta caught a flash of something new. She leaned forward, parting the tangle of leaves and limbs in front of her: ochre cloth. Movement.

Men.

It took her a moment to place what she was looking at. In her time, Buddhist monks wore brightly colored robes that ranged in color from saffron to a kind of burnt tangerine. These were a duller yellow, stained with splatters of mud; they clung to the men as they took shelter beneath the looming gate on the opposite end of a crumbling bridge.

"I suppose that's the gate with the bridge you spoke of," he said, close to her ear.

She nodded. It seemed to be the only one with a pathway across the moat that was still standing, but even it looked like it was slowly being pulled apart by the jungle.

The monks seemed to be discussing what to do. One of them waved his hands toward the jungle, where they were hiding, and Etta and Nicholas flattened against the ground.

"We can't just . . . go, can we?" she whispered.

He raised his brows. "Do either of us look like we might reasonably belong here? That there's a logical explanation for our presence?"

Okay, fair point. If time traveling was the art of blending in, she supposed it might be a little difficult to explain their appearance and clothing in the jungles of Cambodia.

"We aren't traveling with a guardian who can explain away our presence," Nicholas continued, his voice low, "and if they record seeing us, and that record survives . . ."

It would change history. A small ripple, maybe, but . . . Etta wasn't willing to risk either of their futures.

She couldn't say how long they waited—long enough that, as she leaned against Nicholas, pressing a cheek against his bare shoulder, she started to nod off. It was the sound of voices that pulled her out of her exhausted haze. The warm, solid weight next to her shoulder slipped away as Nicholas sat up. He tracked their progress as the monks left the shelter of the gate and made their way out onto the bridge.

Etta rubbed her face, listening to their quiet murmuring and their footsteps through the damp, sucking jungle. She watched them until they found some sort of path and the foliage swallowed them up. There had been ten in all. Nicholas waited a few moments to see if more were leaving the confines of the city, trailing after the first group. When he seemed sure there were not, he helped her up. Etta put some weight on her aching leg.

"It's all right," she promised when he cut a sharp, worried glance toward her. She could handle it.

"Your mother must truly be a fearsome creature," he informed her, taking her arm to help her over a felled tree, and then keeping it in his. "A revolution, a world war, a remote jungle—I'm almost afraid of what's next."

"Paris," Etta breathed out. She could see the painting of the Luxembourg Garden so clearly, could practically smell the sweetness of the grass, the trees, the endless flowerbeds. After the rain, the jungle had taken on a stronger smell of rot. With the cover of clouds, night was creeping in early, spreading its fingers over the skies, deepening the gloom. What was her mother's—or her family's—connection to *this* place?

"Good God. Let me guess: the French Revolution? The Reign of Terror?" He pinched the bridge of his nose. "I'm not quite sure I'm willing to lose my head in this search."

Etta had no idea, but at the terrifying rate they were going, she wouldn't be surprised if her mother threw in a guillotine as a challenge. She understood, sort of, that the point was to discourage travelers from following her trail, but . . . really?

She stretched her arms, her back. If her mother had been tough enough to make it, then Etta would be, too.

Home, she thought. *Home, Mom, and . . . what?*

"Is that anticipation I detect on your face?" he asked, with a small, knowing smile. She warmed at the sight of it, still feeling the soft, sweet touch of those same lips against her own.

"I don't . . . mind this so much," she admitted for the first time. What they could do—their ability—*was* exhilarating and absurd and terrible and wonderful, and it made her heart race. It made her feel, for the first time in a long time, a drive to step outside her bubble of strings and competition and endless practice. It made her feel capable and strong that she'd survived this far, that she was still surviving; it made her feel curious about all of these hidden eras that now, if she desired, could be spread open before her like a deck of cards, only waiting for her to pick one.

He kissed me.

She'd kissed him.

And it hadn't been an accident. It hadn't been a moment drunk with relief; not entirely. It had felt as natural and familiar as his hold on her now. She'd known instinctively that they'd been building toward something, and she was only glad it had been the same "something" she wanted. And maybe she *was* a pirate after all, because she would fight like hell before ever voluntarily surrendering the treasure she'd already found.

Glancing over at Nicholas, taking in his strong profile, one thought caught at the front of her mind, and she couldn't shake it free. It was a neat, easy solution, and she felt herself latch on to it in desperation.

328

If Cyrus would punish him for letting her get away with the astrolabe, then . . . maybe he *should* come with her to avoid it. Travel into the future, where he could have access to all of the modern marvels she took for granted; he could find work, go to school, and—

Never see Chase or Captain Hall again. The family he'd made for himself. Never own the ship he wanted so desperately.

It was selfish, she knew, to want him to come with her—and yes, it was mostly because she wanted to make sure he was safe, but she wasn't ready to never see him again, to never know what became of him, to never recapture that little groan he'd made when he kissed her. Etta would never kid herself into thinking that her time was some kind of post-racial utopia, where no one would ever hassle or harm him for the color of his skin, but it wasn't the eighteenth century. He could have a life there, one he could fully control. . . .

She blew out a long breath from her nose and reached up to touch his hand on her arm, still there from helping her navigate the moss-slick stones.

You can't decide that for him. She could only make decisions for herself.

Home was a clear path forward. Home was New York City, the debut, her mom, Alice, and . . .

The air was cooler than it had been in the minutes leading up to the storm, and she shivered hard enough for Nicholas to fold her into his side as they made their way up the path, toward the arch of one of the dark stone gates. Etta craned her neck back, to better see the enormous face looking outward over the same jungle that had sprouted through the pockets and cracks of the stone. The pointed peaks of the tower were carved down in tooth-like layers, seeming to enclose each other like the petals of a lotus blossom.

"Let's rest for a moment," Nicholas said, once they were under the cover of the gate's arch. The rain was still misting down around them—*spitting*, Alice had always called it—but the trees and structures were dripping wildly from the storm. She wanted a moment to try to wring out her dress, but . . . she wanted to keep moving. Etta understood, in a way she never had before, that time held intrinsic value, and that they were wasting it. She understood. So why was that small, secret part of her grateful that they were slowing down, even for a few minutes? To have one small sliver of time just to be near him, feel his skin against hers, hear his thoughts. Etta wasn't sure when the realization had come, if it had been shadowing her this whole time waiting to be acknowledged, but now it was here: the sooner they found the astrolabe, the sooner she'd be gone. And he'd told her many times that he didn't intend to travel after this, meaning that *gone* would be *for good*.

Stop it.

"We should keep moving." And stop thinking about options that weren't options at all. Stop stalling because she wasn't ready to let go of whatever this was.

Mom. The more she thought her admittedly flimsy plan through, the more Etta realized she would need to do all of this in *less* than the seven days they had left. She would need the element of surprise to get back to the future and pluck her mom out of harm's way—not to mention, she needed to use some of that extra time to figure out *where* she was being held.

"Etta, please," he said. "I know we're losing time, but you need to eat, and I need to make sure that there isn't anyone else around. I'll locate the passage. You tend to your . . . the wound."

The pleading quality in his voice pulled a protest from her lips. But as he stepped out, his gaze swinging over the city, she reached up and caught his wrist.

"I don't want to split up," she said. "Please, just . . . stay. I'll rest and eat for a few minutes, and we can find it together."

His expression softened. "All right, Etta. All right."

She sat down in the mud and leaned back against one arm of the gate as Nicholas settled across the other. She finally saw what he'd been doing when he had left her by the stream: cutting wood into bowl-like shapes. He held one out to catch the rain in its hollowed belly and passed it to her. Etta gulped it down in a single sip, then held it out again to collect more, as he did the same. Digging into the sopping wet bag, he removed his soaked shirt with a mournful look and passed her a bright little bundle—bananas.

Etta greedily tore into the first one, breaking its soft center into pieces as Nicholas gave up on wringing out his shirt and tugged it back on. Raindrops dripped from the arch in soft patters, catching the dim light. The water collected and flowed down the paths worn by hundreds of years of footsteps. In the distance, if she squinted, she could see pale-limbed trees growing into some of the structures, devastating whole sections of walls with their roots and branches.

It was the return of the singing birds that made her close her eyes, simply breathe in the damp air. When she opened them again, Nicholas was watching her, his knees drawn up, his expression inscrutable.

She could feel him drifting away on the tide of his thoughts, so she swam out to meet him.

"How about a kiss, hey?"

Etta liked that she was still able to startle him, just a little. The blank look of concentration broke as he barked out a laugh.

"I don't know if that's a wise idea. We'd never leave."

There it was: the bold line of his smile. Her blood heated at the sight of it, and despite her own flirting, Etta felt herself blush at the promise underlying his words. But just as quickly as the smile appeared, it slid away. He reached for her injured leg, inspecting the healing cut. Nicholas shook his head as he unwound the wet bandage. One hand grasped her ankle, the fingers stroking the curve of bone, while the other ran up the length of the muscle, skirting around the puckered red wound. Etta felt a prickle of goose bumps rise in the places he touched. A different kind of ache hollowed the pit of her stomach, and the echoing heat rose up over her chest, her neck, her face, until all of her ached with the need to touch him in return.

He leaned forward, pressing a faint kiss to a bruise on her shin she hadn't cared to notice until now.

"It's not your fault," she said softly. If she had been paying attention, she would have been able to avoid the snake in the first place. Etta had never doubted that for an instant.

The reply was whispered against her skin. "I'll come to see it that way eventually. For now, let me wallow a bit."

Etta smiled sweetly, pushing up onto her knees. She crawled the distance between them, listening as his breathing grew more ragged. His gaze focused on her face. His hands curled over the top of his knees, and they were shaking as she put hers over them.

Picking up his right hand, she pressed a soft kiss to the rough, scarred knuckles, and as he shuddered she felt an answering shiver low in her stomach. She set his hand back down and rested her arms over his hands, trapping them against his knees.

"You make . . ." Nicholas trailed off as she leaned forward, brushing a faint kiss across his lips. When he didn't lean back, when she breathed in his soft exhale, she did it again, applying a little more pressure. She felt him try to tug his hands out from under hers, but she held firm, watching as a look of amazement spread over his face. She worried, just for a moment, that she was trading one obsession for another—trading the high of performing for this strange sense of freedom, for the way a wild, unfamiliar part of herself was opening up around him. He made her feel brave; he let her be who she was unconditionally, without judgment, and because of it, she felt life shifting around her into something that felt much more beautiful and clear.

He said the words so quietly, she wondered if she'd imagined them. "Then it's the same for you?"

She ran her nose down the length of his, and there wasn't a part of her that wasn't humming, that wasn't rejoicing in this tiny, perfect symphony of happiness.

"Release me," he said hoarsely. He was strong enough to pull his hands away by force; her thoughts spun in a dizzying dance of want and confusion and desperation. "Etta—"

He leaned forward and captured her lips, stealing the kiss himself until she had to come up and gasp for breath. Nicholas pulled her back under, and this time she did let go, only to take his beautiful face in her hands, to let his hands tangle in her hair, around her shoulders. If the sky had opened again just then, Etta didn't think she'd feel the storm at all—not when she was caught so deeply in this. Time was tugging at her back, insistent and demanding, passing faster and faster, but all she wanted was to stay there, to smell the sea on his skin and press her face to that part of his neck where it seemed to fit perfectly, as if it had been made to hold her and her alone. If there was a place to go where time might forget them, she wanted to find it.

He was breathing hard enough that she felt his heart jumping against her ribs, and she knew hers was doing the same. She turned, running her lips along the curve of his ear, her fingers pressed against the solid muscles of his back.

"We can't," he said into her hair, half-pleading, "we can't make this so bloody difficult."

Too late.

What was she even doing—torturing herself with what she couldn't have? She could fight this, whatever force it was that dragged her back to him, that knotted their yearning. *Attraction.* She would go home and he would go home, and whatever kept pulling them back together would be dissolved by distance and time and death.

He's been dead for hundreds of years by the time you're born.

They weren't supposed to have ever met. Maybe that's why she wanted it so badly—it was impossible, and both of them were too stubborn to let themselves be told what they could and couldn't have.

Right now, she didn't care.

Right now, *he* didn't care.

Etta wasn't sure who reached for the other, only that she was kissing him again until her lungs burned and her body ached for him to be closer. Her back collided with the wet stone of the gate, and she imagined she could taste the storm in him, the battering winds of desperation and frustration that met and matched her own, blow for blow.

His lips softened against hers as his hands slid from the nape of her neck to brace his weight against the wall, trapping her against it. She felt Nicholas give in to the slow exploration of her. The tenderness of his touch made her hands curl in his wet shirt. The world dissolved around her, as if she'd stepped through another passage.

Passage.

She pulled him closer, trying to will the world away. Nicholas made a small, hungry noise in his throat.

Astrolabe.

Sliding her hands around his waist, her fingers went searching for the warm bare skin beneath his shirt.

Mom.

"Etta," he was murmuring, turning her name into a secret, "*Etta . . . we . . . the passage . . .*"

There's no time.

"I know," she managed to say against his lips, "I . . ."

Etta didn't have the strength to push him away, to end it, the way they both knew they had to. Even now, the knowledge only filled her with more desperation, made her unbearably feverish beneath her skin. She gripped him tighter, refusing to let go.

No time for this.

This had to stop the same way it had begun. Together. She felt him slow; the lazy, drugging quality of his kisses faded to a ghost of a touch.

No time for us.

She let out a shaky breath and turned her face away. Nicholas leaned down and rested his head against one of his hands, trying to catch his breath.

After a while he said, his voice hollow, "Rather proved my earlier point, didn't I? We need—we need to go, before Ironwood sends a traveler after us. If he hasn't already."

Etta kept her gaze on the wet stones, the winding rivulets of water slipping between them, and nodded. *Why this?* The thought seared through her. *Why him? Why?*

"Do you know where we're meant to go?" he asked quietly. He lifted a hand to touch her face but let it fall away, as if thinking better of it.

"It's . . . I think we're looking for the Elephant Terrace," she said when she'd found her voice. "That's what my mom's painting was of—a view of it from slightly above. I don't know where it is inside, though."

"That's all right, we have a way of quickly finding it. I imagine we're close enough for it to catch the resonance." Nicholas reached into the bag and blew into the harmonica. The call of the passage echoed back twofold, volleying through the empty stones around them. Etta strained her ears, picking through the layers of its call, until she could orient herself in the direction it was coming from. There was something about it, though, a hum she didn't recognize.

Her whole body tensed. "Does it sound different to you?"

"It sounds as atrocious as it always does." Nicholas shifted the bag back onto his shoulder. "Shall we?"

She shook off her concern and followed him through the abandoned city. A part of her wondered how long it had taken the jungle to erase most of the evidence of human life—Etta wished she could remember the exact reason why both Angkor Thom and Angkor Wat had been abandoned, but she thought it had something to do with war, and the ever-shifting tide of power that eventually brought down even the greatest of civilizations. Without the resonance the passage had bounced back to them, she wasn't sure she would have been able to find it at all. While her mom had shown her maps of the city, pointing out where she'd done her dig—if there had even been a dig in her past at all, Etta thought—the pathways were nearly so overgrown, the stone and remnants of wooden structures in such disrepair, she just barely recognized the Bayon when they passed it.

"That's the Bayon," Etta explained, catching Nicholas's appreciative look at the massive structure. "My mom said that there are over two hundred faces on it, if you look—some people believe many of them are of the king who built the city. Jayavarman the Seventh."

"I suppose that's one way to ensure you'll be remembered," he said. "He's a rather handsome devil. How do you think I'd look on one of these temples?"

Etta laughed. "How would I look?"

"I couldn't bear the thought of even your face here, left alone, for only the jungle to admire." He shook his head. "Never. I'd never allow it. The only thing is to hire an artist to turn you into a figurehead for a ship, so some part of you will always be venturing out to sea where you belong."

Etta was so stunned by this earnest speech, she lost all capacity for speech herself. He seemed to notice, and ducked his head in scowling embarrassment.

"All right," she said. "But only on the condition that you give me some kind of a sword. Maybe even an eye patch? Use your best discretion on what will be more terrifying for your future prey."

"Aye," Nicholas agreed, exaggerating and deepening his accent, "the very sight of you will strike fear in the hearts of all men."

She grinned.

The bas-reliefs along the sides of the temple were darkened by rain and clinging green plants, but Etta could still make out the

carved panel of what looked to her like a market—people barter-
ing and selling, with fish swimming above them. They walked
quickly past images of warriors marching alongside elephants to
war, a scene of an enormous fish swallowing a deer, and what had
to be a royal procession, following the barest hint of a footpath
through the mud. The rain had washed away any evidence that
the monks had ever been there, but Nicholas didn't relax, didn't
lower his guard, until they spotted the passage's glimmering wall
of light floating above what Etta knew was the Elephant Terrace.

The same one her mother had painted and hung above the
couch in the living room.

The Elephant Terrace stood a short distance away from the—
her mind reached for the name—the Phimeanakas, the city's first
temple. The one that housed a sacred tree buried within it, where
her mother had actually done her dig. She eyed the steep stairway
that hugged the stacked layers of the temple; the stone seemed
almost red compared to the elaborate gray structure that sat on
top of it.

What was her family's connection to this place?

She turned back toward the raised platform in front of them,
accepting a hand up from Nicholas as he climbed it. The king
had used this terrace to survey the march of his victorious army,
and carved around it, chipped away from the supports, were elephants. The platform looked as if it was resting upon their backs.

"*Stand on the shoulders of memory,*" Nicholas breathed out. The
clue made sense to Etta now—elephants were celebrated for their
memories—but it didn't explain the way the passage made the
air feel like it was hiccupping. The sound coming off it, its usual
bellow of thunder, almost drowned out a second, lower beat. It

reminded Etta of the way that you could sometimes feel your pulse in another, unexpected part of your body.

"Whatever is the matter?" Nicholas asked.

"Nothing, just . . ." Etta looked back at the city, slowly turning to take in the sight of the trees that seemed as if they were stepping over the walls, the faces on the Bayon that watched her with tranquil, serene smiles. When in her life would she see this again—see the city at this moment, before humanity came flooding back into it?

Never.

This was the danger, the seduction of time travel, she realized—it was the opportunity, the freedom of a thousand possibilities of where to live and how to start over. It was the beauty open to you in your life if you only stopped for a moment to look. Those things drowned out even the most basic dangers of collapsing passages, of being lost, of finding yourself in an unfriendly time.

"It's time," Nicholas said quietly, offering his hand.

Again, she felt her desire for music swelling in her like an ache. Her fingers pressed against her side, and she imagined how she would try to coax a song of hidden depth, and warm, wild life, from the strings. And when she passed through the damp jungle air into the electric, shivering fingers of the passage, she mourned the fact that she would never see this place again.

PARIS
1880

FIFTEEN

ETTA FOUND HERSELF AWAKE, SPRAWLED OUT ON THE grass beneath a generous cover of shade, ears ringing, head throbbing—but awake. And not just awake, but also free of the sickening swoop of dizziness that had come hand in hand with the last passages.

She sat up, brushing a red leaf out of her hair. The crisp autumn air was practically golden as it came down through the fiery shade of the leaves overhead. When she turned, Etta wasn't the least bit surprised to see the Luxembourg Garden laid out in front of her, a vision in the warm afternoon light.

"You were correct." Nicholas was sitting with his back against the same tree, rubbing his face. *"C'est le Jardin du Luxembourg."*

Etta couldn't stop her small, ridiculous smile. "Say it again."

"Pardon?" he asked.

Say it again, she thought. His voice did something incredible to the French language. The words moved through her like warm honey.

"C'est le Jardin du Luxembourg," he repeated, visibly bewildered.

343

"So . . . what day do you think it is?"

"The same day as when we woke up in London," he answered. He knew what she was thinking.

Etta's dress had torn in several places at the hem, and had turned from sky blue to a brown usually reserved for muddy rivers. Her boots were crusted with dried dirt and mulch, and she didn't need to touch her hair to know that it was standing straight up in several places.

Nicholas took a quick look around—to make sure they weren't being watched?—and began to smooth her wild waves down, collecting her hair at the nape of her neck. He was careful not to touch her skin as he pulled a ribbon from their bag and used it to tie the mass of it back. Etta was careful not to give in to the urge to lean against his shoulder and wrap her arms around his narrow waist.

Seven days. Less.

"Shall we?" she asked.

"Let's make a slow and careful approach of this," he said. "I want to make sure we don't raise too much alarm. . . ."

And she wanted to make sure that it would be safe for him.

The odd thing was, as they passed through the last of the trees and stood on the edge of the path, Etta couldn't get a sense of where they were in time. The women's fashions were somewhere between the nineteenth and twentieth centuries—brightly colored, finely tailored jackets with long skirts that were bustled up in the back or decorated with layers of ruffles, exaggerating the natural curves of their bodies. Hair was hidden beneath bonnets and hats, all decorated with flowers and ribbons.

The men accompanying them, or playing games of cards or chess, wore suits and top hats. Some strolled around a large basin—a central reflecting pool—with canes. Children ran through and around the artists and their easels; women sat beside one another on benches, talking idly. It was not all that different from the Luxembourg Garden of her own time. At the head of the garden, past the large reflecting pool, was the palace itself, as stately as she remembered, standing like a section of Versailles that had broken off and wandered away.

"We should be all right," Nicholas said, keeping his voice low. "The trick is not to meet anyone's eyes—"

It was like he'd been caught on a hook—one minute he was standing beside her, as tense as any of the marble statues, and the next he was running, off like a shot, jumping over the nearest bed of flowers and ruffling their bright heads. Women shrieked as he passed, men screamed after him—Nicholas didn't bother with the crowded path around the reflecting pool, but simply cut through the water, splashing through the shallow pool and leaping out on the other side. Two little boys attempted to follow him before being snatched back by their nannies.

For a moment Etta stood still, her arm still outstretched after him. Something cold was pressed into her palm by a passing, kind-faced old man: a few coins.

"Wait—no!" she began, trying to give them back. "I'm not— never mind."

She pocketed the coins and ran after Nicholas, trying to let the sting of being mistaken for a beggar roll off her shoulders. First time for everything, and all that.

It was easy enough to follow his dark shape through the crowds as he ran past the statues of French queens, toward the path that would lead them to the nearest road. Finally he stopped, but his shoulders blocked out what, exactly, he'd been chasing until Etta was standing directly behind him, with the gawkers collecting there.

It was a woman—older, if the lines on her face were any indication, but elegantly tall. Her dark skin was the shade of deep earth, her hair hidden beneath a plain sort of hat. Compared to the other women around her, she was dressed simply, almost as if the outfit was a uniform.

An overturned basket had crashed at her feet. Etta moved quickly, trying to gather up the tins that had gone rolling out of it down the path. When she turned, Nicholas's hand was still on her shoulder as he spoke in gruff French. *"Je suis vraiment désolé. Je croyais . . . ma mère . . ."*

At that, the look of terror on the older woman's face disappeared. *"De rien."* She smiled at him, patting his hand. *"Tu es un cher garçon."*

Etta righted the basket, passing it back to her wordlessly. Nicholas looked stricken, as if the whole of his chest was caving in.

"Au revoir," the woman said, with a small wave.

"Au—uh, *au revoir,*" Etta managed, watching her as she hurried away.

Nicholas stared after her, swaying on his feet. Water dripped off his pants, out of his shoes.

"It'll be best if we go unnoticed, huh?" she said.

Nicholas didn't reply—he just stood there, rooted in place.

Better to keep moving than risk being seen by guardians nearby, or by the police. Etta hooked her arm through his and led him off the path, weaving through the trees and picnickers until she found a spot she recognized—the Medici Fountain, and the long pool stretching out in front of it.

She negotiated his big body onto the nearest bench. "Are you okay?"

He shook his head, swallowing.

Etta looked through the bag at his side, digging through it to find some kind of food to give him. Nicholas was in some kind of shock. Turning up nothing, she said, "I'll be right back."

With the coins the old man had given her, and some careful gesturing, she was able to buy a loaf of bread and a small glass of lemonade from a vendor. A sympathetic man was willing to move the queue behind her along by translating, and giving her the last bit of money she needed.

By the time she had made it back to Nicholas and the fountain, he'd come back to himself and was on his feet, pacing—looking for her. The relief that crashed over his features made her rush over to him, careful not to let too much of the lemonade slosh out onto her hand.

He pulled the food and drink out of her hands, setting them aside, and wrapped his arms around her. She did the same, standing on her toes, arms locked around his shoulders, and did what she'd wanted to do from the moment she'd left him there: hold him until he finally stopped shaking.

She didn't care about witnesses. When she rocked back onto her heels, releasing him, she gestured to the bread. "I paid good money for that! You'd better eat every last bite."

"Every last bite," he promised, even as he tore a piece off for her. He took his seat again with a sheepish look around them. "I have to confess, I'm surprised they haven't marked us as vagrants and thrown us out yet."

Etta decided not to tell him where the money for the bread

and drink had come from. Instead, she watched his fascinated, puckered reaction as he took a sip of the lemonade.

"My God," he coughed, pounding his chest. "When does it stop burning?"

"In all of your travels, you never had lemonade?" she asked. "What? Only beer and wine for you?"

"Better than diseased water." He tore the small loaf in half, bringing his piece up to his nose to smell it. The obvious pleasure on his face gave her a flush of happiness, too.

"What happened?" she asked softly.

He took a steadying breath, looking out over the water again. "I thought that woman . . . I caught a glimpse of her as she was hurrying across the park, and for an instant, I truly believed she was my mother."

Etta felt the world shrink around them painfully, tighten around her shoulders, until it hurt even to breathe.

"I know it sounds mad, that it was bloody reckless, but the resemblance was uncanny. Of course it wasn't her. She's long dead by this year. I know it, but it was as if—" He folded his hands in his lap, shaking his head. "It was as if, for a moment, the clouds of the past cleared and gave her back to me."

Etta leaned against his shoulder, wishing there was something she could say. "Did you ever find out what happened to her?"

He nodded. "While I was gallivanting with Julian, Hall finished the work I'd begun in searching for her—she died in South Carolina, in 1773, of a fever." Nicholas managed to choke out one last word. "Alone. I'm not even sure where they buried her. Hall thought that, even with my papers, it was too dangerous to attempt to find the grave."

"I'm so sorry," she breathed out.

He rested his face against her hair.

"I haven't many regrets in my life," Nicholas said, "and I suppose I should be grateful that there's just the one. As much as I do blame Ironwood, I can't divide myself from the guilt. I should not have accepted Ironwood's offer, and left the sea to travel. Then, perhaps, I might have found her in time, and purchased her freedom. Julian would not have fallen; I'd be free of every shackle this family has tried to place on me."

Etta understood all too well what this kind of regret felt like as it burrowed deep inside of you. She would do just about anything to relive those last few moments with Alice, but even traveling was out of the question. She couldn't exist in the same place—the same year—twice.

But Nicholas hadn't been in 1773. At least not all of it. She was almost afraid to ask.

"Isn't there a passage you could take to that year? I know you can't save Julian, that it would change too much. And if she was sick, not even you could have kept her alive. But maybe . . . maybe it would bring you both some peace?"

He shook his head. "There isn't a passage to that year. I've thought this through a thousand times—I've considered how I could get a message to Hall in the past, to keep myself from going. But as much as I wish I'd made a different choice, I can't bring myself to be quite that selfish. To risk all of those changes rippling out."

"When you told me I couldn't save Alice, you spoke from experience."

"I should have told you the whole of it," he murmured.

This memory was clearly something he kept buried deep, a dagger he kept wrapped in layer upon layer of distraction, to avoid cutting himself by brushing up against it. She understood and respected that.

"That's an easy fix, though," Etta said. "Before, you didn't have the astrolabe."

He sat up, pulling away. She'd managed to shock him again. "Etta—"

"No—don't shake your head like it's impossible. It isn't. We could take the time to create a passage for you, before we . . ."

"Before we give it to Ironwood?" he prompted, with obvious suspicion in his eyes.

She nodded, hating the lie. "This is all simpler than you want to think it is."

His lips compressed into a tight, unhappy line. Why couldn't he believe that this was a true possibility, that he could have everything he wanted? Why was he reluctant? Nicholas didn't want to continue traveling; but one last trip to see his mother, to be with her and ease his mind—wouldn't that be worth it?

"Regardless, we need to find the bloody thing first, which means that it's especially lucky that I've figured out the clue." Nicholas spread his hand out on the stone banister that ran along the water's edge. "You brought us right to it."

"You mean . . ." Etta followed his gaze back to the fountain. *"Bring a coin to the widowed queen."*

"This is the Medici Fountain, built by Marie de Medici, the widow of Henry the Fourth of France, isn't it?" Nicholas gestured to the fountain. "Julian brought me here to chase the skirt of some girl he'd seen on the street. If there's one thing that's true of all Ironwoods, they love to lecture and give unsolicited history lessons."

Etta nodded. The stone on the fountain had been carefully worked; two figures sat atop columns that were interspersed with more sculptures. At the very center were three more statues: *Polyphemus Surprising Acis and Galatea*, with the hulking bronze cyclops, Polyphemus, peering over a boulder, and the ill-fated lovers carved out of white marble. Her mother loved and specialized in the conservation of works from the Italian Renaissance, and this fountain had used elements of that in its classic grotto style. To Etta, it was an obvious connection.

Nicholas blew out another ragged breath, burying his face in his palms. Etta reached over, stroking his hair in reassurance. She wasn't sure what was upsetting him more: that he had drawn so much unwanted attention to himself, or that he'd let himself get his hopes up. When he still seemed distraught, his muscles tensed, she took his hand and threaded their fingers together. He returned her soft squeeze with one of his own.

"Bring a coin. . . ." she muttered. Of course—you brought coins to fountains to make a wish. "I think you're right."

She pulled the harmonica out of the bag again with her free hand and brought it to her lips. Her shoulders locked as she braced herself for the deafening ripple of noise to wash over them.

"Wait," he said before she could blow into it, his hand closing over her wrist. "Etta, I need to tell you something—"

The sudden crack of the passage sent them both to their feet. The harmonica skidded to the edge of the water, forcing Etta to dive in order to save it. Nicholas's arm lashed out as she started to rise, keeping her down as he craned his neck around.

"I didn't—" she started to say. *I didn't play the chord.* But if the passage was letting out its usual blistering cry, then—

Two figures stepped out from behind the fountain, dropping bags and shrugging out of black tuxedo jackets. One, a tall chestnut-haired man, clawed at the bow tie around his neck, laughing deeply at something the shorter, blond young man beside him was saying. Both were handsome, and there was something familiar about them—Etta couldn't place it, not until the one with dark hair looked up, and his icy blue gaze fixed on her.

In that moment, she wasn't sure who was more shocked: Nicholas, who sucked in a sharp, alarmed breath; her, as she realized that this man had the same eyes as Cyrus; or the man himself, as he went chalk white and called out, "Rose?"

Nicholas hauled her up from the ground and said a single word: "Run."

Nicholas's longer legs ate up the ground with ease, forcing her to double her speed just to keep up with him. The men and women taking in the sunset scattered.

"Rose!" the man shouted. "Rose!"

"Damn it all," Nicholas swore.

The gunshot sent the Parisians scattering in every direction like a colorful array of feathers. Another shot rang out, blistering the skin of the tree beside Nicholas and sending down a shower of leaves and bark.

Before she could think about why it was a bad idea, Etta reached across Nicholas into the leather bag. She closed her fingers around the handle of the gun and whipped it out. The back of the gun's body had a kind of hook— Her thumb caught it, pulled it back, and with the slightest pressure on the trigger, a bullet exploded from the gun.

The reverberation shot up through her bones; her eardrums

winced at the deafening sound. But it had the desired effect. The travelers broke off from behind them.

"Bloody hell!" Nicholas swore, spinning to look at her. "You liked that, didn't you?"

She shrugged. Maybe a little. Enough to want to try again, and actually aim this time. Wisdom, however, prevailed, and she surrendered the gun to the more experienced marksman as they ran.

Nicholas led them across the garden's green lawn and through the trees, until they were outside of the park and darting across the street. He followed the curve of the road, shouldering through startled onlookers, and ducked into a tight alley. When he crouched down behind some stacked crates, she followed, her chest burning so fiercely she was afraid she'd be sick.

"Bloody hell," he said again, shaking harder than before as he touched a cut on his shoulder. Had the bullet actually grazed him?

"Who?" she panted, leaning forward, trying to see around the crates.

Nicholas leaned his head back against the dank stone wall behind them. "My father. Augustus Ironwood."

Etta had suspected—she'd seen those eyes and recognized the look of Cyrus, his nose, his brows, on the younger man. But more than that, she'd seen the flash of anguish cut across his face as he'd called her by her mother's name.

"Are you all right?" she asked, touching his arm.

"Not the first time that man's nearly killed me," he said off-handedly, "but hopefully it will be the last. Christ, I didn't think I'd ever see him again. Bloody time travel, bloody—"

Oh my God—Etta thought she'd understood this before—that,

even after a traveler died, there was still the chance of bumping into them again at some point in history. Each passage was fixed to a specific year and location, but not a date. What were the chances that they'd managed to land on the exact time that a past version of his father had decided to show up?

"The irony of seeing him . . ." Nicholas shook his head, accepting her touch as she ran the backs of her fingers down his face. He caught them, twining them between his own. His gaze was on the opposite wall, but she saw the emotions storming within him.

Why would her mother hide the astrolabe in a place where the Ironwoods clearly had access to the passage?

Because she hadn't.

When Etta closed her eyes, thought of the wall of paintings, traced the line of her mother's stories to the last one she could remember, it brought her here; it was about her being accepted at the Sorbonne for art history. That was the last piece on the wall.

No.

Etta sat up so suddenly that Nicholas turned to her, worry etched on his face. The painting of Luxembourg Garden wasn't the last one on the wall—or at least her mother had told her she was planning to switch it out, for—for that new painting, the one she had done of the desert in Syria. She had told Etta she was going to replace it. She had woven in that story about the earrings, the market in Damascus, the woman who had sold them to her. And, as Etta was discovering, her mother apparently wasn't the type to do something for no reason.

Are you listening, Etta?

You won't forget, will you?

"Remember, the truth is in the telling," Etta said slowly. *In other words, what she told me overrules anything she's written?*

Maybe her mother had moved the painting at some point after writing the clues out—or had it been meant to be a false lead, on the off chance that Ironwood figured out her set of clues, and picked up her trail? In either case, they were in the wrong city, the wrong time.

"We have to go back," she said. "We missed something. We're not supposed to be here."

"But you said . . ." Nicholas's brow wrinkled. "Are you certain?"

"Positive," Etta said. "Can we get back to the passage to Angkor?"

"We can damn well try."

As they both feared, the authorities had been called to Luxembourg Garden after the disturbance, and Etta felt a shiver work through her at the thought of it being written up in the papers—of there being a witness, a record of the event. They'd been so careful until now. . . .

"I wouldn't worry," Nicholas said. "I think . . . perhaps this was supposed to happen."

She looked up, startled. They were keeping to the very edge of the garden, weaving in and out of the outer ring of trees. The uniforms of the police blended in with the dark suits of the men giving their statements and accounts, offset by the pops of vivid color that were the women.

"In Virgil's letter he referenced a sighting by my—that Augustus had, of Rose in Paris. Perhaps this was it?"

Perhaps. But that was almost too insane for her to accept. It took away the idea that she had free will in any of this; it seemed to suggest there was a set path that they were already on, and had been on from the beginning.

"Or perhaps it's only a coincidence," he said.

The passage was only humming by the time they found it, rippling in the darkening air. Nicholas forced her to wait a moment while he prowled through the trees, his pistol drawn, to make sure they were alone. When they finally stepped through the passage, the crushing pressure felt familiar, like a too-tight embrace, but not like an attack against each one of her senses.

The entrance spit her out at full speed, and Etta found herself slipping forward onto the stone, pinwheeling her arms to try to slow down. Her weight carried her forward until her toes hung over the edge of the terrace, forcing her to sit to avoid falling on her face.

"Etta? Where are you?"

The darkness in her vision wasn't from traveler's sickness, then—the sky was as black as coal around them.

Same day, she thought wearily. *Different time-zone.*

A heavy set of clouds blocked out the moonlight and the stars. In response, her other senses came alive again: the sweet, rotting smell of the jungle as it decayed and bloomed in turn. The sound of small raindrops striking the stones and leaves. Nicholas's hands brushing the top of her head as he felt around in the darkness.

"I am praying to God that that's you and not another tiger."

Etta laughed. As if in response, a cloud peeled back just enough for a thin shaft of moonlight to sneak down and make the puddles glow.

"Quick—where's the harmonica?" said Nicholas.

He released a single, powerful breath and winced as the passage screamed back in response.

Her ears, already sharp, were beyond sensitive when all of her other senses were swamped; it reminded her of all of the times that Oskar had demonstrated a technique and asked her to close her eyes to truly focus her ears on the difference in tone or sound quality. The layers she heard before were easier to separate now, like sections of an orchestra.

There. She'd been right before.

"Do you hear that?" Etta asked.

Nicholas said, "All I hear are Satan's hammers and the war drums of hell, thank you."

Etta shushed him.

He fidgeted impatiently. "I mean no disrespect, but perhaps . . ."

"Listen," Etta said, and then began to hum, matching the pitch of the low, growling snarl. It changed without warning; she adjusted the sound until it was sharper, higher, a match to a trilling his ear had ignored.

Each gate seemed to deliver a veritable mess of sounds as they struck the air, but these two were so different in their nature, cast at such different pitches, that she was angry with herself for not investigating it before. There were two calls woven together. Two passages.

"So there is another one here," he said. "I can hardly hear it. . . ."

Etta turned, trying to decide where it was coming from; the stones bounced the sound around, disguising its true source.

Nicholas swung his gaze around wildly, searching for the ripple of air, the glimmer of the second passage's entrance.

When he turned back to her, he was smiling. "I know where it is."

"You do not!" Etta said, standing on her toes and searching herself.

"I do believe that one goes under my tally," he said, obviously enjoying her outrage.

"Have you been keeping score?" she demanded.

"You haven't?"

All right, fine. "I figured out how to find the one in London."

"We found the passage to Paris together, and the old man figured out the location of the passage in my time," he said, "so, no points awarded for those. We're one for one, pirate. An even draw."

That . . . didn't sound so terrible after all. "How are you so sure?" she asked.

"You may be a lady with the ears of a dog, but I've the eyes of a hawk," he said, pointing up at the top of the Phimeanakas, the temple across the way. Hundreds of steep stairs led up to the grand entrance . . . and to a wavering blanket of air that sparkled like its own starry sky. "And I do believe *that* is the passage we've been searching for."

DAMASCUS
1599

SIXTEEN

IT SEEMED TO NICHOLAS THAT THE KEY TO PASSING
through these time gates and landing on your feet lay squarely in
the approach, and required a great deal of faith in your balance.

A confident stride through the rippling air resulted in only
the slightest push as you came through to the other side—you
emerged at a brisk walk, rather than feeling as if you were being
shot from a cannon. There was no way around the disorienting
pressure and darkness on the journey, but if your mind knew to
expect it, there were ways to prepare for the strike.

Etta released a soft "Oofph!" as her feet struck the floor, and
they were suddenly wrapped in cool, dry air. Nicholas's grip on
her hand tightened as the world fell into place around them.

They weren't falling off the side of a cliff. They hadn't been
shot dead on sight, run through by sword or bayonet. And they
hadn't emerged into a crocodile-filled swamp, or in the middle of
a crowded market, or for that matter, in a burning building. So
he supposed he should be grateful. But he was mostly exhausted.

He had no way of knowing what time it was, only that it was
clearly night; hopefully, the same night as the one they had just

left in Cambodia. Distant voices prickled in his ears, the words muffled by distance or cast in a lyrical language he couldn't decipher. It was as if the air itself had been seasoned with the richest and rarest of spices, so thick he was certain he could taste it on his tongue. The breeze carried other scents that were familiar and strange all at once—there, beneath the warm sweat of beasts of burden and smoke, were notes of a heady, floral fragrance.

His eyes eventually adjusted to the darkness, well enough for him to make out the shapes around him. The room was large, and there appeared to be an elaborate wooden bed in the far corner, as well as some sort of desk or table, so laden with piles of objects that he couldn't quite tell what it was.

Etta fumbled around the room, and with a flash of white, pulled a sheet off of the chair it covered. She did the same with another sheet, uncovering a low table stacked with newspapers and books.

"Some sort of home?" he ventured. The passage's gate thrummed behind them. The sound wouldn't fade entirely, but within an hour it would start to lessen.

"An apartment," Etta agreed, stepping closer to the bed. "Here—here, matches." She held up a small book of them. "Do you see any candles?"

Matches had yet to be invented in his time, but Julian had showed him how to use them during their travels—how to strike the small strips of wood against the rough strip on the jacket containing them. Clever little buggers. As Nicholas marveled again at this small luxury, singeing multiple fingertips as he located a few half-melted candles, Etta moved toward the shutters lining the far wall.

"Don't—" he said, catching her arm. "Not yet."

They didn't need to open themselves up to being caught by someone passing on the street below.

Etta stepped back, holding her hands in the air. "All right, all right. Should we light a fire?"

Nicholas glanced toward the small fireplace, but shook his head. They could use the additional glow from the hearth to see, but the smoke might also draw undesirable attention. "Leave it for now. If you're chilled, I'll warm you."

Etta laughed, pushing him away playfully. What surprised him, perhaps more than his disappointment, was the way her eyes lit at his words, sparking the way the matches had.

Stop this, he commanded himself, ripping away the nearest bed cloth to reveal a distinctly European leather chair. What did it matter that she was clearly as intrigued as he was, that she'd looked at him as though he was the last treasure to be had in the world? Why be so eager to allow her to capture his heart, when it would lead to precisely one thing: nothing?

And yet, he was gripped by the images glittering through his mind, flashing like the sunlight on open water: the memory of her melting beneath his hands, how she'd tasted of rain and earth and sweetness—

There were countless mirrors and portraits to be uncovered, all of which had been taken from their hooks and leaned against the wall, frames and all. English ladies from his time, powdered and pouting; French princesses whose silk gowns seemed to drip from their bodies; fierce Spanish ladies. So the owner clearly recognized beauty when he saw it—tried to collect it and hoard it. He—or she, he supposed—also seemed to love nothing so dearly as landscapes of green pastures. Nicholas made a disgusted face as he turned the next painting around to reveal . . . yet another scene of sheep idling in a flower-spotted field.

Leaving the paintings for a moment, he turned to a large

bench-size object covered with another cloth; upon whipping off the cloth, he found himself staring into the snarling face and exceptionally long, talon-like teeth of a tiger.

He fell back onto the ornately woven red rug beneath them and lay on his back, stunned, as a shower of fine dust fell over him.

"You get that out of your system?" Etta asked, stepping around his prone form. His hand lashed out, closing around her ankle like an iron. The woman was mad if she thought he'd let her take another step forward—

"It's dead," she said, looking down at him with an amused smile. "As gross as it is, it's been preserved and stuffed to be displayed. Look."

He inhaled sharply through his nose as she reached out a hand to stroke its head. As promised, it did not move. It did not blink. The tiger was dead.

"What are the chances your mother killed and stuffed it herself?"

"Pretty good, I think." Etta held up a framed photograph of an older man in the garb of an early twentieth-century explorer, who was holding a rifle. The tiger lay dead at the toes of his boots, and beside it was a grinning, tiny, blond girl—a younger version of the woman in the other photograph he'd seen. Rose.

And he'd wondered from whom Etta had inherited her casual disregard for danger.

She hesitated before reaching out to run a hand along its curved spine. The coat was orange, striped handsomely with black all the way down to its clawed paws. Having missed the tiger that Etta had seen in the jungle, Nicholas allowed himself to marvel. He'd read of Europe's menageries, seen descriptions and etchings of the exotic beasts, but to see one for himself . . .

And yet, what right did a man have to take the life of such a powerful creature, to prop up his own esteem?

"I guess this explains Mom's connection to Cambodia. And here I was, hoping Benjamin Linden was a Buddhist. I'm going to yell at her for this," Etta vowed, giving the thing an affectionate pat on the head. "Tigers are endangered now, you know."

Well . . . all right.

"The older gentleman in this photo is likely your great-grandfather, given what we know about how your mother was raised," he said, passing it back to her waiting hand. She squinted at it, rubbing a thumb over its dusty face.

"I can see it," she said quietly, studying Benjamin Linden's face. "He has her eyes. Her mouth."

Features she had inherited herself. Etta seemed both intrigued and rattled to finally have proof of him—proof that her family existed beyond her and her mother.

"Alice is right. They should have destroyed it," Etta said.

He hesitated a moment before clarifying. "The astrolabe?"

She nodded, and the now-familiar poison of guilt and dread worked its way through his system; he would have preferred to avoid the topic altogether rather than think about his own deceit, how it would crush her to know he had to bring it to Ironwood.

"You won't be able to use it if you do," he was quick to point out. *And Ironwood will never let you or your mother escape.*

"I know you're right, but I can't see a way out of this without huge consequences. I still have a few more days . . . not that many, but a few. I just need to figure out how to avoid giving it to Ironwood, but save Mom." Etta said, sensing his thoughts. "And then, I guess we'll . . . disappear."

His heart clenched at the word.

"What about the violin? Performing?"

"What about a different future, one I never could have predicted?"

He drew his legs up, bracing his arms over his knees. Some part of him knew the truth of what Chase had seen—he felt an equality between himself and Etta. But now and then, in moments like this one, when she casually tossed out ideas he didn't understand and was too ashamed to ask about, he fully realized the differences between their upbringings—how much their worlds had been shaped by where and when they'd been born. She knew things beyond his imagining—what could he give to her, other than history lessons?

He'd lied to her, of course, about not wanting to know. Nicholas did. Even if it meant living with the knowledge of all that his life lacked. A part of himself he did not recognize, one he'd learned to silence as a boy, began to demand the attention he'd always denied it.

I want to know. I want to seek. I want to find.

For the first time since Hall had taken him from that frigid house of terror, he felt the touch of a changing wind blowing through him, pushing him toward a different path. All of these things he desired, he could have; if not on a ship, then by seeking out the passages that could carry him where he wanted to go. And he would have her: the lady with whom he wished to travel.

He spotted the leather notebook a short distance away, near the foot of the side table; it was embossed with the emblem of the Linden family, their tree, but the interior pages were blank, waiting to be filled with dates and memories. Waiting for a traveler to mark his trips through the passages.

"This must be one of your family's homes," he told her.

"Ironwood seized all property belonging to the other families, but it's possible that, like the passages we used, he doesn't know that this one exists."

Etta spun around slowly, taking in the room, breathing in its air, as if trying to become part of it.

Nicholas looked back down at the journal in his hand.

He could return to the Dove—but he doubted the old man would have left his small bag and belongings untouched, if he thought he could somehow use them to control Nicholas. No, he could seek out Chase and Hall one last time to tell them what his intentions were, and then . . .

Go.

He loved the rough beauty of the sea as he loved nothing else in his life, even as it punished him; even as it reminded him of his insignificance in the face of its stormy wrath. It waited, always, for men brave enough to conquer its shimmering skin; for men to use it as their tool to discover fortune, land, themselves. Surely there were places left to be discovered in his own time, islands and kingdoms of ice, routes to be charted that would close the distance between civilizations? Would that not feed the ache he felt inside him at the realization that this was the final clue—that this hunt, this small journey through fear and wonder, was nearly at its end?

No, he thought, rubbing the back of his hand against his forehead. Who could be satisfied with seeking out the four corners of one small world, when there was the whole of time to be had? No, indeed.

"Oh, wow . . ." Etta again broke into his thoughts as she knelt down beside him.

"And what is that?" he asked.

She reached for something leaning against the tiger's hind legs.

It was another creature, one that looked like a large rat or mouse; only, it seemed to be able to stand on its hindquarters, and wore red breeches with yellow buttons . . . and shoes . . . and gloves?

Etta shook the dust from it, and then inexplicably hugged it to her chest. "Something that doesn't belong here," he guessed.

She nodded, replacing the stuffed rodent on the floor, and moved on to the remaining sheets, tossing them to the ground while he remained sitting. Nicholas had a perfect view of the lower half of her bare legs. The women of his time kept themselves covered from the tops of their heads to their ankles, and it had taken every ounce of his will and honor not to dwell on the devastatingly smooth skin that had been revealed to him over the past two days.

The makeshift bandage was beginning to slip down her calf, revealing the edge of the blistered bullet graze. They'd need . . . what had he been taught about germs and disease? To . . . sterilize it, with alcohol of some kind. To rewrap it in clean linen, and pray to God he hadn't scarred her.

When Etta turned toward him, leaning back against the desk, he wondered at the exhaustion and dismay he saw etched so deeply into her fine features.

"Whatever is the matter?" Nicholas asked.

Etta dismissed the question with a shrug.

"I cannot read your mind," he said. This was another man's home, and until they confirmed that it belonged to the Lindens and no one else would come upon it, he wouldn't be able to shake his discomfort.

Etta managed a small smile at that. "Sometimes it feels like you can."

Their thoughts did head in the same direction often enough,

ALEXANDRA BRACKEN

but there were times when Etta remained as mysterious as the stars in the sky. Nicholas pushed himself up off the floor and crossed that short distance to her side again.

"I don't know why it upsets me," she said, fiddling with the ends of the ribbon he'd tied in her hair. Nicholas caught her hand, clasping it between his own. In that moment, she looked so ruffled that he feared she might very well fly out of the window. And of course there was that heady floral scent, driving him half mad, making him think of silky night air, and the moon hanging like an opal at midnight, and—

"Are all travelers like this?" she said, using her free hand to gesture toward the space around them. "Collectors? Tourists to different eras? Going off to have a laugh and pick up souvenirs to show off? Tokens from events"—she picked up a scrap of parchment—"I mean, someone bought themselves a ticket for passage on the *Titanic*, and there's a box over there labeled 'Pompeii' that I'm not even going to open. Is there a point to it, other than to amuse themselves? Sophia claims they protect the timeline, but it just seems like they're protecting their interests."

It did look as though the room was just a collection of trophies from a scattered life. They had nothing in common beyond the obvious—they belonged to different eras. Clocks made in strange, clean-lined styles; swords mounted to the walls; porcelain trinkets; silk robes and garments beyond his wildest fancies; brittle broadsheets and newspapers, dried to yellow crisps—all stood beside each other, as if the mixture was the most natural thing in the world. It was either a hoard of the family's treasure, or their own personal museum.

"Is that so wrong?" Nicholas asked. "Amusement is a privilege few are granted. It's hardly a crime to seek it out. Even *you've* felt the awe of traveling. Do you not qualify it as a pursuit of knowledge?"

"Right," she said. "But I can't help but think that that's not what the passages were meant for. There were generations of travelers who made them, right? How did they discover how to do it, and why did they stop?"

He released her hand, his mind already at work scraping up some sort of weak segue to a safer conversation. She was too clever by half, and Nicholas knew that she would see through his deceit too clearly when he took the astrolabe out of her hands. It was obvious to him now that Etta had no plans of giving it back to Ironwood; he had a feeling the plan she was keeping to herself was as as dangerous as it was daring—that she would try to use it to return to her time, and save her mother herself. And while he could admire her courage, and lament her recklessness, Nicholas needed her to see how foolish it was to believe she could ever escape Ironwood. As it stood, the old man would know that his leaving without permission was hewing to the spirit of their agreement—following her at any cost—so long as he returned with the astrolabe. But how could Etta be so certain of his forgiveness for this act of defiance?

She would hate him for double-crossing her, and he could live with that. But he could not live with knowing she was in constant jeopardy. That Ironwood had stamped out her bloom and buried her. This was the only way he could save her, her mother, and his future that didn't end with one or all of them dead.

Etta would see that. In time.

Perhaps.

"Why do you think they went?" she asked, her eyes a soft, sleepy blue.

If the question had come from any other person, he might have dismissed it with a wave and carried on with his business; but it mattered to him that she sincerely desired his opinion, even knowing who he was. He recognized the want, as it mirrored his own.

Want. His exhaustion had boiled him down to his basest instincts. He wanted her lips, her touch, her esteem, her mind. Inside her. Beside her. With her. *Impossible,* he reminded himself.

Perhaps it was a blessing that he couldn't cross paths with himself, lest he be tempted to shoot himself before making the deal with Ironwood.

"What man can resist the temptation of riches waiting to be found?" he said, running his thumb along the carved edge of a dark wooden desk. "Or woman, for that matter?" he added, thinking of Sophia.

"Maybe," Etta said slowly, turning to sort through the papers on the desk.

"You disagree?"

"No, not really," she said. "I'm sure that was motivation for most of them, especially the ones who came later on. But the first travelers didn't know what they would find, did they? That takes a lot of courage, to charge into the unknown."

"Or blackmail and fear," he said pointedly.

She laughed. "I don't think that was it . . . at least, I hope it wasn't. These were people who overcame the impossible; they figured out a way to break every law of science. They opened up whole worlds within their own. Maybe they saw themselves as explorers, or scholars. Or maybe they saw it as a kind of calling to find out what lay ahead and make adjustments." The force behind her words increased as she spoke, driving her point forward. "Maybe Alice was right—they made too many changes, and everything got out of hand."

"A calling?" He couldn't keep the sardonic note out of his voice.

"Sure," she said. "You don't believe in that?"

"I believe in choosing your purpose and a direction to head—not that there is a path out there just waiting for me to stumble onto it."

"So you wouldn't consider sailing your calling?" Etta asked.

"No. It was the only opportunity that was presented to me, and I saw how I could make something of myself with hard work."

Nicholas couldn't quite believe that he'd managed to distill that cloudy feeling into simple truth.

"I enjoy it," he continued, shifting under her scrutiny. "I love the challenge that the sea presents at every turn. It's allowed me to see more of the world than I ever dared to imagine, and it feeds my desire to see more. And I happen to be damned good at it. But it does not change the fact that the occupation was chosen for me by another. And it was not a divine hand."

Had Hall been of a more business-minded nature, he might have placed Nicholas with a tradesman as an apprentice, and reaped the rewards of his skills until Nicholas had saved enough to purchase his own freedom. Instead, his freedom had been a fact, not an agonizing question; not something that needed to be contemplated. The Halls loathed the institution of slavery not only for what it did to the slaves themselves, but for the way it seemed to pollute the souls of those who participated in it.

As a captain, Nicholas would have the means to support himself, plus the ability to prove his own merit in the eyes of the world. As the owner of a company, with wealth beyond imagination, he could make his mark on the world.

Tell her, he thought, fists squeezing at his side. *Tell her the truth, you sodding bastard.*

"I always thought having a natural talent for something was a sign that it was what you were meant to be doing," Etta said. "That's what got me into trouble in the first place."

"Do you consider the violin to be your calling?" he asked. "Will you see it through after all, then?"

Etta's hand froze over a small, glossy wooden box she'd dug out from beneath a pile of ledgers. "I think . . . I'm not even sure it's possible at this point. My life is so different now. I don't think I could ever go back to the way it was. But . . . maybe there's also something else for me—something I couldn't even imagine before."

Or that I'd want to.

"Rest assured," he said, when he managed to find his voice, "there will always be a position for you on my ship."

Her face brightened with her clever, beautiful smile. "Will you let me climb up into the rigging? Reef the sails?"

A burst of thunder rolled through him. "Absolutely not."

She laughed again. "As if you could stop me."

In spite of all of the voices in his head demanding that he be reasonable, that he listen to his own damned advice and not make more of this than it could be, he reached over to smooth the hair away from her face.

And holy God, when she looked at him the way she did now . . . he felt like he'd stepped into the blue-white heart of a flame. The dark centers of her bright eyes expanded as her teeth caught the corner of her lip, and he had the extraordinarily unhelpful thought that if anyone should be biting those lips, it should be him.

Nicholas fought his scowl and stepped back, feeling as if he were surfacing from underwater. "What . . . what precisely are we meant to be doing?"

"I don't know," Etta said, with a cheeky little smile. "You're so handsome that sometimes I completely lose my train of thought."

He turned to assess the room, struggling to suppress his own grin.

"There's a desk over there. There might be something useful inside to tell us where we are," he said. "I'll have a look through the chest."

She nodded, turning back to the piles with new urgency. The heavy wood-and-iron chest was unlocked, but save for some sachets of lavender still releasing their fragrance, there were only a few blankets tucked inside. Nicholas turned at the sharp *thunk* behind him, and watched as Etta fought with the stubborn bottom drawer of the desk.

She blew a loose strand of hair from her eyes. "It's locked."

Nicholas tested it for himself; even with his full weight and strength, the only thing he accomplished was to break off its metal knob.

"Did you think I didn't know how to work a drawer?" she asked, taking the thing out of his hand with a shake of her head. "Why keep all of this out in the open for anyone to find and question, but lock this one drawer? What's the point?"

"Because," came a silky voice from the shadows. "You were not given the key."

SEVENTEEN

ETTA JUMPED BACK IN ALARM, KNOCKING AGAINST THE desk in surprise. Instinctively, her hands scrambled for something to protect herself, fingers rummaging in the paper until they brushed up against the letter opener she'd seen only a moment before.

When she looked over at him, Nicholas had gone as rigid as a blade, his expression sharpening with the kind of lethal intent she'd seen only once before—when he'd launched himself at the man who had grabbed her in London. He made his way around the furniture between them.

"Do not move." The accent was heavy, the words formal and stilted. "I will feel no guilt in killing thieves."

Nicholas seemed to believe those words, stopping exactly where he was, a few feet behind her.

"Who are you?" Etta asked, brandishing the letter opener in front of her. Whatever good that would do.

"The one who should be asking this question is I," the man said, stepping out from where he had managed to slip through the doorway unnoticed.

He was hardly a man at all; his deep voice was at odds with a soft, rounded face that seemed to indicate his age was close to their own. His skin was a dusky brown, his eyes dark and severe beneath generous brows. His long, white robe rustled as he took a step toward them, bare feet padding across one of the room's many patterned rugs. Etta recognized the style of his dress—it was a close, luxurious approximation to what you might see in her time, in the Middle East.

Bare feet. Even with a haze of exhaustion drooping over her, that small fact stuck in the front of her mind, forcing her to think it through. *I will feel no guilt in killing thieves. . . .* meaning, this house—or apartment, or whatever it was—belonged to him? Now that he was closer, Etta saw red lines marring his cheeks from pillows or sheets; the glazed look of someone still half-asleep.

But . . . didn't this house belong to the Lindens?

Nicholas reached into the interior pocket of his jacket, and the young man raised the wickedly curved blade at his side.

This was about to go exactly one way, and that way involved bloodstains on the beautiful rugs.

"We were told to come here," Etta said, halting both of their movements. "By Rose Linden."

The young man exploded with movement, launching himself forward at her.

"Duck!" Nicholas called.

Etta dropped to her knees and Nicholas's fist sailed over her head. By the time she climbed back onto her feet, the two men had fallen to the floor in a rolling pile of limbs, crashing through chair legs as they tried to batter each other with their fists. The sword was knocked away, spinning toward the door.

"Stop!" Etta cried out. "Stop it!"

It was like breaking up the worst kind of dogfight, when you know the only way to separate the animals is to risk getting bitten yourself. She gripped the back of Nicholas's jacket with both hands, muscles burning as she hauled him away.

"Nicholas!" she said. "*Stop!*"

He shuddered, the breath steaming in and out of him as he pressed his bruised, bleeding knuckles against his mouth. When Etta moved toward the other young man, Nicholas jerked forward as if to stop her. She gave a sharp shake of her head. With some reluctance Nicholas backed off, understanding, and instead went to pick up the discarded sword from the floor.

"You know the name Rose Linden, don't you?" Etta asked.

He shrank back from the hand she'd offered to help him up. Etta sensed she'd committed some kind of offense.

"What about Benjamin Linden?" she asked, wondering if Nicholas had knocked him hard enough to make his ears ring. The pulse of insects outside swamped the room in sound; she wished she had opened just one of the shutters to let the rich floral scent in, to fill the air with something other than fear and sweat.

The young man closed his eyes, dragging in a wheezing breath. When he spoke, Etta had to lean forward to hear him.

"Abbi," he said. "Father."

THE YOUNG MAN, HASAN, WOULDN'T ALLOW HER TO HELP HIM clean his face—he wouldn't even allow her to follow him out to collect clean cloths and water, so a reluctant Nicholas was forced to trail after him to keep an eye on him—but surrendered the sword to Etta as a show of good faith. The few minutes they were gone gave her a chance to consider something that still seemed impossible.

Time was relative and all that, but . . . how insane, to think that her great-grandfather had a son who was her age. He was technically her mother's uncle, which made him Etta's . . . great-uncle? Or . . . no, a first cousin twice removed?

"You look like her," Hasan said as he brought one of the damp cloths to his face. "Sweet Rose."

"That's probably because she's my mother," Etta said. "You know her?"

He nodded, his eyes flicking over to where Nicholas stood glowering behind her.

"Abbi . . . he and Rose lived here for a time before he left it to Ummi—my mother—and then myself, when she died." Hasan shook his head. "You said you were told to come? But . . . this does not make sense, for Rose has come and she has gone, only days ago."

Her stomach rolled. "What do you mean?"

Rose had escaped from Ironwood's men? She was safe—but they'd already missed her?

Nicholas put a calming hand on her wrist and asked Hasan, "Rose—was she young, or was she older than you remember her?"

Oh.

"Young," Hasan said, suspicion edging back into his voice. "Too young to have had a child your age. She had come here with a special purpose, but she would not tell me what this was."

Nicholas glanced at her, clearly taking in her startled reaction. It wasn't her mother—the mother who had raised her. Because of the way the passages worked, they'd nearly bumped into the younger Rose as she'd come here to hide the astrolabe in the first place.

"Why didn't you go with her?" Etta asked, curious.

"Because I cannot. Some would call me a . . . a guardian, but I do not perform a duty beyond the care and keeping of this home," Hasan said. "I do not answer to the Grand Master's call. I will not be an Ironwood."

"Did Rose leave something here?" Etta asked, her words toppling over each other.

Until that moment, Etta hadn't thought to anticipate this problem. Had her mom or Benjamin Linden warned Hasan of the other families, or told him to only trust Rose with the location of the astrolabe?

Nicholas grabbed the collar of Hasan's robe, tightening his grip.

Because, yes, *obviously* what they needed was *more violence.*

Hasan wet his lips, his eyes flickering around the room. The water from the cloth ran down the side of his face like sweat.

"Answer the lady," Nicholas grated out.

"I vowed on my life," Hasan said, dropping the cloth back into the basin. "I cannot simply take your word. You may not be who you say you are. There are many who would trick me—who would trick those of us still sworn to the Linden family and to its secrets."

Etta's mind reached for that one last, real chance. . . .

"The only reason I knew to come here was because my mom told me a story. . . . She told me many stories about her travels that were true and false at the same time. The last one I heard from her was about a woman who sold her these earrings in a marketplace here in Damascus." Etta unhooked one from her ear and handed it to him. "She said a woman named Samarah sold them to her."

Hasan's hand was shaking as he took it from her, running a light finger over the curve of the hoop. The silence between them seemed to stretch into an hour, until he finally said, "Samarah did not sell them to her. She gave them to her. I know this, for Samarah is my wife, my love, and I was there to see it."

Hasan moved to the desk. Reaching into the open neck of his robe, he gripped a long, silver chain, brandishing the thin silver key dangling from it.

"We could have just broken it open," Nicholas muttered, staring at the drawer, but Hasan slid the key not into the lock on the face of the drawer, but beneath it—into a lock they hadn't seen at all.

The drawer gave a satisfying *click* as the tumblers turned, and it slid open on its track.

Nicholas immediately tried to use his height to lean over Hasan and see what was inside. Hasan gave him a cold glance before rifling through its contents. Finding whatever it was, he stood and slammed the drawer shut with his foot.

"You remind me . . ." He held out a small, cream-colored envelope. She unfolded its flap, letting its contents spill out in her hand. The first thing was another black-and-white photograph, again of her mother, only so much younger. She had a sweet smile on her face, and was dressed in some kind of school uniform; her hair was curled and pinned back, her hands resting in her lap. There was a secret tucked into her smile.

On the back someone had written: *Rose, age 13.*

The other piece of paper in the envelope was a letter addressed to: *Etta, my dear heart.*

"You had that all this time, and you still questioned her?" Nicholas asked, outraged.

"Stop being so unreasonable," Etta said. "How could he have known for sure?"

"I am a protector of this family," Hasan said, his chest puffing out. "Rose is the cherished daughter of Abbi's son, beloved by all of us. So I think, when I see this girl, she looks like Rose. She looks like my faraway English papa. She has his sky colors. But so do many from his country. On his last visit, Abbi seemed as old as the desert, the *bādiyat ash-shām*. He was confused in the mind, very frightened about what was happening to the other families. I would not risk her life for anything less than a certainty."

"I understand," Etta said, grateful and touched by how much passion he had invested into protecting the person she loved. "Thank you."

She smoothed the letter out on her knee, looking around for some kind of pen. *My dear heart . . .* another sweet nickname her mother had never used for her before. Nicholas dutifully retrieved a fountain pen from a cup on the desk.

"Rather dangerous to keep all of this out," he noted.

Hasan shrugged. "In the event it is discovered, the house and its contents will be burned."

Etta shook her head at that, roughly sketching out the shape of a heart over the run-on sentences and non sequiturs, until she had isolated what she thought was the true message:

I am so sorry. I wish there was another way. I tried to protect you from this, but if you find this I've failed. Trust no one save those who share our blood. Ironwood will destroy your future, he will erase everyone and everything to save one life, and the Thorns mean to do the same. It must be destroyed. No one can decide what is or what should be. Bring jasmine to the bride who sleeps eternal beneath the sky, and look for the sigil. I will find you there as soon as I can. Forgive me. I love you.

Etta looked up, surprised to find herself crying. "I don't understand—what does that mean, Ironwood wants to save one life? Whose? Augustus? Julian?"

Nicholas knew, but Hasan answered. "His first wife. Minerva."

"What?" She fought the urge to reach over, to force Nicholas to explain why he looked like the world was crashing down around him.

"He wants it all, then," Nicholas said finally. "Bloody hell, the bastard—"

Hasan cleared his throat with a meaningful look in Etta's direction.

"Minerva was married to him for a few years when they were both young," Nicholas continued. "I don't know the details of it, only what Julian's told me. It was a love match, rare for travelers, but it occurred during an incredibly unstable and violent time in the war between the families. His rivals from the other families took advantage of the fact that Ironwood had hidden her somewhere in the past for her safety. They discovered her location, and waited for a year in which there was no passage for Ironwood to use to intervene, then murdered her in retribution. In effect, they rendered her murder unpreventable, unless Ironwood chose to warn himself to return and live that year straight through—to be present when she was killed in 1456. That would have, of course, altered his fate and the shape of the world around him. If he'd given up and lived a normal life with her that year, not traveling around waging his little war of terror, he would not have garnered the power or alliances he needed to become Grand Master."

Oh my God. The letter fell out of her limp hands onto the floor. "He chose power."

But that—that didn't make sense. He loved this woman enough to sacrifice sons and grandchildren to find the astrolabe, in order to save her . . . but his first choice had been his newly acquired wealth, power, and control over the families.

The one thing he truly wanted had been taken from him. Had he always been the way he was now, or had the loss torn some vital part of him away? Would he be the person he was now if she hadn't been killed?

"He remarried Augustus and Virgil's mother, but . . . my God," Nicholas said. "He must have figured out which events were crucial to his success and seen there was still an opening to travel back and save her. He could get a message to his past self—or get the astrolabe to himself. And September thirtieth? His wife was killed on October first. He set that deadline with the goal of immediately acting."

"There are rules, but rules may be rewritten if only one hand holds the ink." Hasan nodded. Etta spun toward Nicholas. "If he changes the past, won't that prevent your father, and then you, from being born?"

He shook his head. "No, I'll simply be orphaned by my time—thrown to whatever last common point there was between the old timeline and the new. My future, and the guardians' . . . they are at stake, as is yours."

Could such a change ripple out so far, so wildly, from one act? Why should saving one life mean so many more—Alice's and Oskar's, and all of the millions and billions of people living and working in the world—might not exist, or would not exist as they had?

"These *ašwaak*—Thorns—they are no better. These travelers and guardians desire it for similar reasons—to undo everything Ironwood has built for himself, and restore the world they know," Hasan said. "Rose was swayed by their passion, by how many of our family had been slaughtered by Ironwood for refusing to come to his table. Abbi was destroyed when Rose left to seek them out, but how could she not? Ironwood had taken her parents. She was furious that Abbi only wished to hide."

So. Her grandparents—Rose's parents—hadn't been killed in a Christmas car accident after all.

"It's so extreme," Etta said, trying to reconcile this angry young woman with the one who had raised her. "I understand her motivations, but—changing the whole future?"

Hasan made a thoughtful sound. "At first, all the Thorns wished was to bring Ironwood to his knees—to restore the council of families, save their loved ones from service to him. The timeline they knew *was* the original timeline, you see. Can you argue that it is meant to be, more than the one that exists now?"

Meaning that she really *had* grown up in an altered timeline of what was actually meant to be. Everything she knew was a product of the changes Ironwood had made in his conquest of the families. So—which timeline deserved to exist? Hers? Theirs?

The full weight of her exhaustion hit her at once. Etta felt as though her head was stuffed with cotton, her knees suddenly hollow. The room tilted sideways a second before two hands caught her; they held her steady until the black spots cleared from her vision.

"Etta?" Nicholas's face floated in front of hers.

"I'm okay," she promised. "Just . . ."

Hasan's face transformed, sharpening. "Who are you to be so familiar with my little niece? Remove your hands before I do."

"*Familar?*" she repeated, just as Nicholas's grip tightened and he said, "Her husband."

Etta choked. Nicholas's hands squeezed her arms once, in silent warning. He wrapped both arms around her shoulders—a mimic of a loving embrace. When she dug her heel down into his foot, he barely grimaced.

Excuse me? Excuse me?

If the lie lit a fuse in her, it had the opposite effect on Hasan, stamping out the flare of fury that had turned his handsome features almost ominous. Mostly stamping it out, anyway.

"I do not think Abbi would approve of this match," he said.

"Why?" Nicholas said challengingly.

"She looks as if she desires nothing so much as to feed you to a lion," said Hasan.

Etta managed to wriggle free. She wasn't sure what it was—the way his expression softened, more vulnerable than she'd ever seen it, or the simple fact that Nicholas rarely did something without good reason—but she held her tongue instead of calling him out on the lie.

"Next time we're on a ship," she said, turning back to Hasan with a conspiratorial smile, "I'll feed some important bit to a shark."

"A sailor?" Hasan scoffed, turning to assess him again with this new knowledge. "A pirate, no doubt."

"A *legal* pirate," Nicholas said tiredly.

"The only pirates I know are those from the Barbary Coast," Hasan said, eyeing Nicholas. "They are not so friendly to

Europeans, you see. They trade in slaves, and their tastes are vast. They take from Africa. They take from Europe. A girl such as this would be prized: her skin, her hair, her eyes. A man would pay a price for her."

Etta actually gasped. "What are you getting at?"

"I believe he's trying to ask if you are my concubine," Nicholas said with a humorless smile. "If you need rescue."

"No!" she choked out. "Neither of us are even *from* this time, and the fact that you think he's even capable of doing something like that—"

Hasan visibly relaxed, even as Nicholas put a calming hand on her shoulder. "One hears of such things—sees them—and so I worry. If Abbi is not here, then it falls to me to protect you. But if he is your husband, as he says, he shares in the responsibility."

"I can take care of myself," Etta muttered.

"This is the truth," Nicholas told him, stooping down to pick up the letter. He glanced over it again. "But we're in a hurry, you see. Ironwood has 'sweet Rose' at his mercy and is threatening to kill her, and very likely will, if we can't figure out where she's hidden something. Does this last phrase here mean anything to you? *Bring jasmine to the bride who sleeps eternal beneath the sky?*"

"My papa was very fond of riddles such as these, but I cannot say I have heard this one before." Hasan's steps were light as he made his way through the room, running his hands along each possession; all were clearly prized. He picked up the photograph of the tiger hunt and brushed the coating of dust from its glass face, continuing, "He is gone, but I have hope that I will see him again. Perhaps not as old as he was, but a young man, discovering this era for the first time. Perhaps he will not yet recognize me, but I will know him. And until that day, I will care for our family, and ask that you stay as my guests. When I am gone, you may use my home as your own."

"Thank you," Etta said. "But what do you mean, *when you're gone?*"

They had . . . How many days was it now until the thirtieth? Only six?

"I must go to Baghdad to collect my wife, little cousin," he said, an almost goofy look of happiness passing over his face. And once again, she tried to judge exactly how old he was, and came up with seventeen at the most. "Samarah will be greatly displeased to have missed you. She has gone to be with her sister and their new child. I will remain here to sell my indigo and pearls, and will fetch her as soon as the goods are gone and there is a caravan or others to travel with."

"A merchant, then," Nicholas clarified.

Hasan nodded, his smile slightly crooked with the swelling on his face. "It is natural. Abbi brought me many books, taught me many languages. English, Turkish, French, Greek. So you see, I cannot travel in your way, but he has helped me to go far on my own feet."

"I'm glad we met you," Etta said sincerely, struck all over again that he was her family; her concept of the word had changed again. "When do you think you'll be leaving, though?"

"I would have left a week ago," Hasan replied, "but some of the tribes make the desert a dangerous place to be alone. So, I wait—it should not be long now."

"Indeed?" Nicholas said. "And what desert would this be?"

Hasan nearly dropped the photo, a surprised laugh tumbling

out of him. "Perhaps that is where we can make another beginning? My new friends, may I be the first to humbly welcome you to the Queen of Cities, *Dimashq.* Damascus."

NEITHER ETTA NOR NICHOLAS HAD KNOWN WHAT TIME IT WAS when they came through the passage, but after Hasan gently informed them that it was three o'clock in the morning, his initial hostility made more sense.

"Rest now," he said, taking one of the candles with him. "Tomorrow, I will show you the house, the city, and we will try to understand Abbi's riddle."

Nicholas's lips parted, his shoulders tightening as if he was about to protest this, but Etta put a hand on his arm and said simply, "Thank you. Good night."

When the door shut firmly behind Hasan, Nicholas pulled away, crossing over to the bed in several rapid, stiff strides. Rather than sit down on it, he pulled the top blanket off, and without sparing even a glance at her, moved to the opposite end of the room to spread it out over a few floor cushions he gathered on the way.

Etta felt a sharp twist in the pit of her stomach. What had she thought? That they'd be sharing the bed? That they'd pick up where they left off earlier that day?

Nicholas could put such a cool distance between himself and others. She felt him trying to do it now, letting the silence speak for him, keeping his back to her as he shrugged off his filthy shirt and folded it neatly. She was almost too aware of him now. He filled a room just by standing in it.

This was a completely different Nicholas than the one who had literally kissed the breath out of her. She'd felt his heartbeat chasing hers. He had been the warm wave that had carried her away from everything else, and he hadn't needed to say a single word in order for her to know that he was as desperate for her as she was for him. She wasn't inexperienced. She knew what that felt like.

Then it's the same for you?

Nicholas had kept any number of things from her, and he was well within his right to do so. He showed only a fraction of what he felt, even when he was being insulted in the crudest, vilest ways imaginable. But alone with him, she'd felt him let go, and she'd recognized what a rare privilege it was to be able to find him beneath all the stiff layers.

Etta tried to run her hands back through her hair and failed; she turned to look for the old silver brush she'd seen on the desk. Her thoughts were still churning when she sat back down and began to work the brush through the tangled ends of her waves.

Nicholas was back up on his feet, pacing the room, his hands clasped behind his back. Etta could feel the weight of his thoughts take shape between them as he put out a few of the candles at the other end of the room.

She wanted to know what he was thinking, but was afraid to ask, on the off chance that his mood had something to do with how quickly they were approaching the end of this. There wasn't enough time.

You are leaving, she thought, even as a small, traitorous voice whispered, *but not yet. . . .*

"Come here a second," Etta said softly.

Nicholas stopped, his hands going slack at his side. He didn't move.

"Please," she said, kicking her shoes off and standing again. She wove through the discarded rainbow of silk cushions, the carpets soft and plush beneath her feet. She took up the basin of water Hasan had left behind.

Returning to her perch on the bed, Etta dipped the last of the clean cloths into the water and carefully squeezed out the excess. Nicholas hesitated, but moved toward her in the end, approaching like a wary cat.

Before he could protest, Etta took his right hand and held it firmly, picking up the cloth to dab at the broken skin he'd reopened across his knuckles. The cuts were already scabbing over, but she worked as delicately as she could to clean away the blood. His fingers squeezed hers, almost reflexively; his eyes were hooded as he watched her work.

"I wish you had gone a little easier on him," she said.

"He came in here thrashing a sword around. Was I supposed to stand idly by and do nothing?" he huffed.

"Well, you weren't supposed to try to rearrange his face with your fist."

"I wasn't," Nicholas protested. "He lunged up into it several times. I was only in the way."

"You're ridiculous," she informed him. "Will you please apologize to him tomorrow?"

"If you wish, but I'm not sure it's necessary," he said. "He didn't respect me until he saw that I was capable of defending you. We've made our peace. And if you think I wouldn't do the same again, let me relieve you of that notion now. If the situation calls for violence, I will use it."

She didn't want to pick a fight, and she sensed that he was trying to start one in order to push her away. It was enough for her to understand why he'd done it, even if she felt he'd gone too far.

I need to tell him. He understood the stakes of it all. Nicholas would see that they couldn't just give the astrolabe back to Ironwood and wash their hands of it.

"I have to tell you something. . . ."

"Shhhh . . ." he whispered. "Not yet. *Not yet.*"

Agitation melted away from him as he exhaled and sat beside her. The stubble along his jaw rasped as he brought his cheek up to rest against her hair.

It's not over yet.

It doesn't have to be over.

Come with me.

Etta swallowed, forcing the words back down her throat. She was tired, and she felt her emotions far too close to the surface to be reasonable about this. The truth solidified inside her, a wisp of hope burning, re-forming, becoming as shatterproof as a diamond. The crazy, stupid truth was as irrational as it was selfish, and she knew that—she knew it—but it didn't seem to matter.

As much as she respected and admired his beautiful, sharp mind, there was such a gentle heart stowed away beneath the stormy colors of his moods, his rougher layers. She didn't want to leave it behind; she didn't want to leave any part of him, and pretend like none of this had happened.

Come with me.

She turned, kissing the place on his neck where she could see his pulse fluttering.

Come home with me.

His fingers slid away from hers—to draw her leg across his lap, unwind the dirty bandage, and begin cleaning the wound on her calf.

"Why did you lie to Hasan?" she whispered.

Nicholas knew exactly what she was talking about.

"By his accent and manner of dress, I assumed he is a Mahometan." At her blank look, he elaborated. "A follower of the prophet Muhammad."

What she thought of as a Muslim. She nodded.

"I only know a little about their faith—stories, really," he explained. "But I assume it matches certain tenets of Christianity, a rather important one being, of course, that unwed women are not to be left alone with rogues whom they are neither related to by blood or bound to through marriage."

"I see," she said mildly.

"I won't pretend I've never done anything disreputable or had a dishonorable thought," he said quietly. "It simply wasn't a question for me. He would have brought you to another room, and I wouldn't leave you alone in a strange place, where anyone could come in and harm you with me none the wiser. But . . . if anyone were to find out I'm staying here, rather than in a separate room, your reputation would be irrevocably damaged."

"I don't care about being judged by another century's standards," said Etta. "Especially one that I'll probably never see again."

"I know," he said, tearing a clean sheet into a bandage to wrap her leg. "But it matters to me. Had I known the idea would be so unappealing, I never would have suggested it."

Was that . . . *hurt* she detected?

"It's not that. I just hate that it's even necessary, you know?" she said. "That a woman doesn't exist as a whole person. I was surprised when you said it. I thought you were joking, but only because I was thinking like a person from my time. Seventeen is a little young to be married."

Nicholas pulled back, that guarded look of assessment sliding back into place.

"Most people don't start considering marriage until they're in their mid-twenties," she continued. "There's years of school, and most people want to find jobs and be somewhat settled first."

"I see," he said, in the same tone she'd used.

"But it's not young for you?" Etta asked, sensing he was beginning to drift away again. "Really?"

"I'm nearly twenty," he told her. "Of course it isn't. But it's not a thought I'll entertain."

Etta could see by the shadow that passed over his eyes that he'd said more than he wanted to. When he released her and stood, she felt the absence of him like the burn of empty lungs. His words had been lanced through with a trembling undercurrent, and she should have known better than to keep pushing him to understand why. She should have.

"Why?"

He turned, a flicker of anger moving through his features. "Must I really answer that? Would you have me catalog all my faults? All the reasons I'm unsuitable—" Nicholas caught himself, pressing the heel of his hand to his forehead, squeezing his eyes shut for a brief moment. "Go to sleep, Etta. Rest. We've much to do tomorrow."

She stood.

There was this dream she used to have, when she was younger and her stage fright was at its crippling worst. The most terrifying thing was how real it felt; each night, she felt the warmth of the stage lights on her skin as she stepped out and let herself be blinded by them. It never mattered what song the orchestra started to play—it was never the one she knew, never the one she had mastered—and she could never seem to improvise, but only choke on her own frustration at her inability to play the right thing on demand.

It was that same desperate feeling that propelled her forward now. She reached for the right words, but came up with nothing but air. She might have understood who he was as a person, but she hadn't experienced the life that had made him that way.

There was something about this that he wasn't telling her. Whatever his secret was, it was like a chasm between them, preventing her from reaching him. Anything she tried—her words, her glances, her touch—spilled into it before it could even get close to his heart.

He had worked his breath into short, hard measures when she threaded her arms beneath his, wrapping them around his center. For the length of a heartbeat, he let her. And in the next, he was pushing her away.

"Don't"—he swallowed roughly—"do not act as though this is more than it is—"

Etta reached for him and pulled him down to her level. He struggled for the excuse he needed to do it again, even as his hands tightened around her shoulders and held her in place. When she kissed him, there was nothing gentle about it. No hesitation. Nicholas stood rigidly, his body hard against hers.

But just when she was sure she had badly fumbled this, he moved with a harsh sound, his hands going first to her loose hair, then to the small bow holding the neck of her blouse together. He swallowed her gasp, lips wild and hungry as they moved from the corner of her mouth to her jaw, her throat. Blood beat against her skin, relentless, and she was being walked backward before she realized it. Etta was dizzy with the feel of him under her hands, grateful she could lean against something just as her legs went soft.

She couldn't hear what he was whispering into her skin, and she wondered if he felt as drunk as she did, sinking too fast to reach for the life preserver.

Etta shifted, angling toward the bed itself; she might as well have been drawing him into a lit fireplace. He pulled back so suddenly, she fell back onto the stuffed mattress. Nicholas spun on his heel, keeping his back to her as he strode to the other side of the room, rubbing his face, his hair, trying to catch his own breath.

"Don't pretend like it isn't real!" she managed to get out. "Don't you dare be a coward about this!"

"Coward!" Nicholas barely managed to keep from howling as he crossed back toward her on unsteady legs. "Coward? You play at things you don't understand—"

"I *would* understand," she said, "if you'd trust me enough to explain them to me. I want to be with you—it's as simple as that. And I think you want to be with me too, but there's something you're not telling me. It makes me feel foolish every time. Just tell me—if I have it all wrong, then tell me now."

She must have caught him off guard, because he took a moment to collect his thoughts. "What is there to explain? You will go home. I will go home. And that will be the end of it. Think about this, Etta. You scarcely know me—"

"I know you," she interrupted. "*I know you*, Nicholas Carter. And I know it doesn't have to be that way."

"And I know you've never planned to give Ironwood the astrolabe," he said sharply. "That you've got it in your head you can escape him and his reach."

She felt a peculiar, hopeless kind of relief to have it out in the open. "I can get it, and I can save my mother—"

"And myself? You expect me to simply let you go, knowing you'll be in grave danger?" he demanded, stooping to look her directly in the eye. Finally, the wall was down. Nicholas looked the way she felt—exhausted, fraught. "You were simply going to leave me behind again, weren't you, without so much as a word?"

"No!" she said. "*No!* I've been trying to figure out another option for us—I don't want you to have to give up the life you have."

"What is this 'other option'? You return with me? Even if we could hide from the old man's wrath . . . to what end? We'd still be in hiding. Even if you could stand the months I'm away at sea, there are laws—enforceable laws, Etta, with years of prison as a sentence—preventing any such union. Not just in America, but in the rest of the world. I could live with the shame of being a criminal, but I would never ask this of you. And I would not risk your life, knowing that others may enforce their own prejudices outside of the law."

There was her answer.

She hadn't realized until that moment that she could feel any more foolish or naïve than she already did.

She didn't know anything. She really didn't.

"Etta . . ." he began. "That came out harsher than I meant it to be. I can see it in your face that you truly didn't know—but it's all I've ever known. I've had to live by it my whole life. If there's a way around it, I want to hear what you think it is. Can you not see it? Can you not feel how badly I want you? I'm a selfish bastard, I'm worse than you'll ever know, but I'll answer to God or anyone else who tries to stand in our way so long as I know you're safe. Tell me how to keep this—tell me the path forward. I beg you."

She felt the tears thick in her throat, warm on her face. "You could come with me. I won't lie to you and say my time is perfect, or that the country doesn't get worse before it gets better, but those laws are gone."

He seemed to consider this, rubbing his jaw. "What would I do there? How would I support myself? The one thing that I know, that I've worked for, would be unrecognizable. And is there a way to prove or earn citizenship?"

God—how would he? No Social Security number, no birth certificate . . . no passport. How had Mom done it? She could help him establish an identity, couldn't she?

"Or would you, your mother, and I all have to keep traveling, struggling to stay one step ahead of the old man?"

"I'm not dismissing those questions, because they're real and I'm not totally sure how to get around them," she said, "but I'm willing to try. My mom did it. Travelers have clearly figured out some system. I feel like all you're willing to see are the problems, and none of the benefits—medicine, for one thing. Education. You could attend school, choose a job for yourself." She took a breath. "I'm not trying to play down how terrifying it would be to start over in a new era—"

"I'm not frightened," he interrupted, only to soften his voice as he continued. "How could I be, knowing I had you there? I know you think I'm being obstinate. . . . I keep asking myself, what sort of joke is this that we've found one another, but all the while there's no true way forward? There's something unnatural in what we can do as travelers, and maybe this is a punishment for it."

"Don't say that," she begged. "It's complicated, I know, but it's not impossible."

"But what if it doesn't work? What if we can't sort everything out in your time? Your era is one small sliver of time compared to all eternity—there is only one small place you and I can be safe together. But even so, how long would it be before missing home and our loved ones became unbearable to one of us? It all ends the same way, with us breaking apart. Isn't it better to have it done with now?"

"No," she said stubbornly. "We could find a place. We could make our own."

"I knew you'd say that. If you can't accept those terms, then can you understand . . . I realize this may sound foolish to you, but I have my pride, Etta. I've bled and sweated and given myself to the making of my life. I could not bear being a burden to you. I want the whole of you, and would never give you less of me."

Nicholas held her face, smoothing away the tears. The small smile he offered was meant to steal one from her, she thought, but it only broke her heart a little more.

"We have done the impossible," he said, bringing his lips to the shell of her ear. "We have stolen what time we could, and it won't ever be taken from us."

"It's not enough," she whispered.

"I know, Etta, I know," he said, already stepping back. "But this cannot be forever."

His words continued to ring in her mind over and over again as she lay on her side on the bed and stared through the curtains, past the dust drifting down from the heavy canopy. One candle was left burning near where he had stretched out across the floor, his back to her; the flickering glow illuminated the long, strong lines of his silhouette. She knew by the cadence of his breathing that he wasn't asleep, either.

They were afraid of what could happen; their sights were set on the future. And there would be time for that. There was work they had to do to maintain the timeline, and one last riddle to solve. But she wondered if, in moving outside of the natural flow of time, they had forgotten the most crucial point of life—that it wasn't meant to be lived for the past, or even the future, but for each present moment.

Etta had lived through a sea battle. She'd survived the scheming of old, power-hungry men; the Blitz; a tiger; a cobra; and a gunshot—and she was denying herself this, out of fear that it might hurt later?

What would hurt worse: the regret that she tried, or the regret that she didn't?

She was protected. She cared so deeply for him that he seemed to live like a second heart inside of her. She wanted him, and he wanted her. To hell with forever. This moment was theirs, and she'd steal it if she had to.

She slipped out from under the quilt, working her fingers down the row of buttons on the back of her dress until it slipped down her front and pooled at her feet with a whisper of sound. Her shadow moved against the wall, blending with his own. His breathing caught as she lifted the blanket and slipped in behind him, curling around the heat of him; her hand slipped over his side, along the muscles of his stomach, until he caught it and turned over slowly, taking in the sight of her.

"Etta . . ." he whispered against her cheek. *Are you certain?*

She tilted her head back, pressing her lips against his square jaw, letting her fingers follow. "Forever isn't right now. It's not even tomorrow."

Etta propped herself up, leaning over his shoulder to extinguish the stub of the candle before it could burn itself out. A bright happiness spread through her as she lay back and his solid weight settled over her. He ducked down, kissing her, and she moved against him, urging him to touch her, to find the secret self that only ever seemed to exist with him. Etta felt him come alive in his own skin, felt the sheer strength of him as he moved over her, with her, and she let herself fall into it, dissolving into him. And what she found in that soft, warm darkness had no beginning and no end, for this time was their own, and it created its own eternity.

EIGHTEEN

"I HAVE BEEN THINKING OF YOUR RIDDLE," HASAN called as they descended the stairs and stepped out into the warm, glowing afternoon air of the courtyard. "I may have an answer for you."

He was set up at a table near a shallow pool, in the shadow of a tree that jutted out just far enough over the water to drop its enormous waxy leaves into the still waters. The walls were tiled in intricate patterns that mimicked the natural, curling growth of the nearby plants. Chimes and bursts of green leaves were interspersed among them, including the source of the fragrance that perfumed the entire house.

Jasmine.

The small white blossoms were scattered across the ground, and dropped like tears onto her hair and shoulders from the ledges lining each of the second-story windows that looked down at them. The outside of the house was incredibly ornate, and last night they had discovered the inside was just as beautiful. As soon as there had been natural light and they could open the shutters, the room had revealed itself in a riot of color and pattern that ran along the walls, through the carpets, and even to the bundle of clothing that had been left outside of the door.

The careful consideration that had gone into crafting the courtyard was staggering; everything was in brilliant balance. There had been no hesitation to invite nature into the heart of the house. Instead, nature had been given a place of honor, a patch of sunlight to thrive, and a perch on which it could be admired. The effect was breathtaking.

The sun warmed Etta's back as she walked toward Hasan. He stood and busied himself with piling bread and fruit on two plates, and poured steaming cups of sweet-smelling tea from a gleaming silver pot.

Nicholas's hand finally released hers as he moved to sit at the opposite end of the table, still lost in the winding paths of his own mind. Etta had woken that morning to find him sitting in front of the tiger, staring into its face. She had sat beside him, smiling as he pressed a kiss to her bare shoulder. His skin smelled sweet, like milk and honey, and he'd shaved and trimmed his hair. Etta ran a hand over it.

"You're looking especially clean this morning," she said.

"I couldn't sleep," he said, "so I brought water up for a bath, and then more for you. The water should still be warm."

Pure joy exploded in her. "I could kiss you for that!"

"By all means," he said coyly. "Don't hold yourself back on my account."

Etta kissed him soundly, then followed him to the next room, where a porcelain claw-foot tub squatted, completely at odds with its surroundings. Nicholas washed her back in comfortable silence until she asked, "What are you wearing?"

A white undershirt was partly hidden by what was either

a luxurious gold vest or snugly fitting jacket, over which was another long patterned crimson coat that hung down over silky, loose pants. A gold sash had been knotted around his waist.

"According to Hasan, *shalvar*," he said, pointing to the pants, "a *kusak*," gesturing to the sash, "and an *entari*," landing finally on the robe-like overcoat.

Nicholas left to retrieve her own clean set of clothes, and she was momentarily stunned by the beauty and richness of their fabric as he laid out the layers: a sheer *gömlek*, an under-tunic; a *chirka*, a short, tight under-jacket of emerald that buttoned up over her bust; next, *shalvar*, loose gold and sapphire brocade trousers that narrowed at the ankles; and an *entari* of her own, in a matching fabric to the *shalvar*. Finally, a small gold cap she pinned to her hair, and a white veil, a *yashmak*, that affixed to it and covered everything but her eyes.

When she finally washed the grime off her skin and out of her tangled hair, Etta stood and began toweling off, scrubbing until her skin was pink. Nicholas drank in the sight of her with a tenderness on his face that just about did her in.

"Am I a scoundrel?" he had asked, clearly more to himself than her.

Etta smiled, stroking the lines and scars on the back of his hand. "I believe *I'm* the scoundrel in this situation."

He gave her a long look she didn't understand—his eyes were heavy with a darkness that sent a chill straight through her center.

"Do you regret it?" she whispered, suddenly self-conscious.

Nicholas seemed startled by her words, shaking his head emphatically. He took her face between his big, warm hands and kissed her so deeply, she felt her toes curl against the floor. "Never. *Never.*"

But those had been the last words he'd said; he hadn't even managed a cheerful greeting to their host. Etta couldn't understand it—if that look hadn't been about what they'd done, then what was he thinking about?

"Eat, eat!" Hasan said, his warm smile at odds with the rough bruises on his face from his fight with Nicholas. "Little niece, you look beautiful. How do you find our manner of dress?"

The first word that leapt to her mind was *overwhelming*, which was hardly fair. The *entari* and *shalvar* were beautifully crafted; the layers of sapphire and emerald silk and brocade were beyond luxurious, even if they were heavy. She was glad for them, though, not just because her dress from London was nearly in tatters, but because she did feel more comfortable blending in, and being respectful of the customs in this place and era.

"Wonderful," she said. "Thank you for taking care of us."

Etta accepted the heavy plate of food gratefully, barely sparing another breath before she dug in, practically swallowing the first pieces of pomegranate and figs whole.

Nicholas was slower to come around to eating, his attention focused on the surrounding courtyard, searching for shadows and hidden corners that didn't exist.

"*Baha'ar*, my new friend," Hasan said. "Eat, please. I do not keep servants in this house. There is no fear of discovery. I would not be so careless."

"*Baha'ar?*" Nicholas repeated.

"Sailor," Hasan explained.

Nicholas gave a wry smile, breaking off a chunk of the bread in front of him. "What was this about the clue?"

But it was a testament to how seriously he took his role as

host that Hasan would not so much as approach the topic until he was satisfied that they'd had their fill of food.

"The riddle?" Nicholas pressed again. Hasan's brows rose.

She bristled at the insistence in his tone, as if every second they spent here was wasted. "Thank you," Etta said quickly, "for a delicious meal. We would love to hear your thoughts about what you think it means."

Hasan seemed to take this bit of rudeness in stride. "*Bring jasmine to the bride who sleeps eternal beneath the sky*—that was it, no?"

She nodded.

"I have tried to break it apart into pieces, to understand," Hasan said. "I thought, surely, Rose meant Damascus. There are many names for this place. The City of Jasmine, but also the Bride of the Earth. But this clue . . . it implies a kind of travel, would you not say? *Bring jasmine to the bride.* She wishes for you to leave this city, the City of Jasmine. So it must refer to another bride."

"And?" Nicholas interrupted, his fingers drumming against the table. "Go where?"

Hasan held up a hand. "Patience—"

Nicholas's hand came down hard enough to make the plates and platters jump across the table.

"Hey!" Etta said, only to be cut off.

"Every moment of delay is a moment that we can be found, tracked by the guardians," Nicholas said. "I don't wish to take any unnecessary risks by prolonging this to the point that Ironwood's guardians can catch us—not when we're so close to finding the astrolabe. Not to mention, we *do* have a deadline, do we not?"

Etta sighed, but nodded.

Hasan nodded. "Then we will make haste. But, *baha'ar*, as

well as you know the sea, you do not know this land. The desert is a ruthless beauty, a punishing empress who bows to no one. It is past midday now, and you should not expect to leave this night. We will make your preparations today and leave tomorrow at sunrise. But first you must listen to what I have to say, or you will not know which direction to go. Yes?"

Nicholas looked down at his hands spread across the richly gleaming wood and nodded.

"As I said before, Damascus is known to some as the Bride of the Earth, but there is another bride—Palmyra, the Bride of the Desert. I think perhaps this is your destination. And what comes next: *who sleeps eternal beneath the sky?* The city itself was a jewel of our trade, a glimmering civilization. But it has since fallen to ruin. There is a valley of tombs remaining, however."

A city her mother had painted for her.

"That's it," she told Nicholas. "We'll find it there." To Hasan, she asked, "Is there any way to narrow down which tomb it might be referring to? Are there very many?"

"Many," Hasan said, almost apologetically. "I have not visited in many years, so I could not tell you. But Rose tells you to look for the sigil, the sign of our family. I think you will recognize it when you see it."

Etta nodded, thinking of the tree etched into the cover of her mother's travel journal. Her hands came up to thoughtfully twist one earring's cool pearl.

"I worry, though," Hasan continued. "It is a three-day ride from Damascus on horse, longer by camel. You may be able to push the horses harder, arrive in two days, but it is dangerous—water is not plenty, and if you drive them to exhaustion you will have to go on foot."

"It's a risk we'll have to take, then," Nicholas said. "We'll need a map, a compass if you have one—water, food—can we go to the markets at once?"

"Well, yes, of course, but you will not require a map nor a compass, for I shall go with you. As your guide."

Nicholas was rising to his feet, but at that, he stopped. "We don't need a guide."

Why? she wondered. Did he think navigating the ocean gave him some kind of magical insight into handling the desert? This was a gift that Hasan was offering. She wasn't about to spit in his face.

"It would be my honor," Hasan said. "It is not ideal to go in a group so small, but I will protect you both with my life."

"I am perfectly capable of—" Nicholas began, stopping only when Etta put a hand on his shoulder.

"I would hope that will not be necessary," she said, "but we accept your help. Thank you."

One to recognize when a battle was already lost—maybe—Nicholas made his way back into the house, crossing the courtyard in long, purposeful strides. He might as well have turned back and glared at them, his posture was so rigid.

"That is a man who does not like to lose." Hasan waited until Nicholas was well out of sight before leaning toward Etta, soft concern on his face. "I would be pleased to kill him for you."

She was so startled by the words, it took his laughter to make her see it had been a joke. "He's been on edge lately. It's been a hard couple of days."

"I am more concerned for you. You seem unhappy this morning," he said. She knew that they were roughly the same age; that, if anything, he had only a few years on her. In that moment, though, his face was so knowing that it felt like she was being offered the opportunity to unburden herself to someone as ancient and knowing as the sun itself—someone who could make sense of what she was feeling.

"We had a bit of a fight," Etta admitted. "We resolved it the best we could, but it's not a permanent solution. He's upset about it and on edge about everything happening. So am I."

"Has he harmed you?"

"No—nothing like that," she assured him quickly. "It was just . . . coming to the conclusion that the . . ." She didn't want to lie to him, but she also wasn't sure how to say it without actually saying it. "That my future might not be what I thought it was going to be."

Not to mention a healthy dose of fear for her mom—where she was, how they were treating her, if she was *hurt*—

"I think perhaps . . ." Hasan caught himself, seeming to consider his words more carefully. "I think perhaps this thing that is between you is not so simple as he would make it sound?"

A shiver of worry passed down her spine.

"Listen well, little niece," Hasan said, clearly sensing this. "I know his reasons. I do not judge, the way others would. Abbi and Ummi were not married—they could not be traditionally bound. It is forbidden for a woman of my faith to marry a man who is not. But Allah in all his wisdom still brought them together. When they were discovered, she was cast out most terribly from her family. He brought her here, to a foreign land, to begin a new life and try to escape the shame that others had tried and failed to cast upon her. He cared for us, provided, but we could not be seen with him without fear of condemnation, and we could not go with him. We never wanted for anything—except, at times, his presence."

Hasan gave one last gentle pat to her hand, continuing. "It is blasphemous, I know; it goes against our teachings and beliefs, but I accept their choices. I cherish them in my heart. I cannot help but think, it matters not who you love, but only the quality of such a love. And so what I wish to say to you is . . . a flower is no less beautiful because it does not bloom in the expected form. Because it lasts an hour, and not days."

Etta nodded again, somehow managing to swallow against the tightness of her throat. It was what she needed to hear, that reassurance, the echo of her own thoughts. "He is very concerned about the judgment of others. I admire the courage of your parents—I can't imagine how difficult it was."

"His wish is your protection; it is a good thing," he said. "I cannot find fault in it. But Abbi described to me what it was to travel, to see the fabric of life spread out before him. He said it was 'possibility.' It is said that there is time enough for every purpose, and so you must continue to believe that there is a time for you."

"What if it's already passed?" she asked.

He leaned forward, a small smile on his face. "Then perhaps you will find a way to make more time. Possibility, dear one. Possibility."

THERE WAS AN EFFORTLESS BEAUTY TO THE CITY. ITS BONES WERE so ancient that one could just as easily imagine a Roman soldier passing through as one could a Crusader, or the brightly garbed Ottoman Janissaries who filled the city in their elaborate robes and tall, plumed hats. It was a crossroads of centuries.

Damascus gleamed white as a pearl, and seemed to fit together like a puzzle; the streets were curved, crooked, narrow, with the large exception of the aptly named Street Called Straight, which provided a firm backbone. Rooms hung out over the stone streets, some creating arches to pass under, all dripping with green plants and shade. At any point, it seemed as if they could turn off a street and escape into a second, hidden world inside of this one. The way the sunlight filtered through the city made her feel as though she were looking at the world through an old pane of glass.

Minarets of mosques stood proudly over homes and covered markets, peacefully sharing the sky with churches. The greatest of these, as Hasan explained, was the Great Mosque, built in the time of the Umayyad. It was the size of a palace, and some part of it always seemed to be visible, no matter where they stood inside the city's walls.

In her era, Syria was in the midst of a civil war, one so destructive and burdened with death and despair that millions of refugees had been forced to flee from it. Even Damascus had not been spared. But it was comforting, in a way she hadn't expected, to understand that the city had stood in one form or another for thousands of years. It had passed through the hands of any number of masters, had faced bloody revolts and subjugations—and it had survived.

"Come, come," Hasan said, ushering them on. "There are Ironwood guardians who make this city their home. We must get to the *souks* and return home as quickly as we can."

Etta walked on faster, searching the crowded streets and squares around them for any sign that they were being watched; beside her, Nicholas's expression was grim as he kept a hand tucked into the folds of his *entari*, on a dagger of some kind.

Each *souk* was a covered market—a bazaar—that coincided with a different trade, each blooming with offerings. If Etta had thought that escaping from the sun for a short time would bring some relief from the heat, she was wrong—there were so many people walking the *souks'* narrow lengths, admiring the fine cages and sweet chirping songbirds of the bird-sellers, testing the weight and strength of the armorers' weapons, examining the copper wares for any flaws, that she was reminded of New York's subways at rush hour.

Baskets hung like clouds from the ceiling, and when they passed the walls covered in lanterns—lanterns of every shape, every color of glass imaginable—she felt her feet shuffle to a stop.

The spice merchants and perfumers provided welcome relief from the less-than-savory smells of the city, especially the smells of those occupying it. Herself included. There was nothing quite like getting a lungful of a fruit vendor's sour breath to remind you how many days had passed since you'd stopped trying to find a toothbrush.

The friendliness of the merchants and local people was unrivaled, and unlike anything she'd ever experienced. Nicholas, through Hasan, tried to negotiate for skins to hold water, as well as less conspicuous clothing. Etta watched the other women around her and hoped she didn't look as awkward as she felt, standing away from where the men were conducting their business. Nicholas had entrusted the satchel to her, including what gold was left after London. When she handed the sack to him to buy the dried fruit, he shoved it back into her hand and allowed Hasan to carefully count out his own money.

"We'll give him the gold," Nicholas murmured, stooping close to her ear. "But to use raw gold and unfamiliar coins so liberally would attract the wrong kind of attention."

Hasan had clearly come up with some viable excuse for their presence. He negotiated in whispers, with laughter, and the occasional stern look, slowly filling their baskets and arms with necessities. While he and Nicholas examined and debated the merits of several different saddles, she was caught in the path of a roving textile merchant who practically flung his silk shawls at her, extolling their virtues in a language she had no chance of understanding.

Etta didn't know what it was, exactly. Even as the sweet-faced man draped a beautiful length of gold brocade over her shoulder, following her as she turned, she suddenly had an eerie feeling, almost like a spider walking up the back of her neck. Etta glanced around, her eyes leaping from woman to man to merchant.

There were two bearded men in black robes nearby, at a mercantile stall with cloth stacked so high on crooked shelves that it actually brushed the ceiling. One had the darker skin of the people around them, but the other was clearly a Westerner, his complexion nearly as pale as her own. They weren't looking at the material they'd picked up and draped over their hands. Their focus wasn't on Hasan, and it wasn't on Nicholas. It wasn't even on her.

They were staring at the young woman standing a few feet behind Etta, tucked against a pillar, who was very clearly watching Hasan. A small section of her golden hair spilled out from beneath the white scarf she'd wrapped around her head. Etta pulled her veil fully aside to see her—to convince herself she hadn't been conjured out of smoke and dust.

412

Etta must have made a sound, because the young woman spun toward her, and her own veil fell back far enough to reveal her face. The blue eyes that stared back at her matched her own.

But . . . how? Hasan had said she'd left days ago. Was she only just leaving now to hide the astrolabe? Or was she returning from stowing it away?

"Rose?" Etta said, voice catching on the name. That was her first mistake.

Running after her when she turned and bolted was Etta's second.

It was easy to track her progress—they were the only ones pushing against the flow of people moving through the bazaar. Angry words rang out behind her, but Etta barely heard them over her wheezing breath and the slap of her soft-soled shoes against the ground. Her mom was *fast*.

Reaching out, Rose tore down a display of silver platters, sending dozens of them slamming to the ground, along with the tables they had been artfully arranged on. Etta stumbled, barely catching herself with a sharp gasp. Rose tossed a look back over her shoulder, and Etta had a full, perfect view of her twisted scowl as her own mother threw a small dagger right at her.

It missed Etta's neck by less than an inch—and only because she had finally tripped, her shoe catching on something jutting out from one of the nearby booths.

"Rose!" she called. "Please, I just want to talk to you—"

The crowd scattered around them—a woman screamed in alarm—but Etta's whole attention was fixed on that face, the way her expression had sharpened like the finest of the blades in the market.

"You can tell Henry or Cyrus or whoever the bloody hell you

413

work for," she said, her accent so clipped it was nearly unfamiliar, "that they'll *never* find it."

"You mean the astrolabe?" Etta asked. "I'm not trying to get in your way, I swear—"

A pair of hands lifted her off the ground, and the last thing she saw before her veil was dragged back across her face was Rose—her eyes wide, backing away.

"Let me go!" Etta said, disoriented. She was lifted off her feet and thrown over a shoulder. "Nicholas, stop, it's her!"

But . . . she sucked in another breath, the veil sticking to her lips and tongue, blinded by the fabric and her own hair. That smell—Nicholas always smelled like the sea, like soap and cedar. And now, with arms crushing around her legs, keeping her in place, all she could smell was camel—animal.

They veered right just as someone let out another cry of alarm. Wood splintered against the ground, and there was the sound of something shattering a second before Etta heard the call to prayer sound over the city.

Etta's back was suddenly drenched in heat, and the world burned a fiery red beneath her closed eyelids. Her hands were trapped beneath her, pinned to someone's shoulders. She thrashed wildly, kicking, her screams muffled by the fabric around her.

I'm being taken—

Etta's foot hit a soft spot that brought the man to his knees. She spilled out onto hot stone and had barely crawled to her hands and knees when a sharp kick to the head sent her back down. Dust and dirt filled her mouth, grinding between her teeth as she tried to crawl away. Black and white exploded across her vision, blocking the sight of her bleeding hand against the pale stone.

There was a howl of fury and a shift in the wind at her back.

Etta fell forward again, but managed to get the veil away from her face. That's when she saw Nicholas barreling shoulder-first into one of the men she'd seen before.

People gathered around, some beginning their prayers, others arrested by the sight of Nicholas throwing his fist into one man's face as the other attacker jumped on his back. The second attacker's hand disappeared into the folds of Nicholas's robe and Etta heard Nicholas cry out as he threw his head back and knocked him off.

No one moved to help, not until Hasan burst out of the bazaar and began to shout for aid. By then, both of the men in black robes were on their feet; Etta didn't see how they managed it, but they ran into the chaos they had created, chased off by the Janissaries.

"Etta—Etta!" Nicholas dropped to his knees in front of her, his lungs working like bellows. "Are you hurt?"

Before her thick tongue could form a response, he swayed, his eyes blinking as if in surprise. She reached out, one hand gripping his arm to steady him, the other going to his side—where a large, wet patch of violently crimson blood was spreading.

"No—" Etta choked out, "no, no! Nicholas!"

She couldn't even catch him as he fell.

NINETEEN

HE KNEW THAT HE WAS IN TROUBLE WHEN THE WOUND did not pain him at all.

Fragments of the last few hours were scattered across his mind, the way the wind had toyed with the white petals dusting the open courtyard. Had that really been only a few hours ago? Impossible. It was dark now. Days might have passed, and he could not surface long enough from the depths of a terrible, gripping sleep to see for himself.

Soft voices carried on above him. Soft hands lifted the bandages at his side to inspect his wounds. Soft cloths mopped away the infernal sweat from his face. If there was one thing Nicholas had not been expecting, it was how soft a touch Death had for him. It seemed unfair, somehow, to not go out fighting. To be denied the chance to burn, to rail against it, to shout it down until his last breath left him. Wasn't that his right? Or did it only feel so wrong because he had spent the whole of his life fighting so bloody hard? To go with a whisper . . . the thought seemed to sit upon his chest, making it harder and harder to breathe.

Perhaps he would think upon it some more, when he was not so tired.

Yes.

THE PLACE WHERE THEY HAD BROUGHT HIM SMELLED OF THE earth. There was a constant shuffle of quiet feet and voices around him. What he knew of their language was irrelevant; it was impossible to concentrate over the roaring of his own blood in his ears. A hospital, then? He forced his eyes open at the first touch of light on his lids.

Around him were walls as white and pale as a tomb, ornamented lavishly with carvings. Nicholas tried to focus long enough to see what was there. A thousand suns. A thousand flowers. The atmosphere was calm and peaceful. Even the water they sponged his face with was sweetly fragranced, strewn with flowers that reminded him of Etta. But, of course, what didn't make him think of Etta now?

Though there were beds open beside him, he was alone in this stretch of the hallway, left to watch the water spilling over the room's fountain, to watch the young men and women who came to fill their basins from it. He was lifted, made to drink tasteless broth. Nicholas might have told them that it was pointless—his throat was swollen and raw, like he'd swallowed the whole of the sun. He knew.

The wound had not killed him.

The fever would.

Despite his weak struggling, they kept him wrapped tightly in the bedding, trapped inside his own heat until there was little choice but to sweat and suffer. All of these people tending to him, and no one would help him.

417

Etta will.

Etta would. Holy God—he'd seen a man try to smash her skull against the stone, and the very last chain of his control had snapped. Was she all right? Where was she? And the date . . . how many days had passed? Would she know to go without him?

When his eyes slid shut again, it wasn't her face that he saw, but Hall's—the way he had looked when he'd crouched down in front of Nicholas, when the boy was barely as high as his hip, and told him that they were leaving. He'd offered his hand—big, so big and warm—and it had closed around his.

Hall . . . who would tell Hall what had become of him? And Chase? Perhaps one of them might seek out Ironwood, only to find that he had no definitive answers, either.

Lost. He would be known not by what he had accomplished, but for the manner of his demise. Most sailors knew to accept the word as final, with all of its deadly simplicity. But Hall and Chase were relentlessly optimistic. Would they be able to shoulder the burden of not knowing? Sold back into slavery, food for the sharks, rotting away in prison . . . there were endless ways for their minds to torture them, and none would even come close to the truth.

He began to measure his hours by the calls to prayer he heard. Every time he sensed someone near him, his body instinctively tensed, trying to reach beneath his pillow for a knife that was not there.

Nicholas woke to the sound of soft humming and ripping fabric, and turned his head to the side to see who it was. A young man sat on a nearby bed, a basket of what looked to be either white linen or rough silk resting beside him. The bolts of fabric were ravaged, ruined by gaping holes and tears; perhaps they had been donated to the hospital for bandages, or perhaps they had once been old bedclothes, repurposed now and given second life. The young man didn't struggle in the slightest as he worked, tearing each into long strips. The holes had weakened the fabric, making it vulnerable to the force of his strength.

Nicholas's mind could not follow a straight path, navigate a single thought, without losing it to the burn of fever. But the image stayed with him, even as his eyes struggled with the weights dragging him back down. What was it about this simple task that spoke to him?

Money . . . power . . .

Tearing. Rending. Fabric. Time.

The reason he was here.

The reason Etta had been forced back.

Time—they were nearly out of time—Etta—

Etta. He needed to speak to Etta.

It was night before his chance arrived, and a familiar voice filled the air. Nicholas cracked an eye open, watching Hasan speak to a barrel-chested older man in pristine robes. He tried to open his mouth, but the sound that came out was a pathetic whimper. Neither heard him until he cleared his throat.

"My friend, let me bring you some water—" The older man, his hair as gray as the inside of Nicholas's head, left with a brief look in his direction. Nicholas caught hold of Hasan's robe before he could pull away.

"Etta," he said, carefully forming the word. "Bring . . . bring me Etta."

"It is late," Hasan said, lightly scolding. "Would you wish for her to see you like this?"

So she hadn't been there at all? "Now," he said harshly. He

thought twice of it and added a softer, hopefully not desperate, "Please."

"Yes, all right," Hasan said. He started to rise from where he had knelt beside Nicholas, only to return to his original position, leaning over his face.

"*Baha'ar,*" he began, his voice soft; grave. "Do not die so far from the sea."

Nicholas closed his eyes, waiting, and did not open them again until he heard Etta's familiar gait hurrying across the tiled floor. It was dark out now, the day edging into evening. Candles glowed around him, warming his bed with their light. He thought of their night together—the expression on her sweet face as she had gazed up at him—and felt his whole chest tighten.

Her steps slowed, and he knew that he must have looked as horrendous as he felt. Her expression tore at his heart, made him want to take her pain away. He wished he could see one last smile before he told her the truth.

"How about a kiss, hey?" he whispered.

She seemed to smile in spite of herself, and slowly lowered herself to the floor so that she could press her soft, cool lips against his. When Etta pulled back, she left her hands on his skin, easing them along his cheeks, his forehead, his scalp.

"Where?" he asked, clearing his throat again.

"Qaymair—a hospital here in Damascus," she said quietly, curling her legs beneath her. "I wanted to take you back to the house, but Hasan was worried about bringing strangers into it. And you needed a doctor, badly."

Nicholas made a sour face and she let out a light laugh. "Hasan has been standing guard. He barely let me in to see you before now. I had to sneak in under the cover of darkness last night."

"Alone?" He gave her a disapproving look that she ignored.

"I got caught, and he dragged me off back to the house. You've been sleeping for most of the past two days."

Two days. Holy God. Only three days, then, to meet the old man's deadline? His heart stirred with fear—for her, the woman responsible for this mad chase.

"The men, were they caught?"

Her hands stilled, and he leaned into her touch greedily to keep her from pulling back. "No. I'm sorry. Do you think they were guardians?"

They must have been, if they had been tailing Rose and realized they'd stumbled onto an equally great bounty with Etta. Bloody hell, they hadn't even managed to go a full day without being caught. What a worthless protector he'd proven himself to be.

"You're sorry I was hurt, not that you ran after her," Nicholas said pointedly, grateful for the steadiness of his voice. "Was it really Rose?"

"Yes—my own mother threw a knife at me." Etta shook her head. "I can't wait to tell her."

"Did she say anything to you?" he asked.

"Just that she'd never let Cyrus or someone named Henry have the astrolabe," Etta said. "I didn't even have time to explain that we weren't giving it to either of them."

Ah.

He knew it was time. He knew that, aside from simply wanting to see her, he had brought her here to finally speak the truth.

But now that Etta was with him, with her lovely face and bright heart, he found himself stalling.

There is no way around, he thought. *Only through.*

She'd pulled back his blanket enough for him to finally free his arms; he used his newfound mobility to reach up and take her hands, press them against his chest. Nicholas knew that she could feel his heart galloping.

Her brows drew together sharply. She looked so tired to him, and he had little doubt as to who was the cause. "What's wrong?"

"I've something to tell you," he began. "You must let me speak the whole of it. It's imperative, you know."

"Can it wait until morning?" she asked. "You need your rest. . . ."

It was just like her to see evidence that his light was fading, and deny it to the last. "I have not been honest with you. It cannot wait."

Etta leaned back, but he held her hands to him, anchoring her.

"I didn't simply come after you through the passage. . . . I was worried that, yes, you do seem to invite a considerable amount of danger into your life, but . . . after you went out that first night, went to sleep, Ironwood negotiated new terms with me." His throat ached so badly, and he lost his train of thought momentarily to the searing pain in his side. "That I would go with you, attend to this matter, and ensure you did not try to make off with the astrolabe or cross him. It was my intention to bring the astrolabe to him, Etta, whether you agreed or not. In exchange, he would surrender his holdings in the West Indies to me, a vast fortune. Now I know the vast fortune will no longer exist once he changes the past and creates a new future."

Etta shook her head, her fingers loosening around his. For several moments, he was sure she was about to speak, but it could have been a trick of the candlelight.

"Say something," he whispered. "Please . . . say you despise me for withholding the truth, that you'll never forgive me . . . say anything, just don't hide your thoughts from me."

"I will," she said evenly, eyeing him past a loose strand of hair that had fallen across her face. "Once I figure out the best way to cut out your heart and eat it."

The laugh that burst from his chest was little more than a weak chuckle. "I wish you would. At least then you might see the whole of the sorry thing, the absolute mastery you have held over it from the moment I saw you."

Etta's eyes slid closed and she turned, trying to hide her expression—as if she could hide from him, after all this time. "I don't want you to . . . to say something like that because you feel bad about keeping that secret. Do I wish you had told me from the beginning? *Yes.* But I kept the truth about not giving the astrolabe back to Ironwood from you for a long time. And it's not like you've already given Ironwood the astrolabe."

"I lied to you. . . ." He couldn't make sense of this reaction; he'd steeled himself for the inevitability of her rejection, her hatred, once she knew what he'd been planning. Nicholas could scarcely bring himself to breathe, lest he shatter the unreal quality of the moment.

"But I know *why* you did. I know that much money would allow you to buy your ship, a whole new life. That's what I want for you . . . to have the things you deserve. I want you to have that, and not feel guilty about how you got it. You told me the truth. You don't have to give me poetry to ease the blow."

"I wasn't motivated to take the deal solely for the reward," he said. "You must know this. I thought I owed it to Julian to finish what we'd begun, and . . . I wanted to . . . I wanted to be near you. Protect you."

"Nicholas . . ."

The truth, stripped bare to its bones, was that if he had cared for her any less, he would have walked away. Not even the full weight of Ironwood's fortune would have been enough to tempt him alone.

It was the quality of her feelings that shattered him—the pure belief and care that she had for him. He'd underestimated her, and he was more the fool for it, for denying this regard . . . this love for him. There was no other word to describe it. It truly was the same for her. The thought flooded him, filled his veins with equal parts relief and agony.

He tugged her forward, until her resistance faded and she curled against his side.

"Would poetry convince you of it? *And now good-morrow to our waking souls,*" he began, reaching into his memory for the rest of the lines. "*Which watch not one another out of fear; for love all love of other sights controls, and makes one little room an everywhere.*"

"Now I know you really *are* unwell. . . ." she began, but he wasn't finished. He could stave off sleep a little while more, for these last few necessary moments. If his own words failed to convince her, Donne's would not.

"*Let sea-discoverers to new worlds have gone; let maps to other, worlds on worlds have shown; let us possess one world; each hath one, and is one.*"

"Just so you know, I'm expecting another recitation of this

when you're feeling better," she informed him. The tremor in her voice stole some of its cheekiness. "Can you try for a time you don't think you're dying?"

"Listen to me," he said, hearing the way his words were beginning to slur. The heat she added to his already-burning skin could have set a man on fire. "You've already been delayed too long. Ask Hasan to take you to Palmyra in the morning. It'll be a hard ride, a long one, but I know you can make it. I know you'll make the right decision about what to do with it. I trust that your heart will know the right way forward."

"No," she said. "I won't go without you—"

"Can you not bend your will to mine, just this once?" he said. "You know what's at stake now. You must go."

"You're my partner," she said, her voice pitching higher. He tightened his grip around her. She was upset now, but only because she could see the truth of his words, the truth of his fate. "Don't you dare abandon me now. I won't go without you. I won't leave you behind."

"You cannot go back," he told her. "You must go forward—always forward now."

Etta pushed herself up, far enough to look him in the face. The tears collected in her pale lashes, but she did not let them fall. Instead, he saw her determination bloom again, and he understood himself so well then, how she could inspire the two warring parts of himself—the half that wished to be the proper gentleman she deserved, and the rogue that wanted her no matter the cost.

"You are going to be incredibly embarrassed when you survive this, and I come back to make you answer for all of that poetry," she said. "I swear, you eighteenth-century men are so dramatic."

"It's . . ." he struggled for the word, rasping it out. The

pounding in his head had only grown worse as his heart had sped up. He wanted to hold her in silence, know the planes of her soft shape again in these last few hours. "I wish it were as simple as choice."

Did people not die of fever in her time? Truly?

"You sound like you've already half given up," she said. "You have things to do for yourself! You're not going to die here—I won't let you!"

The breath wheezed out of him, into him, but his tongue couldn't form the words. He was fighting now to stay above the silver, silky call of oblivious sleep. His strength ebbed, pulling him back, past the point of choice. There was no choice. As much as he wished to strike back, to cling to this life until he wore his fingertips down to the bone, he had seen too much death to believe he could escape. Even with trickery and luck, a man only survived so many fevers before one finally claimed him in the end. But surely, if ever there were a reason to try, it would be her.

Exhaustion crept over him, banished only for a moment as she kissed him fiercely.

"I won't leave you here," she swore. "Promise me that you're going to fight."

"I love you." For whatever small comfort it was worth, he would have the truth between them now. "Most desperately. Bloody inconvenient, that."

"Promise." He felt the first of her tears fall, slide down the length of his cheek. Panic made her tremble, so he drew her close to him again, hoping to steady her. He'd never felt time's grip so acutely; there was so much he wished to say to her, and his chance was slipping away.

"You will live. . . . You must live," he continued. "I think you know . . . the truth of it is . . . I wanted to go with you. I wanted to see your home. I wanted to find that place for us, the one you spoke of. . . ."

"It's waiting," Etta told him. "We just have to go."

She could shatter him with so few words.

"When you play your violin, will you think of me?" he asked softly. "Sometimes . . . not always, or even often, but perhaps when you hear the sea and you remember . . . I should like to have heard you . . . just once. . . ."

"Nicholas," she said sharply, holding his face between her hands, drawing him back from that steep, dark edge again, "if you die, I'll never forgive you. I don't care if that's selfish—I *don't*. Fight."

Love was selfish, wasn't it? It made honest men want things they had no right to. It cocooned one from the rest of the world, erased time itself, knocked away reason. It made you live in defiance of the inevitable. It made you want another's mind, body; it made you feel as if you deserved to own their heart, and carve out a place in it.

You are mine, he thought, watching her, *and I am yours.*

"Tell me . . . just one thing . . . about your time?" he managed to get out.

"Of course," Etta said.

"Do you remember . . . that couple in London, in the station?"

"The ones who were dancing?" she asked. "What about them?"

"Would we . . . be able to dance . . . that way?" he said, finding it harder to catch his breath. "In your time?"

Etta pressed her lips together, clearly fighting to offer him a smile. "Yes."

"Thought so. Will you stay . . . until I sleep . . . ?"

She kissed his cheeks, his eyelids, his forehead, leaving behind a burning trail across his heart. His breathing slowed, his heart seemed to murmur an apology in response . . . a slow *thump thump thump* in his ears that reminded him of a ship's rudder changing course. A gradual slowing, and then . . .

Not like this.

Not a whisper, please God, but a roar. He needed to finish this journey before beginning the next.

"Fight," she whispered one last time, breath warm against his ear.

For you, his pulse throbbed back, *for me.*

NICHOLAS WAS ONLY DIMLY AWARE OF ETTA AS SHE PULLED AWAY; he was locked somewhere between sleep and the fiery hell of fever. There was no feeling left in his arms to reach for her, and his legs might as well have been cut away for all he could shift them. All that was left to him was pain, alternating between the agonizing row of stitches in his side, and the beating inside his skull.

He slept hard, his dreams scalding and bright. He dreamt of the house on Queen Street, that path he took between the kitchen and the hidden door in the dining room to serve the family their meals. *Stay out of sight. Stay in the dark. Stay silent.* He dreamt of his mother's hands—how strange it was to remember their shape and weight and touch when her face was so far away. The pink scars and burns that covered the back of them, evidence of her endless work in the kitchen.

She was always smoothing him—his shirt, his hair, the dirt and blood from his face. He remembered her hands, hideously deformed and hardened by work, but warm, and there when he reached for them—

Nicholas dreamt of burning the house to its bones and pissing on its ashes.

And so it was somewhat startling to be suddenly ripped out of sleep by a splash of warm water.

"*Baha'ar!* Wake! You fool!" Hasan was bellowing, his voice nearly unrecognizable as he slapped a hand down onto the center of Nicholas's chest. He used a word he assumed was a rather violent oath, because it made the solemn doctor standing nearby gape.

The shock of it cleared the smoke clouds from his mind. Nicholas felt much like a cloth that had been wrung out and left in the sun to dry. Every muscle in his body screamed in protest as he drew himself up ever so slightly and leaned against the wall.

"What is it?" he rasped out. "Why are you ranting like—"

"*Fool!*" he barked again. "What did you tell her?"

He missed a breath. "Etta?"

"Who else?" Hasan cried. "Why did you tell her to leave?"

It was at that precise moment that Nicholas knew that he would survive, if only to have the pleasure of throttling her himself. And, well—yes, he was mildly embarrassed by the show he had put on the night before.

"First, you should know it is bloody well impossible to compel her to do anything she doesn't wish to do. I told her to ask you to take her—that she should leave by morning." It was morning now, early morning, before the sun was even ripe in the skin. The darkness diminished with each passing second.

His anger, that immediate, swift response, was fading with it. Etta could be impulsive, yes, but she was not so reckless as to try to make a journey across a desert alone. And even if that were the case, where would she have gotten herself a horse? How

429

would she know where to go? Etta didn't speak their language, she didn't have a map. . . .

A chill rippled down his spine. "Did you look for her at the house?

"Do you think me so stupid I would not look there first?" Hasan huffed. "She did not return there. If she did, it was not to retrieve her belongings."

That same chill turned to ice in his veins. Leaving without money, without their small bag of supplies?

She had not set out alone. Not willingly. Perhaps she hadn't left the city on purpose at all—someone might have taken her, forced her against her will, stolen her away—

With a shameful amount of effort, Nicholas dragged his legs out of the bedding, ignoring the way his wound pulled. "We must ask the men and women here . . . see if anyone saw her leave."

It wasn't a good bet, but it was their only chance.

Hasan nodded, firing a question at the silent, white-haired doctor. He murmured something back in calm tones that somehow made Nicholas's own temper flare. Did this man not see that time was imperative? Why was he walking out of the room, not running?

"Easy, my friend," Hasan said, pressing Nicholas back down onto the bed as he tried to rise. "He will return shortly."

The doctor did—after ten agonizing minutes. A young man, the very same one Nicholas had watched tearing the bandages, trailed behind him with head bowed and hands clasped in front of him.

The young man spoke without any prompting, chirping back answers to all of Hasan's questions. When Hasan finally held up a hand just over his head as if to ask, *How tall?* the last frayed thread of Nicholas's patience snapped.

"What does he say?" he demanded.

Hasan's rich complexion was ashen. "He says he saw her leave this *iwan*—that is, this hall—but she was met by another woman. A Westerner, he says, like herself. And she was pulled away, outside, with the assistance of two other men."

Nicholas fixed the boy with a baleful look. "And he didn't think to say one damn word to someone about it?"

"He thought the woman was her family," Hasan explained, though Nicholas could see his own frustrated anger reflected in his face. As if the color of one's skin was the telltale sign of family.

"What did she look like?" Nicholas asked.

"Young—young as you or I. Brown hair, he says—darker than hers. Eyes like—dark eyes as well. He says he saw her look at an impossibly small gold clock, the like of which he had not ever seen before." He emphasized those last words with a meaningful look.

Fury cramped his aching stomach as he pressed his feet flat against the cool floor. Nicholas took a steadying breath. *You cannot have me yet. . . .* He would fill this weakness in his body, feed it with anger, until either he found her or his body gave out completely.

"Do you know who this is, *baha'ar*?"

Instead of answering, Nicholas asked a question of his own. "Do you know how to do a proper knot?"

"Yes," Hasan said, his forehead wrinkling. "But why?"

"Because," Nicholas said, watching the morning light spread over the tile floor, "I'm going to need you to tie me to my horse."

431

TWENTY

IT WASN'T THE ROLLING FLOW OF THE HORSE'S GALLOP, or even the rope burns around her wrists, that finally brought Etta around. It was the cool mist of the morning air, and the scent of orange blossom on the breeze.

She cracked an eye open, already sick from the riot of movement and the damp, hot press of the man riding behind her. Every breath against the back of her neck made her stomach churn harder, twisting in time with the pain at her right temple. There was no way to know until she had her hands free, but Etta had a feeling that the bump there was going to rival the mountain behind them.

They left Damascus through a series of groves, weaving through the orderly rows of trees. The golden line of the horizon was ahead, and Etta suddenly understood why Hasan had called the desert a ruthless beauty. From a distance, with the sun rising over it, the dust was cast in glorious shades of gold. But the single tone of color hinted at something far more sinister—its barrenness.

"Oh—you're awake."

Her fingers curled around the lip of the saddle as she turned slowly. Etta let her expression fall into a scowl. "Sorry."

When she'd left Nicholas's bedside to find a doctor, or Hasan, or anyone who could confirm that she wasn't going crazy and that his fever really was breaking, Etta had nearly missed her standing there, leaning against the wall. Sophia had called her name, but even then she'd been so deliriously tired she was half-convinced she was hallucinating.

But no. Sophia had been wearing the *entari* and *shalvar* of the women of Damascus in shades of ivory and gold, her head inclined to the side in its usual arrogant way.

"What are you doing here?" Etta had managed.

"You're not an idiot," Sophia had said. "You don't need me to answer that. I'm here to help you finish this task."

Even then, confused, overwhelmed, Etta had known to be suspicious. Sophia could only have found them if she'd followed them—not just through Damascus, but through all of the passages. Or . . . if she'd managed to get her hands on the reports the guardians were no doubt sending back to Ironwood about their sightings.

"I'm not leaving," Etta said. "Not yet."

The other girl's face had hardened behind her veil. "I was afraid you might say something like that."

A sharp pain, and then . . . nothing.

And now, *this.*

"I apologize for the rough treatment," Sophia said as she brought her horse up alongside Etta's with ease. The pounding of the hooves kicked up enough dust in the air between them that she was momentarily shrouded.

"We simply didn't have time," she continued without a trace of remorse. "I could see in your face you weren't going to leave, and in the time it took to convince you, we could have been half-way to Palmyra."

Etta straightened, trying to throw an elbow back against the man behind her. "How do you know about Palmyra?"

"I had these guardians tail you in the market yesterday, and make inquiries. The Arab you were with mentioned your destination to the man who sold you the goatskins. Careless." Sophia shrugged.

I had these guardians tail you in the market . . .

Etta twisted around in the saddle, horror tightening her stomach like a fist. The man was a mess of swelling bruises, a cut lip, glowering down at her.

These were the men who had tried to grab her—one of them had stabbed Nicholas. A wash of white-hot fury flooded beneath her skin, and she began to struggle that much harder.

"Stop it!" Sophia snapped. "I had to pay him twice as much to ride with you—he spouted something preposterous about his faith not allowing him to touch a female who wasn't a relation. Don't test their patience."

Etta gritted her teeth. "You shouldn't have put him in the position of having to do it. That wasn't very kind of you."

The look the man sent her was filled with so much disgust, Etta was sure she was on the verge of being struck again.

"Did you . . ." The words caught in her throat. "Did you hire them to kill Nicholas?"

"What are you going on about?" Sophia's nostrils flared. "If someone attacked the bastard, it wasn't anyone here."

It felt like a freezing hand had wiped all feeling from Etta's face. She stared at the girl, shocked. "Were you there?"

"In the market? Of course not," she said. "I was trying to go through the room—the one the passage opened up into—while the three of you were out. Why? What are you going on about?"

The man riding behind Etta tightened his grip around her center until it felt like one of her ribs would crack. Something sharp dug into her side, and Etta took the silent warning for what it was.

Why didn't the man she was riding with, or the one riding just up ahead of Sophia, want her to say anything? Because they feared this Ironwood's wrath for acting outside the scope of her orders, and it getting back to the Grand Master?

"Someone . . . tried to rob me," Etta said, when she realized Sophia was still watching her. "Nicholas jumped in and got hurt. That's why we were in the hospital."

"What a shame," Sophia said without a hint of pity.

"He's your family," Etta snapped. "And you have more in common than you think—"

The other girl reached out, gripping the reins of Etta's horse so brutally she brought them both up short. The horse whinnied in protest, stamping its feet against the loose dust. When Sophia spoke, her voice was heavy with venom. "I will only say this once, so listen to me: the bastard is not family. If you say it again, you will regret it."

The word she'd used, the way she'd said it—*bastard*. It told Etta everything she needed to know about the way Sophia felt toward herself and her family.

Thank God Nicholas hadn't been raised by these people. She needed to find a way to ensure he'd be out of their hands forever.

"What are you doing here?" Etta demanded finally. "You

PASSENGER

said that you were here to help, but this"—she tugged at her restraints—"implies otherwise. If you were following us through the passages, why didn't you say something? Talk to us?"

Sophia dropped the reins and turned her horse back to the road, speaking to the hired men in what Etta assumed was Arabic. She'd mentioned before that the travelers learned languages as part of their training, but this still somehow caught Etta off guard. There was no way she'd be able to understand their plan until it was too late.

"If you didn't want to be followed, you shouldn't have left in the middle of the night, and you shouldn't have stolen from me," Sophia said finally. "What did you think? He was going to just let you go, and cross his fingers that the bastard held up his end of the bargain?" The other girl gave her a mocking look of pity. "What? Didn't you know about the deal that *Nicholas* made behind your back? That he'd get everything—"

"I know about the deal," Etta snapped. And she'd understood—she had—even as the hurt had sliced through her. It was a good enough reason to align himself with the old man, and it would give him everything he wanted. But to keep it from her . . . "He told me about it himself."

"Did he, now?" Sophia asked. "If he somehow manages to live through that fever, he'll be destroyed for it. When I tried to tell Grandfather he shouldn't be trusted, Grandfather told me that any betrayal on Nicholas's part would ensure he'd never be able to find work on a ship again, let alone set foot on a dock. He'd be wrecked."

"He's not—" Etta's whole mind ached. Had the old man really promised to destroy his future if he backed out of their deal? Her heart was still squeezed in a fist of fear when she said, "He's not going to die."

"Keep telling yourself that, darling."

Etta watched the girl a moment more, trying to work through her own strategy. "So, you must be eating this up. The old man actually trusted you enough to send you after us. Or were his choices that limited?"

"You gave me the opportunity I've been waiting for. . . . I can prove myself very easily, show him how capable I really am." Sophia eased into her horse's pace, adjusting her position in the saddle as if it were the most natural thing in the world. Etta felt like a bag of bones being tossed around, her legs already sore from having to squeeze the sides of the horse. Sophia had to call out to be heard over the horses, and keep her face turned down to avoid getting a mouthful of dirt.

"I'm sorry your pride's hurt that I trailed you both so easily. You made my job very simple by being on the other side of the city as I came through the passage in that charming, secret little apartment. And anyway, you should be grateful it's me, and not one of Grandfather's men. We'll make quick work of finding it, won't we? Have it back by the thirtieth. I'm rather well-versed in meeting his impossible deadlines by now."

Etta shook her head, her fingers toying with the smooth leather of the saddle, debating whether or not to continue. Ironwood had clearly kept the whole truth from her, but Etta couldn't predict how the other girl would actually react if she found out what was at stake for her, too, in all of this. Sophia's loyalty was braided into the family's success and future—everything she wanted was tied to winning the old man's approval. Did she care about anything outside of that attention and respect?

"Told you about the astrolabe, did he?" Etta said. "I doubt he told you the real reason he wants it."

"Be quiet!" Sophia barked, her eyes darting to the man behind Etta in the saddle.

Etta had to try to appeal to her reason. "The astrolabe doesn't read passages, it creates them—"

"Do shut up, Linden!"

Does she already know? And—what—she doesn't care? Sophia had no personal attachment to the future, no one to love or who loved her, no home or place she fit in. Maybe that was what made it so easy.

Etta was jolted, and bit the inside of her mouth as the horse began to gallop again. The man behind her grunted something unintelligible, but she wasn't fooled—not only did he understand English, but there was more here than what any of them were letting on. The men had attacked them in the *souk* without Sophia's orders, or at the very least, without informing her of what had happened. Maybe they only felt true loyalty to the old man?

And maybe Sophia knew this, and that was the real reason she didn't want Etta flapping her gums about the astrolabe for them to hear. She hadn't forgotten what Nicholas had said in the *souk*—how gold, or the promise of treasure, attracted unwanted attention. If Sophia didn't want these men to fully appreciate the magnitude of what they were after, did that mean she was afraid they might decide they wanted it for themselves? But what could guardians actually do with the astrolabe, aside from hold it for ransom?

It was a loose string on a sweater, and Etta was tempted—if she could unravel whatever thin bonds of loyalty they felt for the girl, maybe Etta could slip away in the chaos, get ahead of them, and—

Wander off into the desert?

Leave the other girl for dead?

Etta shook her head slowly. She was a lot of things, and was capable of handling a great deal more than she'd ever known, but *that* was cold-blooded. That was an absolute last resort if nothing else worked.

"I can almost picture it, you know," Sophia began, laughing. "Grandfather's face. His surprise when *I* complete the impossible task."

"Surprise?" Etta felt the same feeling trickling through her. "You mean . . ."

Ironwood didn't know she'd followed them. She'd come by herself, on her own volition.

"Now you've got the shape of things," Sophia said. "I owe it to you, of course. Remember what you said about taking control of my life? If he won't give me the honor of being the heir, then I'll damn well prove to him I'm the right choice."

And it was then that Etta knew she'd need to sort out a different plan, to prepare herself for the absolute worst. Because all the strategies in the world couldn't guard you from the lengths a hungry young girl would go to, to get what she thought she deserved.

HOURS LATER, AFTER THE SUN HAD PASSED OVER THEIR HEADS and was setting at their backs, after the green oasis of Damascus had become a distant memory, Etta realized she had imagined this desert all wrong.

She'd expected piles of sand—dunes they'd sink down into. It was pure ignorance about this part of the world. The land that spread out before them was one of two things: flat, or mountainous. The mountains seemed always to be in the distance, shrouded by a gray haze. The wind whipped around enough to play with the pale, packed dirt underfoot, teasing whatever the horses had kicked up. Its shrieking had a kind of cadence to it. It whispered, coaxed, like it was trying to lead them astray.

The horses devoured the few spots of shriveled shrubbery into the earth when they stopped to rest. Their lungs were heaving, and Etta's horse's body radiated heat until her legs were damp with both its sweet, pungent sweat and her own. She wasn't cut free until it came time to walk the animals.

One of the guardians located a rough well that had been dug into the hard ground. Sophia translated what he said: that it had likely been left by the Romans who'd used this road to travel to Palmyra, and was still in use by the few Bedouin tribes inhabiting the desert. The water was stale and sickly-looking, collected from weeks-old rain, but the horses drank until there was nothing left, and then it was time to continue on.

There was no shade, no water, absolutely nothing save the occasional ancient crumbling structure in the distance. When the dirt settled, Etta could see a hundred miles in every direction; the heat toyed with the air, making it dance like the entrance to a passage. After a while, the thought of looking for a passage became too depressing, and Etta was too sore and tired to try. Even with the protection of the robe and veil, the sun baked her inside out.

Just as Etta thought Sophia would force them to ride through the night, a cluster of pale, low buildings appeared in the distance.

"Kurietain," Sophia said, clearly relieved, as she wiped the sweat from her face with her sleeve.

"How far do we have till Palmyra?" Etta asked, sliding down off the bedraggled horse. The poor thing could barely keep its head up, and shuddered as she and the guardian removed their weight for the duration of the short walk to the village.

"About another day's journey north," Sophia said. "I want to keep pushing after we get water, but our illustrious guardians seem to think we should try to trade the horses for camels."

Switching to camels—animals capable of surviving days without water in the desert—sounded pretty reasonable to Etta.

"What are their names?"

"The camels? How the hell should I know?"

Seriously?

"The guardians!" Etta gestured to the two men, conversing quietly ahead of them.

"Why? Do you want to write them thank-you notes?"

"You know what?" Etta gritted her teeth. "Never mind."

She had more important things to think about: Her mom. The astrolabe. Getting back to Nicholas. Even the debut. That familiar fire lit in her heart when she thought of it now, burning through the dread and apprehension she'd felt about living a life on the run with her mother. She wanted to play—for Alice, yes; so Nicholas could hear her, yes; but even more than that, to take control of her future again, on her own terms.

In Kurietain, men were out talking amongst themselves, smoking water pipes, watching the sunset. They drew a few interested eyes as one of the guardians led them through the maze of sun-bleached streets, heading to what Sophia called a *caravanserai*, but the others referred to as *khan*—some sort of lodgings for weary travelers and their beasts.

And water. Clean, cool water. Etta licked her cracked lips. Her goatskin had gone dry an hour before.

"I overheard men talking about hot springs. I can smell the sulfur, can't you?" Sophia said, taking a deep breath of the evening air.

"Oh," Etta said sweetly, "I just assumed that was you."

Sophia's own smile would have melted the face off a lesser person. "It's a shame you won't be able to clean up. It looks like we rode *you* here."

Her arms felt like she'd tied hundred-pound weights to each wrist, but Etta did summon the energy to flip off the other girl when she turned back to the road.

The *caravanserai* was a simple square structure, almost like a fortress. Its exterior was lined with columns and more arches than Etta could count, broken up by a large entryway. Right now, a group of men was walking through it with an unruly herd of camels.

Two young boys were sent out to retrieve the horses and guide them inside, where they were met by a portly, swollen-faced man in fine red robes. He spoke first to the guardians, who must have told him that Sophia was the one with the gold, for the man fumbled for an apology in three separate languages before Sophia deigned to reply in Arabic.

The *caravanserai* was split between two levels—the upper rooms, where the men slept, and the lower rooms where their camels, horses, and goods were tucked in for the night.

The caravan that had arrived before them had just finished unloading and bedding down its animals. Finished with their sunset prayer, the men began mingling with the other travelers, showing off wares, sharing food.

"In you go," Sophia said, when they reached their room on the second level. Their escorts moved to the next door down and disappeared inside. She heard the sound of them dropping their bags, and the rustle of fabric as they rolled out their bedding.

Etta stepped into the room to find it was a good ten degrees cooler than outside. At that point, she was so used to the artistry that went into even the simplest of these homes, Etta was surprised to see that the room was as bare as a cave. There wasn't a door, only a curtain that fell in place after her.

"Right. Here's a blanket." Sophia tossed her a rolled bundle of cloth.

Unsurprisingly, after spending the day tied to a horse's back, it smelled as bad as Etta did.

She spread it out over the floor, trying to psych herself up for the special agony of settling her already-sore body down onto what basically amounted to flat, packed earth.

At least we're safe for now, she thought, then amended, *I think.*

"There's food in that bag," Sophia said, indicating the cloth sack she'd dumped against the wall on her side of the small space. "I need to see about trading out the horses."

Her eyes flashed with unspoken warning. Etta merely waved her away.

She waited until the other girl disappeared through the curtain before dragging herself over to the bag. Etta pulled out a handful of figs and tore off a chunk of bread as big as her fist before going back for seconds. Next door, she could hear one of the guardians stand up when Sophia called and, grumbling, make his way down the stairs.

Etta eyed the other bags.

The girl had left all of her supplies there, including but not limited to a small pistol, money, her travel log, a gold pocket watch, and a Swiss Army knife.

The compass she'd seen Sophia use earlier in the day had fallen to the very bottom of the smallest sack. She stared at its face, turning herself around the room until it pointed to true north.

Over the last few hours, Etta had imagined five different variations of the same escape plan. While the others slept, she would creep out, take what few supplies she needed, and ride off ahead of them, beating them to Palmyra and the astrolabe by hours. In every version, Etta was long gone before they ever arrived.

But the longer she stared at the compass, the more those plans seemed to slip through her fingers like dust.

Hasan had warned her and Nicholas that the desert wasn't a place to travel alone. Even with a compass, she could still find herself off track, lost, dehydrated, or hungry—and she would wander until someone found her or she collapsed. Etta was a true city kid—wilderness survival wasn't exactly her forte. She needed Sophia and the guardians for their knowledge, and their supplies.

It was getting too close to the thirtieth to waste even a second debating this. All along, she'd been banking on being able to figure out how to use the astrolabe to create a passage back to her own time, to surprise the Ironwoods holding her mother hostage and get her out of there, but now, none of it seemed so simple.

How was she supposed to get to the astrolabe, get it away from Sophia and the guardians before they could take it? And then hide the fact she wasn't bringing it back to Ironwood long enough to get Rose free from him? Her mind began to dissect the problem, cutting it up into manageable measures, testing the tempo, the flow of beats, until finally she settled on a possibility.

The only way to do this would be to get Sophia on her side. To make her complicit in not only destroying the astrolabe, but lying to Cyrus. Etta could force him to set up a trade—to claim she needed to see her mom before she gave him anything. If her mother knew something was going to happen, would she already have a plan?

Or . . . Etta was beginning to feel the tremor of certainty in the pit of her stomach that this might only end with the old man's death. And it might have to be her who dealt the killing blow.

The thought made her sick—her mother might have been ruthless, but Etta wasn't sure what it would make *her* into if she did kill him. He was responsible for Alice's death—the thought should have filled her with the satisfaction of revenge, but . . . it didn't.

Besides, what would she do about the other travelers there? The ones that Ironwood would no doubt have guarding Rose?

As she lay in the darkening room, her mind kept circling back to those words, the ones her mom had written at the end of her first letter: *An ending must be final.*

Final. As in . . . destroyed? Do what her mother and her great-grandfather couldn't, and destroy the astrolabe entirely? Now that she had a clearer picture of her mom's heart, Etta began to wonder if her mother didn't *expect* to be saved—if this, like Alice's last words to her, was meant to comfort her; to direct her; to tell her it was all right.

A flash of bone-deep horror cut through her.

I can't lose Mom, too. Not now, when she had so many questions about her family. Not ever, when they had so many places to go together. If her mom was gone, too, what reason would Etta even have to try to get back to her New York, to the tattered remains of her old life there?

Destroying the astrolabe would be her last resort, she decided. Some part of her was still hoping she could get through to Sophia, to convince her to come back to Etta's own time and escape Ironwood once and for all. That way she could use the astrolabe, somehow, to create a passage directly to her time without needing to find the one in the Bahamas that led to the Met.

Etta slid the compass into the folds of her robe, just in case, and stretched out over her blanket. She forced her mind clear of all of the competing thoughts that sprang up when she closed her eyes.

It'll be over soon, she thought. *An ending must be final.* She rubbed the raw markings around her wrists, and tried very hard not to wish that Nicholas was there. She didn't need a protector, or a rescuer. But she did need him.

Sophia returned half an hour later by Etta's guess, still grumbling as she sank down onto her bedding. Next door, the guardians were talking, laughing, and Etta caught a familiar word passing between them, one Hasan had used: *ašwaak.*

Ašwaak . . . as in, Thorns?

There was silence between the girls as the last lights from the *caravanserai* were finally extinguished, dragging them into the darkness of night.

"Does the astrolabe really create passages?" Sophia asked suddenly. "Not read them?"

I'll give you an answer if you give me one. Etta almost said it, but she thought of Nicholas then, and realized suddenly that she might not need to manipulate Sophia. Not when the truth was on her side.

"Yes. He wants to create a passage back to a point where he can save his first wife without losing his fortune, or his control over the other families," Etta said. "He'll destroy our future, I'm

446

almost sure of it, just to rebuild something he thinks is better. You can't let him have that much power."

"Oh, I was never going to give it to him," Sophia said. "Especially not now that I know exactly how powerful it is—thank you for that piece of information, by the way. My God, this is amazing. I won't just be able to lord it over him—I'll be able to burn his life down around him."

"Sophia—" Etta tried to interrupt, but the girl talked over her, almost trembling with her excitement.

"This is the most powerful object in the world; the travelers and guardians won't just align with me, they'll *kneel*. I won't need to be the heir—I can go back far enough to take him out of the game entirely."

Etta was so stunned, she almost couldn't speak. "You'd really kill him?"

"Not before he lived to regret not choosing me," Sophia said, that false sweetness back in her voice. "I want him to suffer, to see me rise as he falls. So don't worry, darling. He won't change the future, because I'll change it first."

TWENTY-ONE

AFTER NEARLY SEVEN HOURS ON CAMELBACK, ROCKING with the animal's slow gait, Etta was too focused on controlling her ride to notice when the sparse desert had begun to take on some green again. If she'd thought the first leg of their trip had been barren, this last section felt like they were seeing the dry, crumbling bones of the world. Etta's eyes never once stopped watering from the sun's glare cutting through the cloudless blue sky.

But then in the distance, something began to take shape. Not the city itself, but the crumbling fortress on one of the hills that flanked it. What was left after a thousand years of wear and wind looked distinctly Roman, a sea of pillars and columns, hundreds of them that looked like they were holding up the sky.

There was a green oasis nearby, a dense cluster of trees that seemed at odds with the stripped-down land stretching in every direction. But here and there, as they drew their camels into the city, Etta saw evidence of ravines and what looked like small canals.

Now that they were inside the boundaries of the ruins, and Etta had to crane her neck back to look at the carved reliefs on the columns' heads, it was easy to imagine the magnificent scope

of the city in its prime. Hasan had called it one of the most daz-
zling stops along the ancient trade routes between east and west,
a once carefully cultivated jewel that had fallen into neglect,
and then devastation, as new civilizations rose up and the roads
redrew themselves. There was an amphitheater and a large, towering building that Etta assumed was some kind of temple, but
for the most part, they were weaving through the remnants of the
buildings' foundations. Their footprints.

"Well?" Sophia said, turning her camel sharply to cut off the
path of Etta's. Daisy, as she'd started calling the camel, let out a
growl and began to dance around impatiently.

"'Well,' what?" Etta asked, adjusting her hood. The sun was
at its pinnacle, beating down on the top of her head, reminding
Etta she needed to keep drinking the water in her rapidly shrink-
ing goatskin.

"What was the clue? Where are we supposed to find it, now
that we're here?"

Lie to her, Etta thought. *You're already here, you don't need
them, and she won't change her mind. You can go and search by yourself. . . .* Except, of course, that if they got separated, Sophia might
be able to find it first, and Etta would be too far away to stop her.

The last resort, then, Etta thought miserably. The stakes were
obvious to her now, and it felt like every other minute she'd been
biting back tears of bitter frustration. She couldn't save herself
and her future *and* save her mom. Last night, she'd lain awake for
hours trying to imagine the world Cyrus would try to build and
control with the astrolabe. Etta had tried to convince herself that
Sophia would be the lesser of two evils. But the truth was, Sophia
was like a firework with a lit fuse; it would only be a matter of
time before her temper or impatience got the best of her, and her

plans exploded around her. Then, the astrolabe would almost certainly find its way back to Ironwood.

"I'll tell you," Etta said, "but only in exchange for something."

Sophia's brows rose at that. "This silly game again, Linden? *Really?*"

Etta sat up straighter in her saddle, struggling against the rising tears of frustration. *I'm sorry, Mom. I just wanted you to be proud of me. . . .* "You could spend weeks, months, maybe even years searching for it here. I'll help you, but only if you let me create a passage directly back to my time."

To her surprise, Sophia seemed to be considering this. "You actually know how to use the damn thing?"

Etta seized on the small, hopeful surprise in the other girl's voice, and lied. "Yes. It was in my mother's letter. I'll show you, but only if I have your word you'll let me create the passage."

She wouldn't need more than a second to smash the astrolabe. Etta only needed to find a way to get it into her hands.

"All right," Sophia said, holding out her hand to shake. Etta took it, meeting the girl's gaze evenly. "Now tell me what you know."

"We think the clue refers to a burial place," Etta said, hoping she wouldn't live to regret it. "Some kind of a tomb."

Sophia blew out a hard gust of air from her nostrils. "Can't you be more specific?"

Etta narrowed her eyes.

The other girl was all impatience and nerves as she moved toward the guardians, consulting with them in rapid Arabic. Sophia had been in a mood from the moment they left the *caravanserai* that morning; Etta had dismissed it then as the product of too little sleep and too much saddle soreness, but now that she was watching her again, some worry crept in. Frustration might lead her to do something rash.

More than that, thought Etta. She had been watching the guides, her ears tuned in to what few conversations they had, to see if they'd mention the Thorns again. When she'd tried to suggest that they might leave the guardians, or send them back once the city came into view, Sophia had simply snapped her whip and sent her camel into a trot ahead of Etta's.

Daisy spat, rearing her head back, grumbling something in her own peculiar language. Etta leaned forward and patted her neck. She knew the feeling.

As Hasan had said, there were still people living on the outskirts of the city, most of them in tents and smaller, more temporary structures that looked like they were made mostly of dried mud. They kept to themselves as their party moved down what once must have been a breathtaking colonnade, but Etta felt their eyes tracking her progress.

"Where are we going?" she asked.

"Fadi claims there is a valley of tombs just beyond the city," Sophia said stiffly.

"So you do know their names," Etta muttered, watching the backs of the men's heads as they rode steadily in front of them, looking a thousand times more at ease on their camels.

"Of course I do," Sophia snapped. "I'm not as heartless as everyone would make me out to be. Besides, I had to know their names to find them and to pay them, to keep my little adventure—coming after you—away from Grandfather's ears."

"It must have been a real novelty," Etta began coldly, "to make a decision to do something without him ordering it. To actually pull one over on him. It's nice to have a little freedom, isn't it?

Think of what you could have had if you'd actually taken my advice and left the family behind."

Sophia's expression shadowed, but she didn't disagree. Etta heard the girl's hands tightening around the leather reins. They plodded forward through the ruins in a silence as oppressive as the heat.

THE VALLEY OF TOMBS WAS LOCATED PAST WHAT HAD LIKELY BEEN the vibrant, beating heart of Palmyra's city center, tucked into the city's shadows. Had they been alone, without the knowledge of the guardians, Etta wasn't sure she would have ever thought to investigate the buildings. They'd passed right by them on the way in, and she hadn't given them a second look. They seemed almost like defense posts, or watchtowers.

Despite the grand name, the valley consisted of little more than these towers sticking out of the sand like slightly crooked fingers; some of the tombs weren't towers at all, but instead carved out of the earthen hills. If there had been other, more elaborate tombs, they were long gone or buried beneath a thousand years of sandstorms.

They dismounted from the camels and left them tied to a nearby crop of pillars that had fallen onto themselves.

"You think it's safe to go inside?" Etta asked, eyeing the first one. The comparison to fingers hadn't been a bad one—some of the towers were short, only a story high, and wide, the way you'd expect a thumb to be. Others stretched up several dozen feet higher, casting long shadows onto the loose sand and dirt. One looked as though there might have been a balcony of some kind attached to it. Small slits had been left in their imposing sides, likely to allow air and light inside of them.

Still . . . they were tombs. And as eager as Etta was to finish

452

this, just as much anxiety raced through her. She was never going to feel right about trespassing.

"Does it matter?" Sophia snapped with her usual sensitivity. "Let's go get this over with. It's blazing hot out here."

They began with one of the less imposing tombs at the far left; this one was built into the side of the hill, its entrance half buried in the sand. Sophia scattered the sand with her foot as she ducked inside, searching the stone beneath it for something. A sign that there was something buried, maybe?

But Etta couldn't stop looking up.

The walls were covered in frescoes, murals still clinging to the plaster, still showing their faded colors. All around were the faces of men and women draped in robes. Some of their expressions had worn away, leaving them literally defaced; all that remained were the outlines of their bodies and the decorative embellishments beneath. Painted grapevines, their leaves still a vivid green, climbed the support pillars. Gods or angels, or both, seemed to fly across the walls, soar up to the ceiling, which had been painted to look as though it was covered in green-and-red tile. Or . . . Etta squinted. Were they tiles?

You're not here to go sightseeing, she reminded herself. *Stop wasting time.*

Spaced in between the frescoes were rectangular holes, cut into the walls almost like shelves. Some were covered, blocked by solid pieces of stone. Others had been left open.

"What were these for?" she asked Sophia, touching one of the covers. It dwarfed her hand.

The other girl turned, presumably to repeat the question to one of the guardians. She listened to the soft, quick explanation before turning to offer it to Etta.

"That's where they'd place the coffins and bodies, in those openings," she answered. "It would all normally be covered by some sort of façade, but clearly it's been moved. Tomb raiders and grave robbers, most likely."

This seemed to be a unifying problem in all of the tombs—there was hardly anything left to be seen, let alone taken. What low, bench-like sarcophagi they found were broken, their lids removed to reveal absolutely nothing inside but withered bones. One or two were still whole enough that Sophia and the guardians were convinced it would be worth the effort to use brute force and slide the lids off.

"They've already been picked clean," Sophia complained, punctuating the words with a frustrated kick to the side of one of the tombs. "Your mother was a fool to stash it here where anyone could find it!"

"I would call her *many* things," Etta said evenly, "but I wouldn't call her an idiot. She wouldn't have left it here if she thought there was a chance it could be taken."

But even as she said it, she found herself doubting. They'd wasted nearly two hours crawling around in the dark with a single torch between them, trying to find hidden compartments and passages that didn't exist. The guardians even led them down to a series of caves between the main section of Palmyra and the towers, where they found—unsurprisingly—more sarcophagi and no astrolabe.

She rubbed at her forehead, blowing out a long sigh. One of the guardians said something to Sophia, who snapped back in irritation.

"What now?" Etta asked.

"He said that there are more tombs a little ways west of here," Sophia translated, "or we can look around the temples in the city."

Etta didn't think her mother would have left anything in the city proper—not with the small settlements still clinging to the fringes of it.

"Let's check the tombs," she suggested.

"We should have had it by now," Sophia grumbled, heading back toward the camels.

"We'll find it," Etta told her. "She wouldn't have made it impossible, just difficult."

Etta took a deep breath in, trying to get Daisy to remain still long enough for her to climb up onto her back. The others simply struck their camels, either on the head or snout, and got them to kneel. Daisy was as bad-tempered as always, but at least this time she didn't try to shake Etta off like a fly.

They rode deeper into the hills surrounding the city; knowing what to expect this time, Etta's eyes picked out the towering tombs immediately. Many seemed in worse shape than the ones they'd already seen, but there was one in particular that looked almost perfect from the outside. It kept drawing her attention, even as Sophia was hauling Etta to a closer one.

"That one," Etta said, a strange twinge moving down her spine.

"Fine," Sophia said, whistling to get the men's attention.

Etta was right about one thing—this tomb was in much better shape than any of the others. The main chamber was long, leading to the opposite wall, and lined with five busts of men and women. These overlooked more shelves like the ones they had seen in the other tombs, where the bodies or coffins were sealed. Seeing these were all open and there was nothing left inside but loose dust, Sophia took the narrow stairs just to the left of the entryway, nearly cracking her head against the painted stone ceiling. Etta followed, bracing a hand against the wall as she climbed.

Sophia cast one short glance at the second floor before

continuing up to the third, her lip curling in disgust—why? Because the astrolabe of untold value and power wasn't just sitting out, waiting for her to trip over it?

Etta stepped off onto the second floor, letting the guardians pass by on their way up. The stones bounced their quiet voices back to her, and she felt another burst of unease shift in the pit of her stomach. Sophia seemed to trust them implicitly, but Etta wished that she had ordered them to stay outside with the camels.

A small window allowed a stream of warm light to wash into the small space. Etta walked into it and took a moment to settle the rioting pace of her pulse. She leaned out the window, searching for some sign of her mother.

And when she turned, she was face-to-face with a tree.

The startled laugh burst out of her too fast to smother it. And of course, with nothing to catch it, the sound carried straight up to Sophia, who was still pounding around overhead, shaking loose plaster from the ceiling. She came charging down the steps again, nearly breathless.

"What is it?" Sophia demanded.

The second level was lined on either side with the same towering shelves as the chamber below—the only real difference was that many of them still had their coverings, and the busts of their occupants were still in place. While many of the faces were smashed in, or had missing noses, hands, whole sections of skulls, the one in front of Etta was nearly flawless, depicting the familiar outline of a tree. The stone was a shade lighter than the others—a close but imperfect match to those around it.

Everything about it—from the way the branches angled down, to the scattering of leaves across them, to the slight curve of the trunk—matched the sigil she'd seen on her mother's travel journal.

"It's—nothing," Etta tried. "A bird flew by and—"

Sophia ignored her, sharp eyes scanning the room, and, of course, landing on the carved tree. "There! The Linden family sigil." Sophia's whole demeanor changed, a lightning-fast shift from agitation to excitement. Etta finally understood what people meant when they said that eyes could gleam with emotion. Sophia looked ready to tear the cover off with her bare hands.

The guardians used knives—daggers, really, Etta thought—to carve around the edges of the relief and pry it out enough to hold. It crashed to the floor, the symbol of her family smashing into pieces with a deafening crash. There wasn't a stone block behind it; that much was clear when Sophia had the guardians start to wiggle it free. There was a backing, mostly to hold it in place, but nothing so heavy that Etta couldn't have pulled it out herself.

Both girls peered inside, and Etta spotted a lump of something at the back right corner.

"You get it," Sophia ordered. "If someone's hand is going to get burned or chopped off with a booby trap your devil of a mother set, it isn't going to be mine."

Etta rolled her eyes, and with a single, silent prayer, thrust her arm into the opening, stretching as far as she could, fingers closing around the tattered end of the cloth. She dragged it forward to the opening, sucking in a sharp breath between her teeth as she drew out a dusty bundle of faded linen and unwrapped it.

Sophia shouldered her out of the way, breaking Etta's concentration long enough to snatch the thing out of Etta's hands and clutch it between her own.

The astrolabe was bigger than she'd expected; twice the size of her small, clenched fist. Age hadn't dulled its gold sheen in the slightest. The flat disc caught the light from the window and warmed the whole room. There seemed to be markings running along the edge of it, almost like a dial. Etta moved, trying to get a better look at the beautifully etched design on the back.

The other girl seemed so stunned by the fact that it was there—that she had found it after all—there was a long moment where Sophia didn't seem to breathe.

Etta couldn't, either.

An ending must be final.

And this one might just kill her.

"Here," she said. "Give it to me. I'll show you how it works."

The twinge she'd felt outside was back, moving through her veins. The air seemed to vibrate with its power, the buzz racing along her skin until every hair stood on end, until her nerves sang at the same pitch.

"All of that, for *this* . . ." Sophia shook her head, placing it in Etta's outstretched hand. "Go on, then, make it work."

Etta nodded, her jaw clenched as she assessed her options. Finally, she carefully, slowly, set it down in the stream of sunlight on the stone ground, kneeling beside it. Under the cover of her robes, her fingers curled around a jagged piece of rock.

"Get on with it, Linden," Sophia barked.

"With pleasure," Etta said, and before the other girl could even think to move, brought the rock down against the astrolabe's gilded face.

The fire that raced through her was instantly extinguished as the rock broke against it, leaving scratches and dents, but with the device still in one piece. Etta scrambled to pick the astrolabe up and bash it against the floor, until it hopefully fell to pieces.

"You *rat!*" Sophia shrieked, hauling her back by the hair. She turned toward one of the guardians. "Give me your dagger!"

The man lifted it out of its hilt at his side.

It happened so quickly. The man flicked his wrist, flipping the dagger around to slice against Sophia's outstretched palm. The girl gasped in pain as blood sprayed across the stone.

"What do you think you're *doing*?" she snarled. "How dare you! By our family's laws, I could have you killed for this—"

"Yes, if we were Ironwoods," the man said, reaching into his robes for another dagger. The other guardian did the same, holding its razor-sharp tip out in the direction of Etta's throat. "But, sadly for you, we are not."

Not Ironwood? Etta detangled herself from Sophia's grip, and tried to scramble back toward the wall. Then—

"Is that so?" Sophia said, clutching her hand, a thunderous expression on her face. "Is that why you were living in our family's home, using our family's money?"

The guardian laughed, a deep sound that welled up from a belly full of venom and malice.

"Your guardians were easy enough to dispose of," he continued. "How very unsurprising you have never bothered to meet them in your life, let alone learn their faces. And yet, how very fortunate for us."

Etta began to sidestep slowly toward Sophia, the blood thundering through her. She started to lean down to pick up the astrolabe, only to find the dagger's blade a hair away from her throat.

"Step back, girl," the other man snarled. "Hand the astrolabe to me slowly . . . *slowly* . . ."

Fury lanced her, piercing the cloud of confusion and fear. "Get it *yourself*!"

The man backhanded her so hard, Etta's vision blacked out as she hit the stone floor and dust exploded into her lungs.

"If you're not Ironwoods, then who the hell are you?" Sophia demanded.

"Dead men," came a deep voice from behind them.

NICHOLAS STOOD AT THE EDGE OF THE LANDING, ONE FOOT STILL on the step below, Sophia's small pistol in his hands—aimed directly at the man hovering over Etta.

She wanted to drink in the sight of him, to study the way he seemed just slightly unsteady on his feet. The glow of his skin had dimmed. Sweat dripped off his jaw. He was panting, harder than he would have been if he hadn't just crossed a desert with a serious knife wound in a body that had clearly just narrowly escaped a fatal fever.

Now, she thought, *now, now, now—*

Etta threw herself at the man's feet, sending him slamming back with a startled cry. She scrambled to grab the astrolabe from the ground, even as he grabbed her legs and yanked her back. A heavy set of arms locked around her neck.

"Etta!" Nicholas shouted, just before the deafening crack ripped through the air and she felt a sharp, hot pain in her shoulder. She fell forward again under the hot, limp weight of the Thorn, who coughed and sputtered, even as he got the curve of his dagger around Etta's throat, letting it kiss her skin. The hot stench of blood filled her nose, her lungs.

The second man charged Nicholas, knocking him back against the wall, and the gun fell to the ground. Nicholas swung wildly at his face, but only clipped him. The whole world swung beneath Etta as she stood. He wasn't going to be any good in this fight, not in his condition—she needed to get the gun—

The second man already had it in his hands, and was thrashing Nicholas across the face with it. Etta screamed as he stumbled back and slumped against the wall. The man spun back toward Sophia, leveling the revolver at her heart.

"*Thorns,*" she spat, blood spilling out of her palm as she watched him kneel and pick up the astrolabe. "Isn't that right?"

The man gave a mocking little bow that made Etta's stomach tighten to the point of pain.

I have to do this, I have to destroy it, Mom—

I can handle this—

It's my time—

The Thorn holding her pressed the blade so tightly against her throat, she felt a line of her own blood drip down the front of her faded, sandy robes.

"At your service," the first one said.

"Who sold us out?" Sophia demanded.

"Not a soul, though there are many in your so-called family who *would* if given the opportunity for retribution. You left a trail for us to find—you made it *exceptionally* easy, in fact, when *our* leader saw what occurred at the museum. He put out a call for any Thorn guardian or traveler to watch your movements through the passage, to see if you might lead us directly to the astrolabe. And rather than force us to continue to search for you, we set a trap for you to come to us. How well it all worked out." He glanced at the Thorn holding Etta and said, "Tie her up. The desert will deal out its punishment."

The Thorn shifted his weight back, and Etta found herself jerked forward onto her knees. He pinned her hands behind her back, winding something—his sash?—around her wrists.

"The other one as well—"

"Wait—" Sophia said, backing away. "Now listen, just a moment. Do you know who I *am*?"

Have to destroy it—

Can't let Mom down—

Have to save Mom—

"You are an Ironwood," the Thorn said. "That is all I need to know about you."

"No," Sophia added quickly, glancing toward Etta. "I'm a gift. Anything your group wants to know about the Ironwoods, about the Grand Master himself, I can provide. But only if you take me with you."

Nicholas was coming around on the floor, and seemed to rouse just in time to hear this. His eyes snapped open.

The Thorn holding the gun laughed. "You take me for a fool."

"Do you honestly think I was ever going to give the Grand Master the astrolabe?" Sophia asked. "I would have laughed in his face as I tore his dreams apart. If you want to use it to do the same, then I wouldn't stop you. I'd *celebrate* that. The only thing I care about is making his life as miserable as he's made mine."

"You bloody—" Nicholas swore, cutting himself off. "Sophia, it *has* to be destroyed. It doesn't matter if you have it, if they have it—once Ironwood knows, he won't stop until it's in his possession. Think about this—it doesn't read passages, it creates them—"

"I know that," she snapped.

"Once he knows—that you went with the Thorns, that you let them have it—you won't just be exiled. You won't just lose your standing—he will obliterate you. And that goes for all of the Thorns," he added. "Let me destroy it now. Put the blame on me; let the old man come after me and see *your* worth. He'll make you heir, but only if he doesn't have the astrolabe, only if he can't use it to save his first wife and create new heirs. But this . . . this is the path to madness."

Etta saw the flicker of something in Sophia's expression, the fear of confronting that truth. Her lips parted, as if to ask something; but instead she set her shoulders back, eyeing Nicholas like a queen about to order an execution. "So be it."

The Thorn holding Etta down against the stone floor laughed. The one with the gun motioned for him to do something, grating out a few words in Arabic. Etta watched, her mind dragging on a half-second delay, as the man grabbed Nicholas and slammed him up against the wall, ripping the sash from his waist to bind his hands. Finished with that, he punched Nicholas squarely in the jaw, sending him crashing back down onto the stone.

Etta screamed, trying to surge up off the ground, but she was off-balance; Sophia shoved her back into the wall of tombs, half-stunning her. The room blinked out of view as she dropped heavily back onto the stone, her ribs bruised and swollen beneath her skin. Without an ounce of air in her lungs, she couldn't even yelp in pain; she could only wait until her vision pieced itself back together.

"Don't be ridiculous, darling," Sophia murmured, staring down at Etta.

Nicholas bellowed with rage. "I will kill you for this one day."

"It's charming you think that you could," Sophia said with a dismissive flick of her hand. One of the Thorns said something in Arabic.

"It'd be a waste of ammunition," Sophia said coldly. "Leave them for the desert. And I wouldn't get near them with a blade. Both are trained too well. The sun will finish them off for you."

Etta held her breath, her body straining with pain and alarm, but the men seemed to agree with Sophia's assessment.

It was several minutes before the sound of their steps faded completely. Etta breathed in through her nose, out through her mouth, to try to keep herself from throwing up. *I failed, I failed—Mom, I'm sorry—*

I need to get up—

"Etta!" Nicholas said. "Etta! Wake up! Etta!"

She took in a deep breath, still trembling with pain.

You're fine, he's fine, you're fine, he's fine. . . . They could catch up with Sophia and the Thorns, ride hard until they could take the astrolabe back.

"Henrietta!" he barked. "Miss Spencer! Damn you, if you don't wake up this instant—"

She heard the snap of a whip, the grumbling of the camels. Etta didn't have to look to know that they were leading Daisy away, and whatever Nicholas had ridden in on. They were really stranding them, the bastards.

"Etta—" It was the desperate, pleading note in his voice that made Etta push herself upright, so suddenly that Nicholas let out a noise of surprise.

"Are you all right?" she said, her throat aching.

"I'll live, but . . ." he said, looking away. "Damn it all—I'm sorry, I'm so very sorry, we rode as hard as we could—"

"We?" Etta said, testing the fabric tied around her wrists. The Thorn had managed a knot all right, but he'd been too rushed to make sure it was totally secure. She worked her right hand free, sliding it out of the silk binding with a relieved sigh. "Is Hasan here?"

"He came with me, but his horse lamed itself and he had to turn back to Kurietain," Nicholas said. "I'm so bloody sorry. I swear, this isn't the end. We'll get back to Damascus—" His words were edged with fire, but he couldn't bring himself to look at her. "I'll walk the whole of Nassau if it means finding the passage you came through—"

"You would do that?" Etta asked.

He finally looked up. "You cannot fathom the distance I would travel for you."

Despite the pain, despite everything, a small smile broke over her face. "With me."

"Come here," he breathed out, eyes reverent. "Come here . . . come here. . . ."

Etta didn't trust her legs enough to stand quite yet, but she managed to crawl the short distance. A small burst of happiness lit the center of her chest and he tilted his face up, kissing her.

"Untie me, damn it," he said. Etta snorted and reached around behind him. He leaned forward as she worked, burying his face in her neck.

The man had done a better job of binding his hands. The knot swam before her as black began to cloud the edges of her vision. She blinked, leaning back at the feeling of sudden, wet warmth down her front.

Bright blood had soaked through the front of Nicholas's shirt. Her heartbeat throbbed in her ears. "You tore . . . you tore your stitches open . . . careful. . . ."

His eyes widened in alarm, going from her face to her shoulder. She looked down, raising an unsteady hand to the place where she felt a second, white-hot pulse.

Shot, she thought, dazed. *When did that . . .*

"Etta!"

There was a spark of electricity at the base of her spine, scorching through her center, ripping her apart. Air cracked and hissed against her skin, and—

TWENTY-TWO

IN THAT FIRST MOMENT AFTER ETTA DISAPPEARED, DIS-
solving into a million grains of glittering dust, every last trace
of blood seemed to leave his body.

It was impossible to breathe.

It was impossible to move.

Perhaps . . . if he only remained still enough, the moment
would . . . Etta would . . .

His skin was still warm from where it had touched hers, even
as the blood was cooling on his shirt. He felt the imprint of her
lips against his as if they were still there. The rattling heat the air
had taken on seemed to shrink the skin around his bones, to snap
against his chest—and she—

She is gone.

The one clear thought his mind could scrape together from a
flood of the senseless.

She is gone.

Disappeared so completely, as if she'd been dashed into nothing, as if . . .

God, no—God, please, no—

ALEXANDRA BRACKEN

Nicholas slid along the plaster, unable to keep himself upright
when his spine had turned to water. Some part of him was aware
of the fact that he was shaking, as his shoulder collided with the
stone. He choked on the sand and dirt, the disbelief. And the
sound that emerged from that dark, shattered place was a thing
of anguish and fury, inhuman.

Dead. He squeezed his eyes shut, his fingers curled tightly into
fists behind him. *She's dead.*

Sophia had taken the astrolabe, and then—

Etta is dead.

She was—holy God, it was just as it had been with Julian,
from the way the light had broken her apart from the inside out,
shattering her, to the thundering, rolling crack of power he felt as
the passage in Damascus collapsed from the surge of her loss—

He howled. He let the fury pour out of him until he, too, was
shattered. The sunlight tracked across the floor, marking each
passing hour, and he could do nothing but watch it and think of
the ends of her hair, matted with blood; the spectral quality of
her skin as death had stolen over it.

When it no longer felt like he was frozen, Nicholas began to
work at what was left of the knot around his wrists. The wound
in his side pulled, his shoulder ached, and his mind carried him
back, unwanted, undeterred, to that moment again. Her forehead
had creased, as if she had heard something he had not. And there
had been pain—he'd seen it tear across her face, felt it in the way
her fingers had suddenly dug into his wrists, as if she could tether
herself to him. Her eyes had rolled back, she'd gone utterly limp—

Had she known?

Did she know what was happening?

The silk unraveled under the coaxing of his thumb, slipping

against his skin as it fell away. Muscles screamed in protest as he pushed himself up, leaning back against the wall again. He steadfastly avoided looking at the blood that crept across the ancient stone.

Nicholas watched the sun retreat through the window as it set, hatred hardening his core, until he was finally seized by impulse. He snatched a fragment of plaster up off the ground and drew his arm back to smash it against the stone, beat it into something unrecognizable, when he noticed something a few feet away.

An earring.

He scooped it up before the blood could wash over it—clasped it hard enough to feel the shape of the pearl, the prick of the stud, as it dug into his palm—and tried to find her again in himself, to pin down the memory of her face as he'd first seen it on the *Ardent*.

All for nothing. All of this, everything, for nothing.

Why was he so shocked? How had he ever expected life to deliver something he wanted to him, when it had denied him at nearly every turn? And just when he'd finally decided that the risk was worth the reward—when he'd settled on one path over another—Nicholas had been ready to go with her. He would have followed her anywhere.

And he'd killed her. His shot had missed the guardian—the Thorn—in front of him, and passed through her smaller frame.

He had let her change his plans; he'd started to rearrange his future, to become open to the possibility of a different kind of freedom. She had taken all of that with her, and he'd been the one to steal her from the world. To silence her talent and charm and unstoppable, fearless heart.

This. All of this, everything, for this; the cold, unfeeling touch of death and disappointment and grief. Nicholas felt a peculiar sort of envy for his past self, the young man who still existed outside of the barbed knot of time. The one who had not yet been crushed into dust.

He stood, his vision flooding with pops of light and color. His skull felt light enough to float away from his body, to drift off into the night. Was it so wrong to wish it would? If only to escape this . . . this . . .

Nicholas felt his way down the stairs, taking slow, measured steps in the cool darkness, until he reached the lower chamber and stepped outside. As he'd expected, his horse was gone, along with the supply of food and water he'd carried with him.

Rage once again replaced the numbness, flooding his body with a kind of fury that made him unrecognizable to himself. Sophia hadn't fired the gun, but she was partially to blame for this. Together, the three of them might have been able to overcome the two Thorns, but she'd turned on him and Etta, just when it had mattered most. He would kill his cousin, woman or not. When the time was right, when he found her, he would call her out, and he would kill her. Even as a sailor, he'd known how to hunt. He would not stop until he found Sophia.

Nicholas sat at the entrance, leaning his shoulder against the stone, breathing in the night air; it was as dry and harsh as it had been when he and Hasan had camped for a few short hours the night before.

God. He would need to explain this to Hasan. The other young man would know to come looking for them—for *Nicholas*—when they didn't meet on the road.

He shut his eyes. His cracked lip began to bleed as he drew in another steadying breath.

There was nothing to do but wait for Hasan, to try to find a way to save the mother, if he could not save the daughter. His helpless anger spread like a blot of fresh ink on paper until it absorbed her mother, too. She should have protected Etta in the first place. If she had, Etta would be playing in her debut; she would be safe, hundreds of years away from the sweltering, wasting reach of this desert.

The moon was full and bright above him, but he closed his eyes, unwilling to look again. Sleep stole upon him quickly, silently, leaving him confused and disoriented when he woke at the first touch of sunlight.

And then of course he remembered where he was, and he was hollowed out all over again. He could not move, so he did not try. He could not think, so he did not try. He watched the play of light on the sandy hills, the tombs, and felt as wooden and slow as if he had crawled out of one himself.

A few hours into the morning, a small family ambled by on camels. Their presence was so sudden, Nicholas was not quite certain they weren't a mirage until the elder man riding at the front called out to him. Nicholas kept his gaze low, his hands hanging between his knees, and the other man's foreign words rolled off him. The young son, after a brief consultation with his father, slid down the side of the camel and brought a small offering of dried meat and water.

Shocked by the small act of kindness, Nicholas managed a brief nod of thanks. The father lifted his hand in acknowledgment, and called the boy back to him.

Neither hungry nor thirsty, he ate and drank anyway, and was unsurprised to find that it did nothing to fill the emptiness at his core. It occurred to him in the hours that followed that he had misjudged Hall's behavior after Anne's death. The endless nights of drinking and joyless merrymaking hadn't been to dull his senses, or even to numb his pain, but were only fruitless attempts to fill the gnawing nothingness left inside of him, devouring every last feeling.

His back grew stiff from holding the same position, finally forcing him to stretch to reduce the aching in his joints.

I will never hear her play, he thought, and pressed a hand against his chest, hard, trying to dislodge whatever it was that was slowly squeezing his heart.

Or . . . might he? If he found the astrolabe . . . The thought made his skin feel as if there were a hive of bees trapped beneath it. Somehow, he could go back—or rather, forward. Could he warn Etta to be wary of Sophia and not enter the passage?

He'd told her he couldn't save Alice, but damn if he didn't understand now why she refused to believe him at first. Etta must truly have wanted to save the woman with her whole heart.

She would want you to just destroy it.

Could any of it be done? If he prevented Etta from traveling that first time, then he would never have been in the position to find the astrolabe. Would that undo everything, leave them at the place where they started? Had time already played this story through with them before—an endless, self-fulfilling loop of misery?

Or would it just make him Cyrus Ironwood?

How would the old man do it—change the past without preventing Etta from finding the one thing that would have allowed him to pursue that course of action? What was it that he was missing—what piece of this logic?

He settled down again for the night, wrapping his arms

around the stabbing pain in his side. Nicholas needed to think of what he would tell Hasan, how he could ever beg the young man's forgiveness for failing the Linden family, the timeline, so enormously.

But night fell over him and the desert again, and still Hasan did not come, and Nicholas was left with nothing but the suspicion that he'd cost the world two lives instead of one.

THE FIGURE ROSE ON THE HORIZON LIKE THE SUN THE VERY NEXT morning—a distant speck of white that grew larger as it threaded through the hills. For the first time in days, he felt something stir inside of him, rousing the part of him that he had carefully pressed back so as not to suffocate on it. *Hasan.* Finally.

Another horse followed the first on a line. His gaze was so fixated on it, it was a considerable amount of time before he squinted, shading his eyes from the haze of the sun, and realized that the rider coming toward him was no man, but a woman.

A woman with hair like spun gold.

His heart began to beat wildly in his chest, waging war against disbelief. *Etta.* It wasn't a mirage, he could hear the horses breathing, smell the sweat foaming on them, only—

Closer now, steadily closer; Nicholas saw now that the face was sunburnt, but faintly lined with age, and shadowed with experience. The eyes that moved over him from beneath the scarf were sharp, cut from diamonds rather than the sky. The woman searched the empty spaces around him, glanced up toward the second floor of the tomb, and the realization unspooled in his mind.

Rose.

This was Rose—the Rose that Etta had known, the one who

had raised her. Somehow, impossibly, she was here; his heart began to rend itself all over again. She'd escaped Ironwood's men. She'd traveled the desert alone. And now . . .

This was the same young woman who had thrown a knife with deadly accuracy in the bazaar—the very same one who had outfoxed the Ironwoods, even with all of their money and resources, for years. He was somehow both impressed and furious with her that she had taken such a risk with her life. She must have ridden through the desert nearly as hard as he had.

And all for nothing.

Too late.

He watched, the earring clasped between his hands, as she made a steady approach. Dressed as a man, her horse unencumbered by anything but the bare necessities, she had the look of a survivor, a fighter, and he respected the hell out of her for it, especially when she slid the pistol out of one of her saddlebags and aimed at him.

I wish you would.

He rose slowly, so as not to startle her. Nicholas could not bring himself to speak. The quick glance he'd had of her in the bazaar, even the photograph, hadn't been nearly enough to truly appreciate her resemblance to her daughter. Hers was a cool, collected beauty, her features sharpened by age. Etta's appearance struck a person across all the senses at once, like the first blossom of spring. His hand shook, just that small bit, as he raised his hands up and stepped forward.

Rose's words sliced through the air. "Don't come any closer."

He stopped where he was, his arms aching with the small effort it took to keep them up. She would need to come to him, approach carefully. He understood the instinct.

Rose dismounted with practiced ease. When she eyed him, Nicholas suddenly felt as though he needed to fall to his knees and beg for her forgiveness.

"I'm looking for a girl," she began.

"*Etta.*" He scarcely got the name out.

The woman's eyes narrowed. "Where is she?"

He swallowed, trying to clear his ravaged, dry throat. "Gone."

It was the first time he had said the word aloud, and it gained permanence; it solidified. He choked on it.

"She *used* the astrolabe?" Had Rose's eyes actually widened, or was it a trick of the light? "She didn't destroy it?"

Nicholas shook his head. "It was taken by an Ironwood and two members of the Thorns."

Emotions stormed across her face, disbelief whipping into fury and then to despair. Just as quickly, it was all folded away, and her feelings were neatly stowed again behind steely eyes and pursed lips. "Tell me exactly how this happened."

He tried to fill in the pieces of the story she wouldn't know, his throat dry and aching. Rose absorbed his words, soaking them up, until she looked like she might burst.

"How did you escape?" he asked. "Etta was terrified for your life."

"Do you honestly believe I'm not capable of escaping a few Ironwoods?" Rose shook her head. "I fought my way free on the first night, but I couldn't get here any sooner, not without crossing paths with myself."

"She tried to talk to you in the *souk*," he said, suddenly furious all over again. "Instead of listening, you *attacked* her."

"That was me twenty years ago. I'd been running from Ironwoods and the Thorns for months. I couldn't trust anyone,"

Rose said, finally lowering her gun. "I made the connection later, once Etta began to grow."

What could he say to that?

"Why did you not tell her the truth from the beginning? About her true family—about what she could do?"

Her whole countenance tightened, and he wondered if he had trespassed on forbidden ground. But finally she said, "Etta had to be a blank slate for this to work out the way I meant it to."

The way I meant it to? he thought, a thrumming awareness tightening across the back of his neck.

"She wasn't supposed to have training," Rose explained. "Otherwise it would have affected her choices along the way. I met a traveler—one past even the future we lived in. He warned me of what would happen if I allowed anything to change. If Etta *didn't* destroy the astrolabe."

My God. "Who was that?"

"I don't need to tell you that," Rose said. "I don't need to explain myself to *you*. Everything I did—everything I *had* to do, I did to ensure that Etta traveled, that she would know how to find the astrolabe. How did this happen? It was all planned out. . . . Everything . . . everything was to be as it had to be, to save us from that future. I sacrificed everything, I destroyed every complication. . . ." She took a shuddering breath, her hand curling into a fist over her heart. "Alice . . . she . . . I wouldn't have gone to such lengths if I knew it would come to this. And now Alice is . . ."

Nicholas straightened; her words were slithering through his veins like poison. "Alice. It was *you*? Not an Ironwood, like Etta suspected, but *you*?" The words raged out of him, and he saw naked pain on the woman's face, if only for a moment. "The one who called you *Rosie*—who protected you your whole life—you killed the one person who actually *cared* about your daughter!"

Etta would have been destroyed by this, torn apart by the knowledge. He was grateful, if only for a second, that she wasn't there to witness the unraveling of what she loved most dearly.

Rose's eyes sparkled with fury. "This is what it means to be a traveler—to make impossible choices, to serve the good of the world and not yourself. Ironwood will tear the future apart now, do you understand? A traveler warned me of it, of war unlike anything we've seen, of the debts and contracts Cyrus will be called upon to fulfill from powerful men and kings. Etta *had* to travel. The world—time itself—needed her to destroy it. And if I have to justify that to you, to explain my motivations in any other way, then you aren't worthy of what we can do."

How could she begin to justify the killing of kin? Of an elderly woman who her daughter had loved above nearly all else? He could understand the importance of safeguarding the timeline, preventing Ironwood from growing that much more powerful, but the deceit here—the murder of a loved one, the outright manipulation of her daughter, which had led to her death—it all made him wonder if ice water was running through her veins. Even now, there was something so . . . infuriatingly calm . . . about the way she spoke, and he had held back his anger for too long to stop himself. "How can you be so callous about your own daughter's life?"

Rose sent him a venomous look. "I can assure you, I'm not."

"She's—she's gone forever, and you stand there, and you speak of her as if—as if you only care whether she's *useful* to you—" He could scarcely get the words out. "Why . . . why . . ."

"Gone forever?" Rose interrupted sharply. "Tell me exactly what happened."

Somehow, Nicholas did. Each and every agonizing word. Coward that he was, he couldn't bring himself to look the woman in the face.

"When a traveler dies, they don't disappear," Rose said, brushing a hand across her horse's flank, brows drawn together. "If she had died, the passage in Damascus would have collapsed with the surge of energy released as time took her unnatural presence here into account. But it didn't—I wouldn't have been able to come through, otherwise."

His heart was beating so fast in his chest, the pain of it stole his breath. "It's not . . . true?"

"It sounds to me like she was caught in a wrinkle—anything you heard, or felt, or saw, was time reaching out to orphan her when the new timeline took effect. Only a traveler can affect that kind of change—these guardians, the Thorns, they were travelers, weren't they?"

He nodded. If they'd truly followed Sophia as she had followed Etta and Nicholas, then they would have had to be.

"Their presence here instigated the change, then," Rose said. "They must not have been part of the original event—the version of the timeline in which the astrolabe was destroyed."

"Why didn't it shift immediately when the others took it?" he asked.

"Because there was still a chance that it *could* be destroyed, and time would have corrected itself the best it could to smooth over the snag on the timeline that their presence caused," Rose explained.

477

Unless Sophia had planned to go with the men to destroy the astrolabe, or there was a chance it might be damaged or lost on their ride back to Damascus, Nicholas couldn't see how this was possible.

"If the traveler who warned me is correct, the alteration to the timeline will be catastrophic," Rose said. "We must prepare ourselves for that."

"What does all of this mean for Etta?"

"She's been flung to the last common event before the timeline shifted, whenever that may be."

"Why were you not affected? Why wasn't I?"

"Because both of us were born before whatever this last common year is," she said.

Nicholas shook his head, trying to rid himself of that futile hope. "But . . . this is what passed with my brother, when he was killed—he fell to his death."

One of Rose's brows arched again. "Then perhaps he, too, survived without you realizing it."

Survived.

Nicholas had not cried since he was a child, and could not remember what it was to weep, but he imagined it had to be what was happening to him now. It seemed the only explanation for the pressure that rose up inside of him, that broke over him like a wave. He was stunned by the quiet force of it.

"She's not . . ." The words shook as they left him. "He's not . . ."

"Speaking for Etta, I think she's still alive. The wound sounds serious, but not fatal, especially if she can find help," Rose said. "I can't tell you any more than that."

"Can you help me find her?" he asked. "How? Where is she?"

Her expression sharpened, became assessing. "Who are you to her?"

"I'm the one who will always protect her," he said. "I'm the one that will see her home."

Rose allowed a small smile through, and it was so very Etta, he had to press his hands to his side to keep them from shaking. "What's your name?"

"Nicholas. Nicholas Carter." He managed a curt bow despite his disgust and fury. "Your servant, ma'am."

Some of the ice in her expression chipped away as she gave him a small smile. "My, you're serious."

"Serious about this in particular," he told her. "Any help would be gratefully accepted—please, I only mean to—"

She held up her hand. "If I could pinpoint it for you, I would. The only things left are to correct whatever small event it was that caused the timeline to adjust—the astrolabe being in Ironwood hands, likely—and to search for evidence of where the timeline might have thrown Etta. I can be of help with the latter, but can I trust you with the former? I imagine you know where to start looking."

"Will it be enough to take the astrolabe out of Ironwood hands?" Nicholas asked.

"Only if you get to it before they use it," she said. "Tell me once and for all that you can do this—otherwise you're wasting my time."

"I'll find it," he said quickly. Somehow . . . Sophia was bound to slip up, leave a small trail he could sniff out and track. "Thank you."

Rose swung up onto her horse's back. "Then this is where we'll part."

"How shall I get a message to you?" he asked. "After I retrieve the astrolabe, how will I know where to start looking for Etta herself? She won't just be restored to this time, will she?"

"Of course not," Rose said, unknotting the lead on the other horse and tossing him the reins. After casting an exasperated look at his lack of bags and supplies, she untied one of her saddlebags and gave that to him as well. Nicholas felt his pride take a small knock, but stood up straighter.

"I need to return to my present," Rose said, "or Etta's present, at least, in order to see which events have shifted, and I'll try to pinpoint the last common event between the old timeline and the new from there. Can you meet me in Nassau in 1776 in . . . shall we say a week's time?"

It would be easy enough to follow the passages he and Etta had gone through back to 1776, but accounting for the time they would both need to travel to the island from New York . . . He swallowed down his frustration. "Better make it nearer to a month."

If he did not find her sooner himself.

I will tell Etta the truth, he thought, *about what her mother has done.* And, likely, destroy her world all over again in the process. But she deserved to know. She needed to be at the helm of her life—not a passenger, constantly at her mother's mercy.

Rose nodded in agreement, turning her horse back toward the city. "There's one more thing you should know. I have a feeling we won't be the only ones looking for her."

"I know this," Nicholas said. "If Sophia doesn't bring the astrolabe directly to him, Ironwood will assume Etta has absconded with it."

"That's true," Rose said, "but I was talking about the Thorns.

The leader, a man named Henry Hemlock, might attempt to look for her again."

Christ—this was getting muddier by the moment. "I understand."

Rose's face twisted into a sad smile. "I doubt you do. He's a powerful figure, far wealthier and more cunning than you're likely to give him credit for. He's also her father."

Every thought flew out of his head, scattered to the winds.

"Good luck, Nicholas Carter. Don't you dare disappoint me," she called back over her shoulder. "I'll see you in one month's time. Nassau—the Three Crowns tavern."

Nicholas nodded, clenching his reins in his hands as he watched her kick her bedraggled horse into a canter, and then a gallop. He waited until she was well out of sight before the dammed-up air rushed from his lungs and he dropped to his hands and knees. Tears and sweat dripped from his face, and he shook, coughing, laughing, as he pressed his forehead to the earth, trying to master the wild currents inside of him.

"You're alive," he rasped out. "You are alive."

Both of them? Both Julian and Etta? He could scarcely fathom the hope that billowed up inside him, bowing his back like a sail. If Julian were only lost, too, then he would only need to be found.

The horse Rose had left behind just watched him, a picture of serene disinterest. He moved toward it, holding out a hand, until the animal felt comfortable enough to press its nose into his palm. Nicholas ran a hand down its long nose, stroking its dark hair, his thoughts shaken loose again from the ice that had encased them.

Etta was alive, but she wasn't safe. She didn't have anyone or anything now—she was entirely alone.

Not for long.

A surge of purpose worked through him as he hoisted himself up into the horse's saddle. He would bring the exhausted creature to the oasis, give it a moment to rest and water itself, before setting off to locate Hasan. The man might know something of the other passages in this era, and from there . . . well, he would meet those challenges when they arose.

Nicholas had only just emerged from the hills when he spotted another rider weaving through the ruins of the fallen city. The red robe was unmistakable, even at a distance, and yet another burst of pressure left his chest, which no longer felt as tight as a drum.

"Hasan!" he called. The wind aided him, carrying his voice over to where the other man was perched on an unfamiliar horse.

"Baha'ar!" Nicholas was mildly touched that the man sounded equally thrilled to see him. It wasn't until they were within a stone's throw of each other that Hasan seemed to realize Nicholas was alone.

"But where . . . ?" he began, eyes wide with horror.

"She's gone," Nicholas said quickly, gripping his arm. "I'll explain along the way the best I can. I'm afraid I'll need to intrude upon on your kindness again when we're back in Damascus. Where have you been? I thought I might have lost you to the desert."

"My friend, I am touched by your concern," Hasan said, and clearly he was. "After we parted, I was seen by three men of a Bedouin tribe who provided some assistance."

From what little Nicholas had gathered from Hasan, he knew these tribes were rather fierce-spirited, nomadic families who lived in tune with the earth beneath their feet, and who passed their days eking out a humble existence from it. They were not to be provoked. In fact, Hasan had recommended avoiding them entirely.

"Are you all right?" Nicholas asked, looking him over again. While the man's cheerful disposition had dampened somewhat, he seemed whole enough.

"I am humbled greatly by the kindness they have shown in allowing me use of one of their horses," Hasan said. "We must return it to them as quickly as possible."

"Yes, of course," Nicholas said, already turning toward the road out of the city.

"My friend, there is one more thing," Hasan began. "They have something of yours I think you will wish to claim."

THIS PARTICULAR TRIBE OF BEDOUIN HAD MADE A TEMPORARY camp near the halfway point between Palmyra and Kurietain, and were slowly making their way to the former, and to the oasis it provided.

Within a mile of the cluster of low tents, Nicholas and Hasan were met by several men who charged up on camelback, kicking up a dust storm in their wake. The demonstration was impressive, and more than slightly terrifying. An effective show of force to protect their own.

Hasan called out a greeting to them and offered up a bright smile that was immediately returned by the man leading the charge. Nicholas shook his head. The man was incapable of not making friends wherever he went. He had a chronic case of good-naturedness that would have made him the scorn of New England. Even these men, clearly warriors and armed to the teeth, weren't immune.

Initially, he had found the easy bond between Hasan and Etta to be preposterous, inexplicable. But both had such a way of disarming a man, opening doors where none seemed to exist. It was a skill he'd never had himself, and it was surely one to be admired.

They were led into the encampment without further delay, the men talking amongst themselves, never once casting a curious eye his way.

Naturally. Hasan had endeared him to this tribe before Nicholas had even had the chance to meet them.

He understood immediately why Hasan had claimed to be humbled by them. Before Nicholas had even dismounted, they were presented with food and drink, introduced to wives and children. A distinguished elder, his robes marginally grander than those around him, emerged from the largest of the tents. He greeted them not with the simple warmth of the others, but with the polite deference shown to honored guests.

It was only after they had accepted some of the hospitality proffered to them, and went through the rituals of introductions and pleasantries, that the *sheikh*, as Hasan had called him, led them to a tent a short distance from his own.

All three stooped slightly as they entered the open-faced tent, and Nicholas made a conscious effort not to knock into the thin wooden supports that held up the exterior fabric. The inside was less Spartan than he might have expected—rugs and blankets had been spread across the ground, and a number of cushions were strewn about.

"They would like to continue on their way," Hasan said, translating for the *sheikh*, "but they feared moving her. . . . They are offering us a place to rest for the evening, but I think it impolite to delay them further."

Nicholas nodded in agreement. This was a matter that should

never have fallen into their hands in the first place. He stepped carefully over the rugs, to the still figure lying on her back at the very center of the tent. Sophia.

The face was unrecognizable, swollen and purpled as a ripe plum. She'd been stripped bare to her waist, and three jagged stab wounds to the torso looked to be bleeding through the earthy salve and bandages covering them. A thin blanket had been draped over her supine form to protect her modesty.

"They found her in the desert, with nothing but the clothes upon her back," Hasan explained, stepping up behind him. "They believe she was robbed, beaten, and left for dead. What do you think, baha'ar?"

"I think she's a damn fool," he muttered. Years of training should have made her far more careful, but ambition often walked hand in hand with impatience, especially if long denied. "Was she harmed in any other way?"

Hasan shook his head. "The women say she was left untouched save for the wounds that you see."

"And there was no one with her? No other body?"

"None at all."

Then the travelers still had the astrolabe, and, for some reason, had left Sophia for dead. While it wasn't in Ironwood's hands, the Thorns were equally dangerous, equally motivated to see their own agenda through. The astrolabe passing into their possession had been enough to alter the timeline, to orphan Etta from her era—a powerful alteration to the fabric of time.

Would retrieving it, destroying it, be enough to restore the world Etta had known? Nicholas wasn't so sure, but it would be a start. Determination swelled inside him as he took another step toward the girl. He could do this—by land, by sea, over mountains, through valleys—he could track the Thorns, retrieve the astrolabe, and find Etta.

And he would have an unexpected resource at his side.

Sophia wheezed painfully as she drew in her next breath. One eye was so swollen, the lid looked sealed shut. Nicholas would be surprised if she managed to keep it. The other cracked open a sliver, looking up at him with her usual scorn.

The time would come—not at this moment, not even in the coming days, but soon—when Sophia would answer for what she had done. But for now, she was of far more use to Nicholas alive than in the presence of her maker.

"Look lively," he said. "We've a journey to make."

ACKNOWLEDGMENTS

I'VE BEEN BLESSED TO WORK WITH THE INCREDIBLE team at Hyperion for . . . has it really been almost five years? Time flies when you're having fun! Thank you forever and always to Emily Meehan, my editor, as well as Laura Schreiber and Hannah Allaman, who all put so much time and thought into helping me whip this unruly book into shape. (Trust me, it was *not* easy!) Thanks also to Seale Ballenger, Stephanie Lurie, Dina Sherman, LaToya Maitland, Heather Crowley, Holly Nagel, Elke Villa, Andrew Sansone—you guys are the stuff that author-dreams are made of! And Marci Senders? You are a cover goddess.

Special shout-out to copy editor extraordinaire Anna Leuchtenberger. It is such a pleasure to work with you! Thank you for catching all of my crazy mixed metaphors and making me look so good!

To Merrilee Heifetz and the whole gang at Writers House, you are the cream of the crop. I'm so lucky to work with all of you—thank you for taking such incredible care of me and my little books.

I owe a huge debt to my amazing friends, all of whom gave me the confidence and feedback I needed to shape the characters and the direction of the story. Thank you to the inimitable Sarah J. Maas for reading the very first draft of this, back when it was a half-baked mess, and not only giving me the fix that saved the book, but, as always, requesting that there be more kissing. The brilliant Erin Bowman and Susan Dennard both gave me such wise advice about the beginning and helped me reshape it after months of frustration. Wendy Higgins, you are the crown jewel of ladies—thank you so much for reading an early draft of this book and for all of your support! Kevin Dua, I owe you big-time for reading this and giving it your thoughts. And, as always, many, many, many thanks to Anna Jarzab—not only for believing in me and this book, but for always being game to read, brainstorm, and help me untangle the time-travel paradoxes that seemed to pop up daily.

Finally, I'm overflowing with love and gratitude for my family. Not to get too cheesy with this, but I'd be nowhere without you guys. Mom, while you aren't a ruthless time-traveling mama willing to do whatever's necessary to guard the future, you are, in fact, my hero. Thank you for reading so many versions of this story and giving me your notes and feedback—this one's for you!

Also by

A L E X A N D R A   B R A C K E N

THE DARKEST MINDS SERIES
The Darkest Minds
Never Fade
In the Afterlight
Through the Dark

STAR WARS: A NEW HOPE
The Princess, the Scoundrel,
and the Farm Boy

A BREATHTAKING COLLECTION OF NOVELLAS SET IN THE WORLD OF

THE DARKEST MINDS

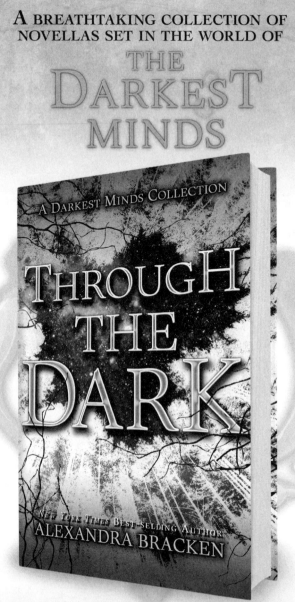

A DARKEST MINDS COLLECTION

Through THE DARK

NEW YORK TIMES BEST-SELLING AUTHOR
ALEXANDRA BRACKEN

FEATURES **3** ORIGINAL STORIES:
IN TIME AND *SPARKS RISE*
(PREVIOUSLY AVAILABLE ONLY AS eBOOKS)
AND A GRIPPING NEW STORY,
BEYOND THE NIGHT.

AVAILABLE OCTOBER 2015

HYPERION